THE DARK ANGEL

F.V.GEORGHIOU

For my husband.

Even now in Heaven, there are Angels carrying savage weapons.
~UNKLE

PROLOGUE

LONDON 2014

ALEXANDRA

The aftermath of a terrorist attack is like a deeply held breath. In a matter of minutes, the city you grew up in is completely foreign. The streets you walk every day leave a different taste in your mouth. Everything is sour. You feel exposed, vulnerable. There's a scar on the land that can't be eliminated. People no longer read a book on the train or listen to music in a world of their own, just in case they miss something; the man mumbling in the corner with his finger on a trigger, the rat-a-tat-tat of gunshots behind them. That world of their own shattered into nervous fragments.

You wake up, get out of bed, jump in the shower, get ready for work, kiss your partner goodbye, perhaps even your children. You call over your shoulder about what time you'll be home for dinner. You pop into the local café, get on the tube, naturally avoiding eye contact with everyone you pass. You tap your oyster card, join the crowds walking from A to B, weaving between others who do this every single day. It's another morning like the rest. But as it progresses, its significance evolves. Because this date is not like any other. This date will become branded into our brains with a searing hot iron. From now on, everyone will remember where they were on August 5th, 2014: the day three suicide bombers strapped three IED vests to their bodies, jumped into three black cabs and gave three addresses of the world's biggest banks. The day they murdered 146 innocent people.

Jed Smart, the Director of Operations for Special Branch Domestic Intelligence, meets our expectant gaze. 'Counter Terrorism received intel that this is a coordinated attack by jihadist leader Imran Almasi.' He has a sharp nose, his eyes are red with exhaustion, his skin is tight and leathery as if it's been stretched across his face. With stress emanating from his body, he rubs a liver-marked hand over his hairless head. 'Almasi was on a CIA watchlist but not known to be active. What we have so far is that he's a British national born in Birmingham. He lived in England with his mother and father until he was radicalised online in 2009. He travelled to Turkey to join an ISIS sleeper cell in 2011. He started his own jihadist state group in 2013. They call themselves The Beatles.'

Simon Haines looks over in my direction. Chatter about this rising jihadist faction had been surfacing on the dark web. This group were being watched by at least three different intelligence agencies.

Smart continues. 'SO15 has recovered information on the first three attacks. And from the intel they've received, there's a fourth assailant.'

'Do we have the fourth location?' Haines asks. 'Is it another bank?'

'We need you to find him.' Smart swallows. 'The first device exploded outside the west office building in The Square at 08:00 hours. The second outside JP Morgan thirty minutes later. The third was HSBC 09:00 hours….' He pauses. 'There's a pattern. We estimate we have another twenty-eight minutes until the fourth goes off.'

'All were wearing homemade vests?' I ask.

Smart nods. 'All of them appeared to have manual triggers in their hands. The CIA has had Almasi in their sights for some time. They say this is how he operates. Never less than four, never more than six.'

'If they'd just shared their intel….' I murmur to Charles McGuire.

'Fuckers never learn.' He replies quietly before clearing his throat and raising his voice. 'Are we sure there's only one more suspect?'

'We located the cell's hideout.' Smart responds. 'Four vests were made.'

'That doesn't mean they aren't using other means.' McGuire mutters. 'This could be the first phase.'

'The vest …' Haines interjects. 'If we shoot at it, can it set it off?'

'Depends on if he's holding the trigger at that time.' Smart replies curtly. 'He would need to hold the receiver and let go for the vest to detonate.'

'We have to kill him before he has the chance to activate the trigger point.' I mutter.

'What's the estimated blast radius?' Haines asks.

'This is Officer Duncan from the EOD support team.' Smart defers to a man in the corner. 'He can answer your questions.'

EOD stands for Explosive Ordnance Disposal. Shifting from one foot to the other, I catch Wayne Gibbs' eye. *We're being sent on a suicide mission.*

Officer Duncan steps into the centre of the room. He's short and blocky but lean. He uncrosses his arms, revealing three missing fingers on his left hand.

'Each black cab has increased the radius of the first three explosions.' Duncan replies. 'A homemade bomb's blast radius alone isn't much but if, like the others, the fourth attacker is in a car, then the petrol tank will ensure optimum destruction. The serious injury radius is roughly five hundred metres.' He looks over to a group packing their blast suits. 'My team are experts in this type of attack; they will accompany you.'

'How much of the surrounding area is evacuated?' I enquire.

'We estimate most office buildings will be clear in an hour.'

I frown. 'But we don't have an hour…'

Smart hesitates, crossing his arms. 'Let us worry about the civilians, soldier.'

'Alright.' Haines steps forward, cutting through the uncomfortable tension. 'Officer, when can your team be ready?' He asks Duncan.

'We're green to go.' He states, without a flicker of hesitation.

Smart clasps his hands together with a thoughtful expression. 'Be vigilant and good luck.' He straightens, tilting his chin. 'Your country thanks you for your service.'

Action erupts through the room, like a nest disturbed by an errant boot. We move with methodical precision, kitting up in ceramic armour plates before throwing assault vests over our heads. We load our magazine pouches, attach our stun and tear gas grenades, check the sound on our internal mics and fasten our helmets. Finally, in case of a chemical attack, I test my oxygen. We've done this countless times. It's second nature.

Gibbs leans against the wall, checking his watch. 'Beat my record by three seconds.' He winks at McGuire.

'You're a cheat.' McGuire straightens the strap of his rifle before nudging his head towards Gibbs' radio harness. 'You left something behind.'

'Ah, nobody uses that Charlie, com'on!'

There's always a good-humoured lightness amongst the team a few minutes before we're deployed into an operation. It's human nature, your nerves get the better of you, your adrenaline spikes and you get a rush. Intelligence agencies have accused B-Squad of being cold and uncaring before. But we need this. A short interlude to shake off the humanity. When we step out onto the field, the shutters come down. Everything that came before is gone. We are no longer individuals but cogs in the wheel that make up an elite team. We have no likes, dislikes, preferences, opinions. We are highly trained instruments to the operational goal.

'B25!' Haines calls out, moving to the front of the group. 'We set and prepped?'

McGuire turns away, saying a quick prayer. Gibbs pops gum in his mouth before making the sign of a cross over his chest. I take a long breath, whispering a phrase my grandmother used to tell me in Greek. *Life shrinks or expands depending on your courage.*

Haines turns to face the group. 'Remember that our determination to preserve our values is stronger than an extremist's will to inflict pain.' He shouts over the noise of anxious activity. 'There can be no hesitation, no second guessing. We will find the last of them and we will take him down.' He takes a moment to meet each of us in the eye. 'You're my team and I know I ask a lot of you. As by your nature, as by your training, you are required to face things others cannot. You are here to protect, to ensure our families, our loved ones are safe, to enable this country to be at peace.'

Ash drops elegantly to the ground like snowflakes, covering The Square with a thick white carpet. Clouds of thick, black smoke float through the air, amidst shadows of white fog. A cacophony of wailing sirens can be heard in the distance. Helicopter blades whirl overhead; Apaches interspersed with the appearance of the odd Air Ambulance. Shoes, briefcases, handbags lay abandoned all over the streets. Almost as if their owners have been plucked from the sky. Shards of glass, metal, and remnants of office furniture litter the pavement. Alarms shriek from every building. My pulse feels like it's beating in time with the relentless warning sounds. I feel I can hear the blood pumping through my body as our boots crumple against the floating pages of deserted newspapers.

'*B25, on the move. OVER.*' Haines informs the comms team.

'*EOD 4 here, B25. We're at your six. OVER.*'

'Mind your back!' Paramedics steam past us, hurtling stretchers across roads and into the reception of JP Morgan.

'Eyes up! Eyes up!' I shout to the team as a group of panicked civilians suddenly spill out of the office building, erupting onto the street.

'Stop!' I command, gripping my weapon. With rapid reactions, the rest of the team follow my lead, pointing their rifles at each of the panicked faces. 'Hands up!' I examine each of them. Their clothes are torn and burnt, their faces blackened and bloody. Tears streak their devastated faces. A boy, the youngest of the group, wears a uniform with a badge that reads *Trainee*.

'It's my first day.' He sobs, trembling. 'The roof caved in. It was just my first day.'

I look away, trying not to absorb the terror in his eyes.

'Can you help us?' He begs in a small whisper, his expression desperate. 'There's so many people stuck in the mall.'

'There are paramedics who can help,' Gibbs interjects, noticing me freeze up. 'We've secured the area that way. Get yourself across the river to the Quay.' He offers before helping one of the women around a pile of debris. 'You get yourselves safe now.'

'Come on,' Haines murmurs, watching them stumble away.

Gibbs spits on the pavement. *He always does it.* I never know whether it's in disgust for the concentration of evil around us or a nervous tick. Either way, I realise I find it oddly comforting. When he doesn't do it, it doesn't feel right. *Crisis craves consistency.*

'Will that building hold?' I ask, craning my neck up to Number One, The Square. The first few floors of which are completely ripped out, as if they've been gutted by a giant. Water pours from the third floor, exposed wires spark, dribbling flickers of electricity onto the ground below. Damaged appliances and desk chairs lay hanging out of windows. We continue towards the car park, nearing the south entrance of The Square, keeping our awareness sharp, focusing our eyes into small corners, directing our attention to other possible entry points. Every so often, we hear the terrified footsteps of other civilians running for their lives, their faces charred, their clothes melted away, scorched into their skin with a mixture of dirt and blood.

'*Eyes up, eyes up.*' McGuire demands into his radio, keeping his voice low. '*Possible target in southeast position of The Square. OVER.*'

'*B25 come in.*' Jed Smart's voice rings in. '*We've got a CTS sniper team on the roof. EOD 4 is in position. You wait for confirmation. OVER.*'

We follow McGuire's intense stare, turning our attention across The Square: our H&Ks braced, our fingers resting on their triggers. There are ways to spot a potential target. It's August. It's hot, but this man is wearing a thick duffel coat. He's walking funny as if lugging something heavy. His arms are by his sides, but he can't rest them against his torso. There's a precision in the way he moves compared to everyone else. He's walking quickly but without fear. He's mumbling. This is something I've seen extremists do before; pray before an attack. He's clean shaven, which is a common ritual. You must enter Paradise purified. A suicide bomber can't be bathed before burial because there isn't a body. Instead, they remove all hair as a way of cleansing themselves. The target's dark eyes are fixed on the entrance of another office block, a building with a large Barclays emblem in the reception.

It's him. He's the fourth.

I hold my breath and look up. Terrified faces crowd around the floor-to-ceiling windows on the first, second, third, fourth floors… as far as my eyes can see. The Barclays building is full of people. Sweat begins to collect in my palms. 'Si, it's him. It's him! We need to act now.'

'Control, suspect is approaching potential fourth target. We need to move. OVER.' Haines informs.

'Have you got eyes on a trigger? OVER.' Smart asks.

'Negative. No eyes on device. OVER.'

'Simon we need to get him away from that building!' I insist.

'Sir, suspect is thirty metres from potential target. Permission to engage. OVER.'

'Hold B25.' Jed Smart instructs. *'We're waiting for CTS identification. OVER.'*

'Sir, with respect, we need to move now, or this is pointless. OVER' McGuire raises his voice over the radio.

'We need to keep him in the middle of that fucking square.' Gibbs asserts, looking urgently between us. 'He's getting too close to that building, Si!'

Haines' eyes flit between the group with an expression as torn as I've ever seen it.

'Every step he takes towards that bank is another dead body.' McGuire continues. 'You want that on your conscience?'

'Target is twenty metres out.' I say, watching the suspect take careful, measured steps. It's like I'm watching him in slow motion. Except we don't have the luxury of time.

'Fuck.' Haines hisses, pressing a shaking hand to his ear. *'Control, what is the hold-up? OVER.'*

'Waiting for confirmation. OVER.' An unfamiliar voice replies.

We all look at each other. *Where the hell is Jed Smart?*

'It is him!' I snap, astonished that we're still being ordered to stand around. *'Control this is our suspect. If you do not give the green now, lots of innocent people are going to die!'*

'Get me Smart.' Haines barks into his earpiece.

'B25, we have CTS on standby, EOD 4 are prepped. As soon as we have confirmation…'

'Fuck this.' I rip out my radio.

'Alex!' Haines shouts.

Without even knowing what I'm doing, I'm running.

Slinging the H&K over my shoulder, I sprint towards the suicide bomber. McGuire screams for me to get back. Gibbs demands the EOD team brace for an explosion. Haines continues yelling for me before instructing the rest of the team forward. Ignoring them all, I race ahead, bound for the sweating, mumbling figure in the middle of The Square. Seeing me charge from the corner of his eye, the bomber falters, halting his determined steps. His eyes cautiously slide in my direction. I take a final leap before hurtling into him, throwing myself on top of his chest; I slam my knees in each crook of his arm, grasping both of his hands above his head. He appears shocked at first, stunned by the fact he's suddenly on his back. Then he starts shaking his entire body, kicking his legs, hurling himself upward whilst screaming.

'Stay still!' I shout in his face, noting the IED vest poking out through the top of his coat, packed with lines of blue and red wires. Quickly, I pull my gun around and press the butt of it against his forehead. 'If you really want to die, *I'll* send you to die….'

He stares back at me with a cold, unrelenting glare. Daring me to do it. Adrenaline seeps from my body and I finally grasp what I've

13

done. I'm sat on top of a homemade IED bomb, chaining my fate to its master.

CHAPTER ONE

COLLINS

The headlights of three service vehicles light up the driveway, illuminating the rain, pelting through the air before it cuts to the ground. Water runs between our feet, pooling in deep puddles around the flower beds. Twenty heavily armed operational officers fan out in a semi-circle around the front of the sizeable mansion. A second group break off and split in half, heading either side of the house to the garden.

Wearing a thick Kevlar vest with a firearm strapped across his chest, Gabriel stands at the door stony-faced. His eyes are dark and determined as he flashes a warrant card in Aldyn Wolfe's face. Being the Head of the Albanian Mafia, Aldyn is no stranger to midnight raids. He's never been stupid enough to keep anything incriminating in his house. Looking at him now, you couldn't guess he ran the largest organised crime network in the world. He stands wearily in his pyjamas, his dressing gown hanging clumsily off his shoulders, squinting through the light of several beaming torches, raising his arm to cover his eyes.

'Shall we do this the easy way?' Gabriel shouts.

Aldyn's jaw hardens before he holds his arms up and takes a big step to the side.

'Every single room, every wardrobe, every hiding place, all loft spaces.' Gabriel calls out. 'Shout if you find anything.'

'I thought I'd seen the last of you when you left the NCA.' Aldyn grumbles in my direction. 'What's MI6's interest in Hellbanianz now, eh?'

I don't respond, understanding his exasperation and admittedly feeling uncomfortable about our presence here.

'Alison....'

Two MI6 heavies block Aldyn's path, their hands tightening around their weapons.

'Let him through,' I signal for them to stand down.

He glares at them both before lowering his head. 'Alexandra isn't here.'

'We're just doing our job.'

'She doesn't want to be found.'

'This taskforce regards her as a person of interest.'

'The taskforce or Gabriel?'

I stiffen, physically stopping myself from saying what I really think. On numerous occasions, I've tried to broach the necessity of these searches, even attempting to reason out Gabriel's pointless vendetta. He merely shuts down and completely closes off. After the death of Mario Christofi, Alexandra put all hopes of a life with him aside and chose to work for SO15, partly to save Gabriel's life but mostly to avenge her father's death. Instead of accepting things as they are, moving on or moving forward like a sane human being, Gabriel has channelled his grief into an unrelenting wrath. Convincing himself that since working for SO15, Alexandra has begun inadvertently obstructing our investigation. He's made her a target. SO15 can't stop him. They're running her off the books, and nobody knows what we'll do when we find her. What I do know is that she's not hindering anything but that's not really what this is about. Gabriel lost something. Now he needs to prove to himself that he can get it back. God knows if it has anything to do with love, certainly not from where I'm standing. His pride is damaged. His career shifted in a direction he didn't expect. He's bloodthirsty. He needs to do this for himself, to cage her like a bird, merely to prove to his father, the person who recruited Alexandra, that he can.

'Collins…' Gabriel jogs over. 'Can you take two officers to the outhouse, check it out.'

'What is it you're looking for…' Aldyn raises his voice. 'She's not here, she didn't leave anything here, didn't tell me anything.'

Gabriel's face remains blank, merely repeating. 'The outhouse.'

Aldyn shakes his head.

'Standon! Hobbs!'

Two MI6 operational officers pace over eagerly.

'You're with me.'

Treading over the wet grass towards the annexe, I turn away from them and take a long breath, trying to quell my impatience. At some point, Gabriel has to get a hold of himself. We can't keep putting resources into this. Paul Brown isn't going to continue to sign off on operations that produce no results. Brown put the MI6 S.A.I.B.R taskforce together to weed out corrupt Government officials, those who were enabling The Singularity and posing a threat to national security by contributing to the growth of their unprecedented crime network. Alexandra Christofi is neither of those things. Our persistence down this path compromises us all but unfortunately, Gabriel leads the team. Somehow, I'll need to find another way to make him listen.

Standon murmurs into his earpiece, keeping his team in the loop as we reach Aldyn's extension. Hobbs holds his fist in the air, signalling for me to wait whilst he and Standon shift silently along the patio, manoeuvring around garden furniture with cat-like agility. They gesture for me to follow, keeping their weapons trained at the glass bi-fold doors. We reach the entrance. Hobbs grips the door handle, looking to me. I nod, giving them the go-ahead and they steam in, their rifles braced for action. Motion-censored lights instantly switch on, revealing a large gym and a small kitchenette tucked in the corner.

'Looks clear, Ma'am.' Hobbs announces, dropping his weapon to his side.

'Check that room.' I point at the door next to the fridge.

'On it,' Standon speeds ahead.

Hobbs follows quickly, both of them disappear.

'Just a bedroom, Ma'am.' Hobbs calls out.

'Search…' I open a cupboard and stifle a gasp. My breath catches, my heart clogging my throat. Alexandra Christofi stares back at me with big, brown eyes. Her blonde hair is wet, her clothes sticking to her as if she's just hurried out of the shower. Her face is frozen, her cheeks damp with tears, her right hand fiercely gripping a knife that's clutched to her chest. Our eyes meet. Her traumatised expression remains unchanging. Her appearance disturbs my logic, like a stone dropping through the surface of water. *Because why wouldn't she feel trauma?* She wants to avenge her father and since she parted ways with Gabriel six months ago, he's scorched the earth trying to stop her.

'What was that?' Hobbs calls from behind.

Alexandra shakes her head, silently pleading with me, begging me to say nothing, to do nothing. I look up to the ceiling and sigh. She shifts, her eyes widening as Standon nears.

I grit my teeth and close the double doors. 'Did you conduct a thorough search?'

He nods. 'Nothing in the bedroom.'

I step away from the cupboard and gesture to the exit. 'Let's wrap this up and move out.'

'You're sure, Ma'am?' Standon asks, looking uneasy.

'Unless you want to take turns on the treadmill?'

He stifles a grin, dropping his head and making his way towards the door. Hobbs follows and both of them spill out into the garden, their stances slightly more relaxed. Despite myself, I hang back, unable to stop from hesitating in the doorway.

'Ma'am?' Hobbs asks, 'everything ok?'

'Yep. Yes. I was just looking for the light switch.'

'They're motion censored, Ma'am.' Standon quips. 'Besides, he can afford the electricity bill.'

CHAPTER TWO

GABRIEL

ONE YEAR LATER

'Gabriel?'

I open my eyes. My brain emerging into consciousness. I move my tongue around my mouth. Dazed and confused, I sit up on my elbows. I look at the clock. Three in the morning.

'Gabriel?'

Battling the suffocating haze of sleep, I squint through the blackness of the bedroom.

'Gabriel?'

I blink slowly, my eyes making out a figure in the doorway. It's dark but I know those features. It's a face I've pictured a thousand times, memorised over and over. The figure takes a nervous step. 'Can I come in?'

I consider the question before nodding. She rushes towards the bed, climbing on all fours: coat, shoes, everything. Golden waves of hair sway as she crawls on top of me until finally coming to lie down. Her heart pounds like a bird thrashing against a cage until her body comes to rest on my chest, head burrowing into the nook under my shoulder. I put my arm around her. She inhales, her hands gripping my T-shirt tightly.

'I miss you.'

I lay back on the pillow and close my eyes with the weight of her pressed into me, breathing in the scent of her hair. Lavender. It's always lavender.

'I know it hurts.' She whispers, 'But it's the greatest privilege...to feel.'

I drift away with the sound of her voice travelling soothingly through the darkness.

'James!'

My eyes squint open, adjusting to the bright overhead lights. I try to turn over, but my left shoulder instantly barges into a cold, hard wall. Groaning, I settle on my back again, staring up at a bland, white-wash ceiling. With my mind grasping for clarity, I reach out; my arm falling off the edge of a tiny, single bed. *I'm not at home.* Desperate cries from distant, isolated voices travel through me, the smell of bleach and body odour encompassing the space.

'Get up, James.' A door grinds open. A loud, cockney voice echoes through the small gap. 'Mummy's come to get ya...' The Custody Sergeant laughs to himself. 'You sober yet?'

'Unfortunately.' I murmur, rolling my bad shoulder.

'Yeah, they ain't made for big lads.' He nods to the single bed attached to the cell wall. 'They'll murder ya back.'

I stare at him, unamused.

'Must 'av friends in high places.' He gives me a knowing look. 'Com'on then.'

I follow him down the corridor, the aggressive howls of other cell occupants growing even louder now, their voices carrying angry protests with frustrated fists and feet bashing metal doors. The Sergeant holds his card against the wall before leading me out to a processing area. Alison Collins waits by the front desk. Her gaunt, wrinkled face is set with impatience. Her blonde bob is shaking with irritation as she loudly chastises a junior officer.

'Here he is.' The officer says with relief, hastily handing her a clear bag of my belongings.

'Finally.' Her pincer blue eyes give me a quick once over before she shoves the bag into my chest.

I join her outside, rolling up my shirt sleeves as the sticky summer air hits me hard.

Collins lights a cigarette, taking a long drag before leaning against the wall. 'You want one?'

'No, thanks.'

She raises her eyebrows, her pinched face full of expectation. 'What?'

'Assaulting a traffic warden.'

'Did they tell you why?'

'Because you were drunk! Because he gave you a ticket, I presume?' She throws the cigarette on the floor, stubbing it out before collecting herself and walking on.

'Did they tell you what happened before I got the ticket?' I follow her. 'The bloody traffic warden helped me reverse into the parking space.'

She smirks, amusement pricking her usually cold gaze.

'It's not funny.'

'Am I laughing?'

'You want to!'

'Go on...'

'I had to go back to the flat, get the last of my stuff. I was literally going to be five minutes max. When I came back... the same guy that helped me was writing a ticket.'

'Where did you park?'

'Opposite the pub.'

'That's a loading bay.' She says, searching in her handbag.

'I know...' I exhale, shaking my head. 'What do you think I was doing? Setting up a car boot sale!'

'Well Gabriel... violence is never the answer.' She points her key forward, waiting for the car to flash before opening the boot.

'Great.' I grumble, ducking my head and getting into the passenger seat. 'He knew what he was doing.'

'I'm just wondering at which point you decided headbutting him would help?'

'I held on to him so he wouldn't fall into the traffic.'

'Thoughtful.' She murmurs, throwing gum in her mouth before starting the engine. 'Let's get your car then, shall we?'

I close my eyes, leaning my head back.

'You're welcome, by the way.'

I sit up and look at her.

'The strings I had to pull...'

'Did you tell them who we were?'

'No... but you owe Julian a drink. Preferably a soft one.'

CHAPTER THREE

ALEXANDRA

I stand in Victoria Street's Counter-Terrorism office, lingering my eyes over Edward James' desk. Post-it notes scribbled with addresses are stuck to multiple files swollen with freshly printed documents. A stack of paperwork sits next to his computer, most of the text redacted. I wonder how many tactical decisions have been made in this very room, probably by men who've never stepped foot in a warzone. I pick up a paperweight and turn it over in my palm, eyeing the inscription at the bottom.

E, from C. x

I grimace, suddenly feeling uncomfortable at the prospect of Edward's personal life. I can't picture him as a '*gifts*' person. He's a very cold, hard man with few redeeming qualities.

'You're not to come here without an appointment, Alexandra.' I jolt as the door swings open. 'You know that.'

Edward strides in, hanging up his rain mac and propping his umbrella against the wall. The air in the room becomes heavy with judgement and expectation.

'You're not taking my calls.'

'When did you get back?' He stands authoritatively behind his desk, his eyes picking at my thoughts like a vulture pulling at a carcass.

'About three weeks ago.'

'You've been in London for three weeks.' He sounds surprised. *Good.*

'As I said, I've been trying to get hold of you.'

24

'Right.'

'I have some important information.'

'Have a seat.'

'I'll stand.'

'Suit yourself.' He unbuttons his suit jacket, sliding it off before placing it on the back of the leather chair. 'Drink?'

'No thanks.'

He raises his eyebrows. 'Not in the mood?'

'It's eleven in the morning.'

Doesn't take a genius to work out where his son gets it from. He pours himself a whisky from a crystal decanter before taking a sip, analysing me above the rim of the tumbler. He swallows, smacking his lips together. 'What is it then?'

'What is it…' I scoff. 'When we started this, you were fixated on being kept in the loop. You sent me out to the desert to track down evidence of Higgs, then you disappear. You're unreachable.'

'We're looking at other avenues.'

'And you were just going to leave me out in Saudi Arabia? Chasing a man who doesn't exist.'

'He exists.'

'Well, he's not out there.'

'What are you talking about?'

'The Singularity wiped Paytak's mafia from the planet. There's nothing of them in Riyadh, Jeddah or anywhere. I think London holds the key.'

He eyes me briefly whilst deliberately making a point of rearranging his desk. 'What is that key exactly?'

'The Foreign Office.'

'Good grief, you're not serious.'

'I've been looking into David Fallows, Minister of State for Europe.'

'Alexandra, you are wasting your time.'

'I have strong reason to believe he's being used by The Singularity.'

'And you've got evidence?'

'Nothing concrete, not yet.'

He drops his gaze back to his papers. 'You should stick with what we discussed.'

'I've investigated every tenuous link, every lead you sent me. If there was something between Higgs and ISIS. I would have found it.'

'And you think you'll find it in the Foreign Office?'

'I want to request that we run surveillance on David Fallows. He has power and influence. From what I can see, over the years, he's amassed quite a debt. Then, suddenly, the debt is just gone. There's been no deaths in the family, no inheritance. His wife hasn't received a bonus or pay rise in the last year. This money has appeared out of thin air.'

'I'll look into it.'

'I would like more resources for a proper surveillance operation.' I pause, weighing up his reaction. 'And any contacts you have within the cabinet.'

'I said,' he raises his voice. 'I will look into it.'

'Didn't you hire me to find Higgs?'

'Precisely. And if you continue sniffing around Whitehall, you'll scare him off.' He gestures to the hefty stack of files next to him. 'Currently, there are other matters that require my attention.'

'What is more pressing than this?'

'Where do I start?' He looks down at them, picking the first one up. 'Bomb factory in Peckham, an extremist recruitment rally in Manchester, a terrorist appearing out of thin air in Victoria... need I go on?'

'What happened in Victoria?'

'Hadid Waqif was spotted by SO15 analysts getting on the Gatwick Express. We didn't even know he was in the country.'

'Did you catch him?'

'He got away.' He confesses grudgingly.

'Which means he's still out there?'

He nods. 'We picked up intel from an ISIS sleeper cell which recently attacked a prisoner camp in Hasaka. Waqif is working for them. They sent him to the UK to scout the terrain. We've got teams looking for him around the clock.'

'How the hell did he get into the country?'

'We're looking into it.'

'Almasi…'

'Excuse me?'

'Imran Almasi used to run the sleeper cells in Syria. After the US campaign against his group called The Beatles, he took everything to ground.'

'And you've been sent to find him multiple times.' Edward comments pointedly. 'Yet never succeeded.'

'Nobody has succeeded.' I snap, taking the bait.

'If Waqif was here, then an attack on British soil is imminent. And if Almasi is involved, then it's going to be devastating.'

'I'll dig up everything I have on Imran Almasi.'

'Well, you better hurry because it's not just us looking.'

'What do you mean?'

'A few days before Waqif appeared… a division of MI6 requested all SO15 background on the attack in Hasaka.'

'You think they know something we don't?'

'It's possible…'

'Surely they would need to share that information.'

'Our government likes to keep its intelligence agencies competing; it's how we whittle out the baddies.'

'Doesn't seem particularly efficient to me.'

He crosses his arms. 'There might be something you can do for me here.'

'What is it?' I ask, knowing it's never straightforward.

'As you know Alexandra, our companions at MI6 report to the Foreign Secretary.'

'Yep.'

'There's a rumour regarding a particular division, supposedly run by Paul Brown, who instead report into the Prime Minister directly. Brown was first desk of the security services for twenty-five years.'

'Ok.'

'Brown requested the intel on the attacks in Hasaka.'

'Right...'

'Brown's division has also been sniffing around our own sealed records regarding Paytak and Freeman Powell Technologies.'

'He's investigating The Singularity too.'

Edward's cold, calculating gaze studies me for a prolonged moment before he clears his throat and picks up an iPad. 'I need you to find out what he has.'

'My connections run deep around the city but MI6 territory, that's not my bag.'

'Did you ever stop to think how Brown got wind of an organisation like The Singularity, Alexandra? Or who might have given him that information?'

'Gabriel.' I murmur.

'I gave my son an opportunity for a fresh start and still he manages to shoehorn his way into this investigation.'

'That is not a good idea.' I swallow past the dry lump in my throat. 'Gabriel is…' I pause. There's no succinct way of explaining what he is or, more specifically, the status of our association right now. 'You made it very clear there was to be no contact. I've held up my end of that deal.'

Edward scoffs. 'I'm not expecting you to invite him over for tea.'

'Then what is it?'

He waits, punctuating the moment; letting me know that my temper will not be tolerated in his presence. 'Knowing my son as you do, he's the kind of man who brings his work home with him… wouldn't you say?'

I think back to Gabriel's Upper Street flat. The files on his bed, the caseload of documents across his coffee table. *I know what he wants.*

'Don't you want to catch a real break?' Edward regards me coolly.

'By investigating the evidence, yes.'

'If MI6 are sitting on key information about an ISIS sleeper cell who have direct links with The Singularity, I guarantee there will be more.'

'You're asking me to steal evidence from an MI6 agent.'

'I shouldn't envisage stealing has ever been an issue for you; you are the daughter of a gangster, after all.'

My eyes burn into his face. 'What is it you're looking for exactly?'

'Anything on Almasi, Higgs, The Singularity and an attack.'

'This isn't exactly what I signed up for.'

'Well…' He tips his glass. 'Better to dance with the devil than stand in his path.'

'Gabriel has two properties… which one?' I ask, feeling sick.

'He sold the London flat. He lives in Oxfordshire now.'

'He kept the house?' I blurt out, my body aching from the memory. 'I haven't been back there.'

'You're a professional.'

I try to breathe through the sadness rising in my throat. 'And if I come back empty-handed?'

'You won't.'

'I want surveillance support on Fallows.'

He sighs. 'Get the intel from MI6... and we'll run the surveillance.'

I grip my hands tightly into fists. 'Fine... when?'

CHAPTER FOUR

ALEXANDRA

Parking the car by a farm gate, I kill the lights and pull the rucksack from the front seat onto my lap, trying to locate a torch. I sit for a while, listening to the steadiness of my breath, going through the protocols in my head. *Conditions. Degree. Manner. Force.* Before B-Squad operations, Simon trained us to think hard on these four things. The conditions of our environment, the degrees we were willing to reach to succeed, the manner in which we would approach and then, ultimately, what force was required. I close my eyes, picturing how this applies here; with all that's happened. *This is Gabriel. This is his home. The place where my father died.* I sit up in my seat and stare ahead. It's a job that needs to be done. And I'm a professional.

Stepping out of the car, I look up and down the dark lane. The perk of breaking into someone's house in the middle of nowhere is that nobody's around. I pull out my phone and check the last message from Edward. It's a picture of Gabriel getting out of his car on a street in Oxford. According to Edward's sources, Gabriel has dinner plans. I stop my mind drifting to what those might be or with whom and begin my journey in the dark. It's roughly half a mile to the first of two cattle grids that lead up to his property. Having enlisted Michael Keough, a world-renowned hacker and an old friend of the family, I was able to obtain detailed information regarding the property's security measures. There's an alarm that trips when cars travel over the second cattle grid just before the gates. Gabriel receives a notification on his phone of the vehicle registration, make and model. He also has another external alarm system that covers the full perimeter of the land with extensive CCTV set up for anyone attempting to enter on foot. The only black spot is the back of the annexe. A large chestnut tree leans partway into the fence, which means he receives regular notifications that there's a breach behind the outhouse. The truth is, it's simply a loose branch or a particularly windy day causing the whole tree to shake. He's been trying to fix the sensors for months. I hate having to know that in such great detail. It feels wrong to hold this access, to put myself in such close proximity, yet ultimately knowing he is at such a great distance.

I slide my gun into the holster around my waist and look up at the big chestnut, its twisted branches hanging over the fence, almost as if beckoning me towards the house. *It's just a place. It's just a place with no meaning.* I check my surroundings once more before sprinting towards the barbed wire. I hurdle over the top, pushing my right foot into the base of the trunk and leaping into the air. Reaching out to grab the first thick branch, I swing myself upward. Gabriel might receive these notifications all the time, but he'll still check the feeds. I clamber on top of the roof and wait, lying flat on my back. He'll be examining all cameras around the outside of the house right about now. After a few minutes, I pull out my phone and call Edward.

'Are you in?'

'No, I'm wondering if you're watching anything nice on TV.'

'We'll kill the power. Gabriel will receive an alert as soon as it goes out. We estimate you've got fifteen minutes until he gets home.'

'Received.'

I hang up and watch the blinking red light on the primary camera, nestled above the door at the front of the house. It flashes a few more times before extinguishing. I jump down and run to the side, checking the light on the second camera before moving to the main entrance. I slide out the key Edward gave me. The symbol of ultimate betrayal. A father's disloyalty to his own son. Then there's me, standing here holding it, plainly marking my deceit. I check behind me before letting myself in. A beeping on the backup interior alarm system tells me Gabriel will receive another notification from inside the house. No doubt he'll be racing down an A-road from Central Oxford, knowing something is very wrong.

I scan the hallway before making my way through to the living room. The place is well lived in but extremely tidy. *He's a neat freak. Always has been.* I avoid looking in the direction of the fireplace. The carpet might be pristine now but the last time I was here, it housed a very different scene; one I'm not able or willing to reimagine. I breathe a little easier on reaching the kitchen, disregarding the memory of blowing Levi Nabilla's brains out in this very doorway. I look around the surfaces, nothing appears to have been left out, but this isn't where he reads case files. I glance up at the ceiling, wishing I didn't have to do it. I could tell Edward that the house was empty, nothing to be found but he'll know it's a lie and he'll do everything in his power to punish me for it. If he can't have this, nobody can.

Having forced myself upstairs, I enter the master bedroom, instantly catching the familiar scent of Gabriel James. *Sandalwood and fresh washing powder.* My body tightens, my mind fights to keep him out, block him away.

Gabriel is gone.

He's not coming back.

Not for me, anyway.

Reaching the walk-in wardrobe, I part his clothes along the rail and stare at the safe. I punch in the code. Janie James' birthday backwards. The light flicks green with a quick beep before the lock relents. The safe reveals three steel shelves; the top one predictably hosts a large pile of case files. I reach in, pulling each one out carefully. Something drops to the floor from the second shelf. My eye catches an agonisingly familiar image. Leaning against the door, I stare down. My body temperature drops. An ultrasound lies on the floor. *Mine.* I bend to retrieve it, running my thumb over the shape. My eyes sting as they fixate on that beautiful light grey blur. *He kept it.* My breathing becomes shallow and tears escape, running down my cheeks. *You're here to do a job, Alexandra. Pull it together.* Touching the picture one last time, I return it to the safe and collect my composure, trying to fight the tightness in my chest.

A distant beeping catches my attention. My body stills. I wait, listening out for it again. *The alarm.* The system is back on. Peering out of the wardrobe, I look across the room, catching the digital clock on Gabriel's bedside table. It's flashing. The red numbers are like a warning, their urgent blinking telling me to speed up. The power is back on. Flicking through the large file, I start taking pictures, not really even reading them properly as I capture multiple snapshots. Something slips out of my hand and onto the floor. An image of a tall, pale man climbing out of a car. Gabriel has written the word *VIPER* in marker on the back. I slide it back in and throw the rest of the files in the safe, bending to collect the loose images. I race towards the bedroom door when the room illuminates. Distant headlights invade the space, causing shadows in the room to leap up and down against the walls. I jog to the window. A black car accelerates quickly through the second cattle grid, its wheels churning up the gravel in its wake. *He's here.*

In those few seconds, I weigh up my options. *Stay or leave. Stay or leave.* His car door slams. I check my gun is holstered before rushing down the stairs. I've got five seconds before he's standing in this hallway. I rush through the kitchen and head for the utility room. There's a door that leads to the back of the house. If I open it before he's inside, the entry sensors will alert him again. He'll know someone is definitely here. He'll chase me down. I have to wait until he's entered, switched them off, then I can slip out. A second car door slams. *He's brought company.* Muffled voices travel through the walls. He warns his companion to stay where they are. I wait, wiping sweat from my forehead, trying not to lean on the tumble dryer in case I switch it on. *Please don't come in here. Please don't come in here.* His footsteps make their way through the living room. He hasn't turned the entry sensor off yet. It's deliberate. He wants to be alerted if an intruder opens another door and makes a run for it. He continues marching around the house, calling out that he's armed as he clears each room, making sure there's no immediate threat or danger. Finally, he enters the kitchen. I hold my breath. He throws his keys down on the marble countertop with a frustrated sigh. There's one place he hasn't checked. *Do I have enough time to bolt and make it to the fence?* No. He's too fast.

'Hi…'

I flinch.

'Yeah. Stand down.'

I breathe out slowly. *He's on the phone.*

'Yeah, it's nothing. Just a power cut.'

He leaves the kitchen, heading for the front door. I hear him open it, calling out across the driveway. The crunch of gravel resounds under the second person's footsteps. They make their way towards the house. Part of me longs to stick around, see who it is, understand how his life has since changed. But I'm instantly reminded of how much that might hurt and the pain this house has already caused me. *There is a reason you left him behind.* Finally, I hear the entry sensors shut off and take one final breath of courage, slipping quietly away, leaving all thoughts of Gabriel James behind.

CHAPTER FIVE

COLLINS

The S.A.I.B.R briefing room smells of fresh paint and new furniture. Dr Emily Meyer, our specialist in forensic science and newest addition to the taskforce, strides elegantly into the room. She's closely followed by Jacob Roe, both quietly taking their seats. A few minutes later, Gabriel stalks in, slapping various files onto the table as if he's got a million other places he'd rather be. He looks drawn and tired. He always dresses impeccably, which is why his most recent spiral of excessive alcoholism goes unnoticed by most. And yet, having known him for twelve years, I can spot the signs: the slightly slack jaw, his unfocused eyes. He never appears drunk, simply distant. Like the lights have been turned off inside. It breaks my heart to see him this way, but I could never tell him that. It has to be handled delicately, or he'll push me away. He's so like my ex-husband Ted. Perhaps that's why I hold a soft spot for him despite his long list of bad decisions and misdeeds.

'Let's go.' Gabriel urges impatiently, crossing his arms. 'Let's get this briefing started so we can get some lunch.'

'Might I remind you that you were late.'

He smirks, enjoying the rise. *At times, his professionalism leaves a lot to be desired.*

I afford him a quick glare for his petulance. 'As you're all aware, from intel we garnered after the attack on Hasaka prison in Syria, we've finally uncovered a link between Imran Almasi's sleeper cells and The Singularity.' I gesture at the screen. 'Recent drone surveillance has captured Almasi with an unidentified male ten miles from Za'atari refugee camp on the Jordanian/Syrian border. We're calling this unidentified male VIPER.' I click the remote, revealing a second image. 'A few days later, in the same spot, we see VIPER with another man, Dante Soridov. Ex – KGB. He's contracted to Freeman Powell Technologies and has worked for Diren Paytak in the past. We believe VIPER could be an identified player nicknamed Higgs and therefore coordinating more breaches of the UK Government using Almasi somehow.' VIPER wears a cap, he's tall and sinewy, towering over Soridov. I flip to a third image, revealing a distorted view of his angular face. Dante, on the other hand, is shorter with a wider build. His large head is shaved save for the top knot at the base of his skull. 'A few hours after this meeting, our drone captured vehicles linked to Imran Almasi travelling in convoy from Port Latakia to Za'atari refugee camp.' I swipe to an aerial picture of four trucks. 'We lost them after this.'

'Lost them how?' Roe interjects.

'Refugee camps are a drone no-go zone. Something to do with controlling press and media coverage.' I inform.

'What could Almasi want with a refugee camp?' Gabriel asks.

'We don't know. But his resurfacing concerns me. It could mean he's planning something big. Bigger than the Wharf Cab Bombings. And if he's stood talking to Dante Soridov, then it's safe to infer that he has The Singularity's backing.'

Dr Meyer clears her throat, her eyes flickering to the screen before she looks at Gabriel. He nods, almost as if giving her permission to speak. It shouldn't seem like a red flag, but I also observe the change in his expression. His eyes linger on her face for a moment too long whilst Dr Meyer's mouth twitches upwards slightly. *That is the last thing we need.*

'You've said in previous briefings that Diren Paytak was trafficking children for The Singularity.' Dr Meyer begins. 'If Almasi is linked to Paytak's associates, could it be that ISIS is continuing Paytak's work…Refugee camps *are* full of children.'

37

'That would be my guess.' I respond, moving on to the next image. 'This is another image of Dante Soridov at Port Latakia in Syria seven days later. Here he's stood watching a crew load a ship called The Corinthia with twenty shipping containers. The ship departed an hour later. Could be that they're using these children somehow.'

'The Corinthia, where was it going?' Dr Meyer asks.

'Port Felixstowe, England via Cyprus.'

'Did you have someone check the ship?' Roe adds. 'Can we question the crew?'

'Cypriot maritime security runs random checks from time to time, we made sure they boarded The Corinthia. It was empty. There's no footage of Soridov getting off that ship. We don't want to alert The Singularity that we know about their vessel. But we're keeping a close eye on the captain and the crew.'

'It doesn't make sense.' He shakes his head.

'Well, we also know that The Corinthia isn't its real name.' I lower myself into a seat at the head of the table, motioning for Dr Meyer to turn the lights back on. 'Imaging from Port Latakia recognises it as a Syrian vessel. And given that all cargo via Syria is sanctioned, a ship like that can't travel from the Middle East without sign-off from the Foreign Office. They would have to know what was on it and exactly where it was going.'

Gabriel sits forward. 'We're running extensive checks on everyone in the FCO. Nothing yet.'

'Will Brown allow us to put a team on the Foreign Office?' Roe asks.

'It's what we're here for.'

Gabriel stands suddenly, collecting his files. 'Roe, can you speak to Brown about bugs in the Foreign Office? Don't put anything in writing. Ask to speak to him personally. Em...' He stops, correcting myself. 'Dr Meyer... run the images of VIPER through every database we can get our hands on. We need to find out who he is. But cast the net wide, we don't want GCHQ alerted to the fact we're looking for him specifically. Mix it in with a few others.'

'Got it.' She says, suppressing a smirk. *Jesus Christ.*

'Any update on the intel from SO15, James?' I ask, reminding him where he is. 'That could help discern Almasi's movements.'

'Not yet, but I'm working on it.'

I wait for Roe and Dr Meyer to exit the room before stepping in and lowering my voice. 'I hope you know what you're doing.'

He frowns, throwing his hands in his pockets.

It's wholly irritating that we have to dance this merry tune before he finally admits to any wrongdoing. *Sometimes, it's like working with a very tall, very irate toddler.*

'Keep it professional. We're finally in a good place with this taskforce.'

He offers a wry smile. 'Noted.'

I shake my head, already exasperated with him. *It's not even ten o'clock.* 'I mean it, Gabriel. We need everyone keeping a clear head. Edward's going to play all the tricks in the book to keep us out. Possibly to the detriment of his own country.'

'I hear you.'

'It worries me. Almasi with Soridov. It's a dangerous pair.'

He nods thoughtfully. 'This city won't survive another attack on that scale.'

I sigh, trying to stave off the feeling of dread. 'At this stage, I'm not sure there's anything we can do to stop it.'

CHAPTER SIX

ALEXANDRA

In our community, the best way to find something out about someone is to go to church. The Greek church is a network of high-functioning, highly motivated people who can spread gossip like wildfire. When I was little, my father would drag me every Sunday. *Hugging, kissing, candles, bread, dried fruit, incense.* Funny what you remember. Most of the Greek I've learnt is from sitting in a pew for hours, listening to a priest. Coming here holds a sense of calm for me. A place to reset, take a breath. When the light floods through the windows and catches the hues of gold on the ceiling, warmth fills the space. The candles burning at the altar represent a sense of infinite tranquillity, like they could go on forever.

A gust of wind travels from the open door as I light one for my father. The flame catches just as I hear the authoritative stride of Edward James on the cold stone behind me. I keep my eyes trained on the flickering blaze, their light creating a glow that seems to thaw his sour presence.

'Is this how you atone for your time in B-Squad?'

'If you've come in here armed, I'll be lighting one for you shortly.'

'You're not serious.' He scoffs.

'You want to test the theory?'

I nod to Atlas, a long-time friend of my father, who lingers in the corner, watching Edward with suspicious eyes. With a sharp look of arrogance, Edward sizes him up, mistaking him as a non-threatening entity. Atlas' eyes dare Edward to make a move, his hand dropping to his side, his tanned fingers grazing the subatomic machine gun hidden under his robes. Reluctantly, he reaches behind him and pulls out a small pistol, placing it in my hand. I hold the gun in the air, ensuring Atlas can see. Satisfied, Atlas nods before turning through a door. I unload Edward's weapon and place it on a pew.

'You'll get it back when you leave.'

He exhales in a way that makes him taller, his shoulders broadening. 'What is this place?'

'It provides a safe haven when needed.'

'Are all the priests armed?' He asks, eyebrows raised.

'Just Atlas.'

'Right, well, I'm pressed for time, Alexandra.'

I pull out my phone, showing him the images from the documents in Gabriel's safe. 'You can take a look yourself but in short, Gabriel is part of an off-book MI6 operations division called S.A.I.B.R, The Security Appointed Intelligence for British Reconnaissance. They report directly to a specialist committee comprised of the PM, Deputy PM, and the Home Secretary. All have had extensive background checks to ensure none of them has any connection to The Singularity.'

'Right.' His mouth thins, irritation simmering under the surface.

'Gabriel's division has found a link between Imran Almasi and The Singularity. There are pictures of Imran Almasi in Syria with Dante Soridov. Dante is contracted to Freeman Powell. He also worked for Paytak.'

His brows twitch. 'He's the go-between.'

'S.A.I.B.R have also been running checks on the Foreign Office. The ship in the second batch of images is called The Corinthia. It's sailing back and forth from Syria. According to Gabriel's notes, the ship contains cargo connected to the Za'atari refugee camp. The ship can't travel in this capacity without sign-off from someone in the Foreign Office. Like I said, putting surveillance on David Fallows is a safe bet. If there's going to be a second attack, we need to get on this now, Edward.'

'Do S.A.I.B.R know anything about an attack?'

'Nothing, they're in the dark too.'

'Za'atari camp, very interesting.' He nods to himself. 'Send me what you have. I'll review the files.'

'There was one more thing.'

He raises his eyebrows as if waiting for a child to ask permission to speak.

'I didn't have time to take a picture,' I lie. 'But in the safe, there were images of a third man. I don't recognise him, but he was spotted meeting with Dante Soridov at Port Latakia a second time.'

'Describe him.'

'Tall. Taller than you. Thin and drawn. Pale. S.A.I.B.R call him VIPER.'

Edward's expression remains neutral.

'He appears to be important. Gabriel's notes indicated that S.A.I.B.R. is still trying to find out his identity.'

'When were these images taken?'

'I didn't see.'

'I didn't send you in there to be utterly useless, Alexandra.'

'Almasi looks older. He has a beard now. And if Dante Soridov is involved, it's certainly within the last eighteen months, or else I'm certain Diren Paytak would be standing in the picture.'

'Let's hope your Cambridge-like guesswork rings true.' He stands, doing up the buttons on his jacket.

'Somebody in the Foreign Office looked the other way when the Hadid Waqif entered the country. It's probably the same person who's allowing The Corinthia to sail to the UK from Syria.'

'I'll put my own surveillance team on David Fallows. If there's anything there, we'll get it.'

'You said…' I stop, too furious to even find the words. 'I brought you Fallows.' I raise my voice, the walls of the church echoing the full force of my frustration. 'That was my lead.'

'I don't answer to you because I happen to be on your turf with a few religious barbarians. You work for me.'

'I work for you as long as it works for me.'

'I said I would keep you updated.'

'You hired me to find Higgs. You're the only one stopping me from doing that.'

'You're the delivery driver, not the chef. You brought me Fallows, the ship, and the camp. And now we do the work.'

'You think Gabriel is going to step aside and let you take this?'

Without any further acknowledgement, he collects his pistol and strides down the aisle, offering the church one last disdainful glare before he exits.

CHAPTER SEVEN

ALEXANDRA

The sticky city heat bears down on me as I wander along Sussex Gardens, cutting off the pavement towards the entrance of The Athena Hotel. A group of confused tourists ask me for the route to Paddington station and I point them in the right direction. I smirk, amused that a few naïve holidaymakers have actually booked to stay here. My father won the hotel in a game of cards, and I don't recall him ever hiring staff to maintain the facilities. Nobody except Michael Keough, of course. Keys is the son of the late Dot Keough, once a terrifying Irish gangster and close family friend. Dot's territory ran in a triangle. From Tower Hamlets to Bow, then up to Hackney. He was well liked, well respected and did more for his community than any politician could. That is, until the IRA assassinated him for making too many friends in the British government. Sensing how London was turning and knowing his control was waning, Dot enlisted our help in case anything happened to him. That's how Michael entered the picture. Mario essentially became the main father figure in his life. He ensured the Keough family had enough money to fund Michael's education, even paying for his degree at Imperial. All seemed to be going well until Michael began attracting the attention of Cyber Investigations. It turns out Dot Keough's son possessed skills that were fervently sought after by the criminal underworld; hacking capabilities that he was using to make a lot of money. After successfully breaching security at Whitehall and attempting to blackmail two senior MPs; Michael 'Keys' Keough was arrested, serving four years in prison. When he was eventually released, Mario put him in charge of The Athena. A poor attempt to sway his interests and keep him on a less dangerous path. Personally, putting a criminal

44

in a room full of other criminals seems counterproductive. But Keys has worked here ever since. Credit to him; he's kept the place in good shape. Occasionally, we get the odd customer, a person who has genuinely booked the hotel for a trip to London but very rarely.

Entering the reception, I approach the antique desk that came with the building, running my eyes over the scratched gold handles, half of them hanging off. I grimace at the thick red carpet and green wallpaper. *This place needs a major refurbishment.*

'Good Afternoon. How can I help?' A young, pubescent boy approaches, dressed in a cheap suit.

'I'm here to see Keys.'

His eyes widen.

The boy hesitates. 'Yes, I urm…' He turns to rummage in an open drawer, quickly presenting a card. He clears his throat before reading. 'Can you tell me where to find the Jasmine Tree?'

I frown. 'Are you new?'

'I started yesterday.'

'Give me that.' I snatch the card from his shaking fingers and read the gold-embossed question. 'Did Keys make you do this?'

'He said if anyone asks for him, they have to answer the card.'

'Avalon.'

'I'm sorry?'

'The Jasmine Tree. It's in Avalon.'

'Oh, yes… yes ok, right.' He says eagerly.

'Are you going to get him, or should I?'

'Yeah… urm, yes.' He begins nodding vigorously. 'Down there.' He gestures to the door under the stairs. 'You'll find him in there.'

'Thanks.'

I approach the staircase, passing two maids whispering in a huddle next to the door. Seeing me, their eyes widen before they

45

shuffle out of the way. The older of the two murmurs to her friend, explaining who I am in Greek. Excusing myself, I shift past them and place my hand on the brass doorknob, twisting it carefully. Peering into the darkness, I fumble for the light switch and head down the stairs towards a muffled beat that becomes more pronounced the further I go. The bottom light finally flickers on, illuminating the end of the staircase. I pull back a thick red curtain, exposing a second door. The wood quivers with the thump of another dance anthem.

'Ms Christofi...' Anthony, the large and menacing doorman, smiles and shifts to one side. 'Enjoy your evening.'

'Thanks, Ant.'

I step into the club, scanning my eyes over huge LED screens; each one flashing a sequence of images. *Fire, vintage cars racing around mountain roads, the sea lapping the beach.* Keys has made a few changes here. A handsome DJ stands confidently on a raised platform, bobbing his head in time with a base you can feel in your bones. So captivated by the scene, I almost miss that his decks have been positioned under a huge red heart, twinkling in an arch above his head. I remind myself to extend my refurbishment project down here and limit Keys from spending any more money. Despite the unique décor, the club still buzzes, filled with patrons of old, none of whom seem bothered by the music rumbling off the walls. The Athena has always had an air of invincibility, like anything could happen above ground but down here, you're a person of your own making. *Special. Untouchable, even.* I pass the bar, recognising a few familiar faces. Aldyn Wolfe lifts his glass in acknowledgement before continuing an intense discussion with a senior member of the Yakuza. I pick up my pace and hope the curling fog of cigar smoke is enough to conceal me. Everyone's wondering what will become of the Christofi empire now and the truth is, I don't know. I spot a group sitting around a poker table nestled in the far corner, each of them deeply focused. One man, in particular, sticks out. Not least because he's dressed the most casually, wearing baggy jeans and a T-shirt that says *My Neck, My Back, My Anxiety Attack*, but his shocking red hair lights up the hazy alcove. Holding his cards close to his washed-out face, Michael Keough mumbles something which causes the other players to laugh. Enjoying his own joke a little too much, he tips his head to the ceiling, chuckling to himself before his childlike eyes zone on me. Abruptly, they widen and his freckles begin disappearing as his face reddens.

'Alex…' He jumps up. 'You're here!'

'I need to speak with you.'

'Sure, sure, sure.' He places his cards down and turns away from the table.

'You turned my father's club into Ibiza.'

'Admittedly, I did a few bits.' He leads me behind the bar, opening the stock room cupboard.

'Can you get rid of that?' I gesture towards the heart. 'I hate it.'

'I've had a lot of positive comments about it actu-'

'And who's the child on the front desk?'

'Oh! He's a friend's son… he was getting a bit big for his boots, so I thought he should spend some time here.'

'You trust him?'

'Oh yeah, yeah. He's harmless.'

'Does he know who he works for?' I cross my arms.

'Not sure how I explain you, to be honest.'

'Can you make sure he knows the score?'

'I'll be sure to do that,' he smiles, busying himself in the cupboard.

'Michael… when my father gave you the responsibility of this place, it was because he trusted you to do right by us; you're still doing that… aren't you?'

He looks offended. 'For eternity, my Queen.' He gestures inside, pulling up a large hatch on the floor. 'The office…'

I examine the ladder beneath. 'You put a stage in the lounge, but you couldn't move Mario's office to a more convenient place?'

'I like it… kinda cool, don't you think?'

'Just know that I am armed.'

'You think I'd kill you in your own club?'

'People have tried more idiotic things.'

I arrive in the office and old memories immediately surge to the surface. I fend off flashes of my father sitting in that creaky leather armchair behind the glass desk, cursing on the phone as he chain-smoked cigars. Keys even kept his vast collection of ashtrays. I move towards one, running my finger over the smooth glass. Every time I took a trip, I would buy him a new one. It became a running joke; the tackier, the better. It was my way of telling him where I'd been and no matter what I was doing, I was thinking of him.

'This is really something to be back here.'

'It's still his… I'm just visiting.'

I nod.

'You can come here anytime you want, Alex.'

I turn my attention to the large fish tank covering the entire back wall. Bright pink fish with spikey tails dart past the glass. 'They're still alive!'

He grins. 'Mario had them genetically enhanced. They'll probably outlive me.'

'Thank you…' I laugh, unable to stop tears welling in my eyes. 'Thank you for keeping it the same.'

'Didn't feel right to change it.'

'What have you got hiding behind there?' I point at the door on the other side of the ladder. 'Mario never let me go in that room.'

'Yeah, well, I'm afraid that's still out of bounds.'

'Is it your bedroom?' I smirk, teasing him.

'Kinda, yeah.'

'Nice.' I say, dropping into the leather sofa.

'Drink?'

'Hmm… yeah go on.'

'What kind?'

'Whisky will do.'

'Quick and dirty.' He approaches the drinks cabinet and starts pouring. 'So what brings you here?'

'Just thought I'd check in, see how things were going.'

'And what *really* brings you here?'

I lean forward, cutting straight to the point. 'I need to know if you've found anything.'

He freezes mid-way through putting ice in his glass.

'Keys, did you?'

'Maybe.'

'Where is she?'

'Alex, can we just…' he sighs, handing me the whisky. 'Can we just talk about where you go from here?'

'I can't go anywhere if you don't tell me where she is.'

'You know what I mean.'

I stare at him blankly.

'Ah, jeez.' He gulps his entire drink, turning to make another.

'She's my sister; it's my choice.'

He groans, looking up at the ceiling.

I raise my eyebrows.

'Ah fuck..' He hesitates. 'The Somalis… She's with King Henry.'

'Excuse me?'

'She's been hauled up with him for a few months.'

Shivers spike my arms as I recall the last time I saw her and the last thing she did before she left. Olivia Christofi; the girl who fell into the black hole of addiction with no desire to climb back out. Never really feeling whole in a world where we existed. Loathing us and herself for her feelings of inadequacy, she quite literally jumped into bed with our family's sworn enemy, helping bridge Diren Paytak's relationship with The Singularity and facilitating the trafficking of thousands of innocent children. I spent months searching for her in Turkey, Saudi, Israel; suspecting she was hiding out with Paytak's organisation. Then The Singularity decided to do some housekeeping and I lost the trail again. All I've ever wanted is to understand why. Why did she murder the most important person in my life without a second's hesitation?

'Alex?'

'Chalk Farm.' I say, my mind throwing up a recent memory. An image of a scribbled Post-it in Edward's office. I knock back my drink, feeling sick. *He deliberately kept her from me.*

'How did you know?' He asks, surprised.

'King Henry is granting her asylum, I take it.'

'Seems that way.'

'Thanks…' I say, holding out the glass for another. 'I'll transfer what we agreed for this and for the house in Oxford.'

'I should warn you…' He pours, watching my face drop. 'It's nothing, you just… you asked me to give you a heads-up, so I'm doing that. I'm giving you the heads.'

'Ok.'

'Gabriel James. He's been down here a few times recently.'

My heart rate rises a notch. 'How recently?'

He shrugs. 'Few times a month over the past year.'

'So what you mean to say is that he's a regular?'

'He knows how to fucking party.' He smiles before wiping the look from his face, catching my scowl. 'Look, he's just here to drink and have a good time.'

'He shouldn't be drinking at all.'

Keys frowns. 'Why?'

'Never mind.' I shake my head. 'Why does Anthony even let him in?'

'When you've got a man that looks like him standing at the bar, it's real good for business.'

I glare in his direction.

'It's simple economics!'

'Can't you just stop serving him?'

'I cut him off months ago. Mesrine Roche just buys him what he wants. Her lot love drinking with him.'

'Mesrine Roche, the head of the Corsican mafia? *That* Mesrine Roche.'

'Well, yeah.' He looks down awkwardly. 'Yeah, that's what I meant.'

'Who else?'

'Sorry?'

'You said *her lot,* so which ones do you mean?'

Keys rolls his eyes. 'You're not killing them, Alex.'

I sigh. 'How many?'

'Pardon?'

'How many of them has he slept with?'

Keys whistles. 'I'd say all of them, like?'

Anger swells inside of me. I have no right to care but I do. *I really do.* 'Stop letting him in.'

He eyes me warily.

I look down at my hands gripping the leather of the sofa beneath me. 'And tell Mesrine she's barred. That will give her something to think about.'

'You're not serious?'

I stare at him.

'That's going to cause issues you don't want.'

'She knows who he is, she knows what she's doing.'

'He's just hurting, Alex.'

Yeah well, so am I. 'You haven't mentioned anything to him?'

'I tend to stay down here when he's in. But the staff say he hasn't asked after you in over a year.'

'Good.' I take a breath, desperate to change the subject. 'Look Keys... about the Foreign Office.'

'You want me to do more.' He states knowingly.

'I have another job.'

'Nope.' He shakes his head vigorously. 'No, no, no!' He points an accusing finger. 'Don't do that.'

'I need you.'

'I'm out of that game. This is what I do now.' He gestures up to the ceiling. 'And I'm doing a fine job of it.'

'You're never really out, though, are you?'

'I told you I'd help with Oxford and Olivia as a one-off.'

'And Fallows?'

'Two offs! You know the conditions of my probation. I'm trying to start fresh.'

'By running a speakeasy for an underworld gangster?'

'That's different, at least! I'm moving on.'

'Then why do you still have a tech lab in the next room?'

He glances at the door, reddening slightly.

'Come on Keys, I know it's not a bedroom.'

'It's for emergencies.'

'This is one of those.'

'I'm not going back to prison.'

'You won't need to.'

'You have to find someone else.'

'Nobody is as good as you.'

'So you're using flattery now.'

'Just listen to the job...'

He shakes his head. 'You know it's like crack to me, Alexandra. I'm clean. I need to stay clean.'

'Keys...'

'Jesus...' He whines, taking a seat. 'You scare the shit out of me, so I can't say no.' He throws his head in his hands. 'But I don't want to say yes because you scare the shit out of me.'

'I won't let anything happen to you.'

'Really?' he raises his eyebrows with disbelief. 'Because the two bullets Gabriel James took for you tell a different story. So forgive me if I don't trust your implicit word.' He notices my expression change. 'Sorry... I just-'

'Who told you that?'

'Alex, when you're at the top, you don't operate in the shadows.'

I snatch the key from the desk and stalk towards the ladder.

'This job...' He says curiously.

I stop, my foot resting on the first rung.

'How long will I be on it for?'

'You could well die doing it.' I reply, honestly.

'How so....'

'So you're interested now?' I ask, studying him.

'That look in your eyes, the fire burning inside of you when I mention Gabriel. I used to have that...'

'I can't promise anything.'

The Dark Angel

'Darling Alex, if it involves you, there'll be a rush.'

CHAPTER EIGHT

ALEXANDRA

Keys' nervous reflection stares back from the mirror as he stands upright in Mikey Sullivan's shop. With a pencil between his teeth, Mikey measures the length of Keys' sleeves before shuffling towards his desk to make notes. *In Stitches*, being otherwise known as Mikey's Tailors, is considered *Switzerland*. Mikey was my father's tailor for years and if you follow mafia code, no underworld business can be conducted on Mikey's turf. You come in here, stand next to anyone; all kinds of enemies and discuss styles, fits, lengths and materials. Aldyn's been known to share a coffee with countless opponents in Mikey's before making them disappear the very next day. Everyone's cordial, everyone's polite. Those are the rules. No business, no violence.

'What do you think of the grey, Alex?'

'Mmhmm, looks nice.'

'Are you treating yourself today, Mr Keys?' Mikey asks.

'Ms Christofi is footing the bill for this one.' He calls out deliberately, making me look up from my phone.

'Sure, yeah.' I murmur absentmindedly.

Mikey heads to the back of the shop, mumbling something about material.

'What time did you tell your contact to show?' Keys asks, his tone uneasy.

'Why are you so nervous?' I whisper, checking for Mikey's reappearance.

'Nothing I do or say can be used against me right?'

'They don't work for the NCA anymore.'

'Where now?'

'MI6.'

'Even worse!'

'Keep your head together.'

'No business!' Mikey scolds, returning with more swatches.

I widen my eyes in the mirror, silently imploring Keys to shut his mouth whilst he fixes back in position.

'You look tired, Lexy. You not getting any sleep?' Mikey asks, measuring Keys' instep.

'Not recently.'

'You need a holiday! Working too hard.'

'I need a chat with HR.'

The bell above the door rings.

Alison Collins steps into the shop. Her face warily takes in the classic mannequins and heaps of material until her bird-like eyes rest on Keys. 'Hello, Mr Keough.'

Keys offers a nervous grin in return.

'Mikey, this is my friend Alison. She's got a dress she wants looking at.'

Collins hesitates, smiling. 'Yes…it's a bit loose. Could I try it on, and then perhaps you can take a look?'

'You can get changed in there.' Mikey replies, beaming at Collins with bright white veneers that stand out amid his sagging face.

'I'll help you with the zip.' I say, jumping up from the sofa.

'Mikey Sullivan's shop?' Collins whispers, stepping into the changing room. 'You think this is wise?'

'It's the only place inaccessible to Edward.'

'Well, it's good to see you're still alive, at least.' She exhales. 'Don't worry, we can skip the pleasantries.'

'I never got the chance to thank you… for that night.'

'I didn't do it for you.'

'Well, I'm grateful all the same.' I offer a small smile. 'And I'm grateful you came today; I wasn't sure if you would.'

'Neither did I...' She admits.

I turn over my shoulder. 'I know you're risking a lot being here. And I'm sorry for what happened back then.'

'That's in the past.' She dismisses.

I nod, distracted by the bittersweet notion of having her here. Alison Collins knows exactly what I've been through, she practically lived it with us, fought just as hard to rid the world of Diren Paytak and protect Gabriel. She put her career and life on the line to save ours countless times. But her loyalty lies with him. *As it should.*

'What is it you need, Alexandra?' She narrows her eyes, assessing me. 'I haven't got much time.'

'Edward knows about your taskforce. I don't have time to dive into everything but-'

'I can't help you.' She bites, her tone stern.

'He knows everything. He knows about S.A.I.B.R and your investigation into The Singularity.'

'You brought me here to threaten me?'

'No!' I step in and lower my voice. 'No. I'm warning you.'

'How does he know?'

I break eye contact.

'How?' She presses.

I look at the floor, my face betraying me.

'You...'

'He suspected you had intel that we didn't.'

'Where did you find it?'

I clear my throat. 'Gabriel... his house.'

'His house?' She hisses.

I nod. 'Edward suspected Gabriel had a link with The Singularity when your division requested intel on Almasi and the prison attack in Hasaka.'

'I knew he'd do this.'

'SO15 are looking for a man named Hadid Waqif. Have you heard that name before?'

She shakes her head.

'He's a known terrorist who was spotted taking the Gatwick Express out of Victoria, this week. He shouldn't have been allowed in the country. Edward thinks there's going to be another attack. He thinks you requested the intel on Hasaka because you know what's coming.'

'We don't... we would never risk national security like that.'

'I know.'

'Alexandra, this has gone too far. You broke into his house. An MI6 agent's house! It took six months...six long months for him to give up on chasing you. Six months for him to admit defeat, to focus on what really mattered. I left you in Aldyn's house that day because we were all desperate to move forward. Christ, what have you done?'

'I wish I had a choice, Alison. Imran Almasi's cells have surfaced for a reason. You know that too.'

'There's always a sodding choice. You could have told him no! Found another way!'

'Listen, I know the mistakes I've made. And I'm certain so do you... but that's not why I brought you here.'

'Then what is it?'

'I have a feeling Edward is deliberately cutting me out, keeping me away from the centre of this. But if a terrorist attack is imminent, if The Singularity is involved... I need to do everything I can to stop it. You warned me he would do this, but it wasn't as simple as that…' I hesitate. 'You know why I left.'

'I don't see what this has to do with me.'

'I can't be Edward's pet anymore.'

'Is that why the world's most prolific hacker is sat outside?'

'I know it seems messy… I'm messy. But I can help you. Keys can help with Almasi. We can stop them.'

'Michael Keough is a criminal, Alexandra.'

'He can work off the books. That is what you need.'

She closes her eyes, considering this. 'How would that work?'

'I have something more, something that might help.'

She waits, narrowing her eyes.

'You know that someone in the Foreign Office had to know about The Corinthia or how else did it get to the UK?'

'Go on.'

'David Fallows. He's the Minister of State for Europe. Keys did a deep dive into the FCO. And he specifically showed flags.'

'What sort of flags?'

'Red ones… addiction issues, debt that's disappeared. Suddenly he's spending like crazy. He has all this money that has come out of nowhere.'

'You had Keys hack the Minister of State's personal information?'

'Almasi is linked to that ship. Fallows could be helping him. I think I know how.'

She rolls her eyes. 'Give it to me.'

'Keys hacked his location tags from his car's sat nav. Fallows drives to the same building site in Battersea twice a month.'

'He could be involved in the construction. Perhaps he's bought an apartment.'

'What is an MP doing on a construction site at midnight?'

'Gabriel will never allow you within a mile of this taskforce.'

'Someone put Waqif back in this country. You know the Foreign Office has to be involved with The Corinthia. Without Kristine Kingley, The Singularity had to find another way to get the children in and out of the UK. What if Almasi and his group are connected to those children now, Alison? Have you thought about that?'

Her face pinches with apprehension. 'Of course I bloody have.'

'Ladies?' Mikey calls out from the other side of the curtain. 'You two alright in there?'

Collins straightens and picks up the dress. 'Just a minute!'

I step in, lowering my voice. 'We need to be watching Fallows when he's next in Battersea. I know this in my gut. If we can get to Fallows, we can get to The Singularity. We can stop another attack.'

'We can't just take him in, Alexandra. If The Singularity finds out Fallows is compromised, they'll back off and we'll lose the lead.'

'Which is why I need your resources. I'm one person. I can't run an entire surveillance operation by myself on that site.'

She shakes her head. 'Gabriel will never agree to this.'

'Don't tell him about me. Just tell him Edward is onto Almasi and that it's linked to David Fallows. Tell him you have a source at GCHQ who's found the Battersea evidence.'

She stares at the floor.

'Please, Alison.'

She sighs, defeated. 'I'll see what I can do.'

CHAPTER NINE

GABRIEL

I kill the engine of the black cab and look up at the tip of the brightly lit towers of Battersea Power Station. The street ahead is empty. No sign of life. No noise. The only sound that can be heard is the distant traffic coming from Chelsea Bridge. The radio on the dashboard crackles; Collins gives details of her position on the roof of a building above my head. Roe is closest to the meeting point, slumped in a doorway of an old mansion block, masked as a vagrant. Emily Meyer chimes in, confirming her location in an empty apartment in Nine Elms, with access to surrounding CCTV feeds.

I pick up the radio from the passenger seat. *'ARES NINE in position. OVER.*

'Copy that ARES NINE.' Collins responds quickly. *'TECH 4, do you have a sufficient angle of meeting location? OVER.'*

'Affirmative. OVER.' Meyer replies.

'TECH 4 from ARES NINE. Can you jam signals for cellular activity? OVER.'

'We're on it, now. OVER.'

'All stations from RAZOR TEN.' Roe's voice announces. *'Car approaching from the east of the street.'*

'Have a visual.' Emily responds. *'Target confirmed as Fallows.'*

David Fallows walks with his briefcase towards a disused office block. He looks around before climbing the stairs and stepping towards the revolving doors.

'All stations from RAZOR TEN. Target is now concealed behind a pillar. Visual lost. OVER.'

'All stations from TECH 4. We can still see his left side. Looking for another angle from feeds.'

'Fuck,' I whisper, craning my neck to see an obscured view of Fallows standing in the shadows. *'All stations from ARES NINE. I can make him out. But won't see if anyone approaches from the west alleyway. OVER.*

'All stations…' Collins chips in, *'Vehicle approaching from Chelsea Bridge. Maintain cover. OVER.'*

I turn down the radio and tap the steering wheel nervously as I scan the street, catching Roe moving slowly between buildings. He's ambling with a sleeping bag wrapped around his shoulders. Fallows spots him and cautiously shifts on his feet, anxiously switching his briefcase from one hand to the other.

'Vehicle approaching at high speed.' Collins rushes out. *'RAZOR TEN, have you got a visual? OVER.'*

A grey Volkswagen van accelerates down the road before coming to an abrupt halt roughly ten metres from Fallows.

'Van is stopping.' I announce. *'RAZOR TEN. You are now fifty metres from both targets. OVER.'*

A car door slams. Fallows steps out from behind the pillar, nodding his head in greeting. An Asian, middle-aged man of average height and build appears from the driver's side, quickly beckoning Fallows around to the boot of the vehicle.

'All stations, anyone got a visual of second target? OVER.' Collins asks.

'Negative.' Emily responds.

'Male. Asian. 5ft 10 roughly. Slight build. View is now obscured by van. OVER.' I mumble into the radio.

'Moving closer to obtain identity of target two.' Roe announces under his breath.

'Negative RAZOR TEN.' I bark. 'Stay where you are.'

'I only need to move down a doorway.'

'Back the fuck off.'

Fallows slides his phone from the briefcase and begins showing his companion the screen. I shift impatiently, wondering if the van covers Roe's position. Fallows checks the street, peering in my direction. I slide down in my seat, watching as they open a set of big doors to the vehicle. The second target hunches over, handing Fallows a second briefcase.

'All stations from TECH4. We have a visual from Roe's body cam. Target two identified as Hadid Waqif. SO15 have an alert on him. He's a known associate of ISIS group The Beatles. OVER.'

So Collins was bang on; Fallows is mixed up with terror groups. Hadid Waqif stops talking suddenly. Something has caught his attention over Fallows' shoulder. I follow his eye line, craning to see out of my left window. A shift in the shadows confirms my suspicion. *Fucking Roe.* Waqif holds up a hand, ceasing Fallows mid-sentence before pulling out his gun and stepping away from the van towards a row of parked cars.

'All stations… Second suspect is armed and on approach to RAZOR TEN. OVER.' Collins warns.

'Fuck, fuck, fuck.' I fumble with my seat belt, trying to free myself. *Can I get to Roe before Waqif?*

'RAZOR TEN, do you hear me?' Collins shouts.

Roe leaps from the pavement, yelling in drunken slurs about climate change and various apocalyptic threats. Waqif jerks back, his gun twitching in his hand before telling Roe to piss off. Roe pretends not to notice, trundling towards the Power Station with his sleeping bag slung over his shoulder. Waqif shakes his head, watching Roe go before he turns back to Fallows, his body language irritated and hostile. Fallows takes a step back, clearly on edge.

'All stations from ARES NINE. Things are heating u-'

A bullet cracks through the air.

Waqif's body falls against the van. He clutches his shoulder, looking up at the buildings around him before scrambling around the side of the vehicle to shield himself. Fallows drops to the ground, inching on his knees towards a parked car as a second bullet hits a wing mirror just above his head. Throwing an earpiece in, I grab my gun and dive out of the taxi.

'ARES NINE. What the fuck are you doing?' Collins calls over the radio.

My feet pound the pavement until I reach Fallows and grab him by the scruff of his neck. I pull him to cover, throwing him between two parked cars. Waqif begins firing in our direction whilst rushing around to the driver's side of his vehicle. I power forward, shooting at the van's tyres. Giving up on starting the engine, Waqif reaches to the left, pulling a semi-automatic rifle from the passenger seat. Rapidly, I change direction and leap up the stairs of the office block, narrowly missing a rapid tirade of bullets launched in my direction.

'ALL STATIONS from ARES NINE.' I whisper, crouching behind a wall. *'ETA on backup would be nice.'*

'Run...' Collins' terrified voice rings through the earpiece. *'You have to get away from there.'*

'And Fallows?'

'Can't see him.' Emily responds, her voice shaking. *'Gabriel, please, you have to get out.'*

'TAC team won't be here in time, will they?'

'No.' Her response comes quickly.

Its finality gives me the push I need. I take a quick breath and brace to stand when a loud, decisive gunshot splits through the air.

'Waqif is down.' Roe announces, his tone shocked and bewildered. *'Waqif is down. Third shooter in play. OVER.'*

What the fuck? Carefully, I edge towards the steps. Fallows cowers by the van, gawking at a masked figure. The anonymous gunman shifts. Their legs are now astride Hadid Waqif, who lies dead in a large pool of his own blood.

'Armed police!' I shout.

The figure doesn't move, their gun determinedly pointed at Waqif as if he might rise from the dead.

'Put your weapon down!'

They turn their head.

'Put the fucking gun down.' I repeat, taking another step.

They slowly lower their hands, making deliberate moves to unload the pistol.

'Stay where you are…'

The shooter drops to the ground, suddenly tumbling under the van with precise and efficient movements.

'*Third target on the move.*' I yell into comms, dropping to the floor, my chest touching the concrete. I peer under the van, watching the suspect hop up to their feet on the other side. Leaping up, I race after them, sprinting in pursuit towards the Power Station.

'Armed police!' I yell with my finger braced to pull the trigger. 'I'll shoot if you do not stop!'

Their legs move with effortless speed. I grip my weapon, watching their hand reaching for a second gun that swings from the strap over their shoulder. I fire a bullet. Their body jolts. Their stride slows. Their legs draw to a halt. I almost expect them to clutch the wound, drop to their knees. Instead, they pivot to face me, wielding the handgun that is now level with my chest.

My eyes meet theirs.

Something in the air changes.

The world speeds up.

They pull the trigger.

The Dark Angel

My body jerks backwards, the breath is thumped from my lungs. I'm falling, tumbling with my gaze tipped to the night sky until finally, I hit the floor.

CHAPTER TEN

ALEXANDRA

The shower runs, suppressing the sobs that won't stop stirring from my chest and spilling from my mouth. I drag air into my lungs, calming my nervous system. Wiping steam from the mirror, I glance through the warm mist at my reflection. I don't recognise this person anymore. Cold eyes encased with dark shadows stare back at me. My face seems hollow. It's as if I'm disappearing slowly, becoming smaller and more insignificant by the minute. *Only living to survive.* That's exactly what my father would say if he were here now. I turn on the faucet, waiting for the sink to fill. My hands shake as adrenaline drains from my body, exposing the pain of the bullet that skimmed my arm. I look down at Aldyn's once pristine white towels. All of them are smeared with red, covered with blood. Picking up the medical staple gun, I grit my teeth and finish sealing the wound in my arm, straining with the effort of trying not to cry out in agony. I take deep breaths, quelling the nausea swirling in my stomach. *Jesus.* The fingers of my left hand tingle with the loss of blood. Using my good hand, I dab the wound with a wet flannel, cleaning the sore, damaged skin. Wincing, I look up to the ceiling, waiting for the wave of pain to pass. *Fallows. The Van. Gabriel.* A shiver twists over my body again, my brain itching with anxiety. *I did what I had to. I did what I had to.* I throw the staple gun down with frustration and turn towards the shower but a solid knock on the door breaks my stride.

'One second.' I reach up, pulling a dressing gown over my body. Sweating from the effort of heaving the robe on, I eventually murmur for whoever it is to come in.

Aldyn stands in the doorway, his expression dropping in shock. 'Alexandra?'

67

I roll my eyes, annoyed at myself for not kicking the dirty towels out of his eye line.

'Are you hurt?' He barges in. 'What is going on in here!' He scans the bloodied tiles, the first aid kit, the staple gun.

I drag the dressing gown to one side, reluctantly revealing the bullet wound.

'You've been bleeding a lot.'

'Yeah, I noticed.'

'You need a medic.'

'It's just a graze, the bullet didn't actually penetrate.'

'I'll call the doctor.'

'I just need to take a shower.'

'You might bleed out!' He runs a flannel under the tap, placing it against the wound.

I reel back from the sudden sting. 'I've patched it up.' I fling the flannel away. 'Ouch.'

'Who shot you?'

'It's part of the job.'

'Who was it?'

'You know I'm not going to tell you that.'

'You want me to help you get cleaned up?'

'Thanks but not really.'

He shakes his head, watching me warily. 'I came to tell you that Alison Collins is downstairs.'

'Did you tell her I was here?'

'She knows you live here now.'

I exhale, trying to expel the impending dread.

'She said you were with her this evening.'

'Briefly…'

He crosses his arms. 'It seems you've been busy tonight.'

I give him a questioning look.

'King Henry said one of his boys was shot in Chalk Farm.'

'Tell Alison I need to shower, and I'll be down in a minute.'

'Why are you screwing with the Somalis Alexandra?'

'I wasn't there to piss off the Somalis.'

'Then what were you doing there?'

'King Henry needs to remember whose patch Chalk Farm actually falls under.'

'He knows it was you or he wouldn't have called me.'

'I shot a Somali gang member with his own gun, did King Henry mention that?'

'Why were you there?'

'I had to put him down. He's not dead... right?'

'You just missed the artery.'

'Exactly.'

'You didn't answer my question.'

'There's been so many,' I smirk.

'What were you doing?'

I twist my mouth in thought. 'I found her...'

Aldyn shifts on his feet. 'Olivia?'

I nod. 'Dead.'

He raises his eyebrows, waiting for the admission.

'It wasn't me.' I confess, unable to hide the thick disappointment in my tone. 'It was an overdose. She left a note...'

I think back to the moment the door opened, the second my eyes took in the fragile body sprawled out across the dirty mattress with years of drug abuse scarred across her arms; needle and track marks telling a long, heart-breaking tale. The crumpled note discarded on her chest. The bitter tang of death in the room. The mixture of my own disgust tinged with loss and grief for the sister I once had, frustration that she got there before I did, the injustice that she took away my revenge, that she got an easy way out.

69

'Down the rabbit hole before you could put me there.'

Aldyn squints, struggling to understand.

'That's what she wrote,' I clarify. 'It's a phrase my father used. Anything that he considered illicit or unreachable, he'd call it the *rabbit hole*.'

'I remember.' He clears his throat. 'Well, whether you pulled the trigger or not... she's gone. The world is better.'

'Not mine.' I murmur.

'When this is all over, you will be free. Then you can mourn the sister you had. But you shouldn't ignore it. Dismissing your pain will make it worse.'

Despite desperately wishing he would leave, his attempt at consoling me still makes me smile. 'Why didn't you ever have children Aldyn...'

'Stop deflecting.'

'That's what I always say to you.'

He chuckles, shaking his head before his face drops into sincerity again. 'Would you have done it?'

I take a moment to consider the question. 'I don't know.'

His eyes soften. 'Don't forget what she took from you... what she became.'

I tense, fighting back tears.

'You need to speak to King Henry.'

'With pleasure.'

'Be polite.'

'Perhaps he can explain why he was harbouring my sister in the first place. Chalk Farm is Christofi turf. If he disobeys me again, the next bullet won't miss.'

Aldyn swears in Albanian before disappearing out of the room, mumbling something about never having daughters. I lock the door behind him and creep slowly into the shower, willing the warm water to cleanse me of this evening, pushing away all thoughts of my sister. *She's gone. Finally gone.* But the world doesn't feel lighter. Not yet.

Having made an effort to wash the blood and grit from my body, I finally head into the bedroom and pull out gym leggings and a grey T-shirt, attempting to put them on as efficiently as I can.

'And here I was thinking you got away unscathed....' Alison Collins' disapproving voice echoes from the doorway.

Failing to hide my exhaustion, I take a seat at the end of the bed. 'How is he?'

'In a lot of bloody pain....' She steps into the room. 'So are you, it seems. Are you going to get that looked at?'

'It's fine.'

'Was it entirely necessary, the rubber bullet?'

'Better than an actual one.' I gesture to my arm.

'You could have just kept running.'

'He's a good shot. He would have killed me.'

'I said you could sit tight and watch how the op played out. But the mere fact you had rubber bullets tells me you prepped for interference.'

'I thought they'd be useful in case we had to keep Waqif alive for questioning.'

'But instead, you shot your ex-boyfriend?'

'You're not seriously making a joke out of this, are you?'

She joins me on the bed. 'If I don't make light of the shit show that is this operation, then I may crack.'

'Is Gabriel going to be alright?' I try to show just the right amount of concern without letting on that the image of him dropping to the floor is already haunting me.

'Well, he won't go to hospital,' she states pointedly. 'So nobody knows the true extent of his injuries, but I've told him to call me if his lung collapses.'

I drop my head in my hands. 'Typical.'

'It's not the injury he's concerned with....'

'He wants to know who shot him with a rubber bullet?'

'Ding ding ding!' She holds up her index finger, scoring me a point. 'Who was the sniper?'

'I honestly don't know... I was watching from a mansion block. But when Waqif and Fallows went to the back of the van, I couldn't see, so I moved to a different vantage point. Then I heard shots. I ran out of there and into the street. Waqif was closing in on Gabriel.'

'You didn't try to shoot Fallows or Hadid Waqif initially?'

'Why would I round up MI6 only for them to watch me shoot two men dead in the street?' I meet her suspicious eyes, my expression imploring her to believe me. 'Perhaps The Singularity found out Waqif and Fallows were compromised.'

'Maybe,' she gnaws at her lip.

'You need to speak to Fallows. He's all we've got left. The Singularity will likely stop all shipments on The Corinthia if they know Fallows has been taken in. But he might know something else...'

'We've taken him to a secure location.'

I sigh, looking up to the ceiling. 'I didn't want to shoot him, Alison. I would never intentionally hurt him, you know that.'

'Not even the tiniest bit?' She smirks, nudging my shoulder. 'You're living here permanently now... with Aldyn?'

I nod. 'For a while, at least.'

'I don't entirely approve but...' She stands, looking around. 'It's good you have someone. Your secret is safe with me.'

'Thank you…' I hesitate, not accustomed to the gentler side of Alison Collins.

'Get some rest,' She says, moving towards the door. 'I'm off to prep for Fallows.'

'Tonight?'

'We're interviewing him first thing.'

CHAPTER ELEVEN

COLLINS

I pretend not to notice Gabriel wincing with every stride he takes down the corridor of our MI6 safehouse. Despite my repeated insistence that he get himself to a hospital, he's making every effort to conceal the true nature of his injuries. Clearly, the whisky I watched him down in the car hasn't numbed the pain as intended. He doesn't even bother trying to hide it from me anymore.

'We've got half an hour before Fallows goes into protective custody.' I remind him, stopping as he leans against a wall. 'Are you going to be ok?'

'Yeah...I think so.' He replies, his voice strained.

'What's the strategy here?' I ask, watching him uneasily.

'Roe has documented most of what we need. We just need to make sure that's all of it.'

We flash our ID badges at a camera tucked above the security door to Fallow's holding room. The panel buzzes and we step inside. Gabriel lowers himself into the chair, his expression set in a sharp grimace.

'You're the one who was shot!' David Fallows' polished face erupts into surprise. His preened eyebrows rising into a perfect arch above ignorant blue eyes. 'Christ, how did you... you're extremely lucky.'

'Not the term I'd use.' Gabriel quips, staring at the glossy MP blankly. *His suit must have cost more than the average monthly salary.* He's handsome for his age but clearly thinks too much of it.

'Ok...' I switch on the recording device, trying to move the process forward before Gabriel throttles him.

'Interview with David Fallows on 20th July.' I begin, without looking up. 'Officers present are Agent James and Agent Collins, from Security Appointed Intelligence for British Reconnaissance. This is the second interview with David Fallows and in light of recent circumstances, Mr Fallows has agreed to help us with our ongoing enquiries. As before, Mr Fallows has declined our offer of legal representation and has agreed to share information related to Operation Yellow Fire in exchange for leniency with regards to his crimes. Mr Fallows has signed a judge-appointed private order which protects the identities of Agent Roe, Agent James, Agent Collins, and associates of S.A.I.B.R. Mr Fallows, as you're aware, from the evidence we've acquired and by your own admission, you are required to provide information on dealings with Hadid Waqif and members of a crime syndicate named The Singularity. You are required to share information about the alleged activities that took place during your communication with these suspects. Activities that include accepting bribes to aid and abet a known terrorist and the syndicate's illegal activities within the UK and Europe.'

'We've identified the man you met with last night, David.' Gabriel starts. 'Hadid Waqif, born in Yemen, ex-Al Qaida, he split from them in 2019 before joining ISIS and finding The Beatles. Had you met this man before?'

'I've already told the Scandinavian gentleman all of this.'

'You're a UK government official who has just been caught making business transactions with a terrorist.' Gabriel fires back. 'You'll tell us again.'

Fallows glares at him across the table.

'Might I remind you…' I interrupt, 'withholding information is going to be problematic for you David.'

'Had you met Waqif before?' Gabriel asks.

'Not him, no.'

'You told Agent Roe that you usually meet Dante Soridov in that location. Dante Soridov is part of an organisation called The Singularity; did you know that?'

'I didn't know they had that name.'

'But you've been in contact with Soridov…' Gabriel says, irritated. 'So you must know something.'

'As I said; in the past, I've only met Mr Soridov until tonight, where my instructions were to meet Mr Waqif.'

'You didn't tell Agent Roe why you were meeting Hadid Waqif.'

He rubs his eyes. 'You don't understand who these people are, the things they'll do.'

'You should have thought about that before you got into bed with them.'

He slams his hands down on the desk, his face turning a reddish-purple. 'I had no choice. They had me over a barrel, I had no choice.'

'Why were you meeting Waqif?'

'Christ… we're all dead. It doesn't matter who you are, how much money or power you have. They'll get you… and they'll make it look like an accident.'

'Answer Agent James' questions.'

'Soridov told me to come to the location as usual. He told me I would be meeting someone who was going to give me another set of instructions.'

'What instructions?' Gabriel asks.

'I didn't get that far. We were being shot at….' He looks up at the ceiling and frowns as if a thought has suddenly occurred to him. 'If that other agent hadn't shown up, I could be dead, and you wouldn't have me sat here at all.'

I freeze in my chair, silently willing David Fallows not to go down this path. *It's not one I can explain, not here, not now.*

'I'm a Minister of State… I'm being shot at from all directions. And you,' he stabs his finger across the table at Gabriel, 'couldn't get close enough to make a blind bit of difference. So thank bloody God for him.'

'Wind back a second.' Gabriel's brow furrows with intrigue. 'Are you referring to the person that shot Hadid Waqif?' He leans forward, quickly forgetting he's incapacitated, before dropping his head, suppressing a groan.

'Yeah.' Fallows replies, taken off guard. 'Are you alright?'

'I'm fine.' Gabriel's hand grips his ribcage, his face pooling with sweat.

'Do you need a minute?' I suggest forcefully.

'You saw them?' Gabriel asks Fallows, ignoring me. 'The shooter.'

'He dropped under the van to get away from you, but I wasn't close enough to see anything.'

'You can't identify them at all?'

'Can't you!?' Fallows frowns.

'Somebody interfered with our operation. We're looking into it.' I state, trying to move past it.

'You saw the way they moved….' Fallows continues. 'Highly professional. Military, if I have to guess.'

I sigh. 'For the record, S.A.I.B.R. has no official connection to this individual.'

'Of course you don't.' Fallows scoffs.

Gabriel works his jaw. *I know that look.* Something is nagging at him. Right now he's probably wondering why someone would kill Hadid Waqif and leave the rest of us alive. It's what I would be thinking.

'How did you come to meet Dante Soridov?' I interject, changing the subject.

'*This* I have gone through before with that other agent.'

'And now we're asking you to say it again.'

'I never met him, not at first.'

'They just plucked your number out of thin air, did they?'

'What leverage did they have on you, David?' Gabriel asks, his voice cagey, almost as if he's waiting to hear something he already knows to be true. He just needs it said aloud.

'Excuse me?'

'You said they had you over a barrel.' Gabriel presses.

Fallows' face drops. Clearly, he had hoped we had forgotten that part of the story. 'They had pictures of me.'

'What sort of pictures?'

'I used to…' He stops, twitching as if a voice inside his head is begging him not to say it. 'I used to pay for sex.'

'Which brothel?'

'There's one in Camden.'

'What happened?'

'Excuse me?'

'Sleeping with escorts, a lot of people do that.' Gabriel shrugs. 'Many of your colleagues in fact. So what happened?'

He breathes out a long, tired breath, his shoulders slumping towards his stomach. 'They set me up.'

'Explain.' Gabriel demands.

'I thought I was talking with this girl online. I got paired with her because she was into the same things as me. She was a working girl, I knew that. But she could, you know, do some of the things I wanted her to do. She gave me her safe word. She told me to book an appointment and we'd enact the… erm… the fantasy.'

Gabriel crosses his arms. 'S&M you mean?'

'She never said the safe word.' His face crumples. 'She never said it. I didn't know she couldn't breathe. I didn't know.'

'She died.' I say, glowering over the table at him. 'You killed her, and they blackmailed you.'

'It was them messaging me all along. This poor woman, she had no idea. She was just a pawn.'

'And then after that, Soridov contacted you, started asking you to do things for him?' I ask quietly.

He nods, ashamed. 'He approached me at a fundraiser.'

'What charity?'

'A Better Place, A Better World…' He shakes his head. 'Something like that.'

'What did he want you to do?'

'They'll get to me in here, you know. They know how to get their way.'

'There was a time to think about that, David.' Gabriel spits. 'And unfortunately that's passed.'

He locks his desperate eyes to mine. 'You don't understand…'

'We understand perfectly.' Gabriel interjects. 'You killed someone, and you wanted to get away with it.'

'What did they ask you to do David?' I repeat calmly.

'Sign some mandates. Shipping transports… I didn't see all the details exactly. He told me to sign and keep my nose out of it. So I did.'

'Does The Corinthia mean anything to you?'

His body stills and his eyes fix on the table.

'David?'

'You know it does,' he grumbles.

'That was the name of the ship, was it?'

'Yes.'

'Louder for the tape, David.'

'Yes!'

'What cargo?' Gabriel asks quickly.

'I didn't see the cargo.'

'But you know where it was going?' I surmise.

He exhales, closing his eyes. 'The ship was going back and forth from Syria.'

'What happened after you'd signed the mandate? Where did you take the document?'

'I had to get it to the meeting point in Battersea.'

'So you'd take Dante Soridov the documents, he'd give you money.'

'Sometimes yes.'

'You've been paid enough money to wipe out all your debts and purchase a flat in St James' Park. You don't mean to tell us that came from signing a few shipping mandates.'

'Well, no. There's...' He stops, rethinking his answer. 'No, it wasn't just that.'

'What else?' Gabriel asks impatiently.

Fallows looks around the room, his face slipping into what looks like panic. The last arrogant spark in his eyes dissolving. 'You have to remember; they knew everything about me. Soridov isn't even the man in charge. Whoever is actually running this...they have the resources, the access, the knowledge to blackmail the entire British government. Saying no... it wasn't an option.'

'How do you know what they have?'

'Soridov would tell me things, you know... boast a bit. All of the stories in the papers about MPs expensing things they shouldn't, affairs, corruption, even covered up crimes. He knew it all. Whoever Soridov works for has enough leverage to run the bloody country.'

'This person he reports to. Did he ever mention names?'

'No, no. They're too smart for that. I never spoke to anyone else. Never met anyone else. Just Soridov and Waqif.'

'What else did Soridov ask you to do for him?' Gabriel raises his voice.

'I verified a visa application! I had to green track it.'

'Whose application was it?'

'I never saw the name, I just had to sign on a line and deliver it back. I didn't see, I promise I didn't see.'

'Only the Home Office can green track a visa....' I murmur.

'Whose signature did you forge?' Gabriel jumps in.

He shrugs helplessly. 'They just told me to copy a signature.'

'How would you have been able to sign it without seeing the information?'

'Soridov told me not to look.'

Gabriel looks at me, incensed. *He doesn't believe a word he's saying.* 'You're telling me you received a visa application; you didn't look at who was applying, you didn't read the signature you were signing!'

'It was a squiggly old thing... I didn't read it properly.'

He scoffs. 'I thought politicians were good liars.'

'I was too afraid!'

'How did you get the application from your department back to the Home Office?' I ask, trying a softer approach.

'I had to deliver it!'

'To whom?'

'They told me to put it in a pigeonhole.'

'Did they tell you why they needed it?'

'Of course not.'

Gabriel stands, looming over him. 'Whose signature did you forge?'

'It was a long time ago... I...' His bottom lip begins to shake. 'Soridov asked me to do it...' He exhales. 'He forced me to go to this event. He said I had to sleep with someone. Try to make it so *she* signed the application. He said she wasn't playing ball, that they needed my help.'

'Who?' I lean forward, puzzled.

'Just wait...' He shouts, his whole body quivering. 'I need you to know the context. I have to explain how and why. It was another charity fundraiser. Soridov told me to accept an invite. He said I had to go there, sleep with her, get close to her.'

'The same charity fundraiser where you met *him*?'

He squints, straining to remember. 'Yes they do one every few months. It's for kids in war-torn countries...'

'Who did Dante Soridov ask you to sleep with?' I stare at him, waiting for this to make sense.

'Please understand I didn't realise what would happen to her. I didn't want that for anyone. I wouldn't wish that outcome for even my worst enemy.'

Gabriel's eyes widen. 'Kristine Kingley...'

Fallows' face pales.

'Soridov asked you to get close to Kristine Kingley because she was refusing to do their bidding, isn't that right?' He speculates.

'Yes,' Fallows whispers. 'I didn't know what they would do to her.' He shakes his head. 'I saw it in the news... terrible, so tragic.'

'A Better World...' Gabriel announces, staring at his phone. 'The charity... that's where you met both Soridov and Kingley.'

'That was it,' Fallows confirms. 'They had an event in Westminster, that's where I met her.'

'And Soridov?'

'I met him at the event in Monaco. There's lots of different ones, all over.'

'Clearly, Kristine Kingley never signed the visa application?' Gabriel asks.

'She was gone before I could put any effort into it, the next thing I know, Soridov is asking *me* to sign it.'

'Whose application was it, David?'

He stares at the table, shaking his head.

'The more you help now, the less shit you'll be in. You know how this works.' Gabriel reminds him.

'Faheem. I think his name was Faheem Shah.'

'Kingley died in October 2021.' I add. 'I take it you signed it after she went missing?'

'It was December.' He admits quietly.

'Faheem Shah…' Gabriel meets my eyes, his face whitening.

Both of us are thinking exactly the same thing.

'Thanks for your time, David.' I stand abruptly, stopping the tape.

'No!' He bellows. 'No please, what's going to happen to me?'

Gabriel gestures for the security guard to open the door.

'Train stations!' Fallows calls out, his face gripped with desperation. 'I heard something about…. about stations.'

We turn to face him again.

Fallows takes a breath to continue. 'Waqif said something before we were shot at.'

'What exactly did he say?' Gabriel lowers himself into the chair again.

'He said everything will change.' Fallows wets his lips. 'He said once those trains leave the stations, nothing will be the same.'

I clutch my stomach as it drops. 'When?'

Fallows shrugs. 'He didn't say.'

'You sure, David?' Gabriel demands. 'Because I asked you before and you said you didn't speak to Waqif. Can you see how it's hard to believe you now?'

'Soridov told me I had to meet him at a private airfield on the morning of August 5th. There could be something going on that day, I don't know.'

'He never gave a reason?' I ask, trying to puzzle it out.

'He said they'd protect me.' Fallows' voice shakes. 'He said I would be safe from what's coming.'

'August 5th...' I murmur, thinking on it.

'I'm telling you because it's the right thing to do and you said things would be better. You said it would be better for me.'

'That will be five years.' Gabriel utters.

I glance at him with a questioning look.

Gabriel turns back to Fallows with a cold expression. 'August 5th will be five years since the Wharf Cab Bombings.'

CHAPTER TWELVE

GABRIEL

I get home and walk straight across the living room to the drinks cabinet. Ignoring the throbbing pain of my aching torso, I place a tumbler on the side, twist the glass top of the whisky decanter, and start pouring. In recovery, you drink, or you don't. You're on the wagon or you're off. I'm under no illusion that just because I'm drinking at what I'd call *maintenance level* means I've got a handle on this. *I don't.* I've been to enough rehabs, enough AA meetings to know the different guises of addiction. Just because I haven't yet disappeared into oblivion doesn't mean I won't. For now, it's just a cycle of treading water until you do something stupid, like crash your car into someone's house or fall asleep at the wheel. That's the kind of end there is for the *functioners.* At least the *rock bottomers* can use phrases like *the only way is up.* Not for us. It's down. All the way down. Of course, Collins has insisted I speak to someone, she's even driven me to a few AA meetings. I've tried but I can't stop. And I don't care. Right now, I'll do whatever I need to get through the day. I take another sip, gritting my teeth as I take a seat on the sofa, my ribs reeling from the pressure. Closing my eyes, I try to forget the last 24 hours, ignoring the cold sweat creeping over my skin.

'Gabriel?'
I open my eyes. My brain emerging into consciousness. I move my tongue around my mouth. Dazed and confused, I sit up on my elbows. I look at the clock. Three in the morning.
'Gabriel?'
Battling the suffocating haze of sleep, I squint through the blackness of the bedroom.

'Gabriel?'

I blink slowly, my eyes making out a figure in the doorway. It's dark but I know those features. It's a face I've pictured a thousand times, memorised over and over. The figure takes a nervous step towards me. 'Can I come in?'

I consider the question before nodding. She rushes towards the bed, climbing on all fours: coat, shoes, everything. Golden waves of hair sway as she crawls on top of me until finally coming to lie down. Her heart pounds like a bird thrashing against a cage until her body comes to rest on my chest, head burrowing into the nook under my shoulder. I put my arm around her. She inhales, her hands gripping my T-shirt tightly.

'I miss you.'

I lay back on the pillow and close my eyes with the weight of her pressed into me, breathing in the scent of her hair. Lavender. It's always lavender.

'I know it hurts.' *She whispers,* 'But it's the greatest privilege…to feel.' *I drift away with the sound of her voice travelling soothingly through the darkness.*

Disoriented, I wake to a flood of distant headlights brightening the room. Groaning, I rise from the sofa with slow, laboured movements. Bottle in one hand, glass in the other, I look out of the window. My alarm system trips as the car reaches the cattle grid.

INCOMING VEHICLE, CAR REGISTRATION
EJ63 SST
CAR REGISTERED TO EMILY MEYER
INSTRUCT YES TO PERMIT ENTRY

'Yeah.' I call out, commanding the gates open, watching her accelerate down the driveway. Forgetting to put the large glass of whiskey down, I open the front door. Emily half jogs towards me, her long bandy legs taking determined strides, her sharp blonde bob shimmering under the moonlight. Despite the darkness, I observe the urgency on her face. Her dainty features are lined with concern and vulnerability. But I've made the mistake of underestimating her before. I'm part of a club of countless others who wrongly assumed that Emily Meyer's youthful skin and wide pixie-like eyes were akin to naivety. She's one of the most skilled forensic analysts in the country, possibly even the continent. She's seen some serious atrocities. There's very little that phases her. And the best thing about her, she has zero inhibitions and a very big heart.

'Gabriel!' She calls out, breathless. 'Are you alright? They wouldn't let me see you…'

She throws herself forward, knocking the air out of me as I catch her in my arms and stifle the urge to yell out in pain. Pushing her away gently, I hunch over, leaning on the doorframe.

'Oh my god,' she steps back, 'Your ribs! I'm sorry. I'm so sorry.' She bends down. 'Are you going to be ok?'

I twist my face and try to stand.

'I tried to get to you. When I saw you go down, my heart was in my mouth. And then by the time I got there, they'd taken you to The Nest. Collins said it wasn't a real bullet. Who was that? And the sniper? What happened down there?'

I down my drink before looking up at the ceiling, trying to work out which question to answer first.

'I'm sorry I held you so tight.' She stares at me with worried eyes. 'Are you going to be alright?'

'Yeah…' I offer a quick smile, 'just, no more hugs… please.'

She laughs, putting an arm around me. 'Come on.'

I grit my teeth with frustration, hating being so incapacitated.

'What are you drinking?'

'The usual.'

She takes the empty tumbler from me, her hand affectionately grazing mine before gliding over to the cabinet to refill it. 'Here.'

I take the glass from her, unable to stop my mind from drifting elsewhere.

'Gabriel?'

'Sorry…Yeah.'

She watches me. 'Are you ok?'

'Yeah…. I urm,' I pause, my brain a little slow from the drink. 'I only got in an hour ago.'

'You need to sleep; you must be exhausted. Didn't they suggest you go to a hospital?'

'They did but I uh… I said no.'

'Can you lift your shirt?' She asks, stepping in.

I raise my eyebrows.

'I just want to take a look.'

I smirk.

'Stop being so arrogant Agent James and let me see.'

I place my drink on the mantelpiece. She takes another step and pulls up my T-shirt. I tense, anticipating the pain, not entirely trusting I won't be prodded.

'Wow… there's significant bruising.'

'Really?' I croak sarcastically.

'The bullet might have cracked a rib but if you've been breathing fine since it happened, I doubt you've punctured a lung.'

'That's something, I guess.'

'You need anything for the pain?'

'No, it's fine…'

'I had hoped to return here under better circumstances.' She reaches up, smoothing the back of her hand over my cheek. 'I miss you when we're at work.' Her eyes trace my features. 'Have you just been sitting here brooding?'

'Kind of.' I shrug, appreciating the way she cuts through my mood, never once put off by the silence. 'Thank you… for coming.' I take her hand in mine, pulling her with me to the sofa. 'I needed the company.'

'Please be careful, I can't watch that again.' She tucks her hair behind her ears before she shuffles forward, studying me. 'Promise to be more cautious.'

I exhale a long, tired breath. 'It's the job, Emily.'

'I know.' She says, looking slightly disappointed. 'Listen, I have something. I wanted to be the one to tell you.'

'Ok…'

'We've analysed all the bullets. There's three from the sniper, a lot from Hadid Waqif, as you know, and we've ruled out the casings related to your weapon. But it's the others…'

'The casings from the mystery gunman, you mean?'

'Yes, I cross-checked the shells with other crime scenes to try and get identification on suspects from other cases.'

'And?'

'I got nothing.'

I linger my gaze, catching her hesitation. 'But…'

'The rubber bullet…'

'Go on.'

'You were shot with a CO_2 handgun… it's military grade. Used in CQC training across elite programmes in the UK. Typically… special units in the armed forces. I watched the footage back. The person who shot you, they've had extensive military training.'

'What makes you say that?'

'Their perimeter surveillance, their approach, the way they move. It's meticulous.'

I say nothing, my mind replaying the scene over and over. Their speed, the lack of hesitation with every shot, every decision mechanical, as if they had done that they're entire life. 'So what does that mean?'

'You were shot by a professional. Someone with an elite army background. Someone who came prepared. Someone who obviously didn't want you dead.' She picks up on my silence. 'Are you alright?'

'Yeah, I'm fine.'

'Do you know who it is?' She watches me carefully.

'How would I?'

She starts shaking her head, 'I'm sorry, it's…None of it makes any sense.'

I look away, thinking back to what Fallows said during his interview; the same insistence that the suspect had significant military training. And more importantly, Collins. I didn't understand it earlier, but she was squirming like nothing I've ever seen before.

'And the sniper?' Emily asks, cutting through my thoughts.

I sit back on the sofa and rest my head. 'I don't know.'

'Look, I know the job, Gabriel. You don't have to take it all on yourself.'

I turn my head, noting the tenderness in her face, the comforting smile, the caring glimmer in her eyes. She reaches forward, almost reading my thoughts, her delicate fingers tracing my hairline. I reach out, placing my hand over hers, my eyes locked to her mouth. She takes the tumbler from me, downing the rest of the drink before placing it on the coffee table. She straightens, her gaze glistening with intrigue, her spectacular green eyes beckoning me closer. Ignoring the screaming pain in my ribs, I grip her arm and drag her onto my lap, knocking a few pillows and various case files on the floor in the process. She smiles, wrapping her arms around my neck, running her tongue along my top lip, leaving me with the burning taste of whisky.

'Always a pleasure Agent James,' she whispers, kissing me.

Carefully, her hands travel down my torso, lifting the bottom of my T-shirt. With great difficulty, I pull it over my head. She bunches the material in her hands, scrunching the cotton to her face. 'God I love your smell.' She moans before removing her own shirt, slipping mine on in its place. I lean forward, gripping her hips, pulling her into me.

'Shall we go to the bedroom?'

'I won't make it up the stairs.' I whisper, kissing her jawline.

I feel her pull away slightly; the tips of her fingers begin tracing the gnarly scar sliced across my shoulder.

'When will you tell me what happened?'

'Another time.' I murmur, returning my mouth to hers.

INCOMING VEHICLE, CAR REGISTRATION
OV68GHD
CAR REGISTERED TO ALISON COLLINS
INSTRUCT YES TO PERMIT ENTRY

'What the hell is that?' Emily leaps up. 'Did that voice say Alison Collins?' She turns, noticing the look on my face as I struggle to stand. 'Are you ok?'

'Yeah. Fine.' I grunt, rolling my shoulder, my body burning from injuries old and new.

'You're falling apart, Gabriel.' She pulls my T-shirt over her head. 'Here, let me help you put this back on.'

91

'Nope.' I snatch it out of her hands, attempting to pull it over my head. The alarm sensors continue bleating with the request of Collins' entry. 'Yes!' I finally shout over the noise.

'Is she here?' Emily asks, dressing herself.

I peer through the window, watching Collins' vehicle drift to a halt; noticing her practically jump out of the car the moment she puts the handbrake on.

'I'm sorry about this.' I mutter.

'Oh, shit…' Emily tries to tidy her messy hair. 'She doesn't know right?'

I reach the front door, pulling it open. 'She does now.'

Collins looks over my shoulder, blinking at the whisky bottle on the table. 'That your dinner?'

'Want some?'

'Not tonight.'

'And here I thought we were having a party.'

'Dr Meyer, Hi? Everything ok?' Collins surveys Emily's wary expression. The realisation arrives on her face as she scans the room. She drops her head and mutters. 'Really Gabriel?'

Emily starts searching for her phone. 'I should go.'

'No, stay.' I say, staring at Collins.

'Gabriel.' Collins warns.

'It's fine, really.' Emily interjects.

'Thank you, Dr Meyer. See you tomorrow.'

'She doesn't have to leave.'

'I need to speak with you.' Collins insists, wide-eyed. 'Privately.'

Emily awkwardly grabs her keys. 'No, really, it's fine. I'll see you both tomorrow.'

I catch the positioning of her feet. *She's standing in the exact spot where Mario Christofi died, the place his daughter begged me to save his life.* More memories flood in; *Alexandra stabbing Rhiannon Benson. Killing Levi Nabilla.* Even the good ones make an appearance. *Alexandra curled up on the sofa. Watching movies enveloped in each other. Eating dinner on the coffee table with our fingers. Lying by the fire, talking about the life we might have. The passionate sex on the floor next to the....*

'Gabriel?'

I look up to see the front door close. Emily jogs across the driveway. 'Hmm?'

'We were right.'

I drop into the armchair and close my eyes. *That hasn't happened in a long time.* 'About what?'

'Faheem Shah's application was buried under a pile of bureaucratic crap. Whoever did this hid it deep. His application was submitted in January 2022 with a green clearance fast-track notice. Those are rare, Gabriel. They're reserved for powerful people seeking political asylum. That's why it was so hard to find anything.'

'Tell me Faheem Shah isn't who I think it is.'

'Almasi...' She swallows. 'It's Imran Almasi.'

I sit bolt upright.

'Do I need to call a doctor?' Collins asks, concerned.

I frown, suddenly aware that my right hand is gripped across my body. 'No...' I shake my head. 'It urm... it's fine.'

'Shah's passport was flagged in Syria last month. He hasn't re-entered the UK since. But they helped him, Gabriel. The Singularity helped Almasi get into this country in the first place. There's a second attack coming.'

'If Hadid Waqif was trying to engage Fallows, they needed him for something. And they'll try again with someone else.'

'Brown is with the PM now. MI6 have increased the threat level. GCHQ are looking for any signs of Almasi. They're using all intelligence resources. Security has been stepped up in the city, across stations and airports. Brown has also alerted SO15 and told them about the prospect of something happening on August 5th.'

'How much have we given SO15?'

'Just that we know Waqif and Almasi have been in and out of the country and that we've picked up intel regarding a potential attack on London transport systems on that date.'

'Good. We're not giving them anything else until we find out who buried that green track application for Almasi. It can't all have been Fallows. There had to be someone else involved.'

'It's locked down. The fact I was looking at…'

'Wait.' I frown, her words triggering something. 'How did you find it?'

'Excuse me?'

'How the hell did you get into Home Office records so quickly?'

She stiffens, her sharp eyes wavering; as if she's weighing up her options.

'Alison?'

She shakes her head.

You were shot by a professional. Someone with an elite army background. Someone who came prepared. Someone who obviously didn't want you dead.

'The unidentified shooter. The rubber bullet. The intel from the Home Office.' I grit my teeth. 'It's her…'

'Gabriel I-'

'Say it.'

'I'm sorry.' She whispers.

'I need you to say it.'

'Fine.' She takes a long, deep breath. 'It was Alexandra. She helped me.'

The room temperature plummets. The mere mention of one single name triggering a vast shift in the atmosphere as if I've been hit by a bullet all over again. Everything finally falls into place. *You were shot with a CO2 handgun. Used in CQC training across elite programmes in the UK. Typically, special units in the armed forces. The person who shot you, they've had extensive military training.*

Collins steps forward, anticipating the need to placate me. 'Alexandra has Michael Keough working for her. He looked into the Foreign Office. Fallows raised some concerns. She brought it to me.' Collins continues. 'She's the one who found out Fallows had been meeting someone. And then Michael helped me track down Faheem Shah's application and travel history through the Home Office.'

'You've let her in on this operation?' I state with disbelief.

'Yes.' She admits quietly. 'Almasi is going to attack this country again and this time, he has the backing of a global crime syndicate. The man murdered 150 innocent people without any help from anyone. Imagine what he'll do now. This will be bigger than anything we've ever seen before.'

'She was the shooter...' I whisper, replaying the scene. *How didn't I see it before? The way she moved, her pace, her precision.* 'She shot me?'

'With a rubber bullet.' Collins clarifies as if it matters.

'She shot me.' I reiterate, louder this time.

'If it helps... I don't think that was part of the plan.'

She took a bullet. I stand abruptly. 'Is she alive?'

'I have absolutely no idea.'

My mouth dries, my heart speeding up. I rerun the scene in my head. The bullet hit. It definitely hit. I watched it happen. I pulled the trigger. She recoiled, clutching her arm. Her pace definitely slowed.

Collins resigns her tight expression, letting out an irritated breath. 'She's alive, Gabriel.'

Relief switches to anger almost immediately. 'She was trying to shoot Fallows. Why the fuck did she kill Hadid Waqif?'

'She wasn't the sniper.' She follows me into the kitchen. 'She intervened to help. She saved your life.'

'You've been taking intel from an unverified source.'

'She's not an unverifi…..Gabriel, this is the woman you once claimed was the love of your life. She wants them just as much as us.'

'Do I need to reiterate the facts whilst I stand here with a handful of broken ribs?'

'She could have killed you easily, if that's what she wanted.'

'Lucky me.'

'Please don't let your feelings cloud your judgement.'

'This isn't about her.'

'Then what is it about?'

'Insubordination!' I yell.

She marches over to me and pulls the tumbler from my hand. 'Someone has to make the decisions when you're off the rails. Every day we risk our lives, trying to finish something you started because you fell in love.'

'You were hunting Higgs and The Singularity long before me.'

'The point is, we put ourselves in danger every second, every minute. It's hard to follow a man who doesn't know that… even worse, doesn't care.' She pauses, taking a moment, her expression regretful. 'Alexandra asked that I keep her involvement a secret and what with the history between the two of you, I agreed.'

'And all of a sudden, anything she says goes?'

'We needed a leg up in this case! We are running out of time!'

'She works under Edward's instruction.'

'Not anymore.'

'How do you know he didn't send her to gather our intel?'

'He has our intel.' Her face reddens. 'He already has it all.' She waves her arms around the room as if indicating violated spaces.

'How?'

'Does it matter?'

I stare at her, devoid of words.

'Edward has forced her to cross the line too many times and now he's shutting her out. She could have gone after Fallows herself, but she chose to come to us because she knows we all want the same thing.'

I start shaking my head.

'I'm just asking you to consider-'

'No, you're not. You're telling me. You've already tethered your agenda to hers. Take it from someone who knows, it will only bring you mountains of shit.'

'Her intel came through; she was right about Fallows. We wouldn't have made this progress without her.'

'She's manipulating you.'

'Gabriel-'

'Send her back to SO15.'

'It's too late for that. She needs our protection.'

I scoff. 'She made a deal with the devil and now she wants out of hell.'

'Do you seriously expect me to believe that you're going to wash your hands of her?'

'This division is meant to be under the radar, Alison. Very few people even know S.A.I.B.R exists, but because of you that's all about to change.'

She slams her hand on the table, the metal of her wedding rings smashing against the wood. 'Everything I do is for this

97

taskforce! If you weren't so bloody erratic when it comes to her, perhaps we wouldn't feel the need to hide anything from you. You can't even say her name. How do you think it would have gone if I'd asked your permission to run an op on information she brought to us.'

'I would have said no because she belongs to SO15.'

'I've just told you she is done.'

'Then why the fuck did she leave me to work for him!' I bellow across the room, suddenly aware that I've given too much away.

Collins' eyes soften with pity. 'You've loved each other for many years. We've all seen it. Even if neither of you can say it. So I know the pain you've carried since she-'

'Get out.' I storm out of the kitchen.

'Please just listen!'

I stop and turn to her, unable to control the venom in my voice. 'You're off this case.'

'Excuse me?'

'You heard me.' I open the front door.

She scoffs. 'You told me you were moving on, getting better. After spending six months acting like a madman, you promised me you were doing what you could to finally live a normal life. But nobody said you had to do it alone. You need people around you. People who know you. We'll talk more tomorrow.'

'There's nothing left to say.'

'She left to save your life, Gabriel. That's all it was. It was merely to save your life.'

I slam the door in Collins' face before turning to lean back, tipping my head to the ceiling, letting out a painful breath. No matter what Alexandra has or how much she's done for this operation; she's kerosene and I'm worried that this time… I won't survive her.

CHAPTER THIRTEEN

COLLINS

Feeling somewhat exposed, I stand on the doorstep to Aldyn Wolfe's ridiculously huge mansion. Using the reflection of the stained glass, I rake the ends of my fingers through the mess of my hair before smoothing out my skirt. I haven't been home. Yesterday's mascara is beginning to crumble, causing my tired eyes to itch. The pain in his voice as he dealt his final words to me is what affects me the most. He likely already regrets the things he said, what he did. I'm certain the guilt has already set in. He can't help himself; he's a bastard but he's hurting. Deep down, he really has nobody else. It's not lost on me, no matter how cruel he can be. Perhaps this is what he needs; to hit rock bottom, to have nobody, in order to pull himself out of this mess.

'You look exhausted.' Alexandra holds the front door open, her irritatingly beautiful face the ultimate mockery.

My shoulders sag, I haven't the energy to pretend I'm alright. 'Can I come in?'

'Urm...sure?' Her big, bright eyes take in my dishevelled clothes. 'Have you been kicked out?'

'I had to go to Paddington to collect my things.'

'Ok.' She stares, perplexed.

'He fired me.' I throw my hands in the air, unable to hold it in anymore.

'To be clear...' Alexandra turns over her shoulder as she leads me into the kitchen. 'Gabriel fired you?'

'Yes.'

'Dare I ask why?'

'Because he's an arsehole. A selfish alcoholic who doesn't like being called out on his shit.' I confess. *It's all true.*

'Don't hold back…'

'Got any coffee?'

'Alison!'

I watch Aldyn Wolfe stand from his chair, his large, handsome face breaking into a wide grin. Remarkable to think that this is one of the most feared men in the city. He's a teddy bear, really. Especially around Alexandra. He expands those big beast-like arms and for a moment, I worry he's going to offer me a hug. 'What a surprise!' He turns quickly, shouting at one of his maids in Albanian, asking her to serve coffee and tea. *That's more like it.*

I shuffle into the kitchen warily, watching him with suspicion.

'It's ok, you can sit here.' Aldyn heaves a stack of newspapers from the head of the table, throwing them on the big marble worktop.

'Hello again, Michael.' I mutter, taking in Michael Keough's nervous expression. 'Thank you for your help last night.'

He merely offers a quick wave from his laptop before his fingers continue clacking against the keypad.

'Do you want to talk about it?' Alexandra asks. 'About what happened with Gabriel.'

'He's just…' I sigh. 'He's off the rails.'

It's almost as if I've told her someone is dying. Her body closes in on itself suddenly, her face freezing, her eyes consumed with guilt. She looks away, taking a deep breath. *What else did she expect?* Uncanny how much pain they cause each other, despite having zero interaction.

'I wanted to talk to you about Fallows.' I offer, trying to change the subject. 'There's some important information.'

Alexandra picks her gaze from the floor, energy returning to her face. She takes a seat, curling her legs to her chest.

'We think there's going to be an attack on August 5th. Fallows mentioned that Soridov planned to get him out of the country on that day. Waqif told him something about train stations.'

'Almasi is going to do it all over again.' She murmurs. 'He's picked the same date…'

'GCHQ have put a flag on Faheem Shah's passport. The next time he enters Europe, every intelligence analyst in Europe will know.'

'Will that be enough?' Aldyn interjects over his newspaper. 'What if Almasi uses another identity? The Singularity will assume you know about Shah's passport now you have Fallows.'

I blink, shocked. *And admittedly a little impressed.*

'I caught him up to speed.' Alexandra confesses.

'We're tightening border control. Every officer will be looking for Almasi and his associates. We're not letting it happen again Alexandra.'

'Can't you just kill him?' Michael looks up from his laptop. His soft Irish accent such a vivid contrast to his words. 'That would sort the short-term issue… if he's planning an attack on London again.'

'If I knew where he was, I would do it myself.' Alexandra admits honestly. 'I've been trying for years.'

Aldyn's housekeeper Anita enters the room, carefully placing a cup and saucer down in front of me.

'Did this come straight from the machine?' I ask, warily looking between Aldyn and Anita.

'If I wanted you dead, I would have done it in the hallway.' Aldyn winks, his eyes filled with mischief. 'Easier to clean.'

'Charming…' I murmur, lifting the cup to my mouth. 'Do you think you could have managed it?'

'Ah,' he waves his hand. 'Probably not.'

Alexandra grins, clearly enjoying the strangeness of this scene. Certainly, it is unusual, I guess: the ex-director of the NCA sat opposite two of organised crime's most wanted people.

'Perhaps we should have something stronger?' Aldyn looks around the table expectantly.

'This is a meeting not a brunch for Christ's sake,' I hiss. 'I'll stick to what I've got.'

'Lexy?'

'No thanks.' She dismisses before looking back at me with impatience in her eyes. 'Anything else, Alison?' *They really are eerily similar.*

'A Better World.' I announce. 'It's a charity. Fallows met Soridov at one of their fundraisers in Monaco. That's where Soridov started blackmailing Fallows. Soridov orchestrated for Fallows to meet Kristine Kingley at their second fundraiser in London.'

'So are we assuming A Better World is connected to this?' Alexandra asks, confused. 'What do they do?'

'They raise money to help refugees in Syrian migrant camps find homes in safe countries. Apparently, they put education and training systems in place to help them travel to get jobs.'

'The charity is for camps in Syria?'

'Yes, Alexandra.' I respond, sensing what she's thinking. 'One main camp.'

'Za'atari.'

I nod. 'The charity was founded by Augustus Fox who appeared out of nowhere about fifteen years ago. He started taking seats on boards of big pharma companies. Then he set up *A Better World.* There was an article in The Times about his charitable contributions to veteran rehabilitation facilities in the US, and in that, they mention he's a recluse. Only a few people have ever seen him.'

'It's him. Fox is in charge of this. He has to be Higgs.'

'Guys…' Michael interrupts.

'They're trafficking children from Za'atari camp…' Alexandra continues. 'Imran Almasi is using them somehow. A Better World is a front for all of it. The shipments are coming from Syria. Almasi was with Dante Soridov in Syria And their charity is in Syria.'

'Guys…' Michael repeats.

'Admittedly, it's a big coincidence.' I add.

'Hello!' Michael yells.

'What is it K!' Alexandra snaps.

'A Better World is hosting another fundraiser.'

I turn reluctantly, noticing his itching enthusiasm. 'When?'

'Tomorrow… Tomorrow night.' He grabs his laptop off the table and brings it closer.

Taking the device, I scroll down the website, reading the fundraiser's location. 'Hotel de Paris, Monte Carlo.'

Alexandra abruptly stands from her seat. 'I have to be there.'

'Alexandra….' I warn hesitantly. 'We should wait for more intel.'

'Fox founded a charity that has direct access to Syrian refugees. The same camp that is connected to every suspect on this case.' She turns to Aldyn expectantly. 'How quickly can you get me a passport?'

My mouth tightens. *I mustn't let her run away with this idea until we know the facts.* 'Just slow down a second.'

'Do you have any other ideas as to how we can move forward without SO15 and S.A.I.B.R. resources?'

Gabriel always warned me; once she's hooked on something, it's very difficult to divert her away. That is the danger of aligning yourself with Alexandra Christofi. And it's easy to fall under that spell, to buy into all that passion and determination. I can see myself doing it and I've never even been romantically involved with her.

'And what are you going to do?' I start, refusing to back down. 'Stroll into that fundraiser, sidle up to the patrons and say, *'oh hey, I'm Alexandra Christofi, are you Higgs?'* *'Have you seen Mr Almasi anywhere?''*

'I don't sound like that.' She scowls.

'If you're going out to Monaco, you need a plan.'

'Lucas Caruso.' Aldyn suggests, despite worry afflicting his plump, leathered face. 'He has a good network in Monaco. He'll be able to look out for you.'

'The Carusos as in… Italian mafia?' I ask, astonished. 'Is there a gangster who isn't going to have a hand in this operation?'

'He lives in Monaco?' Alexandra turns her back to me, directing all her attention to Aldyn. *She knows she's got him.*

Aldyn nods. 'He was exiled from Calabria by the Massino family. The Carusos have a lot of influence in Monaco. Lucas is an old man now but his son, Tino, runs the day-to-day. I'll set up a meet for when you get out there.'

'Thanks.' She places a hand on his shoulder. *This girl is manipulative.*

'She's really doing this?' Michael asks before turning to me. 'You're really letting her do this?'

Shaking my head, I rest back in my chair. 'Aldyn, I think it's time for something stronger.'

CHAPTER FOURTEEN

ALEXANDRA

Tino Caruso lounges comfortably on a crisp white armchair, gazing out over the harbour from the Yacht Club terrace. I walk inelegantly towards him, assertively dropping into the matching seat opposite. Without a word, he offers me a cigarette before lighting one himself. He's lean, a little taller than I expected, with a strong jaw and prominent eyebrows which frame his grey-blue eyes. He rubs his hands over his short, cropped hair as he speaks. His gold rings glint in the sun. Despite carrying that distinct mafia charm, he's not entirely what I expected with his Aryan features but he's certainly Italian in his mannerisms. He uses his hands a lot. Every word, every sentence, a turbulent display of emotion. It's comforting; I feel I always know what he's thinking, which is not something I'm entirely used to.

Tino moves the conversation onto his life in Monaco. I nod along but my eyes are fixed on a particular couple in the harbour. A gentleman is holding out his hand to help his wife or girlfriend leap safely aboard their yacht. She hops across the water, and he pulls her into an embrace. They laugh together before making their way to the front of the boat, greeting and shaking hands with the captain. The picture tightens the knot in my stomach. Not least of all because he's tall and strikingly handsome with broad shoulders, reminding me of someone in particular. But also because they appear to live in a joyful bubble. Not once have they had to survey the surrounding area for danger or had to consider all the hiding places and escape hatches that might be available to them on that boat. A pang of sadness hits my chest as the thought resonates. It happens like that sometimes. I'm looking at something or someone and one small detail jerks my brain back to him, like a tightly coiled spring. It feels good, briefly, to think of him, to remember he exists in the same world as me, and to allow myself to drift back to loving him. The current of my mind so easily drags me out to an unpredictable ocean. And then I remember where I am and what I'm doing. I remember that I'm without him and likely will be for the rest of my life.

Tino continues chatting away, moving on to stories about Mario. I *hmm* and *ahh* in all the right places but I sense he knows I'm not paying attention. When my father died, I used to listen to everything, every fond memory people wanted to share. It helped at first, to know he lived on in the minds of so many people. And then I realised their tales were all the same. *He was well respected, scary, a force to be reckoned with. They didn't get off to a good start but once they realised that Mario upheld the underworld code to a high moral standard, they understood him.* It's tiring; hearing the same thing when I knew him so differently. To me, he was the warm, protective, kind father who taught me how to ride my first bike, told me stories before bed, helped me revise for every exam. In the end, it's a stark reminder that my dad was one thing to me and another to the world. *Now both are gone.*

'Wolfe said you might need somewhere to stay. Best to keep out of town. You can stay at my place in Eze.' He smiles, noticing my hesitation. 'I won't be there. I'll stay at my father's.'

'And what is it you get up to out here?'

He smirks. 'We've got bits going on.'

'How long have you been in Monaco?'

'About eleven years now.'

'The family that ran you out of Calabria, they still have a stronghold there?'

'Yeah.' He shakes his head. 'We used to do good for the community in Calabria. We created order but the Massinos are power hungry, they don't care for the people.'

'Do you want to go back?'

'More than anything. It's our roots, you know?'

'So you know how it feels.'

'Excuse me?'

'To have the one thing that defines you taken away.' I say, with the wind lashing my hair in various directions.

He exhales air through his teeth. 'I lost my mother. We lost our home... I know how it feels.'

'I'm sorry you had to go through that.'

'But unlike us ...' He sits up, gesturing at me with his hands. 'You didn't run and hide.'

'Rebuilding your life isn't hiding, Tino.'

'You know... I've heard things about you.'

I raise my eyebrows expectantly.

'People say your father raised you to live a life beyond his, to seek more than the criminal underworld. They say he was giving you a way out.' He shakes his head. 'Now I see the truth.'

'The truth of what?'

'Mario armed you with skills that made you an unbeatable force. People are more afraid of you than they ever were of him. You have power, Alexandra. You have power because people fear what they don't understand.' He gestures towards the large dressing wrapped around my forearm. 'And you're still not finished. Despite taking out the man who killed your father, you want more; to preserve our way of life, his legacy. Some think you're a hero.'

'Doesn't always feel that way.'

'You wouldn't be a hero if it did.' He stops to take a drink. 'This is nice, you should try it.'

'Are you trying to get me drunk?' I smile.

'Not yet anyway.'

We laugh as I take a sip from his tumbler.

'Hmm… What is that?'

'You want one?' He waves at the waiter and orders another round of drinks in perfect French. 'So, Mario might have nudged you in the right direction but why did you join?'

'The army you mean?'

He nods. 'Tell me…'

I shrug. 'It's probably cliché.'

He waves a hand in the air. 'So let it be a cliché! Humans are so obsessed with being different, it makes us all the same anyway.'

'It's not like I've ever been a patriot. The world isn't split down the middle of right and wrong. I guess… I just always wanted to achieve one specific thing and that has never changed.'

'What is that?' He leans on his elbows.

'Protect the innocent, speaking out for those who can't.'

Tino's dream-like grey eyes study me carefully, as if he's trying to melt away all of my composure. I can't tell if it's a tactic; a way of wearing people down to get them to open up or if he's genuinely trying to gauge the thoughts in my mind. Either way, it causes my heart rate to kick up a gear. Unsettling and thrilling, all at the same time. I'm knocked from the moment as the waiter sets down our drinks. I clear my throat.

'Well,' Tino finally drops his eyes before raising his glass, 'to your father.'

He nudges his cocktail against mine and we each take a sip. 'So…' He claps his hands together. 'My father has managed to get us into that fundraiser you mentioned. What is it you need from me?'

'I'd really like it if you joined me there.'

'What sort of trouble are you getting me into Christofi?'

'Couldn't possibly tell you.'

'The best kind.' He smiles.

I sit up in my seat. 'There's someone I'm looking for.'

'You won't tell me who.'

'It's best I don't.'

'Aldyn said you're using an alias.'

'Carla Borino. A lawyer working for the Hellbanianz.'

'You speak Albanian?'

'Enough.'

'Fine.' He stabs an olive with a cocktail stick. 'What is your reason for being at the fundraiser?'

'I'm your girlfriend...'

He raises his eyebrows.

I smirk. 'We can say that my family were in refugee camps for some time and I want to give back.'

He nods, impressed. 'How long have we been together?'

'Couple of years.'

'Nah...' he looks out to the Port, 'that doesn't work.'

'How do you mean?' I frown.

'By now, you'd already be my wife.' He winks.

'Tino.' I laugh.

'What is it?!' He says with mock outrage.

'Nothing, it's just... my father would roll in his grave.'

'Look, I'm not Greek, but I'm at least a bit Mediterranean.'

I chuckle as the waiter approaches to fetch my empty glass.

'No but seriously, Alexandra.' He says, taking a sip of his cocktail, eyeing me over the glass. 'Something about you makes me want to help...' He shrugs, muttering something in Italian before a small smile plays on his lips. 'Call it intuition.'

CHAPTER FIFTEEN

GABRIEL

'Gabriel?'

She crawls on top of me before finally coming to lie down. Her heart pounds like a bird thumping in a cage. Her hands grip my T-shirt tightly. I lay back on the pillow and close my eyes as the weight of her body presses into me. I inhale, breathing in the scent of her hair. Lavender. It's always lavender.

'I know it hurts.' She whispers, 'but it's the greatest privilege...to feel.'

I wake with my face stuck to a scattering of documents. My head pulsing with the dull ache of a hangover. I move my tongue around my mouth, desperately needing water. I catch sight of an empty bottle of scotch and my stomach turns. *Where the hell did I park my car?* I stand slowly from the office chair, trying to stretch out. Still in the same clothes from last night, I move towards the cupboard at the back of the S.A.I.B.R. incident room. I always keep a couple of spares here; you never know when you might need them.

Finally dressed in a suit with no tie, I half shudder as my phone chimes. Walking over to the source of the noise, I jab the speaker button.

'James.' I croak, my voice hoarse.

'Gabe…'

I squint, recognition dangles in the distance. 'Speaking.'

'Gabe, it's Julian.' He hesitates. 'You alright mate?'

My shoulders relax. 'Jules…' I clear my throat, trying to sound more together than the reality. 'How's things at the Yard?'

'Fucking stressful.' He laughs. 'Never a dull day.'

110

'Tell me about it.'

'Look, I know you're busy. I won't keep you too long.'

'Go on...'

'I've got a few birdies at SO15, lads I play footie with, in the week. They told me that there's a scare coming. Another big one.'

'We've heard that too. Everyone's on alert.'

'Listen, I don't expect you to tell me anything, but I wanted to give you a heads up. SO15 know you have a witness. The boys told me they're bringing in a specialist investigations team in preparation to take over control. They think MI6 are holding back on Almasi. Edward has a meeting with the PM today.'

I clamp my mouth shut, preventing the instant urge to vomit.

'I shouldn't really be sharing this, but SO15 will be petitioning to seize all MI6 evidence against Almasi under grounds of national security. You know what it's like.'

'Right...' I inhale a deep breath to calm my thoughts. 'I appreciate you coming to me with this, mate.'

'My advice is you either need a smoking gun to keep this witness with your division, or you need to prove to the PM that sharing this intel with SO15 will compromise national security even more.'

I close my eyes, lowering the phone.

'Gabe?'

'I understand. Listen... thanks Jules. We'll speak soon yeah?'

'Let's catch up for a drink when we've both got time to breathe.'

'Sure...' I reply without conviction before hanging up.

Making my way downstairs, I keep my head low, not wanting to attract unwanted conversation. Eventually, I reach Paul Brown's office, tapping my knuckles a few times before opening the door slowly.

'Agent James…' He looks up, removing his specs. 'Come in, have a seat.'

I try not to sink into the chair, feeling sweat prickling at the base of my neck, stifling the nausea of a hangover.

Brown stands, his square shoulders straightening as he moves around the edge of the desk and perches opposite me. He's a short man, his boxy torso accentuated by the cut of his suit jacket. I shift back in case he can smell the fumes of alcohol emanating from my skin.

'Got an update for me?'

'SO15 know we have Fallows. They're requesting we hand over everything on Fallows and Almasi.'

He drops his chin to his chest, looking at the floor. 'We need to keep them at bay. Hand over our intel on Faheem Shah and his recent movements but that's it. Do not give them an inch on Fallows. We need to keep him close.'

'Edward knows The Singularity exists. He knows that Fallows is proof of a connection between them and ISIS. Edward is making a play for the whole case, Sir.'

He nods slowly, considering this. 'We could appeal to the PM and the select committee but then, we risk having to divulge key information regarding Operation Yellow Fire. The PM backs this division but if we start creating too much friction with other agencies, it's more trouble than it's worth.'

'And doing that involves more people than we'd like.' I murmur, shaking my head. 'Edward knows that. He knows going up against him will risk giving away too much. He's counting on us wanting to keep it all off book.'

Brown shifts, crossing one leg over the other. 'I'm sorry James, it must be difficult being pitted against your father like this.'

'I'm used to it, Sir. SO15 never look at the bigger picture. My father wants this win for himself. He will happily prevent us from getting to the truth just so he can have the glory.'

'I understand his eagerness to prevent more attacks but working together would be the most sensible decision.'

'He doesn't trust me, Sir. That's the issue.'

He sighs. 'You'd think UK intelligence would have learned something after 9/11 and the Wharf Cab bombings.'

'At least with every intelligence agency on Almasi, we'll find him before his plans come to fruition on August 5th. I just hope S.A.I.B.R find him so we can link him to Higgs.'

'We need something more to bring to the PM. Something tangible as to why all the evidence needs to stay with MI6.'

'Fallows gave us a lead on a charity called A Better World. He was instructed by Dante Soridov to attend the event. That's where he met Kristine Kingley. The charity supports refugees in Za'atari migrant camp. It's not far from where Almasi was meeting Soridov.'

'Good. Keep on that.'

'I might have something else, Sir.' I hesitate, certain I'm going to regret what comes out of my mouth next. 'I have a contact. Ex SAS. She brought us the Fallows intel. She can operate off the books. She might be able to get us ahead of Edward. If we can prove to the select committee we have more weight than SO15, then we can stop their interference altogether.'

He narrows his eyes. 'She's verified?'

I grit my teeth. 'She's got connections, ways of operating under the radar. We can use her for intel then cut her loose when we're done. No strings.'

'What are you suggesting?'

I exhale, forcing myself to come out with it. 'We can use her to pursue anything we need. Fallows, Almasi, Soridov. She's a ghost.

We can keep her close until such time where we don't need her anymore.'

'What is she? A mercenary? Private contractor?'

'Of sorts. She has ways of operating. Ways in which we or certainly SO15 can't.'

'I don't want a tug of war with your father, James.'

'Sir…' I fall short, failing to find the words before I look him dead in the eye, 'knowing this contact as I do, Edward won't have a chance.'

'Her intel has to be clean.'

'I would never compromise this taskforce.'

'Good, we need to be careful.'

'Understood. Thank you, Sir.'

'Where is the contact now?'

'I'll need to locate her.'

'Locate her. I want you and Collins to provide an assessment of her to me in the next 48 hours.'

'Roger that.'

He offers a small jerk of his head. 'Any other updates?'

'I've told Roe to keep surveillance on Port Felixstowe in case we catch sight of The Corinthia. It's not currently docked and no sign of it on any tracking systems. We're trying to track down Dante Soridov. He has a brother, called Ivan, lives in France. He's been on Interpol watchlists before, but his records are sealed. We're in touch with them to check it out.'

'Good.'

I stand and head straight for the door.

'And James?'

I turn back, noting Brown's stern face.

'I trust you when you tell me this contact is of value. But it's your responsibility. Anything goes wrong, I will put it on you.'

'I understand, Sir.'

'That's clear?'

'Crystal.'

'Keep everything off comms. No trace… you hear me?'

Leaving the office, I march down the corridor towards the exit, needing to speak to Collins urgently. Stepping outside, I find Emily standing a few metres ahead, trying to juggle multiple files in her hands.

'You're in early.' She smiles.

'So are you.' I take the folders, helping her reorganise them.

'Thank you.' She steps in, reaching to run her hand gently across my face. 'You look tired.'

I actively try not to pull away, feeling uncomfortable with the public show of affection.

'Gabriel there's something you should know.'

I tense, braced for another blow.

'The gun that was used to shoot Hadid Waqif is a P226. I put out an alert so, if it came up in another crime scene, I'd be notified.'

'Alright.'

'I swear last night, this wasn't there.' She mumbles, handing me a sheet of paper. 'I cross-checked the P226 with past reports of shootings and nothing came up. But this morning, there's that.' She points to the report. 'Preliminary evidence shows that bullets from the very same gun was used to murder two members of a Turkish gang, Diren Paytak and Levi Nabilla. They were murdered about a week apart last year. Both of them took a bullet to the head.'

'Is this it?' I blink, trying to focus on the words. 'No victim? No suspects? Fingerprints?'

'The rest of the records were sealed.'

'You're sure this didn't come up last night?'

'I'm certain. I cross checked the evidence against other crime scenes in the last ten years. Nothing.'

I mull this over. *This has Edward written all over it.* After Alexandra agreed to work for him, he orchestrated the dropping of all charges against her and subsequently me. Any and all incriminating evidence during Operation Sandbank was sealed under his authority. *Until now. Until his little pet went rogue.* It's a threat. To her, to me, to anyone that gets involved. He wants me to know he'll ruin her by any means. He'll even take me down with her if he has to.

'I need to go…' I hand her the stack of files. 'I have to speak to Collins.'

'Anything I can do?'

'No, no. It's… it's complicated.'

Her eyes widen with worry. 'You'll tell me when you can?' She studies my face, noticing my hesitation. 'Sorry… I forget the British are a little more closed off than us Europeans.' She smiles. 'Let's have dinner soon and we'll talk.'

'Sure…' I exhale a nervous breath, trying to stay focused on the conversation. 'Yeah…let's do that.'

'You've only taken me on one proper date.' She hugs the documents to her chest, staring up at me coyly. 'The other night doesn't count.'

'Well, Collins was a curve ball.'

She laughs. 'Look after yourself. Stop trying to get yourself killed for a start.'

'I'll see you later.' I insist, despite the fact I know she knows better. Something in the air tells us that this might be the last time we see each other, for a while.

'Ok.' She looks down at the pavement, twisting her shoe into the ground. 'See you soon.'

She lifts a hand to wave goodbye, and I grab her wrist, pulling her into a kiss; not really thinking about what I'm doing until my mouth connects with hers. She stands on her tiptoes, her body sinking into mine. After a few moments, I pull away, practically setting her back down on the ground. 'I'm sorry, I really have to go.'

She offers a quick nod, her eyes twinkling. 'Be safe.'

I turn away and take my phone out.

Collins picks up instantly.

'Where is she?'

'I take it I'm still under your employment.'

'Yes.'

'Monaco.'

'Can you get me a flight?'

CHAPTER SIXTEEN

ALEXANDRA

I link arms with Tino as we walk through the impressive lobby of Hotel de Paris. Dutifully playing his part, he kisses me on the cheek, fussing with my hair. The hotel's hospitality manager pretends not to notice the overt display of affection as he checks our names off the list and motions us through to the ballroom. Stepping forward, we enter an opulent display of revelry. I look up to see various acrobats hanging from the ceiling; their muscular bodies wrapped in silk ribbons, twisting through the air with hair-raising talent. The sea of tuxedos and cocktail dresses expands as we walk through: the excitement of the event pulsing beneath the soft tune of the music as smoky purple lights splash across the air. Perfectly sculpted women sip champagne, their clear-cut diamonds catching the light as they move elegantly through the room; like beacons flashing amidst a sea of wealth. A small, more attentive crowd marvel at the contortionist who performs on top of a glass bar framed with two large jasmine trees. Others perch on plush velvet stalls, clutching crystal tumblers filled with the burnt orange of aged whisky.

'You look amazing this evening.' Tino whispers in my ear, glancing down at the silk slip that clings to my body. It's the kind of dress that sticks uncomfortably at the first sign of sweat. *But he doesn't know that.* I look into his eyes, trying to read his intentions. It's always the gangsters with the best charm. Before we reach the bar, a waiter in a white tux approaches us with a tray of champagne. I take one and thank him. Tino does the same before we tip the glass to our mouths; each of us downing the drink in one.

'Describe them to me, this person you're searching for.' Tino murmurs, snatching a canapé from another waiter.

118

'I don't know yet.'

'You don't know who it is?'

'I'm looking for the founder of the charity. But I have no idea what he looks like. So right now, anyone with clear influence. Someone powerful who might get us closer to the target.'

'You've just described everyone in the ro...' He pauses, suddenly cursing in Italian.

'What is it?'

'Please excuse me...' He slams his glass on the table. 'I'll be right back.'

'Tino?'

He disappears into the crowd, striding ahead with determination. I crane my neck over the sea of suits and cocktail dresses, trying to make out any familiar faces. I move a little closer, squeezing past gathering groups before finally spotting Tino in a heated discussion with four men. Things look tense. He directs them into a corner before continuing to gesticulate with irritation. The tallest of the group, the one whose hair is pulled back into a greasy bun, steps forward, his face less than an inch from Tino's. A scar puckers his right cheek, almost like the crest of a half-moon. Tino's body language shifts, he plants his feet, pulls his shoulders back, his hands braced for action. *Fuck.* How do I diffuse this situation without breaking cover? Other guests seem none the wiser, the room is too busy, the light too low. I rush over to the bar and collect two full glasses of champagne before plastering a smile on my face and wandering over with false nonchalance.

'There you are...' I breeze into the middle of them, feigning ignorance.

Tino's gaze snaps to me, the anger in his eyes dissipating. The leader of the group shifts his glare with a strong sense of impatience.

I pass Tino his drink and hold out my hand. 'Carla, nice to meet you.'

The man with the scar bends slightly, pressing his lips against my skin. 'Phoenix Massino.' He winks. 'The pleasure is all mine.'

Tino stiffens.

'Sorry to interrupt Mr Massino.' I turn to Tino. 'There's someone I'd like you to meet…'

Phoenix nods curtly. 'Have a nice night.' He mutters something in Italian to the rest of his party, his face set in a cold, hard stare before they swiftly turn towards the exit.

'What the hell was that?' I ask.

'Business.'

'Did you know they were going to be here?'

'He's been following me for days.'

I raise my eyebrows. 'It wasn't enough to run you out of your own country?'

'He wants something.'

'I thought your families hated each other.' My eyes remain glued to Phoenix Massino's back, wanting to be sure, for myself, that he's gone. 'Can you stay, or do you need to see your father?'

Tino frowns, a battle raging behind his eyes. 'I don't scare that easily.'

'Come on, let's head to the other side of the room, see who's…'

Warning signs urgently flash in my mind as my brain works to place the man ahead of me. He looks older now, his body having shrunk somewhat. His face still carries that same tightness, with intense, intelligent eyes that appear to see more than most. Despite the party atmosphere, his mouth remains flat and rigid as he listens to a young woman chatting animatedly in his ear. I haven't seen him since that day in 2014 but I will never forget. He was hailed a hero after

August 5th. But I know him as the man who took no action, the man who nearly condemned hundreds more to die.

'Don't turn around.' I lean into Tino, wrapping my arms around his neck, training my eyes over his shoulder.

'What is it?'

'Someone I never expected to see again.'

'Who?' He asks with concern.

'A man I worked with once.'

'Does he know you?' Tino glances down at me, confused. 'Why is he here?'

Jed Smart continues sipping champagne, his face oozing a leisurely sense of enjoyment as he converses with a group of fashionably dressed men and women. They all seem to know each other quite well. They talk closely, casually, their mannerisms overly familiar.

'He's the Defence Secretary now.'

'The…' Tino blinks, surprised. 'England's Minister of Defence?'

Smart gestures towards the end of the room, tipping his glass to another male in the group. A petite older woman with long brunette hair links arms with him, steering him towards the cocktail bar. I drop my arms and turn towards the stage, concealing my face. With the rest of the lively contingent in tow, he wanders past us, grinning with delight.

Tino fixes his eyes on Smart's back. 'Does that mean he's involved in this?'

I linger my gaze on the group, observing their ease. 'I don't know.'

'This thing you're doing… it runs deep.'

'More than you can ever know.'

'Come on,' he holds out his hand. 'Let's get closer.'

I hesitate, staring at his fingers as he interlaces them with mine.

'You ok?'

'Yeah,' I smile, 'just...thank you.'

He frowns, confused.

'For your willingness to help. You don't have to do thi-'

'You can thank me later.'

Instinctively, I lean in, drifting closer to him, enjoying the feel of his body pressed into mine. Alarm bells sound as I remind myself of the reason I'm here. No good will come from flirting with Tino Caruso. *You're working a job. The alcohol is making you feel things that aren't there. Get a hold of yourself.* I swallow hard, my eyes still stalled on his through the purple haze of the ballroom lights. We're both thinking exactly the same thing: a few drawn-out seconds of being totally taken in as if nobody else exists.

That is, until something breaks my attention.

A striking presence from the corner of my vision.

I'm almost certain I've made a mistake.

I take a deep breath, trying to simultaneously order my thoughts and continue walking. Blinking rapidly, I wait for the crowd to break apart again. The music appears to fade, everything around me sinking into insignificance.

No mistake.

Gabriel James.

He leans against the bar, all six foot three of him towering above the crowd. He stands dressed in a crisp tuxedo, his bow tie loose, hanging around his neck. He swills a drink in his hand with an overwhelmingly familiar arrogance; a bold, menacing presence shining through the obscure light of the room. His stunningly dark eyes pierce straight into mine. A fierce gaze that watches Tino and me with both indignation and disinterest. A look that could stop the human heart in an instant. Even other men stare at him like they don't know whether to hit him or kiss him. *He is so beautiful.* I hate that my instinct is to run to him. It's embarrassing, shameful that my eagerness contrasts so vividly with his own effortless expression of restraint. He downs the rest of his drink, places the glass on the bar and heads towards the exit. I reach the place where he stood, unable to stop from inhaling his lingering scent.

Telling Tino I need to use the lady's room, I immerse myself in the throng of guests and finally step into reception. My heels clack harshly against the gleaming marble floor as I make my way towards the revolving doors, seeing Gabriel pacing outside. He looks up from the ground, training his attention over my shoulder. I falter my stride.

A sudden force grips me, spinning me around.

Instinctively, I move my hand to the pistol strapped beneath my dress.

'I didn't mean to scare you.' A tall Asian man stares back at me, his eyes softening with apology. He offers a smile that looks awkward and crooked on his long face. I say nothing, trying to return my heart rate to normal. He looks over my shoulder and out to the revolving doors, to where Gabriel stands. 'I need you to come with me, just for a few minutes.' He shifts on his feet, his lanky legs fidgeting before he scans the reception. 'Please, come with me.' He licks sweat from his top lip, his eyes dart back to the ballroom.

'I'm sorry, you have the wrong person.'

'I'm a friend… please, you're not safe here.' He throws his palms together, creating a prayer sign. 'I know you are here with Gabriel James. I need to speak with you.' He nudges his head towards the restrooms. 'It won't take long.'

For a moment, I consider taking the stranger outside and depositing him with Gabriel. He mentioned him by name, perhaps this is all part of an MI6 plan. I turn over my shoulder, catching the sharp look of judgement from Gabriel. This is my operation. My call.

'Quickly…' I gesture for the man to go ahead before following him into the disabled bathroom, pulling out my pistol as soon as the door closes behind us. 'You have two minutes. Take off your clothes.'

His eyes widen. 'Excuse me…'

'Prove to me you're not armed or wearing a wire.'

He shrugs off his jacket and unbuttons his shirt.

I step forward, using my left hand to swivel him around. 'Ok, drop your pants.'

'We don't have much time.'

'Then you better do it fast.'

He unzips his trousers, pushing them down to his ankles.

'Ok, now stand against the wall.'

With an exasperated sigh, he places his palms flat against the tiles and spreads his legs wide.

'Speak fast.' I demand, finally satisfied he's clean. 'I have to get back out there.'

He faces me, his eyes frantic. 'Tell Gabriel you shouldn't be here. There's things you don't know.'

My stomach drops. 'What the hell are you talking about?'

'My name is Raheem Kamani.' He places a hand on his chest. 'I'm a doctor. I work for the charity.' He leans against the door, his fingertips clutching the wood as if needing something to cling onto. 'I'm a doctor for the charity.'

'What is it you want, Dr Kamani?'

'I have information. But you need to leave Monaco. You need to go back to the UK. I can make contact with you there.'

'What makes you think I'm interested in anything you have to say?'

'Because I know...I know what you are doing here.'

'Ok.' I respond, recognising the fear and desperation in his eyes. 'I don't understand what you think you know or who you think I am…'

'Just please listen.' He screws his eyes with frustration. 'I know you are here to help.' He digs into his pocket and produces a wrinkled piece of paper, offering it to me. 'But you cannot be here. Call me when you get back to the UK. You have to leave.'

I take the note. 'What are they doing to the children in Za'atari camp?'

He locks his pleading eyes to mine. 'Please, leave. You need to be careful with James.'

'Why? What do you know?'

'I can't let it happen anymore.'

'Let what happen?' I move towards him, eager to know more. 'What is happening to them?'

'I'm sorry, please… please just do as I say.' He turns and rushes for the door, unlocking and exiting in one swift motion.

Shit. I look in the mirror to compose myself, brushing my hair off my face and taking a few long breaths. *We're not safe here.* That's not necessarily new information. *But Gabriel. How did Raheem Kamani know I was with Gabriel? Even I didn't know until a few minutes ago. Did someone send Kamani to seed us out? Does someone else know who we are? Collins, Gabriel, Aldyn, The Carusos. That's the list of people who know the truth.* I entered France under a false identity. The Carusos are allies. *There is no way.* I check the area, ensuring I'm not being watched and step out of the bathroom, pushing all thoughts of Kamani's anxious words aside.

Gabriel stands by reception, the disinterested glare still not stirred from his face. I sigh and make my way over. *No time like the present.* This is bound to be a frosty encounter. He waits for me to get close and without acknowledgement, turns towards the lifts, disappearing down a corridor. Picking up my pace, I follow him, clutching my stomach as it flips with nerves, my brain regurgitating a barrage of scenarios and questions. *Did he know about Raheem Kamani? Does he know about the break-in? Has Collins told him about our agreement?* I inhale slowly, rubbing my sweating palms down the material of my dress. It's just a conversation. He's human like everyone else.

Gabriel stops and produces a key from his pocket before opening the door and gesturing ahead. Without a word, I slide past him and make my way across the room, catching the swift click of the lock behind me. After a few drawn out moments, I turn and face him.

'What are you doing?'

He cocks his gun, pointing it at my chest.

'Gabriel…'

'Stop talking.'

'Look, I don't know what you think has-'

'You broke into my house. You stole MI6 intel. You killed our lead suspect. You shot me.'

I swallow. 'Let me explain.'

'Explain that you're trying to fuck up my operation?' His perfect face becomes dead and cold, void of any familiarity.

'Is that why you're here?'

'I need you to put a plug in whatever you're doing.'

'Can we talk about this?'

'There's no time.'

'I'm not a suspect, Gabriel. And you know, treating me like one is wasting time.'

'Come back to the UK and await further instruction from MI6.'

'As a prisoner or an asset?'

126

He runs a hand through his hair. 'I don't have time for games.'

'Wait…' I splutter. 'Just back up a second.'

'If I leave you out here, Edward is going to kill you.'

'You're saying MI6 will protect me?'

'Aligning yourself with MI6 is your only chance.'

'Doesn't seem like much of a chance.' I nod towards the gun.

He drops the weapon, his eyes briefly shifting to the bandage on my arm. What looks to be guilt replaces the hardness in his face.

'I've heard your concerns but I know the risks, Gabriel. I have to go back out there, I'm working.'

'You're not listening, Alexandra.'

I step in. 'There is going to be another terrorist attack in less than six weeks. It's time we stop running away and meet this head on. All of it. Higgs, The Singularity… everything.'

'The man in reception. Who is he?'

I swallow past the lump in my throat, looking for the deceit in his question. But it seems genuine. He doesn't know more than I do. I prepare myself for the lie but his dark, scrutinising eyes force me to change my mind. He always knows exactly what I'm thinking when I'm thinking it. He raises his eyebrows, waiting for the explanation.

'He's a doctor, he works for a charity called A Better World.'

'What did he want?'

'He has information he wants to share with us.'

'Us? How the hell does he know who we are?'

I take a deep breath. *This is not going to go down well.* 'He knew your full name. I don't know how.'

'So we're both compromised. Already.'

'Seems so.'

'Did you confirm that to him?'

'Of course not!'

'You realise he could be a ploy to get information out of you. Or bait? Did he ask to meet with you again?'

'He said he couldn't but that I should contact him when I'm in the UK.'

'If he knows who we are, then anyone else could.'

'I get the impression he's working alone.'

'You spoke to him for less than five minutes, Alexandra.'

'I don't think he's working for them.'

'Oh did he pinkie swear?' Gabriel crosses his arms.

'He has information to share. He's willing to share it.'

'Seems too easy.'

'I think it's worth the risk.'

'As I said, it's not just The Singularity you have to contend with. Edward is leaking information about you, making as much as he can about Sandbank public. And that's just the start.'

'Bastard.' I hiss.

'It's not safe to be here.'

'We have never been this close.'

'Please Lex, just think about what you're doing.'

I laugh. 'So I'm Lex again, am I? When you want something.'

'I'm not doing this here.'

'I have to go back, Tino is waiting for me.' I try to move past him and reach for the handle.

He slams his palm against the door, preventing me from opening it. 'You will stand down from this rogue operation or you will die.'

'I'm not your responsibility.' I spit. 'Not anymore.'

A glint of sadness taints his eyes. It's gone in a flash. 'You're right. You have it the way you wanted. But I care about my team. I care that what you're doing endangers all of them.'

'You needed to have a life.' I whisper, feeling an overwhelming urge to explain. 'You needed to forget about me.'

He shrugs with indifference. 'I forgot you.'

His words hit like a hammer through the chest. My eyes prick with tears as we stare at each other for a few drawn-out seconds. My breath quickens, feeling both seen and dissected, protected and intimidated, supported yet ultimately alone.

'I really have to go.' I hesitate. 'Meet me tomorrow. Cipriani's. Midday.'

He grimaces. 'Lucas Caruso's restaurant?'

'Tomorrow. Noon.'

He drops his arm, avoiding eye contact before moving out of the way. I lower my head and walk back towards the ballroom, preparing myself to play the necessary part.

CHAPTER SEVENTEEN

ALEXANDRA

I know I will never love anyone like that again. To be honest, it's kind of a relief. Sacrifice demands the things we cherish above all else. A devotion to a cause greater than oneself. Sometimes, I forget what brought me to this point. It's easy to get caught up in the now, lose sense of who you were at the beginning. I'm still fighting the same battle, but I don't know that person anymore. I'm no longer the woman who turned up at Gabriel's door in the middle of the night, begging for his help. But seeing him again has summoned everything to the surface. The memory of that time is a vicious wound that won't heal. And yet I said nothing of consequence. We're simply back to doing what we do best: pretending we don't mean anything to each other. Like being backwards in time, knowing there's someone you should or would rather be.

I approach the doors to Cipriani's restaurant, now owned and run by the Carusos since they came to Monaco, fleeing the Massino family. Looking around, I step under the green canopy to escape the sun and place my back to the door. *Is it a mere coincidence that the Massinos are in Monaco? Why are they following Tino all of a sudden?* That is one battle I can't afford to get involved in. I check the rooftops of the building opposite; all presence of an anonymous sniper making me overly cautious. Ever since my pregnancy, my mind has managed to dictate strange physical reactions to fear. It's worlds apart from the woman I was in B-squad but I'm slowly coming to terms with the fact it's part of who I am now. It's the only time I really allow myself to remember I was pregnant at all. A fact that feels like a lifetime ago; a life that harboured an unfamiliar notion of hope. I close my eyes, picturing the alternative path I might have had; how things might be if I had just walked away from Kristine Kingley. Sometimes I feel I'd give anything to relive that moment, to avoid getting involved. Yet, deep down, I know I'd do it all over again.

Finally, I see Gabriel crossing the road, dressed like something out of a GQ shoot. *It really is unfair to the general population.* He offers a small nod of acknowledgement as his long legs stride in my direction. 'You're early…'

Typical. He could never be late.

He pats his pockets suddenly and pulls out his phone. 'Hey…'

I frown, watching his shoulders shake. He's laughing, looking up to the sky and talking about the weather. Since when did he answer the phone with *Hey?* Which lucky lady gets this perky version of Gabriel James?

'Thanks.' He pauses, lowering his voice. 'I'll call you when I get back to the room. Then we'll catch up…' He laughs again. 'Yeah, I'll call you later. Will do. Ok bye.'

I narrow my eyes, bemused by the politeness, the false tone of his voice.

'What?' He snaps, looking uneasy.

'Nothing.' I smirk, swallowing it all down.

Two blacked-out SUVs pull up outside the restaurant. The lead driver's window winds down and a man dressed in a black suit leans out, an earpiece tethered to his right ear.

'Monsieur, s'il vous plaît…'

Gabriel hesitates, his brain processing various different questions. 'I don't like this.' He steps towards the window, telling the driver he will travel in the same car as me rather than riding in the one behind. I interject, explaining in French that Gabriel is a nervous passenger and needs company. Looking between us, perplexed, the driver eventually agrees.

I stop short of the vehicle, noticing Gabriel's glare. 'What?'

'Why didn't you just ask for one car in the first place?'

'Well…' I widen my eyes. 'I wasn't sure you'd want to go together.'

'Why?'

'Oh let me see… for six months, you hunted me like a dog. Then you accuse me of trying to kill you when actually…' I hold up my arm. 'I think we both know the opposite is true. Then you come out here, try to break up my investigation and accuse me of compromising the safety of your taskforce.'

He grabs my wrist and pulls me close, so close I can smell the fresh scent of body wash radiating from his skin. 'You're the one who asked me to come along to whatever this is. I'm just trying to make sure we get there safely.'

I half breathe a sigh of relief, for a moment, I thought we were going to hash out everything right here. 'Let's just get this done.'

Grumbling under his breath, he takes a seat next to me, having to shift around several times to accommodate his long legs.

I roll my eyes, watching him stare out of the window with a false expression of indifference. 'I forgot you do this…'

'Do what?'

'This.'

'And what is *this*… exactly?' He turns to face me.

'These long passive-aggressive silences.'

'Jesus fucking Christ.' He mumbles, fidgeting again. 'Just tell me what we're doing here… please?'

'I take it Collins has caught you up to speed on A Better World and how it might be connected to The Singularity.'

'Yep.'

'Jed Smart was there last night.'

He frowns. 'The Defence Sec?'

'Yes.'

132

'Did you speak to him?'

'That would not have been wise.'

Gabriel arches his brow.

'I've worked with him before. He knows who I am.'

'All the more reason for us to get out of here.'

'If anything, this is my reason to stay. Jed Smart could be Higgs, Gabriel. I need to speak with Dr Kamani again.'

'Did you call him?'

'Three times. His phone is disconnected.'

'I've asked the team to do some digging.'

I almost share that I've asked Keys to do the same but decide to keep it to myself. *He doesn't need to know about my sources, not just yet.* 'I'll try him again later.'

'Not until we have more intel. I don't want anyone tracing the call.'

'I know how to get around a trace.'

'And they probably know how to get around that.'

'If he's working for them…'

'Which he likely is.'

'Ok great.'

I open the window a crack, needing some air to clear my head. It's been a while since I had so many intense conversations in such a short space of time. The topic of discussion leaping from one subject to the other in an instant.

'Tell me what we're doing meeting Lucas Caruso.'

'The Carusos are the current brokers for the Taliban's opium trade. They protect the trade route, making sure there are no interferences.'

'I know the Caruso family history.' He replies bluntly.

'They have a lot of influence in Monaco and the Middle East.'

'Right.'

133

'They might be able to do some digging for us, find out what Jed Smart has to do with A Better World. And how any of this is connected to Almasi. Lucas has a big network in Monaco. He might be able to find out why Jed is here, who he's seeing. Put a tail on him.'

'Or MI6 could do that?'

'Correct me if I'm wrong, but you seem to be here alone. And who exactly do you trust to do that job?'

'I certainly don't trust a gangster.'

'You never had a problem with it before.' I mutter, facing forward.

'Why would Lucas Caruso do that for us?'

'Let's talk about it when we get there.'

He groans, looking up to the roof of the car. 'This is a mistake.'

'Are you ever going to stop whining?'

He scoffs. 'You won't have to put up with it for much longer.'

'How do you mean?'

'Collins is flying out here, she'll be your liaison.'

'Excuse me?'

'You're her asset, not mine.'

'I never agreed to that.'

He meets my gaze with smugness in his eyes. 'But you two get on so well.'

'You are such a child.'

'It's your choice whether you stick it out with Collins or not, I really don't care.'

'Ok, so you're punishing me.'

'Nope.'

'Well then why are you being this way?'

'What way Alexandra?'

'Awful.' I blurt out, instantly wishing I hadn't.

He closes his eyes. 'I don't want a fight.'

'What do you know about fighting?' I mutter. 'Nobody ever stands up to you.'

He looks away, his jaw flexing.

'I just…' I sigh, wondering how to claw back the conversation. 'I know this isn't you.'

'You've just never seen me like this.'

I know that look, he's officially out for blood.

You should stop this Alexandra. You're pushing him to a place neither of you wants to go.

'And what is 'this' exactly?'

But you can't help yourself. You never can.

'What it's like when I'm not in love with you.'

The last sentence is dealt like a sword through the chest, both of us knowing for certain that Gabriel has come out of it victorious. He takes another breath as if he might say something else but stops himself. We stare at each other in silence. Our chests rising in tandem, the atmosphere filling with a forcible tension. It's as if someone might be polluting the air with every memory we've ever had, like a cloud of nostalgia becoming heavier and darker by the second, ready to burst and unleash a heavy downpour of regret. I tear my eyes from his, training my gaze on the floor, trying to eradicate everything, ridding myself of what it feels like to love him, to have him in arms reach. *He cannot be the crutch on which you prop yourself. I need to focus on what we came here to do.*

CHAPTER EIGHTEEN

GABRIEL

Alexandra's head drops to the floor, her expression pained for a brief second before she turns to look out the window. Anger races through me but I try to keep an eye on her without being obvious. She has always possessed the knack for shoving me into a corner, pushing me to say things I don't mean. I haven't been around her in over eighteen months, and within less than an hour she's under my skin like an aggravated rash. *How is that possible?* Nobody has ever seen me, really seen me, not until her. The ability both irks and thrills me.

The car comes to a halt, and she quickly releases her seatbelt. 'Let's just get this over with.' She mutters solemnly.

A security guard abruptly steps onto the driveway, his hand hovering over the gun strapped to his waist.

Alexandra stops just a few paces away. 'Alexandra Christofi and Gabriel James – here to see Mr Caruso, he knows we're coming.'

He nods and mumbles Italian into his radio. Lex looks up at the hill, counting the armed guards patrolling the steep verges on either side of the long driveway.

'Are you armed?' The guard asks, his eyes running over us.

'Yes.' I lift my T-shirt, flashing the gun strapped to my chest.

Lex's eyes worriedly linger on the bruising across my torso before she turns back to the guard and lifts her white sundress, revealing a knife strapped to one of her very tanned, extremely toned thighs. *Get a grip, James.*

'Give to me.' The guard instructs.

We oblige, handing our weapons over. He chatters into a radio before finally addressing us again. 'Ok. You go through the gate; you get to the top of the hill, and you stop.'

'Is Mr Caruso meeting us there?' Lex asks.

'Si, yes. Mr Caruso will see you.'

I nod, satisfied with the sequence of events. The gates open slowly, and Lex starts climbing the steep driveway, her neck craned to examine Caruso's security patrol more closely. I count fifteen and that's just at the entrance to the house. *Lucas Caruso has a reputation for being a very paranoid man.* On finally reaching the top, we enter a cobbled courtyard. It's empty, save for a white Ford Mustang and a few terracotta pots lying on their sides, positioned in the corners. Four armed guards appear from a set of stone steps on the other side.

'Welcome!' Tino says, holding out both arms in greeting. His cropped golden hair shines in the sun. Despite the heat, he wears a shiny blue three-piece suit tailored to every inch of his body. *Italians.* He takes out a pocket square and begins dabbing his face. 'Alexandra, my love.' He leans to kiss her on both cheeks, staring worshipfully. 'Sorry for this. My guys will need to search you both.'

Lex steps forward and holds her hands above her head. One of Tino's men strides forward and pats her down, sniggering when his hand creeps too far up her leg.

'Ok, that's enough.' I reach out and pull her towards me.

She stumbles into me slightly, resting her hands against my chest to steady herself. I look down, my gaze unwillingly plunging into her bright eyes.

Tino shouts sharply at his men, several Italian profanities rolling off his tongue. 'I'm sorry, they are pigs.' He offers a nervous laugh before motioning towards the steps.

'He's lucky she wasn't armed.'

'My apologies Alexandra…' Tino's blue eyes watch her greedily. 'My father will meet you on the terrace if you'd just like to follow me.' He takes her hand. 'After you….' He smiles at me.

'No mate… after you.'

Alexandra takes her hand back, irritated. 'I'll go first.'

She climbs the stairs, moving in a graceful way that makes me stare, however hard I'm trying not to. My eyes whip to her face as she turns to ask Tino about his day. She's on a charm offensive, one that I know works. *All too well.* Lex is uniquely attractive in her whole being. She has a way of bringing light into a room that others can't. It's a gift very few possess. Looking as if he wants to put his hands on every inch of her, Tino begins listing the extensive amount of exercise he did this morning. Lex smiles, replying with a tone of false admiration. I swallow back the urge to laugh; well aware she's run miles through the desert in full combat gear. Eventually, we reach the top of the stairs and an opulent, pink villa comes into view. Tino gestures for us to take a seat at an extravagant marble table positioned on the terrace. I duck under a pergola of twisted vine leaves and look out to the infinity pool, its shimmering water appearing to merge into the ocean behind.

'Make yourselves at home. My father will be out shortly.' Tino says before disappearing into the villa.

I stay standing, my eyes darting around the open space. A maid appears with a jug of water, beginning to pour it into the four glasses laid out on the table.

'I would suggest sitting where a space has been laid for you.' Alexandra watches me with amusement.

'Are we eating here?'

'Maybe.'

'That's not a good idea.'

'Should I have passed on your dietary requirements?' She crosses her arms and offers a slow, cat-like smile; all evidence of our earlier spat having disappeared. Maybe she's chosen to forget what I said. Part of me hopes she does.

'I'm poison intolerant.' The corners of my mouth lift.

'Good to know.' She winks.

I've missed that wicked sense of humour. 'Why are you so chipper all of a sudden?'

'I don't know…it's nice to see the sea, I guess.'

'How long have you and Tino Caruso been in touch for?' I narrow my eyes.

She frowns. 'Why?'

'No reason.' I shrug, trying to appear casual before pulling out my phone and reading a message from Collins; she's just landed at Nice Airport. I look up at Lex again, irritatingly unable to control my gaze from drifting to her, needing to experience the feeling of merely soaking her in. She's pulling her sun-kissed hair back into a ponytail and glancing over her shoulder, peering through the big double doors. 'Missing lover boy already?'

She rolls her eyes. 'You need to relax.'

'Apologies.' Lucas Caruso's loud voice booms behind me. I turn and watch as he shifts through the double doors with a pace that signifies he works to his own time. Out of breath, he finally reaches the table and wedges himself into a chair, his protruding stomach pressing against the edge of the marble. He looks uncomfortable in this heat. His almost black hair has taken on a significant gleam, especially where it thins on the crown. He fingers a napkin and dabs it against his forehead, all the way down to his neck, flashing a chest darkened with more hair than on his head. Eventually, he throws the serviette on the table and slides his sunglasses down his nose, squinting his eyes beyond the rims. 'Mr James…'

I approach and offer a hand.

Lucas grins, flashing a set of yellowing teeth as he shakes it. 'You know, just because you look like a model does not mean you have to look me up and down like an arsehole.' He laughs, looking towards Lex. 'Wow wow wow. Bellissima, Alexandra Christofi.' He turns to Tino and fires off a derogatory joke in Italian. Clearly, neither of them is aware that she can speak many different languages. 'Alexandra, my son told me about you.'

'Pa, come on.' Tino scolds his father but continues to drink Alexandra in. 'I'm sorry.' He mouths to her.

I would love to punch that smug grin away.

Lucas turns to me. 'Gabriel, I have to be honest, I did not expect you here.'

'You can speak freely.' Lex says, holding my gaze. 'Imagine we're the same person.'

I linger my eyes on her, the statement taking me by surprise. *She's good at getting in your head to get what she wants. Remember that.*

Lucas exchanges a look with his son before he claps his hands together. 'My driver said you bickered like husband and wife the entire journey, so it makes sense.' He pauses. 'Don't worry, he doesn't speak good English.' He looks over his shoulder and calls out to someone in Italian. Another maid comes rushing out with a fruit platter, carefully setting it in the middle of the table. Lucas leans in and takes a large slice of pineapple, shoving it in the corner of his mouth, juices running down his pointed chin. 'Alexandra, Tino told you about our family.'

'Bits…here and there.'

'The Carusos represent a very different category of organisation you know. My son is trying to rebuild our empire.'

'Ok.'

'You would look good on his arm.'

Tino chastises his father again, waving his hands angrily.

Lucas shrugs. 'Parents are meant to embarrass their children.'

I shift in my seat, having to physically bite my tongue. He's trying to rile me up. I won't let him. Lex, in contrast, appears nonplussed, paying no attention to his blatant sexism.

'So, Alexandra...' He grabs a slab of melon from the platter this time, sinking his crooked teeth into the flesh, viciously chomping through it with his mouth open. 'You are what's left of The Christofi family.'

'That's right.'

'There are rumours that you made it so... on purpose.'

'Lucas...' Tino warns.

'I'm merely asking her if it's true.'

Lex pulls back her shoulders. 'That is not true, no.'

'You didn't kill your sister?'

'Would it matter to you if I did?'

The table is silent for a moment before Lucas begins chuckling; a low, wheezing laugh. 'You are like your father. No fear, no shame, just sheer fucking will.' I'm unsure if I catch an edge in his tone but it's gone with his next breath as he stands to shuffle across the terrace, staring at the sun glistening off the shimmering turquoise water. 'Apparently, this is the largest private pool in Europe.'

'Nice...' Lex adds absentmindedly. She's no longer at the table. The mention of her father has cast her back to a time when he was alive.

'It's ugly.' He waves a dismissive hand before turning back. 'Alexandra, do you think your father would have liked his daughter sharing her bed with an MI6 agent?' He digs in his pockets before lighting a cigarette.

My hands grip the seat. Lex fires me a warning look. I grit my teeth and stare at the floor.

'Mr. Caruso, we set up this meeting because we want to discuss a proposition.' She jumps in, ignoring the earlier question. 'Perhaps we should do that?'

'I don't like being told when and what to talk about, my love.'

'Well, I don't have time for idle chit-chat,' she replies.

He breaks into a smile. 'And that is the true Christofi way.'

'Pa, come on…' Tino says, imploring him to play nice.

'I understand my father helped you relocate to Monaco and in return, you have helped me. For that, I'm extremely grateful.'

Lucas takes another drag, flicking cigarette ash on the floor.

'And I'm afraid I need something more, Lucas.'

'Coffee?' Lucas waves his hand in the air.

I frown, flitting my gaze to Lex, both of us frustrated.

'Gabriel?' Lucas asks.

'No thanks.'

'Mr James prefers something a little stronger, I'm told.' Tino chimes in.

Only to smash over your fucking head.

'Alexandra?' Lucas asks.

'No.'

Lucas chats to his maid, giving her very specific instructions on how to make his espresso before returning his attention to us.

Tino sits forward, looking embarrassed. 'I'm sorry for his behaviour.'

'Ok, my dear.' Lucas exhales, returning to the table. 'What is it you want?'

'You have a brilliant network in Monaco.' Lex places her phone on the table. 'I need help with some information. There's a charity called A Better World. As you know, we went to their fundraiser last night at Hotel Du Paris. The man who founded the charity is called Augustus Fox.' She clears her throat. 'I think he's

142

responsible for the death of my father. His organisation hired Diren Paytak to eliminate my family's influence in London, all so they could begin a trafficking operation in the UK.'

'Drugs? Guns?'

Lex shakes her head.

Lucas raises his eyebrows. 'People.'

'Yes. Augustus Fox... if he is the man I think he is, then he has access to government resources. He has friends in very high places. The British Defence Minister, Jed Smart, was at the fundraiser. I want to know how it's all connected. Really connected.'

'You want to know if these people took out your father?'

'I do.'

Lucas shrugs. 'I understand, my dear...but we know how it went down with Mario in London. Have you ever considered that the person at fault is the man sitting next to you right at this moment?'

I stand suddenly, my chair flying backwards, my hands clenched so hard into fists they hurt.

'Gabriel...' Lex stands with me, her tone pleading. 'Please.'

I take a deep breath and look away from her, trying to quell the rage coursing through me. *She believes it.*

'I'm sorry...' Tino offers calmly. 'Lucas likes to draw on people's weaknesses.' He turns in his seat, shouting through the doors to the house.

Another small woman in an apron rushes out, holding a tumbler of brown liquid, nervously placing it in front of me.

I nod a quick thank you and down the whole thing.

Lucas grins. 'Where were we?'

Lex returns to her chair, eyeing the empty glass. 'Lucas, do you remember where you were on August 5th, 2014?'

He frowns as if the answer is obvious.

'I know exactly where I was…' Lex says slowly. 'I was in The Square, laying on top of an extremist, preventing him from blowing up another office building of innocent people.'

I turn in my seat. She's never told me that before and I know a lot about her time in B-squad. The image causes my heart to pound so loud, I'm almost certain she can hear.

'Imran Almasi, the man who coordinated those attacks, the man who murdered 146 innocent people on August 5th, he's back. He's planning something else. A Better World is helping him somehow. I know it's not your country, I know it's not your people but they're attacking our way of life. We can't let them win.'

'What is it you want exactly?'

'I know you run protection for the Taliban's opium trade in the Middle East. A Better World has a refugee camp out there. I want to know what your people have heard.'

'If this Fox is as powerful as you say, it will be difficult to find anything.'

'All I'm asking is that you try…'

'And what happens if he gets wind of this, hmm?'

Lex looks into her lap, unable to respond.

'Everyone at this table knows how you operate, Caruso.' I say, interrupting. 'You've got a lot of tricks up your sleeve.'

'Seems a big ask… this is our only home. If these people have influence, they could run us out of Monaco.'

'We'll help you get Calabria back.' Lex blurts out. Her eyes are alight with a sudden determined energy. *That look is never a good thing.*

Lucas chuckles, a deep, hearty laugh. 'You want to make a deal?'

'Taking Calabria from the Massinos would be a lot easier with MI6 support,' she suggests.

Lucas leans forward, intrigued.

'If you help me find intel on Jed Smart and Augustus Fox, we'll help you take back your land from the Massinos.'

'Alexandra, what are you doing?' I whisper.

Tino turns to Lucas, chatting in Italian. *Massino. Assassin for a price.* That's the only thing I catch but from the look on Lex's face, she understands every word.

'She's not for sale.' I snap.

Lucas looks between us, delight settling in. 'Ok… well I can think about forming an agreement that works to both our-'

'There is no agreement, no deal.' I cut him off.

'Alexandra can speak for herself…' Tino suggests calmly.

'How about you don't speak at all?' I reply, raising my voice.

'Aye aye aye…Diavolo.' Lucas blows air through his cheeks. 'Mr James, the devil really gets into you.'

Tino grins at me and throws his arms out; almost as if to say, *what are you going to do about it?*

CHAPTER NINETEEN

ALEXANDRA

'You agreed to support the Caruso family in a turf war in front of an MI6 agent?' Collins leans over the balcony of the Columbus Hotel, puffing a cloud of smoke into the air, creating a haze over the horizon.

'Well, Gabriel made it very difficult.'

'You really think A Better World is the answer?'

'If Fox isn't Higgs, then it must be Jed Smart. Someone very powerful is allowing Almasi to operate under the radar and it's connected to Za'atari camp.'

'And Gabriel is accepting this, is he?'

'Not exactly.'

'With a friend like Lucas Caruso, who needs enemies.'

'Better the devil you know.' I say, watching Gabriel sprinting down the beach from above. 'How long has he been drinking again, Alison?'

She turns, raising her eyebrows. 'You did that on purpose…'

I say nothing, hoping she wouldn't notice my attempts at catching her off guard. Collins spends most of her waking hours protecting Gabriel.

She sighs, her face pinched with worry. 'About a year. The investigation appears to be the only thing that keeps him going. He comes to work, barely eats, drinks at all times of the day, works out, goes to bed. Put that on repeat.'

'He's been coming to The Athena.'

'I know.'

'He's going to get himself in a lot of trouble if he gets mixed up with the Corsican Mafia.'

'Well, that's all stopped now.' Her eyes flicker to mine. 'He's seeing someone.'

'She makes him happy?'

'It's early days.'

I try to swallow down the bitter pang of jealousy. 'Does she know?'

Collins shakes her head. 'I think he's kept her out of that.'

'All I wanted was for him to have a life.'

'You gave him a chance, it's his choice what he does with it.'

'Didn't MI6 insist he see a therapist after what happened?'

'He sees a counsellor twice a week. Just sits there, refuses to speak.'

'How do you know that?'

'The therapist is a good friend of mine.'

'Jesus.' I laugh, shaking my head.

'Do you still love him Alexandra?'

I drag in a sharp intake of breath, almost like the words have left a burn somewhere inside of me. 'If I had stayed, do you think he'd be better?'

'You saved him from a long prison sentence…' She stops, her mouth withering, holding back the words.

'What?'

'At least he'd still be sober.' She shrugs. 'Perhaps prison wouldn't be so bad after all.'

'To love him is to kill him.'

'Is that what you really believe?'

I lean over the balcony as a warm sea breeze sweeps over us, hoping the salty air will ease the guilt in my mind. 'I wanted him to have a life.'

'You did what you had to because you thought it would save him. But you left him with his worst enemy.' She shakes her hair out of her eyes. 'Himself.'

'I never thought he'd look at me that way. Not ever.'

'You left. He needed to find a way to deal with it.'

'Being around me only causes him pain, Alison.'

'You were all he had.' She takes another drag before throwing the cigarette over the side. 'You made a decision to save his reputation, his career but don't kid yourself, you didn't save his life. He won't let you back in because he's still trying to let you go.'

My lip trembles. I bite down hard. *I will not cry.*

'Don't tell him I said this…' Collins pulls another cigarette out of her pocket and makes to light it, balancing the end between her lips. 'I'll point-blank deny it if you do, but that boy is like a son to me.' She exhales smoke. 'Edward and Camina ruined him. There was never any love, no warmth, just judgement and expectation.'

'He deserved better.'

'You thought you could walk away, and he'd bounce back. I thought keeping you apart would settle him. But nobody ever asks Gabriel what he wants or what he needs. Not me. Not you. Nobody.'

'Edward made those decisions for all of us.'

She fixes her gaze on a group of small children jumping in and out of the pool below. 'You've fought so many causes in your life. Why didn't you fight harder for this one?'

The door bleeps behind us suddenly and both our heads turn. Gabriel walks in, his sweaty T-shirt in his hand, calling out something about room service. He grabs a bottle of water from the mini-bar before eventually joining us on the balcony.

'Good to know S.A.I.B.R. is footing the bill for you to stay in a five-star hotel.' He twists the cap of his water.

'Pot. Kettle…' Alison replies with amusement.

'Self-funded.' He smiles at her, winking.

It's the first time I've seen him jovial since he arrived in Monaco. *It's a side I certainly don't get to see anymore.*

Gabriel and Collins take a seat at the table on the balcony. I move to join them when my phone buzzes in my pocket. I dig it out and answer it quickly.

'Alexandra…'

'Tino…' I exclaim, surprised. Turning away, I walk to the opposite end of the terrace.

'Can we meet?'

I glance over my shoulder. 'Urm… sure?'

'There's just some things I want to discuss. I think it's better in person.'

'Ok.'

'Well, technically, we could talk over the phone,' he pauses, 'but truthfully, I really wanted to see you. I must apologise for my father. That is not how I wanted things to go. I hope you know that.'

'I'm used to it, don't worry.'

'I wish he wouldn't use you as a tool to his own means.'

'It's business. I get it.'

'It's not how I like to do business.'

'Is your father going to take the offer?'

'I think so. We can discuss it when I see you.'

'Where should we meet?'

'You still staying at my place?'

'Mmhmm.'

'I'll see you there. Five minutes of business, then I'll cook you dinner and you can tell me about the rest of your day.'

I look back at Collins' and Gabriel's expectant faces. 'Sounds good, come by around seven?'

'See you then.' He hangs up.

I keep my face to the horizon, not wanting Collins or Gabriel to spot even an inch of apprehension. *I have to keep Tino Caruso on side. He's the one to keep Lucas in check and help us get what we need.*

'What was that about?' Collins calls out.

I try to move past Gabriel to take my own seat at the table but he refuses to shift or allow me to pass. Deliberately, I lean on his shoulder and clamber over his legs. He takes another sip of water, making no acknowledgement of his childish behaviour. *It's cold when he turns away from you, like the chill you feel when the sun goes in.*

Collins looks between us, already exasperated.

'That was Tino, he wants to meet later this evening.'

'That's quick.'

'Yep.'

'Where exactly?' Gabriel asks without looking up, playing with the cord on his shorts.

'At his place in Eze. I've been staying there.'

His jaw tightens as he looks out to sea.

'But he's been staying at his father's.' I clarify. *Why? Why am I explaining myself?*

'Highly unlikely they've got intel already.' Collins surmises.

'Well… he might just want to discuss the terms of our agreement in more detail,' I suggest.

'What time?' Gabriel asks.

I hesitate. 'I think I should do this one alone.'

He scoffs. 'Yeah, fat chance.'

'You didn't really help matters earlier, to be honest, Gabriel.'

'Because I wouldn't allow Lucas Caruso to use you as his personal mercenary?'

'I'm just saying if you want to be included, then you need to learn to control your temper.'

Collins' eyes widen with surprise.

'You'd still be there now if I hadn't stepped in...' He raises his voice. 'Probably polishing Lucas' shoes or worse-'

'MI6 has really gone to your head.'

'Enough!' Collins yells over us. 'You might both love the sound of your own voices but it's incredibly fucking boring for the rest of us.'

Gabriel takes another breath to speak.

'I said *enough.*'

His face drops. 'I'm going for a shower.'

'Sit down.' Collins demands.

He rolls his eyes but takes his seat with surprising obedience.

'Alexandra, you can meet Tino as long as you wear a wire. Our progress could rest on this agreement with his family. It would be remiss of us to allow you to meet an asset and not hear what he has to say for ourselves.'

'You think I'd hide terms of the deal from you?'

'With all due respect, we need to cover all bases.'

'Fine.' I concede.

'Even if he isn't meeting with you to discuss the agreement... I'm afraid we'll still need you to keep recording.'

Gabriel fidgets, looking uncomfortable.

'What is it now?' Collins asks, irritated.

'This doesn't feel like a sensible idea.' He replies.

'I've been on my own with Tino multiple times.'

'In public.' He rebuts.

'He has zero reason to hurt me. The Carusos were allies with my father.'

'*Were* as in... past tense.'

'There's a code, Gabriel.'

'The code died with your father, I'm afraid.'

'The risk is minimal.' I turn to Collins. 'And it's worth seeing what he wants.'

'I know what he wants.' Gabriel mutters.

'Well, there shouldn't be an issue with me going alone then.'

'Ok!' Collins interjects. 'We came out here to get answers. Alexandra is right. We have to take risks. We've got the rest of the team coming out tonight, we'll have more resources after that.'

'We should wait for them then.' Gabriel suggests.

'Why?' I ask, irritated. 'What will a few extra bodies achieve?'

'Roe has friends at Interpol. We could use their manpower.'

'I don't think that will be necessary.'

'What if Tino wants something we can't offer?'

'I'll tell him the decision will have to wait until the rest of the taskforce arrive, how about that?'

Collins nods. 'We can still set up live comms.'

'We'd have to do it here.' Gabriel suggests. 'This hotel is closer to Eze. If she needs support, we can be there in fifteen minutes.'

I frown. '*She* has a name.'

Gabriel looks down, ignoring me.

'You good with that, Alexandra?' Collins cuts in, clearly trying to avoid another altercation.

'Yes.' I respond quickly.

She eyes the both of us. 'Ok… well now we're getting somewhere.'

Gabriel looks at her, disgruntled. 'Yeah and at what cost?'

CHAPTER TWENTY

ALEXANDRA

As it turns out, Tino Caruso had no intention of discussing our agreement with his family. I should have guessed the moment I saw him standing there with three bottles of wine, his eyes alight with mischief.

'You up for a drink Christofi?'
'Depends who's asking…'

The minute he entered the house, I lifted my top revealing the wire strapped to my torso. He'd smiled with a knowing look; almost as if he'd expected it. He certainly didn't seem phased. And despite knowing we were being listened to, he still leaned in for a kiss goodnight. I did my best to cover the mic as I reciprocated. I don't know what I was thinking. I shouldn't be crossing lines with Tino Caruso, especially with MI6 listening. It's important to keep the Caruso family sweet, I need their network and this evening might help us get a little closer to securing their support but I went too far. I'm losing control and I can't allow that. Whether it's Gabriel or Tino clouding my judgement, it needs to stop. I have to block it out.

I unpeel the wire from my skin and toss it on the table. My body instantly feels lighter, cutting off that connection to him. If only I could sever it entirely. I wander around the villa, switching off lights and various appliances; plunging the living room into darkness. Reaching up to close the curtains, I pause for a moment and enjoy the moon's glow illuminating the terrace. Its silver glimmer catches the edges of the bougainvillaea that climb the outside of the property. Looking up, I count along to Orion's belt, picking out Mars, scanning

153

the sky for shooting stars. We used to do this every summer in Cyprus. My father and I would lay by the pool, backs flat to the warm ground, listening to the soothing chirp of crickets whilst watching stars burst across the galaxy. It was perfect. No noise, no light pollution; just us and the solar system. I would give anything to do that with him again. *Anything.* Saying a silent goodnight to Mario, I close the blinds and turn to get ready for bed.

Something feels different.

There's been a shift.

My eyes scan the environment, trying to ascertain what feels off. I look back to the windows, eyeing the drawn curtains. The crack of light seeping over the top seems brighter. The white of the bed's duvet is shining under a heavier glow from the terrace. *Perhaps a security light has come on?* Pulling the gun from the bedside table, I creep down the corridor, grabbing the knife strapped underneath the sink. Quietly, I take my phone and dial Gabriel's number.

'What is it?' He answers coolly.

A car door slams.

'Are you outside?'

'Huh?'

'Are you or Collins outside the villa in Eze?'

'I'm with Collins at her hotel.'

Is it Tino again?

'What's going on?' He asks, his tone urgent.

'I don't know.' I sneak to the front of the house.

'Is someone there?'

'I think so…'

Pressing my back to the wall, I listen out for footsteps or murmurs, waiting for whoever might be shifting in the shadows. I slide into the doorway, trying to make out shapes on the driveway.

'I can be there in fifteen.' He says, doing something in the background. 'I'm walking to the car now.'

'Wait....' My ears prick at the sound of shuffling by the door. It has to be Tino. *But he rang the doorbell when he arrived earlier.* He didn't once act like I was the one occupying *his* space. He behaved like a guest. Why would he now just enter the villa without...

A hand seizes the back of my head.

I drop the phone to the floor.

My face is rammed into the wall.

My lip splits. Blood pours from my mouth and I try to spit it out. The hand grips me again, tightening around my skull, driving me forward. The gun flies from my grip as I hit it a second time. Something cracks. I cry out, dropping to my knees, throwing my arms over my face, shielding myself from another attack. Blood gushes onto the floor. I attempt to jump up but a leg swings into my side. A thick, black boot hurtles into my kidney. My body appears to leave the ground, air is struck from my lungs. I hit the tiles again, splayed on the floor. With my ears ringing, my face feeling as if it's been carved in two, I peer up, seeing my knife roughly a metre away. Scrambling my legs forward, I throw my hands out, reaching for my lifeline. I'm dragged up to my feet; effortlessly plucked into the air. I flail my arms, kicking and yelling, desperately clinging to furniture. Glass smashes around me, ornaments crashing to the floor as I do everything I can to resist my own abduction. The attacker gives up trying to drag me out of the door and I'm thrown to the floor, kicked repeatedly in the direction of the kitchen. Eventually, I crawl up to my knees, heaving myself to stand. That's when I see him for the first time. Tall and broad. He's wearing all black with a balaclava that covers his face. But his eyes are watching me with a self-satisfied, snarling expression, like a hunter who knows he's cornered his prey. My vision blurs. My cheeks are wet. I try to blink rapidly, running my fingers

155

over the deep cut along my hairline. I wipe blood out of my eyes with the back of my hand.

Come on then, you piece of shit. I raise my fists and plant my feet. 'Thought you might need that, did you?' I nudge my head at the gun in his hand. 'Don't think you can do the job without?'

He scoffs, pockets the revolver and charges forward. I duck and slide behind him, leaping onto his back, tightening my legs around his torso, yanking my forearm across his neck, straining to crush his windpipe to his spine. He bucks, flinging his body backwards until we hit a wall. I let go and drop to my feet. He quickly rotates and smashes his fist into my stomach. I groan and hunch over, trying to expel black spots from my vision. Seeing him swing again, I clamber away and make a run for the door but the smeared pools of blood on the floor cause me to slip. I stumble again, now on all fours, trying to ignore the convulsing of my stomach. *Don't fucking vomit in front of this prick Alexandra.* The attacker takes three quick strides before snatching me in his grip once more.

'See…' He jibes in a thick Russian accent, his eyes ablaze with triumph. 'I didn't need it, did I?' He cocks his gun, pressing the cold metal against my forehead. 'Be good, or I feed you a bullet.'

CHAPTER TWENTY-ONE

GABRIEL

There's blood everywhere. It's all over the tiles, smeared across the walls, pools gathered by the front door and on the terrace. Broken crockery and smashed glass litter the villa, covering most of the floor. Lex's phone lays cracked to pieces next to a chair knocked on its side. I bend down to retrieve it, noticing a clump of hair on the floor, the blonde strands bunched together.

Is someone there?
I think so…

I stand and move towards the living room window. She was facing the driveway when she was talking to me then the line went dead. I turn over my shoulder and look to the kitchen, noticing the back door that leads to the pool. If she was facing the front looking out, nobody could have come through the front door fast enough to catch her off guard. The fact the phone cut out so quickly tells me she didn't see this coming. The attacker would have slipped through the back. I tread into the hallway and examine the painting hanging askew with a smattering of blood and scuffed paint next to it. This is where he could have grabbed her from behind, pushed her into the wall. I go back to the kitchen again. At some point, she fought hard; appliances are ripped from the sockets, lying on their side, placemats crushed, mugs shattered into pieces. Nowhere has been spared from the mayhem. I close my eyes, trying to push the image from my mind.

'Gabriel?' Collins calls out. She stands by the wardrobe of the main bedroom, staring inside. 'Everything's gone.'

Contrary to the rest of the villa, nothing of Alexandra remains here. It's as if this room had never been occupied. I head for the bathroom and open the cabinets. *Empty.*

'Roe is at the airport. He's going to organise an overseas forensic team.'

I shake my head, my mind elsewhere. *Only a handful of people knew she was here.*

'You alright?' Collins asks, her face plagued with concern.

I turn away, trying to draw in oxygen, attempting to think reasonably about our next steps. But the reality continues to sink in, like a heavy anchor tearing through logic. *She's gone.* This wasn't supposed to happen. *She's gone.* 'Give me a second.'

Knowing I have to pull myself together, I slip into the bathroom, trying to inhale breath after breath but there's no air. *Pull your shit together James.* I lock the door, leaning both hands on the sink, needing a minute to stave off the fear corrupting my rationale like a virus spreading through a healthy host.

You will stand down from this rogue operation or you will die.
I'm not your responsibility. Not anymore.
You're right. You have it the way you wanted.

'Fuck!' I ram my fist against the mirror, barely feeling the dull impact of skin and bone against the thick glass. The surface cracks under the force, creating multiple tormented reflections staring back at me. *I knew it was a mistake to get involved with the Carusos. I knew better.* Turning towards the toilet, I rapidly lift the lid and chuck up all the contents of my stomach. Screwing my eyes shut, I slump against the wall, grappling for clarity, repeatedly running my hands over my face as if it might conjure up a plan to get her back. Nothing succinct comes. *I need a drink, something to level me out.* Eventually,

I look up as a light knocking resounds from the other side of the door. 'Give me a second.' I stand slowly, turning on the tap and splashing water on my face.

'Gabriel?' Collins' voice travels through the walls.

I open the door, silently meeting her worried eyes.

'It's going to be ok.' She says, examining me; taking in the bloody knuckles, the ashen complexion, the unmistakable fear. 'We'll find her Gabriel…We *will* get her back.'

CHAPTER TWENTY-TWO

ALEXANDRA

Memories drift in and out of my head. Fragments of recollection floating apart, the distance increasing the harder I try. Like slivers of ice sifting across a lake. The world is dark. My hands and feet are bound. The cotton material over my head is getting heavier as the condensation from my breath settles into the fibres. I try to regulate my breathing, but the bag gets wetter with every exhalation. I jerk my hands against the cable ties cutting into my skin. They don't budge. A system beeps in the corner. I listen out for any other sign of life, but I can't hear anything over the whirring of machines. A door slams and someone enters. Their footsteps marking their approaching presence, tapping across a hard floor. The bag is torn from my head and my eyes struggle to adjust to the halogenic lights above me, my brain forcing its way out of sedation.

'Alexandra Christofi.' A hoarse voice sings my name with chilling curiosity. A small, slender man with messy bed hair and a white lab coat sits in a desk chair on my right. He studies me, a gun nestled between pink, bony fingers. There's a signal monitor in front of me. Wires protrude from the machine, leading back to my body; several are attached to my head and face. The machine begins beeping more frantically, notifying the room that my heart rate is increasing. There's another presence in the room. A young girl dressed in a grey tracksuit is strapped to the chair next to me. Her hair is shaved right down to her scalp, and she wears what looks like a VR headset wrapped around her skull, covering her eyes. The man checks his watch and stands from his seat. He moves with determined strides, leaning over the girl's limp body before he carefully injects her with something, his focus trained on releasing a liquid into her arm with steady hands.

'Welcome to our facility.' He straightens, discarding the empty vial before pumping alcohol gel into his hands, rubbing them together. 'You can call me Icarus or Dr Flint, whichever you prefer.'

A facility.

I look up to the ceiling, searching for an exit or a window that might eventually provide an escape. There's neither. *Am I underground?* There's one internal door in the front left corner of the room. *If I could just get off this chair.* Dr Flint doesn't appear much of a threat. All I need to do is slip out of the cable ties…

Another person enters.

His huge shoulders fill the doorway, his body blocking out any light from the corridor. I squint, analysing his face, catching the crooked way he stands. *Dante Soridov. It was Soridov who attacked me in the villa.*

'All is in hand?' Dr Flint asks.

Soridov nods.

'I'll wake her.'

With careful movements, he slips the headset off of the girl and produces another vial, injecting it into her arm, again. She jolts awake, her muscles tensing. Her bloodshot eyes widen, her gaze shifts to her restraints. She begins writhing in her chair, screaming and kicking like a wild animal.

Dr Flint waits patiently, ignoring her desperate protestations. 'Hope, I do not like foul language. This is the only way. Wouldn't you rather this happened swiftly?'

She stills for a second before turning to me. We lock eyes. *Hope.* I silently implore her not to give in. Whatever it is that's about to happen, she has to fight. Flint hunches over, trying to pull the headset over her eyes. Hope's head reels up and she spits at him, the gob of her saliva landing in his face. Without a word, Flint takes a plain white handkerchief from inside his coat, wiping the evidence away calmly. Soridov purposefully strides over, grabs Hope's shoulders and backhands her hard.

Flint finally slips the headset over her face. 'Start the cycle.'

Soridov reaches over to a control panel at the back of the lab, pressing a sequence of buttons. The wall in front of me becomes a screen. An image of an orange ring appears, a large expanding circle of flames. Hope whimpers, shaking her head.

'We can see what she sees.' Flint informs me excitedly. 'This is our work in action, Miss Christofi.'

'Stop it.' I try to sit up. 'Leave her alone!'

Flint approaches Hope, attaching three additional patches to her chest. These ones have a red base, with wires that lead to a small device in his palm. I've seen something similar in Syria. *Electric shock therapy*. Government-backed terrorist cells would use it on teenagers to brainwash them into adopting extremist beliefs. It was popular with the CIA after 9/11. I've been present on two interrogations when this method was used. You turn to it out of desperation if you're up against the clock and you need the prisoner to crack; to turn away from everything they once knew. It's a way of obtaining control of your subject in a cruel, sadistic manner.

CHAPTER TWENTY-THREE

GABRIEL

Tino Caruso storms into the villa, his gaze fiercely whipping around the hallway.

Without a second's hesitation, I close the distance between us, grabbing his collar. 'Where is she!?'

He narrows his eyes, anger seeping into his face. 'What the fuck is going on here?'

'What did you do Tino?' I shout, pinning him to the wall.

'Gabriel, let him go!' Collins yells.

'What the fuck did you do!'

'What are you talking about!? Where is Alexandra?'

'Gabriel stop!' Collins pulls at my arm.

I throw Tino to the floor and take a step back.

He straightens, inspecting his suit before brushing his sleeves. 'I had nothing to do with this. I don't even know what has happened.'

'Then why are you here?'

'I received word of a break-in.'

'From who?'

'I've got eyes and ears everywhere.' He explains, exasperated.

'Well, obviously not enough!'

'Where is Alexandra?'

'You tell us, you were the last to see her.'

'I don't know where she is! I came here to see if she was ok!'

'Sure...'

'You've got a problem, Gabriel.' He points to his head, screwing his index finger into his temple. 'You're blaming me for your own fuck up.'

'The only fuck up was letting her spend any time with you.'

'Alright, enough!' Collins shouts, stepping between us. 'Mr Caruso, can you account for your whereabouts?'

He scoffs, casting his eyes over the mess. 'I went straight from here to a bar in Nice.' He fishes his wallet out of his pocket and hands Collins a card. 'Here, you can call them.'

'Doesn't mean you didn't arrange this.'

'To what end?' He shouts with disbelief.

'I don't know… you come up here, keep her distracted, make sure she's alone then you call your dogs when you leave, get them to come in and take her away.'

'Why!? Why would I do that?' He throws his hands in the air.

'Because maybe you have other plans. Perhaps the deal we made just isn't enough.'

'I'm a man of my word.'

'You made no promises to *me*.'

'I would never hurt her.' He confesses in a low tone.

'Did you tell anyone she was staying here?'

'Listen, this is an attack on me, too.' He stabs a finger into his chest. 'This is my home. People don't fuck with my…'

'With your what?' I scowl. 'Your what?'

'People don't fuck with my friends.' He lowers his voice.

'You better find out who was willing to.'

'You have to understand, I would never hurt her.' Tino places his hands on his hips and looks down at the floor. 'I care about her very much…I'm going to make some calls, see what I can find out.'

'Could it be the Massinos?' Collins suggests. 'Perhaps they thought they'd get at your family through Alexandra.'

'No it isn't them.'

I groan. 'How can you be so sure?'

Tino hesitates. 'Doesn't make sense.'

'What do you mean?'

'This is too sloppy for them.' He gestures around the room. 'They've been following me for weeks; they like to gather information. If they had her, they would already be in contact.'

'Why are they following you?'

'That is my business.'

'Taking Alexandra could be a warning to you.'

'It's not possible.'

'Unless they found out who she is.' Collins says. 'They could have followed you up here, waited until you left...'

'This isn't their style.' Tino insists forcefully. 'I know it's not them.'

'It's the Sicilian mafia...' Collins exclaims.

'As I said, I'll make some calls.' He moves out of the kitchen and down the corridor, looking around his home. 'If you hear from her, you let me know.'

I meet his eyes, searching for the tell, needing to be sure that none of this is his doing.

'Save yourself some time James and look elsewhere. I'm not your guy.' He opens the front door and leans against the frame. 'All I ever wanted to do was protect her.'

I offer a slight nod, unable to quiet the suspicion badgering my mind. *Something isn't right.* I watch Tino jog down the driveway to a waiting car. 'We should have him followed.'

'Here...' Collins utters behind me.

I turn, noticing the clear liquid sloshing around the glass in her hand. 'What is it?'

'Vodka.' She thrusts it forward.

'Any whisky?'

'Clearly Tino isn't a whisky man.'

I take it from her with a shaking hand, downing it in one go. 'You think he's telling the truth?'

'It doesn't make sense for him to have done this.' She hesitates, eyeing me. 'But you think there's more to it.'

'What if Smart saw her at the fundraiser? What if he's taken her?'

'Do you think he could do something like that?'

'I think we're caught in something we don't yet understand.' She nods. 'I hear you.'

'We need to speak to Brown, use S.A.I.B.R's overseas resources.'

'Roe just texted. Interpol is already en-route.'

'Right.'

'He and Meyer are on their way from Nice. S.A.I.B.R. have pulled together an incident response team.'

'Where from?'

'French security service.'

'Did you explain what happened to Brown?'

She nods. 'I told him our asset has disappeared and finding them is integral to this operation.'

'He's going to think this is SO15 trying to make a point.'

'Could it be?'

'Not out here…'

'You think your father couldn't find a way?'

'This seems too… loud, even for him.'

'Well, we need to keep an open mind.'

'I should be out there looking for her.'

'The quickest way to find her is to gather our intelligence resources.' Collins offers warily. 'This isn't over, Gabriel.'

'I said so much shit I didn't mean.'

'You were just trying to keep a distance.'

'And this happened anyway.'

'Listen, you need to push through and focus on finding her. Guilt is useless here.'

'Can you fill that up again?' I hand her the empty glass.

'As long as it helps you focus.' She says, taking the tumbler.

My phone rings. I nearly drop it, trying to answer. 'Hello?'

'Gabriel James? Hi, this is Keys…Michael Keough. Sorry to bother you. Look, Alexandra's phone has been disconnected and I can't get hold of Alison Collins.'

'Who is it?' She whispers.

I put the phone on speaker.

'… and the thing is, I've been helping Alison out here and there.'

Collins' face falls with recognition as Keys continues.

'…. Alexandra had me track her phone. She's been sending me intel.'

'How did you get this number?'

'Michael, this is Alison.' Collins interjects. 'Listen, there's been an incident, Alexandra's gone.'

He swears under his breath. 'I knew something wasn't right.'

'We think someone took her from the villa tonight.'

'Shit. What time? I can look at street cams in the area. Send me the address.'

'Eleven*ish*.' I respond, becoming impatient. 'She called me around that time. She told me a car had pulled up to the villa.'

'The suspect was in a car?'

'That's what she said.'

'Ok, look I'll do my best. But without a reg plate…'

'It's a needle in a haystack.' I groan, running a hand over my face. 'Listen, are you able to track someone else's whereabouts? If I give you their number.'

'Yeah, yeah definitely.'

'Good. I need you to do two things for me. Track Tino Caruso's phone. I want to know where he is right now and keep tracking him.'

'Yeah, I can try. Get Alison to send me his number.'

'On it.' Collins replies, stalking away.

'Gabriel, I…' Keys starts, 'this would be a lot easier if I had access to S.A.I.B.R. resources.'

Fuck it, I'll deal with the consequences later. 'We'll give you temporary privileges. Collins will text you what you need.'

'Got it.'

'I also need you to find out where Tino went last night. And if he's on CCTV anywhere near this villa when Lex was taken, I need to know.'

'Ok, ok. All this… it will take time.' Keys warns.

'Yeah well, she doesn't have any.'

'I'll do what I can.'

I hang up the phone and stare ahead. This is a waiting game that I wasn't prepared for.

'Gabriel?' Emily appears at the door to the villa, quickly donning gloves and shoe covers. 'What can I do?'

'This is the rest of the team from Interpol?' I ask, watching a group of forensics file in. 'Can you ask them to collect all the glass? Every piece. And I need fingerprints. Whoever was here could have left a mark. That's the priority.'

'Ok.' She hesitates, taking in my appearance. 'What happened here?' She reaches out, the tips of her fingers brushing my bruised knuckles. 'Collins said you lost an asset.'

'Yeah, we need to get her back.' I pull away.

She lingers her worried gaze on my face, searching for the answers she knows she won't get out loud. 'You can tell me… there's obviously something going o-'

'Not now.' I feel my phone vibrate and look down at the screen. I step past her and walk out onto the terrace before answering. 'Yep?'

'I decided not to wait, and I hacked into GCHQ. They've got satellite feeds all over the place. Thought I might get a better look of the vehicle there. Did a shoddy job as no time. But they're onto me… got my location, traced my IP.'

'Get yourself to The Nest. I'll send you the address and an encrypted code for entry.'

'Will do.' Keys hesitates. 'Listen, Gabriel… from GCHQ… I think I've got something.'

'Go on…'

'I've been trawling through police chatter in the area in case anyone saw anything in the neighbourhood.'

'Did they?'

'Not locally but there's noise about a black van travelling at speed out of Monaco on the DH17. It caused a commotion through the tolls. It didn't stop and caused a lot of damage. French Police were sent out in pursuit but lost sight of the vehicle around Menton. Last sighting was on the DH17 carriageway, heading west.'

'Can you get a reg plate?'

'I had to jump off the feed and get on the move. But I've got a list of owners who have a black Peugeot carrier with the reg plate that starts EL-475.'

'Ok, make a start on that list. I want you to flag anyone who owns a van like that with connections to organised crime, government corruption, anyone that might have worked for Freeman Powell Technologies. Specifically, I want to know if a van like that has any connection to a man named Dante Soridov.'

'Freeman Powell as in…' I hear his fingers tapping his keypad, 'the security company?'

'Yeah, this particular group we're dealing with like to use them. Use the S.A.I.B.R database. The team here can check that reg plate with other local crimes in the area. That could narrow it down. You focus on Soridov. I'll get Roe to go through known associates connected to this operation, anyone that's on our watchlist and see if a black Peugeot has ever shown up.'

'Sounds good. I'll work as fast as I can...' He hesitates. 'Listen, there's something else.'

My heart sinks. 'Go on...'

'Whilst I was scanning police chatter, I picked up a few callouts that might be relevant.'

'Ok...'

'Two hotels in Monaco reported break-ins tonight. Details of a gunman in one bedroom. The other room was ransacked, guests reported hearing furniture being thrown about the place.'

'Which?' I ask. 'Which hotels?'

'Hotel du Paris and...

'Columbus ...' I finish his sentence. *Our bedrooms.* 'Someone's coming for the whole team.'

'You need to be careful.' Keys says.

'Yeah...' I jog down the corridor, searching for Collins. 'Yeah we will. Thanks for the heads up. Get rid of your phone. Get to the Nest. We'll speak soon.'

'Roger that.'

I find Collins and relay the message. Her eyes dart across the floor as she thinks. 'We've just brought the whole sodding team out to them on a platter.'

'Contact Brown. Tell him this is not the work of SO15. We need a secure location.'

'I can do it…' Roe appears, pulling off his gloves. 'The team will finish up here, then we'll get everyone to a safe house. I'll speak to Brown.'

'The incident response team are fifteen minutes out.' Collins looks between us. 'Won't we be safe here with them?'

'They'll have to come with us,' I suggest. 'Roe, have you got a laptop handy?'

'Yeah.' He turns, gesturing to the kitchen table.

'I've got an intelligence source who has a list of black Peugeot vans that start with the registration EL-475. This van was reported travelling at high speed out of Monaco, west along the DH17, towards Menton. And the timeline fits with when Le…' I pause, correcting myself. 'With when our asset was taken. We need to check all CCTV in the Menton area. Then we crosscheck any reports of a van like that involved in local crime or any association with our investigation.'

Roe sits down in front of his computer. 'Where is this list coming from?'

'You'll get it in your inbox.'

'This is a long shot.' Collins murmurs.

'It's all we have.'

'What should we do?' Roe looks up. 'Go through our list of POIs and check their records, see if they or their associates have ever been reported using a black Peugeot.'

'Start with the Massinos. Then the Carusos. I'm still not convinced this wasn't some fucked up play by them.'

Roe leans down to the floor and pulls a second bag onto his lap. 'Here…' He hands me a laptop. 'Let's share the load.'

CHAPTER TWENTY-FOUR

ALEXANDRA

Multiple images begin flashing across the large screen, illuminating the room around us: *A lab facility. A military camp. A warehouse. Berlin. London. Moscow. Budapest.*

Flint presses a white button on the device.

Hope's body jolts upwards.

Her fingernails claw the leather seat as a current travels through her body and she screams a blood-curdling cry. Blood dribbles from her mouth, her juddering teeth bite into her lip.

'What the hell are you doing!' I yell. 'You will kill her!'

Flint's awe-stricken expression gapes at the machine, pleased with its readings. 'Stable. Good brain function. Repeat the sequence.'

The large screen goes blank. The orange ring returns, engulfing the room. The same images flash into view. *The lab facility. A military camp. A warehouse. Berlin. London. Moscow. Budapest.*

'Stimulation detected.' Icarus looks startled. 'Images Four and Five. That means she remembers.'

New images appear this time: *An orphanage. The streets of a small European town. A couple standing on the porch of an old house. Children playing in a garden.*

'Detecting high levels of oxytocin, dopamine, and serotonin.'

His finger drops to the white button. Another current ignites through Hope's fragile body, her limbs jerking, her cries piercing the walls, howling with agony. Spittle flies from her mouth, her teeth omitting a terrifying, repetitive chattering, her jaw slackening as if it might detach from her body.

'Stop it! Please!' I shout again. 'Please stop!'

'Images Two, Three, and Four.' Flint dictates.

I look back at the screen. *An orphanage. The streets of a small European town. A couple standing on the porch of an old house. Children playing in the garden.* These are pictures of things she knows. Things that are important to her. Hope's breathing is laboured, her hands twitching involuntarily.

'This is barbaric! She's a child!' I struggle against my restraints, desperate to put an end to this.

'This is good. She's responding well.' Flint nods to himself.

Hope's head lulls forward. She must be unconscious at least, if not already dead. Icarus tags a few more wires to her temples. He signals to Soridov. The images start up again.

The European town appears on the screen. Icarus triggers the white button. Hope jerks in her chair; her limbs turning a deep purple. *A couple standing on the porch of an old house.* More electrical current soars through her body; blood spews from her mouth. *Children playing in the garden.* She limply shifts with the voltage passing through her, like a fish out of water; vulnerable and entirely powerless. The screen finally goes blank.

'Again!' Flint calls out.

I pull at my restraints, screaming at him to stop.

The images reappear. Hope's body is launched into the air, her limbs pulsating, her veins standing bold against her youthful skin as if they might burst through her pores.

'Low dopamine, no serotonin, no oxytocin.' Flint murmurs. 'Another few hours and we'll have broken the circuit. She'll be ready.'

CHAPTER TWENTY-FIVE

GABRIEL

I lay on the bed, fully clothed, with my phone on my chest. The turmoil in my mind contrasting with the peaceful sound of Emily's deep breathing. I stare at the ceiling, running through every possible scenario. *Tino took her because he loves her. Jed Smart recognised her. Lucas took her to guarantee we'd help with the Massinos. That fucking doctor told The Singularity who she was. They followed her up here, waited until Tino left and took their shot.* Only two of those situations mean she's alive. I close my eyes, desperate to think of something else.

Wild hair blowing in the wind. I see her huddled down an alleyway, trying to release her bike, swearing like nothing I've ever heard before, aggressively shaking a padlock to no avail.

'You need some help?'

'Not interested.' She grumbles.

'You seem like you do.'

'If you're planning on sexually harassing me, can you get on with it so you can learn the hard way and I can get on with my night.'

I crouch down next to her. 'I'm sober. And I'm really offering a hand.'

She finally looks at me, her eyes widening for less than a second before they glisten with amusement. She stands, gesturing towards the bike. 'Ok...'

I lean forward, jimmying the lock a few times before straightening. 'Yeah that's fucked...' I hold out the broken key.

She laughs, throwing her head back. In that split second, I know I would do anything to hear that again.

174

'I can walk you home instead?'

She eyes me, craning her neck. 'You think I might not make it without you?'

'No... I urm...' I smile, nervously running a hand through my hair. 'I'm sure you're more than capable.'

'Do you like beer?'

'I wouldn't feel comfortable you buying me a drink when, in reality, I just made your situation a lot worse.'

'I'm not buying.' She grins, throwing her hands in her pockets, walking confidently ahead.

'What's your name?' I jog after her.

'What's yours?' She looks up, challenging me.

'Gabriel.'

The corners of her lips turn up, she suppresses a smile.

'What?'

'There's symbolism in there somewhere.'

'You suggesting I'm God's favourite?'

She raises an eyebrow. 'Helpful and modest.'

I smile in the dark. Since the night we met, she's persistently found a way to get under my skin and it's exactly where she's stayed ever since.

I forgot you do this...
Do what?
This.
And what is this... exactly?
These long passive-aggressive silences.

Memories of her keep flooding in as if trying to fill a void. Sleep won't come. I sit up, trying to stave off the circling dread. *I*

175

need to do something. Waiting around is killing me. Careful not to wake Emily, I get off the bed and tread out into the corridor, turning in the wrong direction before doubling back and locating the kitchen. Roe and Collins are still seated at the table, both of them looking exhausted.

'You should get some sleep.' I announce from the doorway.

'That what you're doing?' Roe laughs.

'Why do safehouses always have such terrible mattresses?' I rub my sore shoulder.

'Budget cuts.' Collins says, getting up to put the kettle on.

'Got anything to go on?'

'Tino has an alibi and multiple witnesses. CCTV confirms. He never even checked his phone.'

'Odd, don't you think? He goes to a bar miles away from the scene of the crime, ensures he's on CCTV and doesn't check his phone once.'

'Well, it's all odd to be honest.'

'What about Lucas?'

'Never left his villa.'

'Your pal Keys might have something but we're confirming.' Roe announces.

'Go on…' I take a seat.

Roe looks to Collins, who nods.

'Ivan Soridov' Roe swivels his laptop around.

'Dante's brother?' I lean on the table, examining the image. A gaunt face with a hard jaw and even harder eyes stare back. 'Tell me…'

'In 2015, a black Peugeot van was reported stolen by Europcar in Nice.'

I frown. 'It's not the same reg.'

'I think it's been switched.' Roe continues. 'Someone took a black Peugeot van when it was in the repair shop getting a bumper replaced. The logs say they were never able to fix the damages before it was stolen.'

'It's still got the damage?'

'We've been trawling CCTV through towns and villages around the DH17 towards Menton.' He taps a key on the computer, switching the screen. 'We think this is it… driving into this estate at four this afternoon. It appeared to stop here on its way east. The opposite direction.'

'And the same van was caught on cameras travelling west at speed at around the time Lex was taken?'

'Yep.'

'So here… it's on its way to her?'

'Could have been.'

'And you crosschecked that location with known associates?'

'Ivan Soridov.' Collins pours boiling water into a mug. 'He lives in that estate.'

I stand from the chair. 'Why the hell are we still sat here?'

Collins shakes her head. 'We can't touch him.'

'What are you talking about?'

'Interpol has been contacted; we're asking for a way around this.' Roe explains.

'A way around what!'

'He's protected. The Soridov brothers are ex-KGB. Ivan is working with Interpol giving intel on a classified operation.'

'We're a leading security intelligence agency.' I turn and leave, stalking towards the bedroom.

'Gabriel!' Collins rushes after me. 'We will have the permission we need. We just have to wait.'

I turn to face her. 'If she had waited… if she had waited just one more second to come for me, do you think I'd be standing here in front of you? Do you think this is all I would have ended up with?' I pull my T-shirt to one side, exposing the scar below my collarbone.

Collins' mouth drops open as she tries to think of a response.

Emily opens the door, shielding her eyes from the light. 'What's going on?'

I move past her into the bedroom, picking up my stuff.

'What are you doing, Gabriel?' She asks, observing me.

'We have a lead.' I throw on my vest before turning to compile my weapons kit.

'We need to do this properly.' Collins interjects.

'Tell Roe to get the security team ready.'

'Brown will murder us.' Collins protests. 'He's already furious that we didn't bring Alexandra straight back to the UK.'

'We're leaving in less than one minute.'

'We will not have a taskforce to beat them if we do this, Gabriel!' She shouts, calling after me as I march towards the front door. 'Brown will have our heads. We will be useless.'

'And what will we be without her?' I yell.

'You need to think clearly.'

'Security team will be in the cars in less than a minute.' Roe appears, strapping himself into his vest.

'You're on board with this?' Collins says with disbelief.

He shrugs. 'It's a losing battle.'

CHAPTER TWENTY- SIX

ALEXANDRA

Dante Soridov lowers Hope onto a stretcher, fitting her into more restraints before wheeling her out of the room. I take a deep breath, pushing oxygen to my brain, grappling with logic through the fog. *Flint, the lab, the images, the aversion therapy. How is this connected to A Better World? Are Gabriel and Collins safe? Where are they taking Hope now?*

'Have you ever heard of Disassociation Disorder?' Dr Flint asks.

I nod my head slowly.

'Of course…you're a soldier.' He wheels over a small stall and takes a seat; sitting so close I can smell the sweat perspiring underneath his clothes, see it collecting in the stubble above his top lip.

'What the hell is this place? Why am I here?'

He clasps his hands together, crossing his leg over his knee. 'Here, we deal in extraction.'

'You're creating aversions to memories, is that it? All those images are relevant to Hope and you're trying to cut them away?'

'Sergeant Haines did all he could to teach you. But he couldn't make it perfect. Imagine how good you could have been at your job without the flaws of emotion.'

'What the hell do you know about Simon?'

'*Simon* was on the right track, trying to train your unit to remove emotional attachments, to become cold, killing machines. But the army doesn't have the patience, the resources to do what needs to be done at a grassroots level. They train you from adulthood and in order to make you obey, they close your mind. Your world becomes so small, so rigid.'

'You want subservience, is that it?'

'Do you know what it's like to create true, unprecedented value from nothing? To take something useless, meaningless and turn it into a commodity. Have you ever experienced that before?'

'Is that what you're doing here? Experimenting on people.'

'You're a prime example. You were dealt a hand that you dragged yourself out of. Your path was organised crime, you took a different one. At some point in your life, you were able to think bigger than yourself.'

'What is your plan for Hope?'

He ignores the question, linking his hands behind his head. 'I heard you've had a hard time. Lost a child, your father, your sister…After we're done here, you won't feel pain, remorse, guilt, sadness. You'll be free, free of nature's weaknesses.'

'That's freedom, is it?'

'Tell me Alexandra… how often do you think of the boys you murdered?'

I look away from him, my stomach churning waves of bitter nausea that threaten to travel up my throat.

'Your squadron, your fellow soldiers… there are thousands like them all over the world. SBS, SAS, Mossad, CIA. All of you fighting like with like.'

'And you think you're creating better soldiers by using that.' I throw my head towards the screen. 'It's a delusion.'

He shrugs. 'Haines saw the value in ridding you of emotion.'

'Not like this.'

'But you have to admit, it made you better. Even with his measly attempts at detachment. You felt it. The advantage.'

'You know nothing about me.'

'My dear, we know everything…' He looks up to the ceiling, revelling in the statement. 'We are the Queen on the proverbial chessboard.'

'And who is we?'

'We're the extra mile, the last push.'

'What has this got to do with A Better World? What connects you to…' I stop. *Hope. Children.* 'Dante was in Syria because you're trafficking children from Za'atari camp. You're bringing them to labs to do this.' My voice becomes shrill. I wrestle against the restraints. 'Then what? What is this place?'

He cocks his head, studying me. 'It is a shame that the world got its hands on you before we could make you truly matter.'

'Augustus Fox is Higgs.' I utter, laying it all out. 'Fox is Higgs. And he's doing this for Jed Smart, right? You're working for the British Government but then, what are you doing with Almasi?'

He reaches out as if trying to clutch a thought. 'Higgs is everything.'

'Tell me more about him then.'

The door opens suddenly. Soridov strides in, nodding his head towards Flint; clearly affirming something important.

'Times up!' Flint grins, jumping up from the chair.

Quickly, he slides the machine across the room, depositing it at the top of the chair next to my head. Humming a tuneless song, Flint unravels a fresh set of wires, connecting me to the second device and attaching small pads to my head and chest.

'I've completed years of Army MRT.' I blurt out, trying my utmost to sound measured when the truth is I'm in a blind panic. *They're going to do it to me. What they did to Hope is going to happen to me.* 'And on top of that, months of psychological interrogation training. I can't crack. I don't crack.'

'Everyone cracks.' Flint murmurs, still fiddling with corresponding wires. 'The circuit always breaks.'

I tense. 'You don't want me working for you. I'm wanted everywhere. MI6, Counterterrorism, a few London gangs, a whole bunch of people in Turkey.'

Flint ignores me, carefully slipping a headset over my face. Everything goes dark. My heart staggers with increased palpitations before adrenaline kicks in and it hammers hard against my chest, beating itself free. I take a deep breath. *Zone out, Alexandra. Do what Simon taught you. Distance yourself from the now.* I flinch suddenly, feeling an abrupt sting at the base of my neck. My left hand jerks against the restraint, instinctively trying to locate the source of the pain. I blink a few times, trying to gauge what he's given me.

'You won't feel different.' Flint explains. 'We've inserted a tiny chip into the base of your skull, which we control. It contains several psychoactive serums we've created for the program. Throughout this process, we release them into your brain tissue. They can act as a blocker or enhancer, depending on what we decide. And this...' He injects something into my arm. 'This supports your reactions to certain stimuli. It allows your brain to react in a more truthful way. When an image triggers you, we'll see it all.'

'Just kill me!' I shout, losing all composure, fiercely struggling against the leather straps. 'Kill me and be done with it!'

'Alexandra, you're going to see a series of images.' Flint begins calmly. 'We've obtained these images from various sources, and we know the places, people and things have meaning to you. We'll monitor your reactions. That will give us an indication as to how much work needs to be done. You won't remember a thing.'

This isn't the end.

I'll fight.

I'll fight with everything I have.

CHAPTER TWENTY-SEVEN

GABRIEL

We wait in a van a few streets away from Ivan Soridov's bleak French council block. Collins briefs the security team; eight hard-faced men are crammed shoulder to shoulder, their eyes the only feature that can be seen beneath their thick black bandanas. Despite the sweltering heat, unbearable humidity, and robust TAC uniforms, not one of them appears to be sweating. In contrast, I shift uncomfortably, tugging at the base of my Kevlar vest, trying to cool down.

'Mike Hinchen.' A burly man raises his hand before pulling up the lip of his bandana. 'With the suspect's history in Moscow, is there any indication that he might have explosives training? Or had access to explosives recently?'

'Our intel suggests he's been trying to keep a low profile. Interpol has kept an eye on him since he entered Nice. He's had no contact, it would appear, with anyone from his past or any known associates of Russian FSB agents, with any links to explosives.' Collins explains.

Hinchen nods, satisfied with the answer.

'We've got an explosives team on hand if and when we need. But I think this one is pretty straightforward,' I say, looking down the length of the van. 'We get up there, enter the property, search the place and get the intel onsite.'

'We've spoken to the landlord, and he'd prefer if we didn't break the door down.' Collins shrugs. 'So we're going to knock first.'

'Shall we bring the stack, Ma'am?' Hinchen asks.

'Yes, we might need a ram, if it comes to it.' Collins says reluctantly.

'We'll need you to conduct this operation with the usual approach. Two, two, and two.' I clarify, indicating their formation.

Hinchen nods. 'Six in the flat, two at higher ground surveying the perimeter.' He leans in, divvying up his team, giving them instructions.

'Agent James has agreed to approach the property first. He'll knock once and if no answer, we have a warrant to enter.' Collins lies, giving me a disapproving look.

The assault team nod, starting their preparation; placing their earpieces in, checking the safety on their weapons. We make our way across the street and down the road towards Ivan Soridov's estate. Two of Hinchen's men peel off to climb the stairs of a tower block opposite, gaining higher ground with a clear visual of escape routes or external interference. Hinchen signals for his men to stop a few metres short of the stairwell leading to the fourth floor.

'EXPO BRAVO are you in position? OVER.' Hinchen checks in with his team.

'Green. Area secure. OVER.'

'You're good.' Hinchen nods.

I climb the stairs with the assault team following closely behind. Reaching the fourth floor, Hinchen creeps across the hall, flattening his back to the wall. He surveys the area before giving a thumbs up. I move to stand at the door of Ivan's apartment. Five of his men line up on my left, their weapons at the ready. I pull out my gun and train it by my side before knocking on the door. Muffled footsteps approach and the door opens a fraction. One eye appears below a sweaty forehead, his pupils blown to an unthinkable size. *High as a kite.*

'Who is it?' Ivan Soridov asks in a thick Russian accent.

'Agent James, Security Intelligence Service.'

'If you're police, then speak to my lawyer.' He tries to close the door.

I shove my foot in the way. 'I'm not that type of police, pal.'

'Fuck off...' He spits, shoving my shoe out of the way and slamming the door.

'Ok...' I turn to the team. 'We tried.'

I throw my leg out and force my foot against the lock, not bothering to wait for the ram. The door breaks and Hinchen's men methodically rush in, yelling commands and signals. They work quickly, securing room after room.

Collins puts her hand on my shoulder, noticing my pained expression. 'Be prepared that you might not find anything here.'

'That's what I'm worried about.'

'We're clear!' Hinchen calls out. 'James, you're good.'

We stride through the messy apartment, kicking clothes and empty takeaway boxes beneath our feet. Ivan Soridov stands in a towel between two gunmen. His bony rib cage expands and retracts quickly, his breathing heavy. He could do with a good meal. His panicked, beady eyes watch Hinchen's team. He complains in Russian as they aggressively unload drawers and turn over furniture in search of evidence.

'Here!' One of the team shouts from the next room. 'Someone else has been staying.'

'Collect anything that relates to a second occupant. Any tablets, mobile devices, bag it up.'

'Why are you here?!' Ivan shouts. 'You can't do this!'

'Bring him with me.'

The two officers lift Ivan off his feet, drag him to the living room and throw him in a chair. He begins shivering, mumbling incoherent words, nervously watching the team rifle through his possessions.

'Eyes to me.' I click in his face. 'Who has been staying here?'
'пошел на хуй'
'Roe!' I call out.
Roe strides over, his eyebrows raised.
'Say it again…'
Ivan stares up at me, confused.
'Say it again, what you just said.'
The corner of his mouth turns up in a snarl. He repeats himself slowly as if speaking to someone with learning difficulties.
'He says fuck you….' Roe shrugs.
I sigh, throwing my hand around Ivan's neck, pulling him off the sofa. 'Who the fuck has been staying here?'
He starts whining, dribble running down his chin.
'We've got a bit of a situation here, Ivan. One of our assets has been taken. The vehicle in connection with this attack was seen on this estate, only yesterday.'
'What?' His eyes freeze with fear. 'I don't know anything about that!'
'Do you know what happens to people who fuck with British Intelligence?'
'I haven't done anything wrong! You can't do this. You can't be here!'
'Who visited you yesterday?'
'Nobody knows I'm here!? I don't know what you want!'
I throw him down again; his skinny arms work frantically to rearrange the towel around his body.
'Who else is staying at this apartment?'
He fidgets, blinking rapidly. 'Dante… my brother, Dante.'
'Does he live here?'
'No… no.'
'Where does he live?'

'I swear I don't know. I don't know, I really don't.'

'Why is he here?'

'I don't...' he whimpers. 'I swear I don't know.'

'He's your brother and you don't know a thing about him?'

'He...' Ivan shakes his head, his eyes darting desperately around. 'I help him sometimes. He gets into trouble, needs a place to lay low.'

'Help him how?'

'We're nothing, not bad, just defectors.... You know what that is? We're ex-FSB, KGB, whatever you want to call it. We don't talk. We have to keep apart for our own safety.'

'You have information that Interpol needs, so they put you up here?'

'Yes... yes. But I have to stay quiet. I have to mind my own business.'

'How have you been helping your brother?'

'Give him a place to stay. Give him some money. He...' He hesitates. 'I just want to help him make a new life.'

'What has he been doing whilst he's here?'

'I really don't know.'

'You must have an inkling.'

'A what?' He frowns, looking confused.

'An idea.' I snap. 'You must have an idea what he's doing here, where he's going.'

He shrugs. 'He goes to nice dinners with people. Important people. I don't know who they are.'

'You ever met some of these people?'

'Huh?' His face disintegrates into confusion.

'Have you met these people?'

Collins approaches with a phone dropped into a clear evidence bag.

Ivan starts shaking his head. 'That is mine! That is my phone for Interpol. I have a deal with them...'

I dig into my back pocket, retrieving my mobile.

Ivan frowns. 'Wha... what are you doing?'

'I'm calling the Head of the Albanian Mafia. Got lots of connections in Russia. He'll send out word to the FSB, tell them where you are. I reckon you'll be dead in under an hour.'

'No, no, no.' He holds up his trembling hands. 'Please! Please...'   ʼ

'The people your brother hangs out with...' I say, holding the phone up to my ear. 'Have you met them?'

'No! I don't know who he meets. We don't talk much. I promise I'm telling the truth. Please.' He forms a prayer sign. 'Please don't tell anyone I'm here.'

'Your brother stays here, borrows money. You don't ever overhear him on the phone? He never mentions names?'

'No.'

I swing my arm in the air, making a hard connection against his face. Blood instantly appears from the split in his lip.

'Taste it... means you're alive. Make the most of that moment because very soon, you won't be.'

'Dante will kill me.'

'The Russians will get to you first, Ivan.'

'I...' he looks around the room, lowering his voice. 'I had to pick him up once.'

'Where?'

'I wasn't allowed to go all the way in. They made me stay at the gate.'

'The gate to what?'

'It's a facility. Like a college only, not for students. Somewhere in the hills...'

'Is it a house?'

'There is a house but there are lots of buildings around too.'

'Where?'

He looks off to the side, jumping at the sound of the TAC team crashing through the kitchen. 'I can't be sure. I can't remember.'

'Is it in Monaco?'

'No... no. Not Monaco. Definitely not Monaco.'

'Someone keep an eye on him!'

Two of the assault team strides over and position themselves on either side of the sofa.

'Shoot him if he stands up.'

Ivan's eyes widen.

I walk away and dial the number for The Nest.

'Gabriel?' Keys answers.

'You alright?

'I'm good. I'm safe... I mean.'

'Listen up, Collins is going to send a number for Ivan Soridov's brother, Dante. It'll be switched off now, but I need you to track his whereabouts over the last few days. Any locations outside of Monaco, you let me know.'

'Ok...'

'There's a large property. Lex could be there, but I need to make sure Ivan isn't fucking with us.'

'What am I looking for?'

'He says it's a facility of some kind. It's in the hills. Check if Dante's been travelling outside of Monaco. And then I need you to find this place for me. Check satellite imaging.'

'Right... not a lot to go on.'

'I need you to find this place, Keys.'

'I'm going to try, Gabe... I'll try.'

CHAPTER TWENTY-EIGHT

ALEXANDRA

A burnt orange circle appears.

It burns and pulses.

Swirling, expanding, soaring towards me as it grows, getting bigger and bigger until eventually the edges disappear.

All that's left is darkness.

I'm drifting in the middle, stranded in an empty void.

The screen flickers: an image of my father appears; he's sitting on the floor smiling. I'm sat next to him, my hands placed clumsily on his. We beam at the camera. An image of my sister from her prom. She's wearing an electric blue cocktail dress, the one Mario reluctantly agreed to buy after months of her begging. A third image. A mugshot from when Olivia was first admitted to a psychiatric hospital. My father returns. His corpse lying on a gurney in a morgue. I begin to wretch, struck with anguish. Simon in his military uniform. Sandhurst. Gabriel. His face is a solid gut punch. His dark eyes both inviting and intimidating. The sculpt of every feature, his jaw, his neck. *Perfect.* A fog of dread descends; horror shutting me down. *They know who he is.* I start to shake my head, my brain agonising over that fact. They know what he means. I close my eyes, screwing them shut.

'She's trying to block her readings on images eight, nine, and ten.' Flint observes.

The sequence repeats.

My father. Olivia. Simon. Sandhurst. Gabriel. I shake my head, trying to switch everything off, needing to deter them. My brain won't oblige. I have to focus. *Keep them away from Gabriel.*

'Eight, nine, and ten…' Flint muses with curiosity. 'So it's James.'

The screen goes blank.

The orange ring burns, expanding until it disappears.

Image eight. The violent fuse of the current hits me, pain sears through my body as if my skin is being peeled with a laser. Gritting my teeth so hard I begin to taste blood, I shake in the chair, my nerve endings shattering. *Hold onto the thought of him Alexandra. Don't let him go. It's him, it's Gabriel. I won't disassociate. Seeing him isn't pain. It's not excruciating. It's everything.* Image nine appears. Another surge torpedoes through me. I clutch the sides, my tongue swollen, my whole mouth chattering. My eyes are dry and hot. So hot that I feel like they might fade into dust. Image nine surfaces. The frequency increases, my heart feels like it might burst from my chest, its erratic beats burning a hole in my body. I won't watch this. I squeeze my eyes shut. I will not surrender.

'Alexandra…I know what you're doing.' Flint warns.

Tightening my eyelids, I savour the control, embracing the moment of peace from the haunting images.

'Dante!' Flint shouts. 'These are fresh readings…We need the readings. Make her open her eyes.'

Someone moves towards me. Cold steel presses against my skin, nestling deliberately against my skull. 'I will shoot you right here Christofi. Open your eyes!'

I subtly shift in my chair, positioning my left thumb against the restraint. I begin muttering under my breath, murmuring nonsensical words. I feel breath on my skin; Dante leans closer, trying to gauge what I'm saying.

The first time I deployed my parachute during a B-Squad skydiving exercise, I dislocated my thumb. Never bothering to get it looked at, it tends to pop out from time to time. Mario used to go on at

191

me to get it sorted. He wasn't squeamish, he could take the sight of blood, but bones… he hated the idea of broken bones. I think of my father as I grit my teeth and clamp my jaw down, braced for that uncomfortable, popping sensation. I jolt to the right, causing my body and thumb to travel in different directions. Practically biting through the tip of my tongue, I absorb the spasming pain. My muscles scream, the action tearing my ligaments apart. *Fuck.* It didn't work.

'What is she doing?' Dante yells, confusion in his voice.

'It's registering pain… the machine… it detects adrenaline, cortisol…'

Again.

I jolt, forcing my thumb in an excruciating direction until it dislocates. I cry out, tasting blood, screaming outwardly this time. I slip through the restraint, throwing the headset off my face and punch the gun out of Soridov's hand. I grip his hair, pulling him towards me. With the weight of my body, I headbutt him twice, trying to knock him out; my forehead pummelling his skull with a hard crack. He falters, falling back and hunching over. I sit up and look around for something sharp, something to get me out.

Two things happen.

My ears fill with the sound of a turbine engine.

My body contorts as a current of electrical energy flows through me.

I clench my jaw through the pain, my shaking arm reaching for the gun, but another wave comes. Volts course through my body, my teeth shudder, I clamp my eyes shut, gripping hard to the leather until finally, I float back down, heavy with exhaustion. I can't get out of here alone. It's been hours. *Nobody is coming.*

CHAPTER TWENTY-NINE

GABRIEL

'Got a pen?' Keys says, his tone eager.

'What is it?'

'Get a pen.'

I wave to Collins, gesturing for something to write with.

'Chateau Noir, Saint Agnes. It's in the hills between here and Menton. It was a fortress back in the day. But it was bought and restored by Andrew Magnusson in the 1980s. Magnusson was a Doctor of Cognitive Psychology who worked for UK intelligence but his records are sealed. And I mean, really sealed. Even I can't get into them. He must have been a big timer with the British Government at one stage.'

'Where is Magnusson now?'

'Dead. He was killed in 2005, during 7/7.'

'Can you send me a picture of the house?'

'Yep. Dante Soridov's burner has pinged calls four miles from this place. That's the closest tower.'

'Thanks.' A message comes through on my phone, an aerial shot of the property. I walk over to Ivan, shoving the screen under his nose. 'Is this it?'

He frowns, his eyes fearful.

'Chateau Noir, is this where you dropped your brother off?'

He hesitates, squinting at the screen.

'Is this it!' I shout. 'Is this where you took him?'

'I think so yes, yes. The gates. I know the gates.'

I turn to Collins. 'Let's go.'

We rush across the street towards the van. I climb in the driver's side. Hinchen's men pile in the back and Collins settles into the passenger seat, producing her phone.

'What are you doing?' I ask, starting the engine.

'We need Roe to stay here in case Interpol show.'

'Hinchen's put someone on surveillance in case Ivan tries to warn his brother.'

'And we've bugged his apartment.' Collins confesses under her breath.

'That's going to upset our cousins…'

'We'll cross that bridge when we come to it.'

'You've changed your tune.'

'I've given up fighting you on this.'

I keep my eyes on the road, speeding down the D700 out of Monaco.

Collins fiddles with the GPS system. 'Take a left towards Corrine. Then follow the road up the D223.'

I swerve the car, cutting off oncoming traffic; affording a few groans from Hinchen's men and a handful of very angry drivers who sound their horns aggressively. Flooring the accelerator, I steer the vehicle at high speed into the hills. Collins leans over her shoulder, checking on the TAC Team before looking at me.

'You know she's a survivor. They need her for something.'

'She doesn't break.' I whisper to myself.

'Pardon?'

'Each SAS squadron is trained to endure a lengthy stint of torture to ensure they remain silent under duress.'

'Which means we're in luck. She won't give anything up.'

'But everyone has a breaking point, so the SAS like to work out how long each of their operatives can last. That indicates how much time they have in hostage rescue situations. How much time before a particular soldier starts talking.'

'Sounds barbaric.'

'Each member of the B-Squadron has a record in their file; of the time it took them to break in simulated interrogation.'

'Alright…'

'Simon Haines was the longest on record. He lasted a week.'

'And Alexandra?'

'Inconclusive.'

'What does that mean?'

'They couldn't mark a time. They pulled her out after eight and a half days. Any longer than that and they're liable for a lawsuit. They had to stop.'

'Because she didn't break at all.'

'She didn't.'

'Well then, you need to think clearly, Gabriel. This is good news. If they need her, they're keeping her alive. She'll hold on until we get there.'

'You're not understanding, Alison.' I snap, exasperated. 'Do you know what happens to people who don't talk? The things they'll put her through.'

'She's tough.'

'They'll go to great lengths to get what they need.'

'I hear you.' She says quietly. 'But she's going to be at that facility. We'll have got to her in good time.'

'We don't know that.'

'I have faith.'

I take a breath, preventing my imagination from running riot. 'Did Keys find anything more about Magnusson?'

'Not yet. If he's ex-British Intelligence, do you think he could have been involved with The Singularity way back?'

'It's possible.'

We travel in silence for a time; Collins only speaking up when giving me directions. I try to focus on the road, keeping my mind from picturing what's become of Lex in the hours she's been gone. The sound of her struggling over the phone haunts me, the guilt and dread of sitting there so passively whilst she fought for her life.

'Ok, half a kilometre up here...' Collins says, leaning forward. 'There, you see that track. It's telling you to go up there.' She unstraps her seat belt. 'Listen up.' She calls out to Mike and his team. 'We're jamming the area. Radio's only.'

'Roger that.' He calls back.

'We'll go on your green, Ma'am.' A second commanding officer replies, checking his assault vest.

The gates appear; tall rails of shiny black iron with a gold star emblem in the middle, set against a sparse, mountainous landscape.

'This is it.' I cut the engine.

'Should we back off?' Collins asks, 'Unload somewhere else.'

'Keys has jammed CCTV; nobody can see us on that thing.' I point to the camera.

Mike Hinchen stretches forward and hands me a GPS device. 'We've detected heat signatures from the Northwest corner of the estate, about two clicks from here. Two buildings are used frequently. There's a lot of energy being generated in the first building.'

Collins frowns. 'So it is a facility.'

'Prioritise the first building. Northwest.'

Collins turns to Hinchen, a satisfied grin on her face. 'Get your men, you're cleared to go.'

'Affirmative.' He stands from the bench, pulling his weapon around to his front. 'T MINUS 1 MINUTE.'

CHAPTER THIRTY

ALEXANDRA

My muscles are shrieking. My head pounding. My chest burns, my lungs twisted into hard stone.

'We lost power,' Flint says. 'We're hydrating you.'

'Is it...' I blink through the dark, trying to swallow past the rawness in my throat. 'Am I done?'

'No, dear.' He says, retrieving his lab coat from the hook on the door. The room grumbles as the generators kick in. 'This is just the beginning.'

'What were you doing to Hope...' I whisper. 'Why her?'

He looks off to the corner of the room and smiles. 'My Compliants are very special. They stop wars, change history, save lives... so many lives.'

'Compliants?'

'They're everywhere... everywhere they need to be.'

'Jed Smart, the Minister of Defence... is...' I cough, my body crying out from the sudden movement, 'is he one?'

'Oh no, no.'

'But he's involved?'

'He has his role.'

'Please just kill me...' I plead, meaning every word. 'I won't do your bidding. I'd rather die.'

'Don't you want to be special?'

I shake my head.

'We might have to...' he takes a seat, 'kill you, that is. We rarely succeed in adults. To make a good Compliant, you need a blank canvas. Someone who lacks or struggles with solid attachments. Hope...we worked on her when she was small. She came to us very

197

young. And for years, it was successful. We kept her controlled, obedient.'

'She woke up from it?'

He shakes his head, disagreeing with my choice of words. 'She unravelled. Her chip was old. She was one of the first Compliants.'

'You've been trying to get her back under.'

'Adults are too messy, too chaotic. And you... well, not only have you been trained by the military, but your mind has also been educated, modified, enhanced by life experience; your father, your peers, your commanders, even yourself. Not to mention, your psyche was irreversibly altered by your pregnancy. There's a good chance we can't extract you. And when that happens, well... you will be of no use.'

The door crashes open, the handle slamming into the wall. Dante enters the room with three armed men, his face flushed. 'There's a breach.'

Flint stands with alarm. 'Find out where!' He frantically wanders around the room, collecting files and documents in his arms.

Dante barks orders to the other men. They swiftly pivot and disappear, their boots echoing through the corridors.

'Th- the lab work, the readings...' Flint utters with dread. 'We need to get them out of here.'

'We're going to untie you.' Dante says, grabbing the small remote, waving it in my face. 'But remember, you're still attached. If you even so much as flinch, I'll light you up. You understand?'

Adrenaline tugs at me, nudging gently beneath the fatigue. I try to remain calm, try to stop myself from garnering too much hope. Observing me closely, Dante releases my restraints and hands Flint the device. I rise out of the chair, my muscles feeling like I'm dragging them against a powerful tide.

'Walk with me.' Flint instructs. 'There's a tunnel.'

I drop my head and fall in line. An alarm bellows out, an aggressive red light flashing above the exit. Flint and Dante look to the ceiling. I lunge forward, grabbing Flint's wrist, twisting it in the wrong direction, forcing the device out of his hand before gripping him at the base of his neck. Dante pivots around, raising his weapon, firing a handful of bullets in my direction. I duck, throwing Icarus in front of me, manoeuvring him as a shield.

'Give it up, Christofi.' He yells over the siren. 'You won't get out of here alive.'

'Put the gun down or I'll kill the doctor.'

Dante takes a step forward. 'You have no idea who you are dealing with.'

'I might die in here, but I will not let you strap me to that chair again.'

'You cannot win.' Dante shakes his head. 'You're not thinking clearly.'

I tighten my grip around Icarus. 'If I kill him, all that work with Hope will be for nothing. You need him. Icarus is the only one who can get Hope back under.'

'What you're doing is meaningless, Miss Christofi...' Flint says, struggling against me, 'There are other facilities. Other people who can do what we're doing. This has been the way for decades and as long as governments exist, it will always continue.'

Without another thought, I shove Flint to the floor and leap towards Dante, elbowing the gun out of his hand, watching it fly across the room. Dropping to a crouch, I crawl to retrieve it, but he seizes my hair, dragging me up to stand. I turn quickly, lashing out with my right leg, kicking him in the face, hearing a crack of bone under the force of my foot. He stumbles towards the EEG machine; test tubes and vials shatter across the floor as an equipment trolley topples over. Dante springs up, a needle wielded between his fingers, flying towards me at speed. I throw my arm up, preventing it from penetrating my skin. He pushes hard, propelling his weight downwards, arrowing the sharp point towards my artery. My body shakes. Summoning every shred of strength I have left, I battle him, fighting to keep the needle from piercing the surface. *Don't give up, Alexandra. Don't stop.* Straining with the gruelling effort, I look down at my feet, trying to stay steady, feeling them slipping on the tiles. Wayne Gibbs' voice echoes in my head. *Use your conditions, Angel. Don't let them use you.* I release my stance, allowing my feet to slip backwards and duck suddenly. Dante falls with the momentum; the unexpected movement causes him to smash into the chair ahead. I jump to my feet, grabbing a large beaker from the side, shattering glass into the back of his head before twisting him around and punching him hard in the face, hurling all my weight behind my fists. I hit him again and again. Dante's head lulls in a daze, his eyes unfocused. Dipping my shoulder, I barge him into the wall, throwing my arm around his neck, the other gripping a shard of glass against his pulsing skin.

'Flint!' Dante wheezes behind his bloodied teeth. 'Get the gun, Flint!'

Icarus cowers in the corner, his shaking hands covering his face as if concealing his vision might save his life.

'Flint, if you so much as look like you're about to stand, I'll slit Soridov's throat and then I'll slit yours before he's hit the grou…'

The door bursts open.

I pull Dante from the wall, heaving his thick, limp body in front of me. A familiar voice calls through the room. I squint through the dull light, counting eight-armed gunmen. It calls out again. *That voice. I recognise that voice.*

CHAPTER THIRTY-ONE

GABRIEL

Without waiting, I storm through the door, yelling out for all armed suspects to immediately drop their weapons. Hinchen files in behind, securing the lab with his team; red lights cross every inch of the room as he demands a check for hidden weapons. A short, muscular block of a man apprehends a suspect who's squeezed himself into the foetal position in the corner of the room. Alexandra stares ahead with a haunted expression. She holds a shard of glass against Dante Soridov's neck. Her hand grips the sharp fragment so tightly that blood drips between her trembling fingers and down her wrist. Her wild eyes skim around the room, her mouth set in a determined line. I drop my rifle, letting it hang off the strap and take a careful step towards her.

'Alexandra…'

'Stop. Gabriel. Stop.' She barks, pulling Dante towards her, nestling the blade into his neck. 'Please don't come any closer.'

'We're here now…' I hold my hands up. 'You're safe.'

Sweat glistens on Dante's face, his cold eyes suddenly fearful. He shifts, trying to straighten.

'Don't you move, or I will end your life.' Lex warns him.

Dante shouts something in Russian as she pierces the skin, blood flows from the wound. I take another step towards them both.

'Please, Gabriel.' Lex begs. 'You have to let me do this. You don't know what they did, what he's capable of.'

'He deserves to rot in a dark hole, no doubt…'

She nods, swaying slightly.

'So let us take him in.' I gesture to Hinchen's team, waiting on tenterhooks behind me. 'Let us question him, get the evidence we need to stop all of this from ever happening again.'

She closes her eyes, whispering something under her breath.

I continue closing the distance between us, standing less than a foot away. 'You're ok...' I take her hand, peeling the glass away. 'I won't let him hurt you anymore.'

Hinchen rapidly steps in, pressing the end of his gun to Soridov's head. 'On your knees.'

Glaring at me, Soridov does as he's told, placing his hands over his head before another of the TAC team cuffs him and pulls him out of the room.

Lex drops to the floor, staring at her quivering hands. 'It's over,' she breathes. 'It's really over.'

'It's over.' I kneel with her, offering her some water. 'We'll get you a medic.'

Her expression is weary, her eyelids heavy, as if even the act of drinking is taking every ounce of energy. I reach one arm around her, letting her lean her weight on me. Pathways of tears streak her dirty cheeks, her right eye is bloodied and swollen, her neck is violently bruised with purple marks, her left hand hangs limply by her side.

'Hope...' she croaks. 'There's another girl here.'

Collins crouches next to us, her eyes filled with despair. 'Gabriel, can I have a word?'

'Later.'

'Now, Gabriel.'

'Did you get Flint and Soridov?' Lex asks Collins, a hint of strength returning to her eyes. 'Did you get both?'

'We got them.' Collins takes her in, placing a hand on her shoulder. 'You did it... you survived.'

'Whatever it is, you need to say...' Lex props herself up against me. 'You can tell me.'

'There's a young girl in the next room...' She clears her throat. 'I'm afraid she's urm... she's dead.'

Lex nods slowly, staring at the floor. 'Dante killed her. He killed her so we wouldn't be able to save her.'

Collins glances up at the ceiling, working to regain composure. 'We need this entire facility secured whilst we bring in the analysts.' She fixes her gaze on me. 'Interpol isn't going to help us anymore, not once they realise we interrogated their asset without clearance.'

'Can't Roe just ask the evidence team from Eze?'

'We have screwed our chances with Interpol, Gabriel.' She repeats impatiently. 'Meyer used to work with them, maybe she can wrangle a few favours. I'll tell Roe to throw Ivan Soridov back in the ocean.' She stands, gripping her phone.

I turn back to Lex. 'Come on, let's get you patched up.'

'I'll be fine.' She frowns, clutching my arm. 'Can I see her? I need to see Hope.'

'I don't think that's a good idea-'

'Please. Will you take me to her?'

'Roe says S.A.I.B.R has a safehouse called the Bolthole near Florence.' Collins drops her phone to her side, covering the speaker. 'It's the only place within a few hours that has cells... so we can hold the suspects until we head home.'

'I thought we were heading straight to Nice airport?'

'Brown has suggested we wait.'

'Why?' I frown, carefully leading Lex out of the room.

Collins follows behind. 'Roe says Interpol have already cottoned on. They will most likely be waiting for us at the border. We can't risk them taking our suspects. They're bound to argue jurisdiction in connection with Ivan Soridov…. What are you doing?' Collins asks, losing her train of thought.

'Lex wants to see the victim.'

Disapproval flickers across her face. 'We don't have time.'

'Please….' Lex asks quietly. 'I need to see her.'

Collins' eyes soften. 'She's in the room at the end of the corridor, around the corner on your left.'

I lead Lex out of the room, weaving between Hinchen's men. 'Do you want me to wait out here?

'No.' She replies quickly. 'Can you come in? Can you stay with me?'

I push the door all the way, wedging my foot to hold it open. This lab resembles the other but in reverse. One large screen on the left wall. Two black chairs in the centre of the room with clunky headsets hanging over the arms. Two large EEG machines. White clinical surfaces filled with test tubes and medical freezers. A silver gurney is tucked at the far end of the room. A slender woman is strapped to it. Her deep, blue eyes, permanently open; provide the only colour in the room. Their boldness creating a chillingly morbid atmosphere. Her lank, fair hair is stuck to her pale forehead, which is still coated with a gleam of sweat. I take a lab coat from the back of the door and cover up her limp body.

'She's so young.'

'Who was she, Lex?'

'I saw their faces. Her parents.'

'How?'

She gently caresses Hope's face. 'They showed me.'

I frown, unsure what she means. 'Why was she here?'

'What will happen to her now?' She looks up at me, her eyes so full of expectation. It's as if I hold the key to everything she needs.

'Dr Meyer will come here, run some tests, we'll have to formally identify her.'

'Nobody will mourn her. Nobody is even looking for her. Not anymore. The Singularity took her. She was a child and they took her away. Just like the children in Za'atari.'

I want to press her on the details; mostly so I can enact my own revenge on whoever coordinates this sick fucking place. But I stop myself. Now is not the time. 'They'll pay for this, Lex. For everything.'

'I'm sorry.' She softly closes Hope's frozen eyes. 'I'm so sorry this happened.'

We leave the room and round the corner. Hinchen's men crowd Flint and Dante; the two suspects handcuffed and rigorously guarded. Collins paces at the end of the corridor, her face set in a determined scowl. Meyer stands on the phone, only looking up when she notices our approach. Her eyes flit between me and Lex before her gaze settles on the latter, her mind working to discern something specific.

'Gabriel, I…' Lex takes my hand, pulling me to a halt. 'I couldn't…'

'Are you alright?' I step in. 'Do you need to sit down?'

She supports herself against the wall, taking a few deep breaths.

'You don't have to worry.' I reassure her, placing both hands on her shoulders. 'The IRT has secured the whole place. You're safe.'

She rubs her palms over her eyes. 'You never give up.'

'Neither do you. You're a survivor.'

The thought seems to irk her more than anything else. 'I think it's more than that.'

'How do you mean?'

'I feel you up here.' She taps her temple. 'All the time. I used to hate it; the fact I could never escape you but then, they tried to take it.'

'Take what?'

She pulls her hair from her shoulders and turns slowly, exposing the incision at the base of her skull. 'Can you see it?'

'Yeah,' I clear my throat. 'I see it.'

'Please don't tell anyone.'

'What did they do?' I ask, unable to tear my eyes away from the angry slash across her skin.

She swivels to face me. 'I don't think they completed it. I'm still me.'

'You'll always be you.' I pull her into a tight embrace, my brain packed with questions. 'Nobody will take that away from you.'

'They took it from Hope.' She leans in closer, lowering her voice. 'We just have to make sure they pay for it like you said.'

Something returns to her eyes briefly. A spark of determination, maybe. It fills me with a sense of relief. Perhaps she will recover quickly from this. Despite what they put her through, she's refusing to be broken. She won't let it change her.

'I really want you to see someone, a medic. Ok?'

'Fine.' She utters, looking at the floor. I place my hand on the small of her back, gently steering her towards the rest of the team. Seeing Collins and Meyer, she picks up the pace. Her arms swing with purpose as she marches down the corridor, her blonde hair bouncing with a sudden intent. Half of the TAC team walks ahead, escorting Flint to the exit, guiding him up the stairs. Hinchen stands twenty paces away with two of his men, forming an armed triangle around Soridov. Two at the back, one at the front. With his head dipped low, Soridov shuffles to the door with laboured, reluctant movements. Lex stops dead.

'Are you alright?'

She nods, her eyes fixed on the back of Soridov's head.

'It's ok, we can wait. We'll wait until he's gone.'

'Gabriel...' She whispers. 'You know he'll never talk.'

'Soridov?'

She nods. 'He won't tell us anything. That's not the way he's trained. He's ex-KGB. He'll die before he gives anything away.'

'Yeah, it's likely.'

'I'm going to need you to forgive me.'

Everything from that moment happens in an unintelligible flash. She sprints ahead, powering down the corridor. I shout after her, causing the TAC Team to turn around, bracing their weapons. She leaps up, flying through the air, her right hand sealed around a knife. *That knife.* I look down at my vest, the empty strap. *Mine.* Hinchen's second in command tries to catch her but she's too fast, she hurtles past him, landing on Soridov's shoulders, she wraps her legs around his waist and drives the sharp weapon into his neck. Blood spurts across the lab before she pulls the knife out and drives it in again. Then again. And again. I stand, unable to process, unable to speak, unable to react.

'Gabriel!' Collins' voice screeches, her face gripped with horror. 'Do something!'

Hinchen's men draw their weapons, training them on Lex. Soridov howls, collapsing to the ground. Lex climbs over him, manically plunging the blade into his chest. He kicks out from underneath her, bucking his body, his arms and legs flailing with desperation. The TAC team demand that she drop the weapon, forcefully threatening to take her out if she doesn't comply.

'Gabriel!' Collins screams. 'They will shoot her!'

Her words jolt me into action. I race forward, diving in between. 'Stand down! Stand down!' I shout. 'Hinchen! Please!'

Despite the outrage on his face, Hinchen repeats the order to his men. They lower their guns, their shocked expressions fixed on the bloody mess. Soridov's twitching body finally stills, his strangled gasps for breath dissipating. Satisfied, Lex drops the knife, wiping her face with the back of her hand as if simply having spent a long day gardening. The blankness: the glacial disconnect in her eyes fills me with a sickening swell of anxiety. Within seconds, she's transformed from demonic to detached, completely disconnected from her actions. Every inch of her body is soaked with his blood. She stares at him blankly, like she found him that way.

CHAPTER THIRTY-TWO

COLLINS

The TAC team tread down the uneven path, escorting Flint through the poplar trees and into the old, dilapidated property called The Bolthole. It's an MI6 safehouse that probably hasn't seen human life since the 80s. Gabriel paces the cliff edge, his dark eyes focusing on the swell of the sea against the rocky coastline. I try to get comfortable, fidgeting on the crumbling stone wall that once divided the villa's pool area from the gardens.

'We have to explain to Brown that we lost an asset.' I suggest, watching anxiety settle into his face. 'He's bound to find out we went off book, made a deal with an organised crime group and pissed off Interpol. Not to mention the brutal murder of a suspect in our custody. A suspect that was a direct link to Imran Almasi. Perhaps our only way of preventing the biggest terrorist attack since 9/11.' I sigh, looking up at him. 'How are we going to do that?'

He stares at me for a few seconds before looking back out to sea. 'The point of S.A.I.B.R is that we have the autonomy to bypass paperwork.'

His words trip a switch of anger. *He still thinks he's invincible.* 'Whatever the hell went down in that lab… she needs help. Soridov was a key witness.' I fumble with a cigarette, trying to light it before taking a long drag. 'You don't see sense where she's involved.'

He turns, outraged. 'You're the reason we're both out here. I fought you on this. I did not want to end up back in this place.'

'Admittedly, it was naïve to think you wouldn't let your feelings get in the way.' I flick ash onto the floor, watching him stamp it out as he continues powering up and down. 'Both of you.'

'I told you what would happen…' He concedes.

'You act like you don't have control of your own mind.'

He shrugs, looking away.

'With you now being in charge of this bloody taskforce and it being nearly two years, I had hoped all of that would be behind you. You spend a few hours with her again and she's got you right where she wants you. You allow her to make a bloody deal with the Italian mafia, you risk MI6's long-standing relationship with Interpol, you stand by and watch her kill Soridov without even blinking. This team is at the mercy of your loyalty to her.'

He scoffs. 'And what exactly do you suggest?'

'You two need to get on the same page. Find a way to make it work. When you're at each other's throats, it's erratic and she's impossible to control.'

'And look what she does to you!' He rebuts, pointing at me. 'Look how easily she persuaded you to bring her into this. I made it very clear it was a bad idea; *repeatedly*.'

'What else were we going to do now she's cut ties with SO15? We need to keep her close. In an ideal world, for your own personal bloody sanity, I wouldn't have her in your life at all. You and I both know that if you weren't tied to this case, living a life without Alexandra Christofi would be the best thing for you.'

'But I am tied to it, and she's tied to it.'

'Exactly, neither of you can escape it. So my second hope was that you could work together without causing an insurmountable pile of shit, but it seems I was wrong on all accounts.'

'Yeah, it hasn't exactly worked out.' He runs his hands through his hair, stress permeating his features. 'I tried to keep my distance and she still ended up being taken by...'

'You and Alexandra are two very fragile souls that need time to heal, preferably away from each other.' I flick my cigarette over the edge. 'But you don't have the luxury of doing that. Neither of you.

So… please. Please find a way to work together on this taskforce. You need to stop fighting her on everything because she chose Edward. And she has to stop letting you take control because she feels guilty for leaving. You're both unstable and that ends now. Whatever it is you need to become to each other, make peace with it and move on. We need to unite against these bastards, Gabriel.'

'I hear you.' He mutters.

'You just stood there...' I say, astonished. 'Tell me why you let her take the knife.'

'I didn't. She lifted it from my vest.' He closes his eyes, turning away slightly. 'Where she stabbed Soridov the first time, did you see?'

'Left carotid artery….'

'That's where Mario was shot.' He utters, almost as if he hopes the breeze will catch the words and carry them away.

'That's why you froze.'

'That moment replays in my head a lot.'

I stand, reaching up to place both my hands on his shoulders. 'Since he died, there's been a lot going on up there and it's about time you sorted it out.'

'I'll be fine.'

'Do me the courtesy of telling the truth… for once. Losing one person hurts but it seems to me you lost two.'

'She's not dead, Alison.'

'No.' I gesture up to the villa. 'She's right there in that house but not in the way you thought. She left, Gabriel.'

'I'm handling it.'

'With whisky?'

'It's not like before.'

'And how's that?'

'It's just a drink here and there to take the edge…'

'Gabriel.' I raise my voice before taking a deep, calming breath. *Anger never gets through to him. Never.* 'When you have a drink, it's not like when other people have a drink.'

He stares out at the waves, watching them ebb and flow, his expression broken, as if my judgement is actually causing him physical pain. The image threatens to crush me. There are times since I've known this young man where I wish with every ounce of my being that I had brought him up so that I could have taught him how to navigate through the tragedy that life inevitably brings.

I watch his whole body tense as if having to physically brace himself against a crushing wave of shame. He grimaces, struggling not to let it swallow him whole. 'Her leaving made things very dark.'

'I know.' I say softly. 'I know you loved her very much.'

'Five years gone with one drop.' He takes a breath to say more, the words catching in his throat until he wins a silent battle to keep down whatever wanted to come out.

'You have faced an extremely trying few months. Nobody is handling this. You've tried your...'

'I should be better.'

'You expect too much of yourself.' *Because of them.* I almost add. *Because of the way your parents made you believe you were only worth what was written on a piece of paper.* 'I'll call your sponsor when we're back. All you have to do is show up...'

He grits his teeth, almost wincing at the thought.

'In the meantime, you do whatever it takes to pull it together because we need her. And I need your help controlling her.'

'I don't know if we can...'

'Jesus.' I rub my eyes, feeling impatient. 'Well, you need to bloody find a way. You may not have brought her in this time, but you know for a fact she will listen to you. Get her in line and I'll try to help you retain a modicum of bloody sanity. We can't fail on this, Gabriel. We cannot let an attack happen on our soil. Not again.'

'I won't fail.' He says with defiance in his eyes. 'I don't fail.'

'Good.' I nod, pleased to see that familiar determination.

'It's not normal is it...' He looks away. 'The way she puts me through hell, gets in my head.'

'Well...' I exhale. 'Unfortunately, it's what you like.'

He frowns, offering me a questioning look.

'Pardon me for saying this but you grew up with a narcissistic mother, your father's a borderline sociopath. Graduating from Cambridge, you could have done anything but instead, you joined the police force, hunting the most dangerous criminals in the country. You have a fascination with mayhem.'

'And I pay all that money for a therapist...' He smirks.

'I spend enough time with you already.' I nudge him playfully. 'But you can't allow any more rule breaking because of how much you love someone or because you know you're surrounded by people who will cover for you.' I rest a maternal hand on his shoulder. 'Accept it as it is...You haven't moved on. She's your ghost... every house is haunted by one.'

CHAPTER THIRTY-THREE

GABRIEL

The conversation with Collins nags at my brain as I stand on the villa's large balcony. I drop my head, swearing under my breath, trying to still my jittering hands. *Withdrawal.* Life would be easier if I untangled my world from Alexandra's. I wouldn't even have to give up. Drinking could dull the ache of missing her, enabling me to accept loving her from afar. At least everyone else would be safer.

Emily appears from the master bathroom, and I'm thrown from the thought. She crosses the bedroom hurriedly, her green eyes noting the stress in my face.

'How is she?'

'She's going to shower.' She glances at my hands. 'Are you alright?'

'Is she going to be ok?'

'You're shaking.' She steps forward, taking my wrists. 'And you're pale.' She looks around the room as if she might find the reason until she spots an unopened bottle of whisky. 'Gabriel you can't just go cold turkey.'

I stare at the floor; my thoughts muddling. 'What happened? Did she say... did she say anything to you?'

She releases her comforting grip. Her pretty, petite face is clearly contemplating something as her eyes fix through the double doors on the burning horizon. 'I've never seen you like this.'

I step back, leaning on the antique bureau behind me. 'What's that?'

'Well...' She holds up a clear zip-lock bag. 'This needs analysis. Hair follicles, potential skin particles from under her nails.'

'Rape kit?' I murmur, the words barely audible.

214

'No sign of sexual assault.'

I breathe an audible sigh of relief.

'She has burns on her skin.' Emily continues. 'A dislocated thumb. Loss of hearing in one ear. Her muscles are still spasming from repeated electric shock treatment. She has another semi-healed wound on her arm. That can't be from the lab.'

'Yeah, she was nicked by a bullet.' I say begrudgingly.

'I saw her file.' Judgement laces her tone. 'Daughter of a gangster. Lost a child. Disappeared off the face of the earth. That is, until she showed up during our op a few nights ago. The wound on her arm was you, wasn't it? It was her in Battersea. She shot you with the rubber bullet.'

My head snaps up, meeting her penetrative glare.

'Why is your life so closely linked with hers?'

'She was the first to discover The Singularity.'

'And how did you get involved?'

'I just told you.'

'That's not what I asked.'

I maintain a deceptive look of indifference.

'I'm asking how you know her, Gabriel.'

'That's…' I exhale, looking at the floor. 'It's complicated.'

She watches the sea, nodding to herself. 'I can't believe I was this stupid.'

I frown. 'What is that supposed to mean?'

'How could I expect honesty from a spy?'

'I have never lied to you, Emily.'

'Who is she to you?' She demands in hushed tones, pointing her finger at the floor. 'Tell me who she is that makes you leave the country at the drop of a hat, or lose all sense when she goes missing. Who is she that you're willing to stand by and watch her violently stab a man to death?' Her face reddens. 'I watched you. Your world fell apart when she was taken. Was it yours?'

'Excuse me?'

'The baby. Was it yours?' She rushes out, her face loaded with expectation.

'No...' I twitch my head, briefly reflecting on that flicker of hope amongst the shit. 'No, it wasn't.'

'But by the look on your face, it might as well have been.'

'Emily...' I take a step towards her.

'It's the secrecy. You say you didn't lie but you didn't give me the truth either.' She throws her hands out as if to prevent me from getting too close. 'I'm risking my life to be out here too. I need to know the stakes!'

'When we get back to the UK, she won't be your issue.'

'It will because...'

'Because what?'

'I have feelings now! I know it's ludicrous for me to say it here amidst all of this. But you pursued me. You made me have these feelings that are stopping me from being good at my job. Feelings that make me instantly dislike that poor woman in the next room. Feelings that mean I'm sitting right here, discussing something so trivial with you. Feelings that make me a jealous person! Jealous that you've given up drinking the minute she appears. I don't want to be like this. But clearly, she means something, Gabriel. Look at you!'

I rub my eyes, trying to string a response together.

She pulls something out of the file in her hand and holds it up. 'These are images of you that were recovered from the lab...' she flicks through each one, presenting them to me. 'They were all on a digital file. A file that held very personal details about Alexandra's life.'

My hands grip the desk so hard, the wood groans. 'There's a lot we need to figure out about that lab.'

She dives back in, pulling out another document. 'They were using them to track Alexandra's neurological responses. No pictures of Collins or Roe, just you and her family. Do I have to ask you again, Gabriel?'

I say nothing.

'Do you want to know what Roe thinks?'

'Not really.'

'He said that even when you're not together, you're with each other.' She moves her hand over her heart. 'He said it's always about the other one. In everything you do, everything you say. A bond that could destroy all of us.'

I straighten, losing patience. 'We have heaps of evidence to get through. We have a suspect to interview. I have to figure out how to tell Brown all of this shit. I can't be here, doing this.' I gesture between us. 'I need you to do your job. That is what I need from you.'

She nods at the floor. 'The job comes first.'

'Yeah, it does.'

'But you threw away all consideration of the job when you sanctioned an off-the-book interrogation of an Interpol asset. You threw away all notion of professional integrity when you stood by and let her stab Dante Soridov to death. Do you think I want to know any of this? You think I want to think about it? Care about it? I used to be a professional. I was good. I was the best. I was selected to join this taskforce because of my talent. But then came you. You accelerated this relationship. You. Not me.'

'I know that Emily.'

'Because why? Your heart was broken? Because she left you? Because you needed to get under me to get over her?'

'That's not what it was.'

She rubs her face, muttering into her hands. 'Then tell me the truth.'

'I shouldn't have pursued you.' I admit softly. 'I wasn't ready but you're… you. You're wonderful. And you just… you didn't let me wallow. You cut through the bullshit. You make me laugh. You're fucking smart. Too smart for me. It's refreshing.' I look at the floor. 'It's real. How I felt…how I *feel* is real. I like you, Emily.'

She looks up with a hopeful glint in her eye.

'This… me and you, it wasn't about someone else. It was about you, about being with you. I don't have relationships. I'm not that sort of person. But I wanted to be with you, because it's you. I love being around you.'

'I just…' Her face suddenly falls as the realisation sinks in. 'It *was* about me and you. Past tense.' She groans. 'This isn't me. I don't talk about this stuff at work. I never should have blurred the lines. I'm good at this job. I deserve to be here.'

'We all know that.'

'It was so unbelievably stupid to think this wouldn't end in tears.' She laughs. 'But you really have no idea what it's like to be seen by you.'

'I was trying to move on…' I pause, searching for the words. 'In another life-'

'But not one where she exists.'

'I didn't think our paths would cross again.'

'And now they have?'

'I'm still there.'

'*There* being in love with her?'

I sigh. 'We've been through a lot.'

'Soridov could have been our chance to stop a large scale terrorist attack. Do you even know who she is?' A single tear makes a dash down her face. 'How does she have this hold over you?'

I shrug, looking down. 'At one time, she saw all of me.'

'And I couldn't?'

'I wouldn't let you.'

She scoffs as if she has nothing left to offer. 'You say you want to stop The Singularity because they're monsters. And what they have done is unforgivable.'

'That's still true.'

'What if they're not even close to the person you invited into your bed.' She clears her throat and tucks her hair behind her ears, regaining her composure.

'I'm sorry, Emily.'

'Sorry is what you say when you want permission to stop feeling bad.' Her eyes meet mine before she walks towards me. 'If I'm right about the neurological responses...' She screws a sheet of paper against my chest. 'She loves you too, by the way.'

CHAPTER THIRTY-FOUR

ALEXANDRA

I sit on the edge of the bath and close my eyes, ignoring the involuntarily twitching of my muscles. *Mario. Olivia. Simon. Sandhurst. Gabriel. Gabriel. Gabriel. Gabriel.* I drop my head in my hands, haunted by the people that have gone, hating the pain of missing the people I will never see again. *It's a blessing that child wasn't born into this world with you as a mother.* I stand and reach out for some water, my hands trembling around the cold glass, ignoring the throbbing pain of my thumb, which is now strapped with a splint. I look down at my legs, my skin soiled with Soridov's dried and congealed blood. *Everyone suffers, everyone dies. And I am all that's left, wishing I had gone with them all.*

'Lex?' Gabriel leans against the door frame, halting all my thoughts. 'Dr Meyer says you're going to be alright… you just need a good night's sleep.'

'I haven't had one of those in years.'

He raises his head, his dark eyes standing bold against his sun-kissed skin, frowning suddenly. 'Didn't she tell you to clean up?'

'I thought they might still need evidence.'

'Not anymore.' He says, irritated. 'They're done.'

He walks towards me, taking a small flannel from the towel rail. He reaches out for the tap, and I watch the water rush through the soft, white fibres.

'I can do that.' I croak.

'There's no mirrors in here.' He says, the deepness of his voice travelling through my chest. 'Hold still.'

I tilt my head, relishing the soft touch of his fingertips, the gentle feel of the cloth slowly guided across my face. He breaks every so often to rinse the flannel under the tap before continuing to remove dirt and dried blood. I feel the touch of his thumb, lightly caressing the reddened scar on my arm, the area where his bullet skimmed my skin. 'I'm sorry I hurt you.' He whispers in a low murmur.

'You didn't mean to,' I say, transfixed on the slow, stroking sensation of his fingertips.

'What made you do it…' He glides the flannel over the right side of my face and down my neck. 'Why did you kill Soridov?'

I close my eyes, trying not to watch his mouth.

'He was our way to stop Almasi, Lex. I need you to explain it to me so I can help you. I want to understand.' He runs the tap again and despite having my eyes closed, I can feel the withering heat of his gaze.

'Flint… he explained things to me.' I say, swerving the question. 'It's sort of falling into place. Who they are and what they're doing with the children.'

He steps back, placing the wet flannel on a towel rail, immediately creating a void with the cool air of his absence.

'It does start with A Better World. But Flint is just a pawn. Like Dr Kamani, perhaps. It makes sense now why the charity would hire doctors.' I shrug. 'And Hope…Flint was tasked with getting her back under.'

'Woah, slow down.' He says, watching my chest rise and fall with eagerness. 'Flint was doing what to her?'

'Hope was a Compliant.'

'A what?'

'That's what he calls them. Flint told me they have this way of rewiring someone's brain.' I reach up to rub the back of my neck. 'He injects a chip, like this one…' I angle my body so he can see. 'But somehow Hope became lucid.'

'Lucid from what?'

221

'That facility takes children and brainwashes them. They take away everything that makes them human...' I stumble over my words, recalling the orange ring of light, the wave of electricity. I screw my eyes shut. Suddenly, I'm plunging forward.

Gabriel leaps in, catching me in his arms. 'Here, let's sit down.'

'I can't stop seeing her in that chair.'

'Let's go outside, get some fresh air.'

'No, not yet.'

He follows my troubled gaze before searching the room. 'I have an idea.' He pulls a towel from the rail, gently placing it down. 'Here, we'll sit on this.'

I hesitate.

'It's fine, see.' He says, turning to lean his back against the cupboard. 'Come on.' He holds out his hand.

I take it, crouching to join him, feeling the soft towel underneath me. 'I wanted to help her.'

'It's ok.' He says, putting his arm over my shoulders, pulling me into his chest. 'You don't have to talk about it now.'

I nod my head stubbornly. 'I do. I do because I'm free. I'm alive. I survived and she didn't. How many innocent children have had to endure that?'

He takes my trembling hand, waiting patiently.

I take a deep breath. 'They insert a chip. It contains certain toxins that act as a trigger. Then they inject a serum, something I've actually seen before... in Pakistan. It stops you from being able to access the creative part of your brain. You can't hide anything. Everything is pure and unfiltered. Then they monitored me, using images to determine my recognition to things that made me happy, nostalgic, or sad even. They pinpoint triggers and emotional attachments. Because once they know... they can carve it all away,

222

obliterate the things that make us human, detach us from anything we ever loved to make us nothing.' I glance up at him. 'The Singularity aren't killing people, Gabriel. They're consuming them.'

He swallows hard, his jaw turning rigid. 'They did that to you?'

'They tried.'

'And Hope…' He asks, trying to keep his tone level. 'They kept her like that? To what end?'

'Flint said something about creating soldiers. I think that's why Jed Smart was here in Monaco. I wonder if Flint and the other doctors are doing this for the British Government. Maybe Smart is working and the MOD are working with them.'

'So you think The Singularity took Hope, brainwashed her, placed her in UK intelligence until recently when she became lucid. And Flint was trying to get her back under?'

'Yeah… that's exactly it.'

'How many children do you think they have access to in migrant camps?'

'Thousands. And most of them have no family left, nobody to fight for them. Even if they have parents, they don't have the resources to look for them. It seems Augustus Fox is using the camps to harvest the children, then Flint and Kamani work on them in the labs to create, what they call, Compliants. Once that's done, they hand them over to the MOD, Jed Smart, I don't know… anyone with enough money, including Imran Almasi.'

'Fuck what a mess.' Gabriel looks up at the ceiling.

'I think Augustus Fox is the man in your pictures in Port Latakia.'

'VIPER?'

I nod. 'I think that's Higgs, Gabriel.'

'And Soridov…' He looks deeply into my eyes. 'Why? Why did you do it?'

'I knew men like Dante Soridov, Gabriel. They don't talk. They're trained to die in silence.' I try to swallow past the dry cracks in my throat. 'For once, I just wanted The Singularity to know what it's like to lose someone important. I want Fox or Higgs to know we won't go quietly. We might be outnumbered. We might ultimately lose but we're taking out his key players on our way down. I wanted Soridov to feel how Hope must have felt, to be terrified beyond all measure, to have no escape from your circumstances, for there to be no lifeline, to lose everything and feel every second of it slipping away.'

'I've only seen you like that once before.' He says quietly.

'Soridov deserved to die that way. He deserved to suffer.'

'I know Lex.'

'If I had thought there was a chance we'd learn anything from him, Gabriel, I would have kept him alive.'

'I trust you…' He whispers into the air.

I stare at him for a few moments, waiting for the hesitation in his face. He barely even blinks.

'In the lab…every time I saw a picture of you, they shocked me with high voltage currents of electricity.' I feel his body tense. 'And how crazy is this… despite that happening every time I saw your face,' I take a breath; tears begin rolling down my cheeks, 'I will never associate you with pain. No matter what anyone does, yourself included. Nothing or nobody will ever take away what you are to me.'

Gabriel tightens his hold but looks away.

'Gabriel…'

'Hmm?'

'Do you still feel it?' I ask in a tiny whisper. 'Is there any part of you that feels that way?'

He glances down, his eyes uncertain.

'I'm sorry, I don't... I shouldn't have asked.'

He exhales. 'It's an addiction. With addiction, only one of you thrives. And from experience, it's never me.'

I think back to that day at my father's funeral and all the time spent wishing I could reverse all the decisions I've made.

He lets go of me and rises from the floor. 'You should get cleaned up. Take a shower. I'll get you some food. We'll talk later.'

'Gabriel... wait.'

He freezes, the muscles in his back tensing under the thin material of his T-shirt. This is my moment. *I have to know.*

'What are you so afraid of?'

'You.' He admits softly. 'I'm afraid of you.'

Four words that I never thought I'd hear him say.

Four words that have pierced me straight through the chest.

He gestures towards the bedroom. 'With Emily, it's easy. There's no darkness, no pain. She doesn't have any fucked up traumas...at least until today.' He rolls his eyes. 'She doesn't disappear without explanation, doesn't make it impossible to have a different opinion, doesn't overthink my silences, doesn't push me to the limits of my sanity. She doesn't know the quickest way to kill a man, she doesn't know how to make someone suffer. She hasn't been to war, she's not a fucking trained assassin. The country doesn't depend on her. She's normal!'

'Gabriel...'

'The thought of her leaving doesn't make me sick to my stomach. The thought of living in a world without her doesn't make me want to give up and fucking die.' He crosses his arms, irritated with himself. 'It's simple.'

I stand, tears streaming down my face. 'But I had to walk away. I had to save your life.'

'That's not love, it's control.' He hisses, his voice thick with anger. 'All of this is infatuation. It's not real.'

'Of course it is. It's real, Gabriel.'

He shakes his head. 'All I know for sure is that despite hating that you left, hating that you chose to work with Edward and at times even hating *you*, I still jump at any chance to be close to you. I crave you: the sight of you, the feel of you, the sound of your voice.' He steps back. 'Like I said, it's an addiction; only one of us comes out on top. Never both.'

'You understand you would have gone to prison? If I had rejected your father's offer…'

'You didn't give me a chance to show you I loved you more than I loved being free. You made a decision about *my* life without my knowledge. We're not good for each other Lex,' he says with finality. 'Look what happens when we're together. To you, to me, to everyone else.'

I reach both hands up to his face, stretching up to press my mouth against his. 'I made a mistake. It was a terrible mistake.'

His expression remains guarded, his body rigid. 'I don't know what you want from me.'

I take a breath to reply but he moves unexpectedly, struck with a sudden force, as if he has no control over his actions. He grabs my face and pulls me in, taking my mouth with intense possession. We kiss like we might never see each other again, as if being this close just isn't close enough. The hairs on the back of my neck stand to attention and he lifts me up, perching me on the side of the sink, pulling his T-shirt over his head, discarding it on the floor, before returning his hands to me, holding my head in place, his tongue caressing mine. I reach up, running my thumb over the thick, ragged scar on his left shoulder; the wound inflicted by the bullet he took for me. *He's always saving me. All I do is cause him pain.* I straighten, pulling away. Gabriel pants, his dark eyes watching me apprehensively. My muscles twitch, my eyes blink rapidly. *The Singularity know who he is because of me. They know he's important. I'm always putting his life in danger.* Sensing my mind has gone elsewhere; he steps in and kisses me on the forehead before pulling me against his chest, hugging me tightly. *What is that noise?* I look around the bathroom, reaching up to touch my face. It's wet.

I pull back, confused. 'What is that?'

His eyes fill with sympathy. 'You,' he says gently. 'It's you... you're crying.'

I look up at the ceiling. 'Everyone just keeps dying. I don't think I can...' Gripping his arms, I collapse with the crushing weight of the last eighteen months. 'I need it gone.' I weep, staring at the blood on my hands, reaching for the flannel. 'Get it off of me. I need it to go away. All of it has to go away.'

He lifts me from the sink and carries me to the shower, leaning to switch it on before he steps under the water. 'We're supposed to hate and grieve and be destroyed,' he says, kneeling with me in his arms before shifting to rest his back against the wall. 'You'll survive this. Just... let go. You can let go now.'

He holds me tight, and I exhale a long, agonising wail of grief. My tears become lost in the spray of hot water above us. I sob into his chest, pleading with him to stay until I can be at peace once again.

CHAPTER THIRTY-FIVE

ALEXANDRA

I hadn't noticed before for obvious reasons, but Icarus is a very slight, short man. He stands on the shoreline, his wiry figure so fragile against the vast backdrop of the ocean. I find it hard to believe that such a person could inflict so much destruction on the world. With his trousers rolled up to his ankles, we amble from one end of the beach to the other. He stops every so often to feel the waves rushing over his bare feet.

'Thank you for agreeing to speak with me.' He says, looking out to the horizon. 'Everyone has tried to keep you away.'

'And why do you think that is?'

'It's an excuse to see daylight, at least.'

'Yeah, I don't imagine you'll be seeing too much of that in the future.'

'Not if they have their way.' He gestures to the armed security team fanned out on the hillside.

'Dr Flint, the chip you injected into me. Can it be controlled remotely?'

'Icarus…. Please.'

'Icarus…'

'Why? Do you feel different?'

I linger on his small face for a beat. His features are rodent-like; all of them peering in on each other. 'I don't.'

He shakes his head. 'We needed more time.'

'I'm going to remove it, but I want to understand how it works.'

'Your potential.' He whispers. 'If I had more time to get the serum right. I could have made it work…' He whistles. 'You'd be a God.'

'So it needs the right serums.'

He nods. 'And the aversion programming.'

'The electric shock therapy, you mean?'

'It takes time.'

'To make Compliants?'

'My gifts.'

'You said Hope was the best Compliant you had.'

'She was my best girl.' He admits, saddened.

'What happens when you make a Compliant, Icarus?'

'They start their work, make their mark on the world.'

'What work is that?'

'You want it to stop.'

'I do.' I reply, honestly. 'I want to know everything so I can terminate this program.'

He stares off into the distance. 'There are very few doctors in the program.'

'Is Jed Smart purchasing Compliants from you? Does anyone else purchase them?'

'Hope was the best. My best gift.'

'Who did Hope work for?'

'We knew. We always knew that he would love her.'

I sigh, sensing this is going nowhere. 'Za'atari camp in Syria. Is that where you take the children from?'

'That's not my field.'

'Who is in charge of getting the children from the camp to you?'

'They have their ways.'

'Who?'

'I might not be an assassin or trained like you people… but it will take a lot more than a trip to the beach to make me sing like a canary.'

'This is your one and only chance to tell us what you know in a civilised manner.'

Icarus smirks, squinting through the sun. 'And I'm having a wonderful time.'

I sigh, moving on. 'How many Compliants have you created in your lifetime?'

He shrugs. 'Hundreds.'

'Then you sell them on, right?' I try again.

'If you give something to everyone, it becomes obsolete.'

'Then who is it specifically? The British Government?'

'When I create my gifts, I know where their strengths lie. Not everyone is the same. That's why Hope was so unique… she was good at everything. Despite our life's work, you can't erase someone's whole character. They still have instinctive flaws or weaknesses they've inherited that they fall back into over time.'

'Who is this man, Icarus?' I hold up the image of VIPER. 'Can you tell me who this is?'

He flits his eyes to the image briefly before looking away.

'Is this man Augustus Fox?'

'I'm tired of talking.' He mutters, grinning at the sun.

I pocket the picture, giving up. 'Fox founded A Better World and Magnusson owned Chateau Noir. Did Magnusson sell it to Fox? Was he part of the program?'

'Oh no… no, no.'

'Do you know where we can find Fox?'

'I do not.'

'You only work from Chateau Noir?'

'Yes.'

'And you've never met Fox or Magnusson?'

'Not that I recall.'

'Who have you met, Icarus? Is it Higgs?' I push again, sensing he's shutting down. 'You had to have been hired by somebody. How did you become involved in the Compliancy program?'

'You're nearly there… it's fascinating.'

I look away briefly, trying to moderate my impatience. 'Tell me about Imran Almasi, is *he* paying you for Compliants?'

'We don't talk about our buyers. That's what he tells us.'

'Who?' I ask, my tone forceful. 'Who tells you that? Where does Almasi fit in? Is he using Compliants to attack the British Government? Is Higgs selling Compliants to both sides?'

'We don't talk about our buyers.'

'You really don't see the issue with what you're doing?'

'The problem with human beings is the selective activism-'

'It doesn't bother you that you're making soldiers for a terrorist organisation? Not to mention you are taking hundreds of children from their families. At best, they become cyborgs.'

'You see hardship and you think you're witnessing rare injustice. But our very existence is an injustice. You wear clothes, you stay in hotels, you've been to bars, you take medicine. All are products of forced labour. I don't see you fighting their cause. *You* don't even question the people around you.'

'That isn't the same.'

'It's not the same because the actions of someone like Gabriel James or Aldyn Wolfe doesn't taint your view of the world. You grew up in organised crime. You know it and you're comfortable with it. So if your boyfriend murders someone on your behalf, you barely blink. But what I do makes you uncomfortable because you don't know it.

And the mere existence of something you don't know spoils your privilege.'

'You don't know my view of the world.'

'Tell me.'

'I've lived the horror, dealt the pain, suffered from it. This is wrong because it's wrong. Not because it shattered my pretty view of humanity.'

'You know the world and yet you chose to protect it.'

'Not all of it but being a good, decent person requires standing up for those who otherwise are too vulnerable. And innocent people will die if I do not do something.'

'You think you'd have the freedom to be a good, decent person without me?'

'You're saying that Compliants facilitate democracy?'

'The Singularity protects a world where you have a choice. Without us, you think civilisation would hold its own against dictatorships. Do you think we'd thrive as we do now?'

'You are robbing innocent children of a chance. And now you're selling them to the very people you claim to protect us from!'

'I'm giving those children something they would otherwise never have.'

'That is a delusion.'

Icarus leans forward and points his index finger at the sky. 'Do you know what a Singularity is?'

'A group of sadists.'

He laughs with a patronising tone. 'The term. Do you know what the term means?'

'Something to do with a black hole.' I reply impatiently.

'Close. A Black Hole Singularity is the very definition of no man's land. It's the centre of nothing. A point where time and space do not exist.'

'Ok...'

'From nothing comes everything. The absoluteness of *nothing* unleashes so much potential just by the sheer possibility of everything.'

'Is that how you see your Compliants?'

'It's almost perfect.' He stops grinning to himself, looking at his toes sinking into the wet sand.

'What is?'

'Poetic, really.'

'How do you mean?'

'Your squadron had a nickname for you, didn't they? They used to call you *The Angel*.'

My blood runs cold. 'How did you know that?'

'An Angel is meant to advocate a message from God.'

'It was never about religion. It was a term used ironically.'

'Higgs Boson comes from the God particle.'

'Ok.'

'It embodies everything we're doing.' He repeats, pleased with himself. 'So I've got creation, I've got God. And then there's you...'

'And what am I exactly?'

'You are what could have been. Like Lucifer, you have the ability, the power, the propensity to be on top. You're the First of the Fallen, too stubborn and proud to see your own potential. Not an Angel, no. Not to me. You, Alexandra, are an Abyss... and you'll drag everyone down with you.'

CHAPTER THIRTY-SIX

ALEXANDRA

'You weren't there when I woke up…' Gabriel steps in, the worry visible in his dark eyes. 'I didn't know you were speaking to Flint until Collins told me.'

I reach into my top and pull the wire from my chest. 'I just needed to get it done.'

'Where did you go?'

'Hmm?'

'This morning.'

'Just took a walk.'

The truth is, I didn't want anyone to notice we spent the night in the same bed. *Least of all, Emily Meyer.* But I knew I wouldn't be able to sleep on my own and last night; I've never needed him more. I take a quick breath, remembering the feel of his body next to mine, the way he held me whilst I drifted off. I've never felt more safe.

'I just needed to think.'

He looks over his shoulder, ensuring he's out of earshot. 'Our conversation last night… it was intense, we both said a lot of…' he trails off before meeting my eyes. 'We need to work together. We owe it to the team to keep it professional. This is beyond our personal history. We have to do this right. I said things in the heat of the moment.' He runs a hand through his hair. 'We need to put all of that behind us and draw a line. You know, move on… move forward.'

My heart sinks.

But this is who Gabriel is. This is who he's always been. He gives and then he takes away. Two steps forward, three steps back.

'It's all there.' I hand him the device, moving past the moment. 'Flint wouldn't divulge anything on Almasi. I don't think he knows much.'

'Yeah, I was listening...' He takes the wire from me.

'I didn't ask him about Dr Kamani in case Flint finds a way to get a message to someone and it breaks Kamani's cover. If he's still alive, that is....'

'Good thinking.' Gabriel lingers his gaze on me for a few seconds longer, the cogs of his brain fractiously whirring away until he catches sight of Roe at the end of the terrace. 'Excuse me for a minute...' He begins to walk away before quickly doubling back. 'What Flint said about Lucifer...' He utters, looking me straight in the eye. 'Lucifer actually means bringer of the light.'

I take a breath to respond but he's already stalking determinedly towards Roe.

'Going to need a hand.' Collins approaches with Icarus in handcuffs, closely followed by five security officers. 'This wonderful bunch are doing a shift change. I need someone else to escort me back to the steel box.'

'Are you taking me to my cell?' Icarus asks.

The roar of an engine diverts our attention.

The security team brace in tandem, readying their weapons.

I turn back towards Gabriel. He stops on his approach to Roe. All of us look up the hill, our hands prepared. The car rounds the corner, accelerating into the driveway at speed.

'It's Meyer.' Gabriel announces with relief.

Noticing Emily Meyer frantically park and jump out of the vehicle, he starts jogging up the hill.

'Do you think she's been followed?' I ask Collins.

'She's too smart for that.'

Reaching the driveway, Gabriel bows his head as Meyer talks quickly in his ear, gesturing to a folder of documents under her arm. Eventually, she spots us on the terrace and motions for him to follow her around the back of the house.

'Looks important.' I mutter curiously. Part of my brain drifts into wondering what she thinks of all this and more specifically what Gabriel has told her about me.

'I'm sure we'll find out soon.' Collins nudges her head towards Icarus, signalling that we should get a move on.

'Time to say goodbye to the sun for today, Flint.' Roe appears, opening the door ahead of us.

'You might get another walk tomorrow, if you'd be up for sharing more.' I suggest looking to Collins.

She shrugs. *We both know that will largely depend on Gabriel's mood.* The door closes behind us and we step into the darkness, waiting for the halogenic lights to turn on whilst we make the short trip down the metal stairs to the basement of cells. All three of us surround Icarus like a protective shell as we walk slowly down the corridor to Cell Eight. Collins punches in the code, waiting for the locked door to release. The keypad beeps and the panel turns green.

'Someone will come down to give you food.'

'I won't eat.'

'That's fine.' Collins breathes with exasperation. 'But we have to feed you anyway.'

'Oh, Ms. Christofi.' Icarus calls out. 'It was an honour.'

I pause in the doorway, noting his gleam of excitement.

'You are exceptional.'

'Please eat... we need you healthy.' I step out of the cell, gesturing for Roe to reseal the door.

'This place depresses me.' Collins whispers.

Icarus begins to recite Corinthians through the walls. Roe widens his eyes, tapping the side of his head. Standing on the bottom step, I stare into the darkness for a while. Something doesn't feel right. *The jeebies.* That's what Gibbs and McGuire used to call it. If something felt off or if we were on an op that seemed about to take a turn, they'd always make a call to back out, check again, cover your six. And the scary thing is, they were rarely ever wrong. With what's happened over the last forty-eight hours, I can't trust my gut. There's no certainty what effect Flint's work has had on me yet. I'm not sure what's me, what's fear and what's potentially been put there by someone else. I run my finger over the bump on my neck.

Thankfully, Collins opens the basement door and sunlight floods through the murky space. Instinctively, I move towards the warm air, needing to feel the breeze. *Enclosed spaces aren't my favourite.* Stepping outside, I angle my face towards the sun, hoping the heat will burn away some of the raging anxiety in my mind.

'I'm going to check on Meyer.' Collins announces.

'What's up?' Roe asks, blocking the light.

'Nothing,' I open my eyes, trying to shake it all away. 'I just…since the lab, I guess nothing feels right.' I hesitate. 'I don't have any answers about Almasi. I just feel we're missing something with Icarus.'

His face alights with a sudden nervous energy. 'You don't think he's being honest?'

'He knows a lot more than what he's told us so far. You should have heard him talking about Hope. If I can get him on her again, he might reveal something more.'

'What did he say?'

'That she was the best. He treats her like a vanity project.'

Roe nods, thinking on something. 'We'll figure it out.'

'Do we have any background on her yet?'

He shakes his head. 'Meyer had to get her body transported to a private lab in Pisa. Still waiting on details.'

'If we find out who she really is, we can determine how she fell into their hands and perhaps who was involved.'

The skin around his eyes tightens. 'Orphans aren't easy to trace. Not all of them keep records.'

'I might try and speak to Flint again…'

'Want some company?'

'Sure.' I smile, grateful for his understanding.

He opens the door, gesturing for me to go first before we make our way back down to the depths of the steel box.

CHAPTER THIRTY-SEVEN

GABRIEL

'You were right to suspect the Carusos.' Emily fans multiple files out, organising pages upon pages of documents.

I move to join her, placing my palms on the table. 'Go on…'

'Please don't lose it.'

I catch the stress in her voice. 'Ok…start from the beginning.'

She takes an exasperated breath. 'Keys has been going through the devices we found at the lab. Dante has several and that's all documented here.' She points to a thick folder at the top of the pile. 'But then, there's also a laptop found at the scene, which we think belongs to Dr Flint. That's all in this one.'

She hands me a thicker green folder, opening the binder. 'I extracted as much as I could, trying to make sense of all of this.' She unclips a few sheets and hands them to me. 'Here is a list of all calls made to and from Dante's devices over the past week.'

I peer down, following her index finger.

'Interestingly, Dante received a call from this specific number twenty-four minutes before Alexandra was taken at around ten thirty-two. The call lasted about five minutes. He then contacted that same number after she was taken, at four minutes past eleven.'

My face drops. *Caruso. The Carusos are the current brokers for the Taliban's opium trade. They protect the trade route, making sure there are no interferences.* 'Caruso sold her out.'

'It seems that way. About an hour after you met with Lucas and Tino, Dante Soridov received a call from another number but this one was untraceable. That call lasted just under an hour. A text then followed. That message detailed your agreement with Caruso. This anonymous contact informed Soridov that Caruso was going to help you and Alexandra. Whoever this was… they were the middleman in setting up a meet between Caruso and Soridov, to stop the agreement from going ahead.'

'You can't trace that second number?'

'I've tried. Keys has tried.'

'Someone close to this fucked it up deliberately. If Caruso aligns himself with The Singularity, he gets paid to protect the trade route, he gets Calabria back. He gets protection. Of course he wants in.' I shake my head. 'This someone made sure Soridov knew what to offer. Fucking bastard.'

'Lucas Caruso has eyes everywhere. We aren't safe in Italy, Gabriel.'

I meet her gaze. 'You're right, we need to leave.'

'If you ask me, we'd be much safer in the UK.'

I stand from the wall. 'Yeah, we need to find a way to safely contact Brown. Tell him the situation has changed. We need to get out of here ASAP. It makes no sense to have all this evidence and a prime suspect sitting here like ducks.'

'I'll have to speak to Roe. He's got Brown's secure line.' She collects the files from the table.

'Just Roe?'

'Brown gave it to him before we came out here. Roe said only one of us should have it for security purposes.'

I stare ahead, watching her wander away, something nagging at me, tapping at my brain with desperate urgency. Words swim around my subconscious, regurgitating with dogged insistence.

Caruso sold us out.

Whoever this was… they were the middleman.

This someone made sure Soridov knew what to offer.

We'd be much safer in the UK.

Roe's got the secure line.

Someone close to this fucked it up deliberately.

'Emily...' I call out, nerves jumping around my stomach.

She turns, looking at me expectantly.

'Roe told you that Brown said we had to wait out here?'

She nods. 'Brown said to wait.'

'You just said only Roe has the means to speak to Brown. So Brown didn't tell you that information himself?'

'Brown's orders were to wait until everything blows over with Interpol, then we can make our way back once he got back in touch.'

'Who told you that? Roe or Brown?'

'Jesus, Gabriel. What is the issue?'

'Icarus is back where he belongs.' Collins rounds the corner. She stops, abruptly noticing the look on our faces. 'What's up?'

I march over to her, placing my hands on her shoulders. 'When was the last time you spoke to Paul Brown?'

'Pardon?'

'Who told you that we needed to stay at the Bolthole?'

She frowns, taking a step back. 'Why?'

'Answer the question.'

'What is going on?'

'I told you we had instructions to go back to Nice airport. And *you* told *me* we had to come to the Bolthole.' I drop my arm near my weapon, hovering my hand near the trigger. 'Who told you that we needed to wait a few days? Who told you we needed to come here?'

She blinks, looking flustered. 'Roe...' She raises her head. 'It was Roe.'

CHAPTER THIRTY-EIGHT

ALEXANDRA

There's a buzzing in my head. A resounding nagging that I can't shake. Icarus' voice hums an eerie tune as we travel down the shadowy corridor towards his cell. The deceptively joyful melody carries a sinister edge amongst the unnerving silence of the steel box. With Roe closely behind, I peep through the hatch. Icarus lies on his back with one arm behind his head, the other outstretched to the ceiling, his index finger trailing through the air as if tracing a drawing. The whites of his eyes widen with excitement at the invisible masterpiece.

'You think you're going to get much sense out of him tonight?' Roe whispers.

'Probably not.' I murmur, shivering suddenly.

'He's not going anywhere.' Roe pulls out his phone, checking the time. 'Perhaps we can try again tomorrow.'

Something occurs to me, and I stare at him for a few drawn-out seconds. 'Hope Clarke was an orphan.'

Roe raises his eyebrows.

'You said she was an orphan?'

'I'm sorry?' He smiles politely.

'You said it would be hard to track her background because she's an orphan.'

He shrugs casually. 'Yes....'

'How did you know that about her?'

'Sorry?'

'I didn't tell you that.' My hands drift to my waistband, my fingers skirting the handle of my weapon.

'You must have.' He laughs. 'Come on, let's go back upstairs.'

'No,' I place my hand on his chest, stopping him. 'I didn't even tell Gabriel that.'

'Meyer must have told me.'

'Meyer doesn't know.'

'Jesus, Alexandra.' He raises his voice. 'What's the matter now, eh?'

'How did you know that about Hope?'

He frowns, trying to shove past me. I strengthen my stance, gripping my hand around the gun.

'Alexandra…' He hisses. 'Please stop.'

'Tell me.'

'I need you to remove your hand from your weapon.'

I look down.

Roe's own hand is gripping a pistol, the end of it pressing into my ribs. 'Give me your gun.'

'Jake…' I splutter.

'Give me the gun.' He demands, his face blank.

'Excuse me?'

'Come on, Alexandra. Don't make this difficult.'

I swallow, my throat constricting. 'Jake-'

'The gun.' He raises his voice.

'Ok, ok.'

'Hand it to me.'

I do as he asks. 'What is happening?'

'Hands on your head.'

I raise my arms. The sudden screech of car brakes reverberates from above. 'Wait, who's here?'

'Don't move. Please don't do anything stupid.' He wipes sweat from his face with the back of his hand.

My eyes shift to his trembling fingers.

'I know how your mind works.' He snaps. 'If you move, Alexandra, I will shoot you. And if you die, they will kill Gabriel as consolation. Be smart about this.'

'Who is they?'

'Is that what you want!?' He shouts, his voice strained.

'No. It's not… it's not.'

'I thought so.'

'How long?'

'Pardon me?'

'How long have you been working for them? Was this always the plan? Get yourself into the taskforce, report everything back.'

'Shut up.' He shifts on his feet, sweat dripping onto the floor. 'I didn't want it to happen like this.' His tone descends into panic. 'You have to understand. One mistake…just one wrong decision can tear your whole world apart.'

'You can tell me what happened, we can figure this out.'

'I gave in.'

'To what? Who is behind this Roe?'

He scoffs. 'If you knew who you were up against.'

'Then tell me!'

'I've really had no choice.'

My head snaps up to the sound of machine guns above.

'Don't even think about it.'

'Is it Fox? Or Smart? Are they here for Icarus?'

He glares at me, his eyes red with anguish as if he knows things that he wished with all his heart he didn't.

'Who's upstairs, Jake?' I repeat.

'Just fucking wait.' He yells, the veins in his head bulging.

'You're a good person.' Desperation lands in my voice. *I have to find a way to get up those stairs.* 'You're honourable. I know you.

Let me help you. We can go up there together, we can face this together. You don't want to do this.'

'Of course I don't want to fucking do this! There is no choice, Alexandra. Not all of us have an entire bloody underworld at our fingertips.'

'Did you tell The Singularity I was staying at Tino's?'

'It doesn't matter.'

'Are you the reason they were always one step ahead? Right from the moment you met Gabriel.'

'They will always find a way. If not me, then it would have been someone else.'

I think back to when things started to speed out of control. *Right back to Roe.* 'You organised to meet Gabriel in the church hat night.'

'Stop it.'

'You sold him out.'

'I don't have time for this!'

'I had to put his body back together with a fucking needle and thread!' I yell, every shred of oppressed anger rushing to the surface. My hands tremble, my body shaking; only now realising how much I needed someone to blame. Ever since it happened, there was nobody left to hold accountable. *Paytak and Rhiannon Benson dead. Olivia disappeared.* 'I had a miscarriage.' I whisper, my eyes boring into his. 'I lost my baby because of you.' It's the first time I've said the words out loud since. The first moment I have ever openly acknowledged what happened. 'And if it wasn't enough that Gabriel could barely sit up by himself, it wasn't enough that I had lost my child, you gave away our position at the house. You made sure Olivia knew where we were. You brought her to us. You killed Mario.'

'I didn't want to.' He shouts, tears rolling down his face. 'You have to know I didn't want to do any of this.'

'I need to know why… I need to know what drove you. I need to know how you could cause that much pain?'

'Stop. Please stop!'

'You haven't paid…for any of it. You've just kept on living as if nothing was of any consequence.'

'I hate who I am…' He admits, his mouth trembling. 'I do.'

Icarus' singing becomes louder, his voice travelling down the corridor. Gunshots echo from around the house. My whole body tenses. *Just focus on getting out.*

'You need to make this right. This is your chance.'

'None of you will survive this.'

'Whatever it is, you don't have to do this anymore. You need to stop. Let me help you.'

'I can't go back. I can't.'

'Tell me who it is and what you've agreed to do.'

'I need to find a way to make you disappear.'

'Just me?'

'Just you.'

'What about Gabriel and the others?'

'With you gone, we'd return to the UK.'

'And then what? You continue to sabotage the investigation from the inside?'

'I… I don't know. I just had to keep you here. I did what I had to!'

'It's just me *they* want?'

'Yes.' He sighs. 'I had to find a way to separate you from *him.*'

'From Gabriel?'

'Yes! Now please… please turn around and walk slowly towards the stairs.' Roe commands with desperation.

'I'll protect you if you stop this, Roe. We can do it together.'

'Turn around Alexandra!' He presses the weapon into the small of my back.

'Is this the man you want to be? If you help them, you are supporting Imran Almasi! You are responsible for whatever happens on August 5th. You've fought against people like that your whole life. You don't want that on your conscience! You don't!'

'You gave it a good try but it's not going to happen. I've made my decision.'

He pushes me up the stairs, his hand fiercely gripping his weapon, his finger resting on the trigger. We emerge out of the steel box. I stumble slightly, struggling to find my bearings as my eyes adjust to the natural light. Roe forces me towards the pergola, driving me down the path that snakes to the cliff's edge.

'Where is everyone else?'

'Keep your head down, do as you're told.' Roe gestures towards a semi-collapsed stone arch intertwined with vine leaves. 'Through there.'

Cautiously, I duck under and emerge next to the large swimming pool. Collins and Meyer are knelt in a row by the treeline, their hands are bound. Both of them look decidedly pale and uneasy. Collins stares ahead with resignation. Meyer's eyes dart between the two heavily armed gunmen looming above them. Instantly, I recognise the familiar faces of Lucas Caruso's security detail.

'Gabriel...' I murmur.

Roe freezes, his worried eyes taking in the look on my face.

'Where the hell is he?'

Roe's gaze shoots to the opposite side of the pool area. Following the direction of his fretful expression, I see him. He's knelt on the floor with a third gunman of immense height towering above him. His head hangs low. His arms are tied behind his back. He's soaking wet from the waist up, his hair dripping on the patio beneath him. The large man steps forward, yanking Gabriel's head upward, whispering something in his ear with a snarl. Gabriel's eyes find me across the water, despair falling into his features.

'Alexandra…' Lucas Caruso appears through the arch, his thick, purple fingers clutching a Glock. 'Sit quietly,' he motions to a deck chair. 'Like the others.'

'What the hell are you doing Lucas? What is going on?'

His mouth quirks in a near smile. 'Well, for starters, we thought we'd take your boyfriend for a little swim.'

'If you touch another hair on his head.'

'Yes, yes… we've heard it before.' He widens his eyes.

'She's all yours.' Roe pushes me into a chair and steps forward. 'We had an agreement.'

'Yes.' Lucas signals to the two men guarding Collins and Meyer. 'We will let you have the women back. You three can leave.'

Roe turns over his shoulder, appearing flustered. 'That's… No, that's not what we agreed.' He rushes out, shaking his head at the floor. 'You wanted Alexandra. You have her. The rest of the taskforce come with me.'

'You take the women; you get out of here or none of you leave.'

'I kept Alexandra in Italy for you. You have exactly what you required. The deal was that the rest of the team must come with me.'

'And do you think Gabriel James will let you live after you give up his girlfriend? It's better this way.'

'That was not the deal!' Roe shouts. 'If you do not let me leave with the whole taskforce, there will be consequences for…'

Caruso's hand jerks so quickly that I barely hear the shots. Roe's words fall away. His mouth drops open, confusion marring his imperturbable face. Swaying, he lowers his head, observing the scorched holes in his body. Bright red spots appear on the material of his light blue T-shirt, expanding rapidly. Blood suddenly pours from the wounds, becoming thicker and darker by the second. He tries to turn away before stumbling, falling face forward and plunging into the water; tainting the ripples of the pool with deep red.

CHAPTER THIRTY-NINE

ALEXANDRA

Meyer screams at the top of her lungs, caught between yelling Roe's name and begging Caruso to let us go. Collins' eyes are anchored to Roe's body. Gabriel stares out at the horizon, his expression cold and unyielding. I take a long breath and check the distance between myself and his armed guard. Counting the steps, I run the scenario of disarming him in my head. With Roe out of the equation, it's four against four. That would be the best scenario: disarm Caruso, take him as a hostage, get the others to surrender. I turn over my shoulder and glance up the long grassy hill. It's too exposed and yet it's our only means of escape.

Caruso stares into the water, somewhat regretful. 'I don't like to make rash decisions.'

'How do you think this is going to end for you?' I spit. 'You think it's smart killing an entire MI6 taskforce?'

He turns, squinting through the sun. 'It's funny the way you speak to me when you don't need me anymore.'

'Where the hell is your code?'

'The code is dead!' He shouts, causing birds to flee from the trees. 'The code died when your father helped the Massinos take Calabria.'

'No! He would never…'

'He helped them steal it from us. He betrayed my trust.'

'He was the one who helped you relocate to Monaco, he offered you protection, kept you safe!'

'Mario was working both sides.'

'I don't believe you!'

'The Massinos paid him. It served your father to have both of us in his pocket!'

'Who the hell told you that?'

'I saw the payments for myself.'

'Did Soridov tell you that?' Gabriel throws in. 'Why would you listen to a word he says?'

'They're poisoning your mind!' I add. 'They wanted to ensure you split from Aldyn, from me. They want to use you!'

'We're going to run protection on their trade route and we're going to get very fucking rich!' He grins, his yellow teeth glinting in the sun.

'You're an idiot Caruso.' Gabriel laughs. 'They will kill you the minute they're done with you.'

'We'll make them money!' Lucas replies. 'Money talks. We are building a new empire.'

'Where is your fucking honour?' I swallow, my breath catching at the thought. 'You are partnering with an organisation that kills children. They're helping a terrorist!'

'I'm tired of this.' Lucas exclaims, his eyes wild and indignant. 'Get Gabriel up.'

'No!' Meyer cries. 'Please, stop this!'

The mountainous security guard drags Gabriel to his feet. Terrified, I jump to stand.

'Stay where you are Christofi!' Lucas yells, the veins in his thick neck straining with his impatience. 'James, stand here.' He angrily points to a spot a metre away from me. 'Face Alexandra.'

Gabriel plants his feet, refusing to move, his deadened gaze trained above Lucas' head.

'Fucking face her!' Lucas steps in, craning his neck to meet Gabriel's eyes. 'Do as you're told, or Angelo will shoot her in the head, turning all that beautiful hair a very dark sticky red.'

The tendons in Gabriel's jaw tighten, his fists clenching. Lucas cocks his weapon, waiting. Reluctantly, Gabriel shifts, resting his eyes on me. Angelo strides forward, shoving the end of a Colt Python revolver under Gabriel's chin.

My pulse jumps, my stomach dropping. 'Lucas, please. This has nothing to do with him!'

'If I kill Gabriel James, you will finally have nothing, just like your father left us with nothing.'

Angelo jams the gun harder, but Gabriel doesn't react, he doesn't even flinch. Despite what might be going on inside his head, he would never give Lucas Caruso an inch of fear.

'If you kill us Lucas, you will have no peace. MI6 will come. Aldyn Wolfe will not let you live long.'

'Perhaps I will keep you alive, Alexandra.' He muses, as if discussing what shoes he might wear that day. 'I want you to feel what I felt when we were ran out of our homes. My wife murdered; my family tortured.'

'I do! I already know what it's like to lose everything, to not have a home, a family. I've suffered exactly what you have.'

'There has to be justice for what your father did.'

He jerks his head. Angelo swings his arm, slamming the gun hard into Gabriel's face. With his hands still bound behind his back, Gabriel merely grunts under the force, his chin dropping to his chest, his nose pouring with blood.

'You already have your revenge!' I shout, willing him to stop. 'Mario is dead.'

'Mario's betrayal took the woman I love.'

'Then take me!'

Caruso narrows his eyes, intrigued.

'Alexandra…' Gabriel warns, spitting blood on the floor.

'If my father took away your family, then you need to take the last of his. Take me. I'm the last.'

'Caruso don't you fucking dare.' Gabriel threatens. 'Lex stop...' He pleads, his expression pained. 'Don't do this.'

I glance at those beautiful, chestnut eyes, hesitating for just a second. *I don't want to leave him behind. But he has to live.* I nod, adopting a false look of certainty. 'Shoot me. I'm your justice.'

'Stop it, Alexandra!' Collins shouts, her voice cracking.

'If you kill all these people, you will never stop looking over your shoulder.' I continue. 'Gabriel is the son of a very powerful man. Collins and Meyer are MI6 intelligence operatives. If you murder them, you will never be free. You want justice? Take me and be done with it. Take me and let them go.'

'Caruso!' Gabriel bellows. 'If you touch her, I will kill you myself.'

Lucas stares at the ground, mulling it over. 'And what will really become of Gabriel James?'

'Gabriel will...' *Be broken. He'll be broken.* I tighten my mouth, gritting my teeth. 'Gabriel will finally be free. Aldyn will make sure he holds up his end of the deal.'

'Lex!' Gabriel implores. 'Why are you doing this?'

'Do what you must but let the others go.' I shout over Gabriel's frenzied threats. 'Taking me is enough, you will have wiped the Christofis out entirely. That's what you want, for my family to be gone. You say your pain started with my father. It can end with me.'

Gabriel lurches forward, struggling against Angelo. 'No, Caruso stop. I will come for you! Are you listening to me!?' He roars, fighting against Angelo's grip. 'If you do this, you will never be safe. I will hunt you down. I'll make your life a living hell.'

'Aldyn will have to give me his word. Gabriel will live but he must never return here.'

'He won't. Just let them all go, please.'

Caruso nods to himself. 'I will send you to hell with your father, your sister, and your bastard baby. That where you want to go?'

I nod, closing my eyes, braced for the shot to end everything. The cold steel of Caruso's pistol settles against my skin. I try to zone out Gabriel's pleas, to dull the sound of his voice, to forget about his existence entirely. I'm abandoning him, I know that. But I have to trust that Caruso will keep his word. I have no other choice.

With Emily, it's easy. There's no darkness, no pain. She doesn't disappear without explanation. She doesn't know the quickest way to kill a man, she doesn't know how to make someone suffer. She hasn't been to war, she's not a fucking trained assassin. The country doesn't depend on her.

In the long term, this will be better. I won't interfere in his life. He can move on. One day, this will be a memory. A painful one, perhaps, but it will be distant. He could be happy. I take a final breath, picturing the bullet waiting for me in its chamber. I'm not scared to die. *Not anymore.*

Gunfire echoes from up the hill.

My eyes fly open.

Caruso turns towards the barrage of shots pelting through the trees. He stumbles backwards, falling on top of me, dragging me to the ground. I scramble to move away, trying to flee behind the wall for cover. A sticky sensation of blood causes me to stop. I pause, waiting for the sharp influx of pain. I shift under Caruso's weight, checking my torso, feeling my arms and legs. *More blood.* I claw myself out from the thick bulk of his body. Grabbing either side of his face, I raise his head, taking in the frozen, unblinking expression.

Finally, I slide out from underneath him. More bullets are flying across the pool. I look down at myself again, taking full stock, feeling around for bullet holes. *Nothing.* It must be Caruso's blood. I reach forward, peeling the weapon from his hand and crawl across the terrace. *I have to find Gabriel.* I crouch, scouring the patio, trying to get a closer look at the dead bodies scattered around. I catch a flash of peroxide hair. Collins and Meyer sprint under the pergola and into the house. Ducking amidst another tirade of shots, I brace to follow.

'Alexandra!'

I freeze, reluctant to turn, dreading the striking familiarity of that voice. Clutching Lucas' weapon as tightly as possible, I meet Tino Caruso's bold grey eyes. His expression is blank and unreadable. He looks down at his father, his shoulders slumping, his body dejected.

'Tino… I…' Words fail me. I know what this is like. The shock, the grief, the rage. All of it fused together and nothing making sense. Nothing but the immediate desire to inflict the pain that you feel in that moment. The need for revenge.

I lower the gun.

Tino says nothing, shaking his head.

'I'm sorry.' I whisper. 'Tino, I don't know what to say…'

Still clutching his revolver, he wipes a tear from his cheek and looks up to the sky.

'Tino…I understand if you-'

'It's ok, Alexandra.' He stares regretfully at his father's deadened gaze. 'I came here to help.' He sighs, slowly making a sacramental over Lucas' body before turning away and pocketing his revolver. 'You're safe with me.'

Phoenix Massino rounds the corner, clutching a white pocket square, wiping sweat from his face. He moves purposefully towards

Tino, muttering something in Italian with a low, urgent tone. Tino nods, agreeing with him before suggesting he rounds up his men.

'That's...' I linger my gaze on Phoenix. 'You're with them now?' I clutch my head. *None of this is making any sense.*

He reaches out a hand. 'Come with me to the house, I will explain.'

I look around, feeling unnerved. 'Are you going to let us go?'

His face drops with disappointment. 'Of course. I would never...' He takes a few careful steps towards me, touching my arm. 'I would never hurt you.'

'Your father.' I take a seat, still not able to comprehend it fully. 'This is a lot to take in.'

Tino crouches in front of me, taking both my hands in his. 'This is not how I wanted things to be.' He exhales a long breath. 'But this has been a very long time coming, Alexandra.'

'You were going to overthrow him?'

'The Massino family and I had set the wheels in motion. But when you were taken, I confronted Lucas; I knew it had to be him. Only the two of us knew where you were in Eze. Then I discovered he was going to trade you to the very people who killed your father.' He swears under his breath. 'That is not our way. It's not the code we follow.'

'I'm sorry it came to this.' I look over his shoulder at Lucas. 'I hate that so many people have to suffer.'

'This was not your doing.' He reaches forward, running his fingers down my face. 'Do not blame yourself. I want to help you. I want you with us.'

I frown. 'How do you mean?'

'Phoenix and I are joining empires. About six months ago, we realised we have more in common than we knew. We both want the same for Calabria. Our parents have caused too much hardship for the people there. The underworld needs to set aside old conflicts. It is time for something new. Something smarter. And with your input, we could be…' he exhales, smiling. 'We would be some of the most powerful people in the world. I have plans, big plans.'

'Tino, I…' I squint, trying to find the words. 'I'm truly thankful to you, for everything. I don't know if I can ever repay…'

'You need to protect your father's legacy.' He nods knowingly. 'You need to finish what you started.'

I nod. 'If I came with you, it would become your fight, that's not fair.'

'I respect your honour…' He looks over at Lucas' corpse. 'That is how I want the people of Calabria to see the Carusos someday.'

'You have a new legacy to create there, and trust me, I would love to see that. But I can't run. It will catch up with us. The Singularity will continue to tear everything apart. Everything I spent years protecting. They have to pay, Tino. They took everything from me.'

'Let me help you.' He moves closer. 'What can I do?'

'No.' I say firmly, remembering Flint's words. *You're an abyss.* 'I can't drag more people down with me. I can't watch you die for this cause. It's not your fight. You have a plan for your life. You should follow it.'

'And once you're done protecting the people you love, setting things right… would you reconsider?'

'Tino, I…'

He shifts, his eyes meeting mine with intensity. 'Alexandra, we both know that the life I can give you, the life I *lead* is much better suited to who you really are. Your father is Mario Christofi. The most infamous gangster in the world. It's in your blood.'

'I know.'

'You felt the thrill when we were together. You saw how powerful we could be.' His eyes search mine.

'I can't...' I place my hand on his cheek. 'I'm sorry but I can't.'

'Because of your vendetta or because of Gabriel James?'

I look down.

'Does James see you for the truth? Or does he see what he wants to make of you?' He places his hand on his chest. 'You know he can never understand you or your world. Not the way I do. There's mafia blood in you, Alexandra. That will always be who you are. I could still give you the life you deserve. No more sadness, no more loss. You would be a queen. Tell me you wouldn't want that.'

'I don't know...'

'Tell me...'

'Tino...'

'Tell me the truth.'

'Yes...' I breathe, finally. 'Of course. Of course that's what I want. I want for this to never have happened. I want for Mario to still be here. I wish...' I look down at his fingers holding mine. 'I wish I had met you years ago. I wonder what my life with you might look like. I yearn for things to be that simple; to hold your hand, to kiss you, to go to bed with you, to feel you next to me every night, wake up to you every morning. I wonder what it would be like to be protected, to feel safe. I daydream about all of it. And in that world, none of this exists. No pain, no suffering, no grief. In that world, I'm happy. I know that in my core...'

'Choose happiness.' Tino stands. 'It's yours... if you want it, it's yours.'

'Mario deserves justice.'

'Mario would want you to be happy. He would want you to have everything you just mentioned.'

'Tino, it's not real life.'

'It can be…it can be your life.'

'Lex?' Gabriel's voice travels across the pool.

I stand abruptly from the chair, meeting his troubled expression. Without a second's hesitation, I race towards him, throwing my arms around him. 'You're ok… oh thank god.' I hug him again. 'I was wondering where you'd got to.'

CHAPTER FORTY

GABRIEL

Paul Brown sits with a pallid expression. He hasn't said a word since I entered the room. He's been stewing for almost twenty minutes with a furious glare fixed on a random point on the floor. A heavy quiet rests in the room; the kind of silence even I find uncomfortable.

'Call her.' He announces quickly, his sharp eyes suddenly zoning in on me.

'She said she'd just be another minu-'

'Call her James!' He bellows, spittle flying from between his thin lips.

The door swings open suddenly and Collins rushes through. 'Sorry… sorry I'm late.'

'Have a seat, Agent.'

She lowers herself into the chair without a glance in my direction but her apprehension flurries in the air. Brown stands, beginning to pace as he watches traffic on the Westway flyover.

'Only yesterday, the select committee determined that S.A.I.B.R keep Operation Yellow Fire over SO15. The prevention of this attack, the elimination of The Singularity, rests on my shoulders.'

'Sir, we-'

'Don't.' He holds up a hand. 'I called you in to tell you exactly what you will be doing in the next few days and exactly what you won't be. Because I will be busy trying to keep this case in our hands and stopping the PM from shipping you two off to a very remote place. Do you understand?'

'Yes, sir.' Collins replies shakily.

'Despite the NCA sniffing around and asking how an entire mafia organisation can disappear from Monaco, MI6 have cleared up your mess. Tino Caruso is now a witness who will need to be carefully watched and placated for years to come. Congratulations to the both of you. The first taskforce in the history of MI6 to rely on a mobster to save your skin. Moving onto SO15, if they haven't yet figured out that we commandeered their asset, they soon will. You might as well have announced your allegiance with her via French air traffic control. Cut all contact with her immediately.' He checks a document on his desk. 'Next...I've had to concoct a story for the press about the break-ins of two hotel rooms in Monte Carlo. Not to mention explaining the mass shooting at a villa in Italy, which subsequently exposed an MI6 safehouse. That's just the headlines and it is still a whole career's worth of shit in a matter of days.'

Collins takes a breath, 'Sir...'

'No.'

She lowers her head again.

I exhale a loud, exasperated sigh.

Brown stares me down. 'The only reason you are even a part of this taskforce is because I signed off on it. Me.' He stabs a finger into his chest. 'Your future is in my hands. I suggest you keep your opinions to yourself, James.' He glares at me before picking up a pen and fiddling it between his fingers. 'Here's where we're at.' He takes a seat and leans forward. 'The girl in the lab has been identified as Hope Clarke. She was reported missing in Hungary in 2005 by her foster parents, Viola and Hernan Kerti. She disappeared from her front lawn when she was just three years old.'

'The Singularity had her all that time?' Collins whispers.

Brown shifts, looking uncomfortable. 'Roe was the Junior Investigator on the case.'

I raise my head. 'Jake Roe investigated her disappearance?'

'Dr Meyer and the analysts are combing his devices as we speak. We'll know more soon.' He opens a second folder. 'In addition to this, there is currently no evidence linking the safehouse massacre to you. I've shelved it. Let's hope it stays that way. James, you're suspended pending an extremely detailed review of your actions. I've wrapped up as much as I can but what remains outstanding is the incident with the Interpol asset and the death of an agent in your command. No doubt the PM will want heads on a plate. If she asks, I'll be giving her yours. I told you to run an assessment on an asset, I told you to submit a report. I did not tell you to activate them in the field. If SO15 gets wind of this, they will use it as grounds to re-appeal the PM's decision...'

'Sir, I-'

'This country is at its highest threat level. There's an impending attack and the last thing we need is squabbling between intelligence agencies.'

'Sir, we have Flint. We have all the devices from the lab. We have intel from our asset. We have enough to act.'

'We can't bloody use that asset's intel James!'

'Sir, if I may...' Collins starts.

He shifts his eyes across the room. 'You may not. You sanctioned an off-the-books operation with a gangster, not to mention standing by during an interrogation of an Interpol-protected witness. Nothing you have to say is of use to me. Which is why you're joining James on suspension.'

Collins' sheepish expression switches to outrage in an instant. She opens her mouth to speak but Brown cuts her off.

'I advise you both to lay low whilst we wrap up the enquiry into the death of Jacob Roe. As far as the press is concerned, an intelligence analyst has been killed in an armed robbery whilst on holiday. Understood?'

'Sir, with all due-'

'Yes or no, James.'

I stare at him blankly.

'I'm puzzled by this air of entitlement you seem to be harbouring.'

'We made mistakes, Sir. But we couldn't have foreseen the attack on us, the break-ins at the hotels or Roe. We can't be held accountable for how his actions impacted our investigation.'

'Flying out to Monaco to chase an asset with whom you failed to mention you're romantically involved. *That* I can hold you accountable for.' He raises his eyebrows, offering as a side note. 'Spies are the worst gossips; you should know that by now.' He takes a long, drawn-out breath. 'Losing said asset, *that* I can hold you accountable for. Breaking international relations with our cousins to get her back, that I can hold you accountable for. Allowing the death of a suspect in your custody, that I can hold you accountable for.' He stands, throwing both palms onto the desk and leaning forward. 'Oh look… All that and I haven't even mentioned Jacob Roe's name. Let's not beat around the bush here James, your P45 might cite Agent Roe's death as the reason you were let go from the service, but you and I both know it's much more than that.'

I look up to the ceiling, swallowing all the words my brain strongly urges me to say.

'You both need to hand over your security passes, your identification, your weapons and all evidence.'

'Sir,' Collins clears her throat. 'Meyer's still working on evidence from the lab. She should continue…' her voice falters as she collects herself, 'if you take a look at our report, we have evidence that Jed Smart, the Minister of Defence, is involved. We might have fucked up on a monumental level but please be careful when handling this evidence. This runs deeper than we thought. Fallows was coerced into allowing a known terrorist into the country, this is not the time to lose momentum. Icarus Flint inferred on tape that Almasi is a buyer. I'm just asking when you select a team, can we brief them properly, make sure they know the stakes?'

'I'll think about it.'

My head snaps up. 'Sir, if you'd been there-'

'If I'd been there, I would have done my due diligence. I would have flown the asset back to the UK for further analysis of their intel *before* proceeding to run an undercover operation with a crime syndicate and the Italian mafia. I took a risk with you James because of your connections but it's clear to me that you're not fit to lead this team.'

Collins rises from our chair. 'Our own people are exploiting the tragedy and suffering of refugees, taking children from camps, promising their parents a better future, and then brainwashing them to become killers. You hired us because our government knows. You hired us because you said it keeps you up at night. We didn't promise that putting an end to this would be easy or tidy. And now you want to hand it all over... take us away from everything.'

'Do you think anybody wants this division to exist? Do you think the *powers that be* want a department constantly sniffing around the misdeeds and slip-ups of their powerful friends? It's already a fight. You two have made it ten times harder.' His face turns a shade of purple, his eyes bulging from their sockets. 'We need to keep this case with S.A.I.B.R. If SO15 take over, we are done for. They will make a pig's ear of this; we all know it. In order to keep it in our hands, I need you both out. If we're to stop this attack on August 5th then I need a taskforce who plays by the rules.'

'Rules! There are no bloody rules in this game! What we've given to this... what we've lost.' Collins shakes her head, her face swelling with frustration. 'Everything we've sacrificed. If we walk away now, it will be for nothing. All of it will be for nothing. How can you reasonably expect us to do that? My husband left me because I gave too much to the job. I can't sleep at night because I'm frightened that these people know where I live. I'm scared. All the time. But I carry on because this is right... what we are doing is important. It's going to save people. It's going to save innocent lives.'

Brown exhales, some of the usual colour returning to his face. 'The question remains Alison; will your methods save as many lives as you're taking in the process?'

CHAPTER FORTY-ONE

ALEXANDRA

Aldyn opens the door to his mansion, a burden of guilt weighing heavy on his face. It's a look that almost breaks me into a thousand pieces. I leap over the threshold, wrapping my arms around his broad shoulders, comforted by the itch of his white beard against my face.

'I failed you.' His voice becomes muffled as he envelops me, squeezing me tight to his chest. 'I would never have sent you out there if I had suspected Lucas would side with them.'

'I know.' My words become lost in the hug. I inhale the overpowering scent of his cologne, mixed with mints and tobacco.

He strokes my hair, muttering in Albanian. 'I should have known, should have thought better.'

'It's ok.' I lean back, glimpsing the moisture in the wrinkles around his eyes, shame inhabiting his usually tough exterior. 'Nobody could have foreseen that Aldyn.'

'It is my job to know who our enemies are, Alexandra.'

'Not yours alone.' I tilt my head, imploring him to forgive himself.

'Come…' He gestures inside. 'We'll eat and talk.'

'Whose clothes are those?' Keys lingers at the bottom of the stairs, smirking. 'You look homeless.'

I cross the marble reception, taking him into an embrace.

'I missed your horrible personality.'

He winks, guiding me to the kitchen.

'Thank you for everything you did. Without you, I'd be…' I look at the floor, my hand reaching over my shoulder, my fingers tracing the scar on my neck. 'I'd be gone.'

'It was Gabriel really. The man is truly relentless.'

'You found me Keys…'

His bright blue eyes soften. 'There was no question.'

'How's it been here?' I look around Aldyn's mansion. 'Looks the same.'

'Fucking stressful, to be honest.' Keys pulls at his red mop of hair. 'When Aldyn found out you'd been taken… I've never seen him that scared. This was another level. Then, when we got word that Tino Caruso had rescued you lot from near execution, Aldyn sent Hellbanianz to Monaco. Some of them are still out there now.'

'Oh God… what for?'

'Aldyn tells me there are rules that need to be discussed.'

'Your name is Christofi, which means you are under Hellbanianz protection.' Aldyn interjects from the kitchen. 'The boys are drawing up an agreement with Tino and Phoenix.'

Keys shrugs, leading me to the dining room. 'Aldyn is just doing his due diligence, making sure the threat is truly gone. And obviously, his boys need to check out the details of this new deal Tino Caruso has with Phoenix Massino.'

'You think it could be false?'

'The Carusos and Massinos have been enemies for years. The mere thought of them taking a modern approach and combining the empire…it doesn't seem right.' Keys takes a seat at the table.

'I saw the look on Tino's face as he stood over his father's body. Seemed real to me.'

'Phoenix always said he wanted to take the Massino family in a new direction after the death of his mother.' Aldyn shrugs.

'And do you think Tino was always planning on killing Lucas?' Keys looks between us.

'He told me it was a long time coming. And when Lucas tried to pursue the deal with The Singularity, he had to act.'

'Tino has his own agenda.' Aldyn takes a seat at the head of the table. 'Do not underestimate him because he made eyes at you.' He shakes a disapproving finger in the air before looking at me pensively. 'You look ill, too thin. You need to eat.'

'Oh...' I glance down at myself. 'Thanks.'

Keys opens his laptop, busying himself with something on the screen. Aldyn calls out to Anita, instructing her to bring in a long list of snacks.

'I'm sorry, I can't sit still.' I stand from the table. 'Gabriel and Alison are likely being arrested as we speak.'

'They can't arrest them, that's too public.' Keys chimes in. 'They'll just make them disappear.'

'How reassuring.'

'Sit down.' Aldyn demands. 'Anita is bringing food, whisky and rum.'

'Both?!'

A drinks trolley is carefully wheeled through the door and around the table, stopping just beside Aldyn. He straightens, scanning the expensive selection of spirits. 'Alexandra, what would you like?'

I grimace. 'I haven't been able to drink whisky since university.'

He stares at me judgementally before pointing to a bottle of Wray and Nephew. 'Rum it is.'

'Any mixers or...' I watch Aldyn pour me a double. 'No, ok then.'

'I'll have the Johnnie Walker.' Keys interjects excitedly.

Aldyn hands me the crystal tumbler before decanting the whiskey for himself and Keys.

'What's the deal with you and James now?' Keys asks, taking his first sip.

I catch eyes with Aldyn, uncomfortable having this conversation in front of him; like a teenage girl being asked to recite secrets from her diary. 'How do you mean?'

'Well, is he still with that French girl?'

I tense. 'I think she's Danish.'

'Whatever, I'm only asking because he chased you all the way to Monaco, you told him you're still in love with him, he practically announced he'd skin Caruso alive if he laid a hand on you. So, now what? You just go your separate ways?'

'If MI6 have their way.' I frown. 'And how the hell do you know any of this?'

'Collins,' he throws out casually.

Aldyn shrugs. 'They like to gossip.'

'If you must know...' I start, irritated. 'Gabriel came out to Monaco because I had a lead he was interested in. He wants to get ahead of his father. And yes, I told him how I feel but he's made it very clear that we cannot go back to the way it was. He doesn't feel the way I do.'

Keys narrows his eyes. 'I don't believe you can be this stupid.'

'Can we just... forget it, please. It's bad enough I have to endure the rejection from him, let alone talk about it out loud.'

'Has he actually said the words *Alexandra I do not love you?*'

'Yeah *actually* Michael he did. He said those exact words.'

'Oh...'

'Granted, that was before all the shit we went through.' I swallow a large gulp of rum. 'Why do you care anyway?'

'No reason.' Keys says in a higher pitch than usual.

'He made it all very clear...' I take a breath. 'He wants to keep it professional. Move on.'

Aldyn groans. 'Alexandra…Everybody knows Gabriel has wanted to be with you for most of his adult life.'

'Yeah well, we both have to move forward.'

'Come on, Alex.' Keys interjects.

'God…' I throw my head to the ceiling. 'Why does this matter so much to you two? You saw how hell-bent he was on punishing me before. He chased me for six months! We can't go back!'

Keys' eyes shift to Aldyn. 'You need to tell her.'

Aldyn turns away, busying himself with the drinks trolley.

'Tell me what?'

'It is not our place.' Aldyn states disapprovingly.

'I think she needs to know.' Keys insists.

'Tell me what?' I repeat, sliding my empty glass to Aldyn.

He shakes his head, pouring another drink. 'I made a pact.'

'You're scaring me.'

Aldyn's face slumps. '*We* made a pact.'

'Aldyn, what pact?'

'Gabriel he…' Aldyn stops, sliding me the rum. 'I don't even know where to begin.'

Keys groans, rolling his eyes. 'A month after you left him to work for SO15, Gabriel paid Aldyn a visit.'

My heart thumps like it might jump up and out of my mouth.

'He predicted that your priority would be finding your sister and the rest of Paytak's mafia. Which is what you did for the first six months.'

'Yes…'

'Gabriel knew Edward would do everything in his power to keep you under his control. He told me his father never intended on letting you have your own justice.'

'He also didn't trust his father to keep his end of the bargain.' Keys adds. 'Especially if Edward suspected for even a second that you and Gabriel might still be together.'

I swallow past the dryness in my throat. 'Ok.'

Aldyn downs his drink. 'So we made an agreement.'

My body runs cold. 'What kind of agreement?'

'Gabriel suggested, in order to let you do what you needed, he would act as a diversion. I would tell him when you needed help disappearing, he would make a big show of searching for you somewhere else; somewhere he knew for certain you wouldn't be.'

'It kept Edward off your trail when you wanted to slip away.' Keys informs. 'And it worked.'

'And Gabriel knew where I was all along?'

Aldyn nods. 'He wasn't looking for you, Alexandra. He was protecting you.'

'Sad, really…' Keys ponders, dipping into the bowl of nuts. 'Imagine having Edward James as your dad.'

'Oh...' I take my seat again, feeling sick. 'But he was at The Athena all those times?'

'Edward has a lot of spies. Gabriel wanted his father to think he was off the rails. So he used the club to create false speculation.'

'He had me fooled.' Keys confesses. 'He's a clever sod.'

'What about Mesrine Roche… the Corsicans?'

'We would meet at Mesrine's club to discuss the next diversion and how we could keep Edward from tracking you.'

'Gabriel nearly caught me once. Collins found me here.'

'You weren't meant to be home. You came back unannounced, but I knew he wasn't going to harm you.'

'Was she in on it?'

'No.' He sighs wistfully. 'She's just a decent person.'

271

'He loves you, Alex. He loves you even when he hates you.' Keys says forcefully. 'You have good friends, brave people who want to help you. He protects you because he believes in you. He flew to Monaco to stop Edward from exposing you. When you were taken, he practically had me hack every intelligence database in the bloody world to find you. Once again, he's risked his life and career. He might not be able to say it out loud, but he chooses you Alex. All he does is bloody choose you, time and time again. Just like we all do! You need to start paying attention.'

I grit my teeth, trying to stop the tears from pooling in my eyes, my mouth aching from the effort of maintaining composure. 'I just want everyone to be safe.'

'You're our family.' Aldyn interjects. 'You have our loyalty whether you want it or not.'

'Listen.' Keys leans across the table. 'You've proved before that you're the only one who can come at these fuckers so hard that they will never get back up. We need you. But you… you need him.' He shrugs matter-of-factly. 'You need him, Alex.'

The sound of the doorbell ceases all conversation. 'Could it be them?' I look around the table apprehensively.

'Nobody else would have got past the security.' Aldyn says, handing me his gun. 'Here…take this.'

I exit the room, leaving them both in an anticipated silence. Looking through the peephole, I expect to see Gabriel's impeccable face and impatient dark eyes. Instead, Aldyn's head of security waits next to Collins and Emily Meyer. Emily holds a briefcase in her left hand, her right smoothing her bob. Collins paces anxiously. I open the door, unable to hide my puzzlement. *Where is Gabriel?*

'Can we come in?' Collins asks, irritated.

I don't move. 'Gabriel?'

'I saw him an hour ago leaving the Paddington office.' Emily admits uneasily. 'He said he had to see a dog?'

'A man about a dog.' Collins clarifies.

'I didn't know he had a pet?' Emily shrugs.

'It's a saying.' I reply.

'When do we need to worry?' She asks.

'There's no need to worry…' Collins adds, looking down at her phone.

'He looked like he needed a drink.'

'He's an alcoholic.' I mumble. 'He always looks like that.'

'He hasn't had a drop since he found you in that lab.' Emily's face becomes fierce with indignation. 'You haven't noticed?'

I say nothing, admittedly a little shocked by the outburst, the drink slowing my ability to process anything in real time.

'Shit…' Emily's face crumples. 'I'm sorry… uh… you know it's been a long day.

'It's ok.' My heart sinks. *She's right.* We all plough on, nobody really asking the others if they're alright. We need to pay more attention. 'We should find him.'

'Trust me, he's fine.' Collins shows us her screen.

'What is that?' Emily asks, curious.

'It's a tracking app. I know where that boy is at any given time.'

I squint at the screen. 'Hard Rock Café?'

'See!' Emily raises her voice. 'He is at a bar getting 'pissed' as you Brits say. He needs to be more careful, he has a target on his back. We all do!' She breathes, infuriated. 'He's more fragile than you know. He needs support.'

I stay quiet. *I cannot go there. I will not go there.*

Collins steps in, lowering her voice. 'Gabriel James is like a son to me, so I have this on good authority. People think he can't

273

handle adversity because he's got a charmed face. People think he doesn't know how to look out for himself because he grew up rich. But that boy has faced more hardship and heartbreak than most. Despite what you think you know; he will likely be the one left standing when the rest of us are gone. He's not in danger. The Hard Rock Café is actually a good thing. It's where he meets his sponsor. So trust me when I say leaving him to do what he needs to do is the best course of action.'

He's meeting his sponsor. I breathe an audible sigh of relief. He's getting the help he needs.

Collins' attention diverts over my shoulder. Keys lingers by the entrance to the kitchen, holding the bottle of Johnnie Walker.

'Speaking of... *I* need a bloody drink.' Collins barges past me without another word.

Emily hesitates in the doorway, suddenly sheepish. I gesture her inside with an attempt at a welcoming smile and close the front door before walking through to the living room.

'As you might have guessed...' Collins reappears with a tumbler of whiskey. 'Gabriel and I are off the case, so we've lost all access to evidence. But Dr Meyer might have enough to go on.'

'You want to run this off the books?'

Collins raises her eyebrows. 'I'm not stopping now.'

'Brown has a new taskforce starting tomorrow.' Emily starts whilst opening her briefcase. 'In the meantime, I downloaded the data from Caruso, Soridov and Roe's devices onto my hard drive. It has put together quite the picture.' She pulls out a large file. 'Firstly, the unknown number texting Soridov about the deal between him and Caruso, that was Roe.'

'He convinced Caruso to give me up to The Singularity?'

She nods. 'Roe supplied Caruso with evidence that your father helped the Massino family take Calabria. That pushed Caruso towards a deal with Soridov.'

'What evidence exactly?' I ask, more sharply than intended.

'I'm sorry, I don't know yet. But it's clear that Roe convinced Caruso to contact Soridov about taking over the trafficking operation and give you up.'

'Flint knew intimate details about my life. He had pictures that I've never even seen before. It's like he was given a file.'

'Well, we know Edward has made your file accessible to anyone with a power socket.' Collins suggests.

'It appears Soridov was happy with the arrangement and The Singularity were going to pay Caruso a large sum of money to continue the trafficking operation. Lucas also demanded that if he was to work with Soridov, The Singularity had to help him take back Calabria.'

'I don't understand how Roe managed all of this in such a short space of time...' Collins frowns, thinking aloud. 'And for what?'

Unconsciously, I hold my breath, recalling our exchange in the steel box. *Roe's insistence that we couldn't win.* 'Someone was blackmailing him, that's the impression I got. Was there anything on his phone about who that could have been?'

'Not who but I think I know how.'

'Because Jacob Roe was a Junior Investigator on the Hope Clarke case.' Collins informs. 'He's been involved for years...'

Emily looks up to the ceiling, thinking. 'About a year ago, someone texted Roe a message that reads *HC. Let's talk.* I take the initials to mean *Hope Clarke.* Then, before Roe flew out to Monaco, he received another message which read *Deal with her.* I presume the second was about you, Alexandra.'

'So Roe was in constant contact with The Singularity…' I say, feeling an overwhelming anxiousness. 'If Roe was an investigator on the Hope Clarke case and he was being blackmailed, then did he have something to do with her disappearance?'

Emily sighs. 'It seems whatever happened was being used as leverage against him.'

'He said he made a mistake.' I recall. 'He said one mistake had changed his whole life.'

Collins pinches the bridge of her nose. 'Edward put Roe and I on a taskforce together in 2017.'

'So Edward brings Roe to the table and Roe is the one selling us all out…' I say, almost trying the words out for size. 'Do you think Edward knew?'

'Admittedly, that was the first thing that sprung to my mind in Italy.' Collins says, shaking her head. 'But Roe actively worked to keep Edward out of the loop and as awful as that man is, do you really think he's capable of trying to murder his son?'

'Yeah…' I exhale. 'You're right.'

'It's also worth mentioning…' Emily begins, rifling through more documents. 'Over a year ago, it was Roe who texted Diren Paytak telling him which route he was taking when he was transporting an Operation Sandbank witness named Amber Brookes.'

'Roe got rid of Amber?' I ask with disbelief.

'Exactly…' Emily stands, flexing her ankles. 'That was around the time Roe ended up in hospital, right? Their communication correlates with that.'

I look to Collins. 'That's how Paytak found Gabriel in the chapel. Paytak ambushed the vehicle, killed Amber, took Roe's phone.'

'Is that how he got shot?' Emily places her hand on her hips, glancing between us. 'His bullet wounds…' She elaborates. 'Gabriel thought he was meeting Roe in the church but instead, Paytak was there. It was your gun that killed Diren Paytak. You were there. You saved his life.' Realisation strikes her face as she speaks the final words. It's as if the notion provides an explanation to something that's been nagging at her for a while.

Collins' eyebrows shoot up. 'How the hell did you work that out?'

'We need to figure out who has been blackmailing Roe.' I say, trying not to think about how many times Meyer has seen those wounds on Gabriel's body. 'It can't be Soridov. Roe was in contact with him separately. It can't be Paytak. He's dead.'

'If Roe has been in contact with The Singularity for years, then why didn't he just give you up before now?' Collins asks, looking up. 'That would have been the quickest way to stop the investigation.'

'He didn't seem like he actually wanted to hurt anyone… he was remorseful.' I shrug. 'Perhaps he just couldn't bring himself to.'

'What if he's not being blackmailed by them at all?' Collins suggests. 'Could that number belong to Jed Smart? He's connected. Roe was only told to get rid of you when you got close to Hope and the lab. Smart could have been using Roe to cover up his dealings with The Singularity.'

'That is entirely possible.' I say, casting my mind back to my first interaction with Smart during the Wharf cab bombings. *He must know exactly who I am.* 'We should look at any connection Jed Smart might have had to Roe before Hope Clarke. Or if they've had any dealings since.'

'I'll ask Keys to look into that. We need to speak to Smart anyway.' Collins bites down on the corner of her mouth. 'It's the next logical step.'

'Could it be Imran Almasi?' I ask, my mouth running dry at the thought. 'Roe just kept telling me we wouldn't be able to beat this.'

'Almasi is a recent addition to all of this. Whoever this is, it's closer to home, somehow.' Collins utters. 'I know he was a traitor. But I just can't picture him working with a terrorist.'

'Perhaps Flint's devices can tell us more.' Emily suggests. 'I didn't get a chance to run reports on them yet.'

'Are we going to be able to?' I ask.

'One of the S.A.I.B.R analysts is a good friend.' She states with confidence. 'She's having issues cracking the laptop. I said I could help but that it needed to be off-book. I'll have it in the next twenty-four hours.'

'What if Brown finds out?'

'If Keys can decipher something that stops an attack, it's worth the risk.'

'Thank you, Emily.'

She nods determinedly. 'You've all risked so much already. It's the least I could do.'

'Gabriel might be able to look at this from another angle.' I suggest. 'We should wait for him to come back, then we can put our heads together again.'

'Good idea.' Collins stands. 'We'll wait for Flint's devices, regroup. Emily, care to join us for a drink?'

At first, she stares at us as if we've spoken an entirely different language. 'Ok,' she finally breathes. 'What the heck.'

CHAPTER FORTY-TWO

GABRIEL

I press my thumb on the bell again, ringing impatiently. Baffled by the music blaring from Aldyn's house, I peer through the window to the hallway, trying to get a look inside. Aldyn's Head of Security shrugs at me, equally puzzled. When the door finally opens, Alexandra sways with her eyes blurred and unfocused.

'Gabriel's here!'

I smirk. 'Are you wasted?'

'You have so much luggage…' She says, distracted. 'Are you staying?'

'Yeah, can I come in?'

'Oh sure!' She grabs my arm and pulls me inside. 'Earlier… oh my god Meyer was so angry. So serious.' She giggles before lowering her voice to the kind of whisper that could be heard in the next room. 'She thinks you went to see a dog.'

'She…' I frown. 'Hang on what?'

I step over discarded coats and shoes; the reception looking as if someone has been rifling through Aldyn's cupboards. Glancing into the living room, I see Keys and Emily dancing in front of the fireplace, swinging each other around as if performing some sort of ritual.

'Yeah…' Lex stops, watching them. 'No idea.'

Following her into the kitchen, I nod a quick hello to Aldyn, who sits with a group of Hellbanianz gang members amidst a thick fog of cigar smoke. Not one of them looks bothered or perturbed by the blaring music. Lex slumps into a chair at the table, plucking a cigar from a mobster's mouth before taking a drag. I walk over to Collins, who stands at the sink, rinsing a glass.

'Can you explain what's going on?'

Turning, she looks up at me with bleary eyes.

'Oh not you too.'

'It's been a hard day…' she throws out her arms inelegantly. 'And we deserve some joy.'

'Whose idea was this?'

'Alexandra said we should have fun. And I said… God, I need fun.'

'Mmhmm.'

'Snap!' Lex yells from the table.

I note the confused Albanian faces. *Clearly, none of them have the heart to tell her they're playing poker.*

'Meyer was furious, and I told her you wouldn't be dead.' Collins picks up a dusty bottle of Wray & Nephew, thrusting it in the air. 'Cheers!'

'Ok… I'll take that.' I sigh, prying the bottle away.

'Hypocrite!' She snatches it back, taking a gulp.

I roll my eyes and return to Lex. 'Can I talk to you?'

The Albanians all turn in my direction, observing me like a pack of angry hyenas. Aldyn gives me a warning look. I nod, acknowledging the message before escorting her to the hallway.

'Here…' I hand her a pint of water. 'Drink this.'

She takes the glass and leans against the wall. 'Shh Gabriel… come here.' She wheezes with hilarity, accidentally tipping water onto the floor. 'I…am… absolutely wasted.'

'No shit…' I help her up. 'How about you actually drink that instead of spilling it everywhere?'

'Bossy.'

'All of it.'

She downs the water. 'Ok, let's go!'

'Wait, I'd really like to talk to you.'

She exhales a disapproving breath. 'Ok but be quick, I'm hosting a party.'

'This isn't your house.'

She scowls. 'You're a rude person.'

I lower my head, amused. 'Excellent point.'

'I know what you're going to say ok? We're moving forward. Moving on. Drawing a line. Message received.' She salutes. 'Loud and clear. Professional. We will keep it purely professional.' She widens her mouth. 'Wow… that was really hard to say.'

'Exactly how much have you had to drink?'

She makes a small gap between her index finger and thumb, struggling to focus on keeping her fingers still.

'I'll get you another water.'

'How many times did you have sex with her?' She calls out.

'Who?' I look over my shoulder and pull her around the corner. 'What are you talking about?'

She drops her head into her hands. 'You don't care, so why should I?'

'What do you mean, Lex?'

She looks up. 'How many have there been?'

'Can you put the crazy aside for a second and just tell me what you want to know?'

'M-e-y-e-r.' She spells the word out. 'How else would she know about the wounds on your leg and your shoulder, hmm? She's seen them all. Everything.'

'Ah…'

'Ever think I should have been a detective?'

'Not with your family history.' I sigh, taking a seat on the bottom of Aldyn's staircase.

'I know what it looks like to love you.' She joins me on the step, leaning against my shoulder. 'And that is how she looks.'

281

The music changes and ABBA blasts from the speakers. Keys gesticulates enthusiastically from the fireplace, attempting to beckon us over for a dance.

I offer him a quick wave. 'Can we go somewhere private, please? I really think we should talk about this elsewhere.'

'Do we have to go through it all again?'

'Through what?'

'I already know what you're going to say.'

'You don't.'

She narrows her eyes suspiciously. 'Do you have trouble understanding me, do you think?'

'Well…right now yeah.' I scratch the back of my head. 'You've had a pirate's ransom of rum.'

She yawns. 'I'm going upstairs, do you want to come?'

'Sure…' I exhale, helping her up.

'Please can you stay the night?'

'Sure.' I repeat.

'Sure… as in yes?'

'Yeah, I was going to ask Aldyn if I could crash in one of his spare rooms anyway.'

Her eyes light up, she dives forward to hug me, nearly knocking us both down the stairway.

CHAPTER FORTY-THREE

GABRIEL

Lex kicks her slippers towards a large double bed. Since university, I've only ever been in her room once before, back when she had the flat on Essex Road. This is similar in that everything is white and cream. The walls, the bedding, the throw, the French armchair in the corner. It's a serene, tranquil space; completely at odds with the whirlwind woman in front of me. Struggling to pull her shirt off, she holds her hands up, signalling for me to assist. Laughing at her lack of coordination, I pull it over her head.

'What was it you wanted to talk about?' She asks.

I turn and face the wall whilst she undresses, studying a framed picture of her leaning against the bonnet of an armoured truck between Charles McGuire and Wayne Gibbs. Despite being dressed head to toe in military combat gear, all three grin joyfully at the camera.

'Gabriel…' Lex tuts behind me. 'You can look… you've seen it all before.'

I peer over my shoulder slowly. She's perched on the edge of the bed, wearing one of my old T-shirts.

'You kept that?'

She looks down, pulling at the material, her eyes tracing the faded National Crime Agency branding. 'Of course.' The corner of her lips twitch. 'Come.' She pats the mattress. 'What was it you wanted to say?'

I inhale, drawing in the confidence, trying to calm my heart rate. *I need to get this out.* I move to sit next to her. 'I'm sure it hasn't escaped your notice that I've been drinking again.'

'I know…' She whispers softly.

I pause, plucking up courage. 'If I hadn't, things might have gone differently in Monaco. I would have sniffed a rat with Roe. I wouldn't have allowed you to be in Eze on your own. When you were taken…that was rock bottom for me.'

She places her hand on mine, the golden flecks in her eyes catching the light as she looks at me. There's no judgement, no pity; it's just her. And that feeling, the touch of her skin, gives me the strength I need to continue.

'I can't even look back and figure out how or where it went wrong because I was drunk, Lex. I've been drunk for over a year. And the point is, I'll never know if that was what contributed to the shit we're in.'

'Please Gabriel, don't put it all on yourself. It only leads to more guilt. You have to want to get better for you, not because you want to balance the scales.'

'I do, I do want that…'

'Ok…' She smiles.

'I saw my sponsor. I'm getting back on the program, but I can't move forward unless I'm honest with the people around me.'

She tightens her grip. I can't tell if it's an encouraging squeeze or an instinctive reaction for fear of the truth.

'I had this epiphany when we got back yesterday. I wasted so much time wearing a mask around you when we were away. Forgiving you meant moving forward. I didn't want to move on. I didn't want to stop being angry. My twisted logic told me that anger allowed there to be something significant between us still.'

'You have always been significant to me, Gabriel.'

'There's so much I should have said, so many opportunities lost. That became abundantly clear when faced with the fact I might never get to tell you again. I can't be in that position anymore. I don't know what's going to happen to us, but I want to tell you the truth.'

She shifts along the bed, her legs touching mine. 'You can tell me anything, you really can.'

'I uh…' I sigh, finding it slightly easier now she's not looking directly at me. 'You lost so much and instead of respecting your decision, instead of accepting that what you did ultimately saved my life, I wanted to believe the worst of you because that made it easier.'

'I understand. Trust me, I do…'

'What I should have said in that bathroom in Italy is that I physically struggle to tell you how I feel because there aren't adequate words. It can't be condensed into *I love you*. That doesn't even begin to illustrate what you are to me. I'm anchored to you in a way that even I don't understand. I'll never escape that. I've never wanted to. I'm tethered to how you feel, what makes you laugh, causes you pain, who hurts you, the music you listen to, the food you like. Sometimes it's too much. Sometimes, it paralyses me. Being bound to you makes me incredibly vulnerable. Especially when the thing I fear most in the world is losing you.'

'We're two halves.' She nods, staring at the floor. 'And sometimes, it's messy.'

'But it doesn't scare you. It wakes you up, it drives you to fight. I admire that; how brave you are. It makes me want to be brave. And because I love you, as in 'chase you across Europe' *love you*, I want to be worthy. I want to be the person Mario wrote about in that letter. The man he deemed deserving of his daughter.'

Tears spill from her bright, beaming eyes. 'You are that person.' She takes my hand. 'You will always be that person and that is why I have always been so in love with you.'

My shoulders seem to physically drop with relief. 'Listen, I heard what Tino Caruso said to you in Italy. And I contemplated letting you go, watching you walk away and be with him.' I confess, honestly. 'Everyone around us thinks we should be apart. They think that healing will take distance.'

She takes a breath to protest, her face tightening.

'But I don't think that's what we need. And I know it's not what I want.'

'I want to be where you are.' She says suddenly, wiping tears from her face. 'I'm not better off without you, Gabriel. I want to heal with you. I go where you go.'

'Good…' I grin. 'Because having you around again but so far from my reach is torture. I can't function…' I stoop, placing my forehead against hers. 'I just want you with me, Lex. I've always only wanted you with me.'

'I'm here.' She tilts my chin, so my eyes meet hers. 'I shouldn't have doubted you. You're always there. Even when I don't see it.'

'Obviously, I'm still working on things, and it'll take time, but I want to get better, to be better.'

'I know,' she nods assuredly. 'I know you'll always fight.'

'I hope you're sober enough to remember this conversation because I don't know if I can repeat it all tomorrow.' I wink.

She laughs, more tears escaping the corners of her eyes.

'I'm sorry for all the nasty shit I said, I was scared.' I bring her closer to me, running my hands through her hair. 'You're not a vice. You're not an addiction. You're the sunshine. Bright, blinding, constant, warm. I can't waste another minute trying *not* to love you. It's fucking pointless and it never works.'

Her eyes fixate on mine, the only sound between us, our synchronised breathing. 'Promise you won't take it all back tomorrow? Promise this is real?'

'It's real…' I pull her onto my lap, taking her in my arms, caressing her mouth with mine. 'You taste like a distillery…'

'Sorry.' She offers an apologetic laugh. 'So much rum.'
'Whisky is more my thing anyway.'

CHAPTER FORTY-FOUR

ALEXANDRA

'Christ!' Collins croaks, massaging her neck. 'Anyone got any painkillers?'

'That's the downside to parties.' Aldyn warns, settling into his seat at the head of the table and opening his newspaper.

'Thank you for letting us wreck your house.' I offer warily.

'The house needs to be used. Did Gabriel find his room?'

'Mmhmm.' I respond casually. 'Did the boys have a good time?'

He lowers his paper and smiles. 'Anywhere there's whisky, cigars, and women, they are happy.' He winks at Collins.

She grimaces and switches on the kettle.

'Morning Campers!' Keys greets us all, strolling in.

'Urgh, why are you so cheerful?' I lean over the table, stealing a slice of toast from Aldyn's plate.

'Where's Gabe?' Keys asks.

'Gone for a run...' I pause before adding, 'I think.'

'Is he going to become really smug now he's sober?'

'What do you mean become?' Collins grumbles.

As if on cue, Gabriel appears in the doorway. Pulling an earphone from his ear, he smiles with sweat glistening across his face and chest.

Collins holds up the cafetière in his direction.

'Yeah, thanks.' He responds before looking around the group. 'Emily didn't drive home, did she?'

'If you walk ten paces behind you and look under the coffee table, you'll have your answer.' Keys replies, buttering some bread.

Collins hands Gabriel a steaming mug. 'You're looking better.'

'Just needed a good night's sleep.' He murmurs, taking a sip.

'Is *that* what you call it?' Keys blurts out.

Gabriel's lips creep up behind his cup.

'Ouch! Stop it!' Keys jerks away from my elbow. 'I'm just saying the walls are thin!'

'These walls are strong!' Aldyn protests without looking up from his newspaper.

'I'm just impressed like.' Keys continues before lowering his voice. 'Did you really not even have to fake it onc-'

'Ok everyone…' I shout over him. 'Let's eat and then we need to get our heads in gear.'

'Keys did you get anything on Flint's phone yet?' Gabriel jumps in, doing us both a favour.

Keys moves to the kitchen island and shakes his mouse to wake up the desktop. 'Nothing new. We've confirmed that Jed Smart is indeed buying Compliants from The Singularity. Flint and he were exchanging a few texts about getting Hope Clarke back to the Monaco lab for *repair*. Their words, not mine.' He scrubs a freckled hand through his hair. 'Apparently, she snapped out of whatever weird trance they had her in during an operation in Moscow. Smart had to pull strings to get her out alive.'

'What about the laptop?' Gabriel asks.

'Yeah, about that… I can see why your pals at S.A.I.B.R were struggling with access. The Singularity took big measures to protect their data.'

'You're saying you can't do it?'

Keys eyes him incredulously. 'I'm saying it will take time.'

'We don't have time.' Gabriel insists. 'Emily will have to get those devices back to Paddington before the new taskforce step in.'

'Look, I'm a good hacker, but I'm not *Leo Eden* good. Not yet anyway.'

'Who's Leo Eden?' I ask.

'Only the Da Vinci of hacking. A pure artist at work.' Keys scoffs, like a kid explaining social media to his grandparents.

'Where is he now?'

'How much time you got?'

'No but seriously, is he contactable?'

'Don't get any ideas.' Keys warns. 'He's in a maximum-security prison. MI5 barely even let him use his electric toothbrush.'

'He's *that* good?'

'The best.'

'How about you?' I ask Gabriel, who looks a million miles away as he pours more coffee. 'You know him?'

He shrugs, his expression unreadable. 'Heard of him.'

'Hmm…'

Keys sighs, defeated. 'I'm trying to find any connections between Roe and Jed Smart, aside from Hope Clarke. So far, nothing. You might need to find a way to speak to Smart yourselves. Even if he wasn't blackmailing Roe, he's still a key player in all of this.'

'I'm convinced it's Smart.' I turn to Gabriel. 'I think I have an idea of how we can reach him. Have you got time to come to Soho with me today?'

'Yep…' A hint of suspicion lands in his voice. 'If we go before my AA meeting, this afternoon.'

'Sure. It's a long shot, but I have a feeling we can get close to Smart if we speak to…'

'My head!' Emily cries, her voice carrying from the living room.

'I would have thought she'd danced it all off.' Keys murmurs as she enters. 'Oh wow.'

Emily hobbles into the kitchen, her hair stuck to one side of her face. 'Has anyone seen my other shoe?'

'You threw it in the fireplace.' He informs her.

She turns, squinting at him. 'What?'

'We told you not to.'

'Was the fire on?'

'Yes and it smells everywhere of burnt leather.' Aldyn interjects, irritated.

'Emily, if you need to shower, you can use my room?' I suggest, wanting to extend a semi-peace offering.

'Collins' is closer.' Gabriel rushes out, his eyes urgent. 'She has a better shower.'

I frown briefly. *How would he know that?* Then the realisation hits me. His clothes are strewn all over my room.

'I'll get you a towel.' I disappear out of the kitchen and up the stairs, making a mental note to tidy up.

CHAPTER FORTY-FIVE

ALEXANDRA

Mesrine Roche, owner and Madam of The Red Door, stares into the empty fireplace with big, liquid eyes. Her long red dress, which could easily pass for lingerie, skirts the floor. She clutches a tumbler with elegant fingers, swirling it in circles. She's the type of woman you might think was born with a red lip. It's her war paint. Despite the young, pretty '*waitress*' announcing our arrival, Mesrine hasn't moved, not even turned her head in our direction. She looks as if nothing has ever surprised her and nothing ever could. A second member of staff appears, a man this time, tall but still just a few inches shorter than Gabriel. His shirt is open at the collar, revealing the tip of a tattoo on a tanned, broad chest. He deposits a jug of water on the table, offering a friendly smile before returning to tend the bar. Noticing my lingering stare, Gabriel shifts impatiently behind me. I flit my eyes away.

'Gabriel James…' Mesrine twists her plump lips into a sumptuous smirk. Her voice is deep and commanding. 'I was wondering when you might return. It really is good to see you.'

She flicks long raven hair off of her shoulders; revealing a neckline plunging so low it causes Gabriel to clear his throat.

Noticing my glare, he moves his gaze, his eyes practically twitching with the effort. 'I'll wait in the car.'

'Good idea.'

Mesrine breaks into a beautiful grin as she watches him leave with hungry green eyes. 'Le travail de Dieu.'

I cross my arms. 'Don't ever let him hear you say that.'

'Parlez vous francais?'

'Amongst other things.'

292

'Ah, Alexandra,' she says patronisingly. 'You surprise me.'

'Good.'

'You know…' She waves her drink at the door before taking a sip. 'You should be careful. Men like that need to be adored.'

'He's fine.'

'He is back under your thumb, I presume.' She curls her bottom lip. 'Such a shame. What an unbelievable body, so much raw intimacy. He was one of the best lovers I've ever had. Very, very generous.'

I keep my expression cool. *This bitch will not see me as much as blink in response to her provocation.*

'I'm busy, Alexandra.' She turns towards the bar, ordering another drink.

'You've been frequenting my club quite a bit, I hear.'

'You have the best whisky.' She admits grudgingly. 'Which, of course, is Gabriel's favourite.' She rolls that nugget of information off of her tongue casually. *A tongue I'd like to cut out right now.* 'Is that why you stock so much of it, to make sure he comes back to you?'

'I'm not here to talk about Gabriel.'

'You know if you wanted…We could have an arrangement. Perhaps I start with him, and you could watch?'

'Mesrine…'

'I'll show you the things he likes, teach you how to keep his interest. Because if you don't try, he will stray.' She shakes a manicured finger in the air. 'Men who look like that always do. The power gets to their heads.'

'I just need some information.' I continue, blocking her out.

'Aren't you the least bit intrigued? The things he begged me to do, the reason he came back time and time aga….'

The pistol is out so quickly I don't properly acknowledge the feel of it in my hands until I'm pulling the trigger.

Once.

Twice.

Three times.

Mesrine's mouth falls open, suspended in shock. The three grotesque China vases on the mantlepiece explode behind her: shards of bronze and ceramic burst into the air. Quickly, she clasps her hands together, her shoulders hunched to her ears.

'I don't have time to play this game.'

'You think I'm intimidated by you?' She masks the shake in her voice well but it's there. *I hear it.*

Gabriel flies through the door, his eyes wild. 'What the…' He stops suddenly, taking in the mess. 'Are you alri…' His face drops with irritation. 'Alexandra… really?!'

Mesrine eyes widen with innocence. 'Please don't leave me alone with her. Don't let her do anything more!'

'We're fine.' I say flatly.

'Stay!' Mesrine cries out. 'Please do not let her…'

I step forward, digging the butt of my pistol into her ribs. 'Please don't mistake his fucking you for caring about you.'

She exhales an exasperated breath, dropping the doe-eyed act. 'I have had people killed for less than this.'

'And I'm the one who knows how to do the killing.'

'Ok, let's rewind.' Gabriel suggests. 'Lex, can you put the gun away?'

'Nope.' I shove the end in a little harder.

'Do what Daddy says, Lex.' Mesrine quips, amused.

'It isn't for your benefit.' Gabriel snaps in her direction. 'I don't want her to kill you because I want a life with her when we're done here, and ending yours is more hassle than it's worth.'

A shocked realisation strikes her face as if she's just swallowed a stone. Eventually, she sighs, feigning nonchalance before grabbing her cocktail and dropping back into her armchair like a bored schoolgirl.

'Mes...' Gabriel begins with a placating tone. 'You have a network; you know things others don't.'

'What is it you need?'

He steps forward. 'We know powerful men come here. We know they like to use the services you offer.'

'Men like you, you mean?'

'Come on, Mes.... Please.'

I exhale, looking up to the ceiling. *Mes is starting to grate on me.* 'You know of David Fallows, don't you?'

She curses in French, spitting at my feet.

'Your choice but make the most of things as they are now.' I gesture around the room. 'Shame really... you've decorated it so well.'

She jumps up from her chair. 'You want to continue threatening me like a stupid little girl!'

I lurch forward, gripping her chin between my thumb and index finger. 'Listen to me, you crazy bitch.... David Fallows and Jed Smart are two MPs mixed up with a crime syndicate and a terrorist organisation. This syndicate are not afraid to bulldoze their way through the underworld; they've figured out that we, more than anyone, know how to operate in the shadows. They will attack this city and squeeze us dry. They will own our world and everyone in it. Including this club, including you.'

'What if that suits me just fine?' She spits; the smudging of her mascara the only indication that she's the least bit distressed.

I release her. 'You've worked hard to build an empire here. When you took over from your husband, Soho was in a real state. But you changed that around, you look after your girls. You give them an autonomy they've never had. You even set them up with a pension! You respect their choices. You changed the game. You earned your reputation. Why would you let someone take that from you?'

Her mouth tightens.

'Jed Smart?' Gabriel holds up his phone, showing her a picture of him. 'Has he been here, or have you heard any rumours about him using other houses?'

'I would remember him. I watch the news.'

'And Fallows?' He asks, softer this time.

She sighs, a little of the tautness leaving her face. 'Only once, then the press found out about him. He didn't come again.'

'Anyone come with Fallows?' Gabriel continues on a roll.

'He came alone.'

'How often do you get politicians in here?'

'Confidentiality is integral to this business.'

'Is there anyone that sticks out in your mind?'

'Get rid of her…' She nudges her head in my direction. 'I will tell you what you need to know.'

'Not going to happen, I'm afraid.' Gabriel rebuts.

She smooths her dress. 'You love her more than you love the thrill of this place, Gabriel huh? Seriously!' She becomes irate. 'The most unbelievable experiences, unrivalled pleasure… something new every time. You would throw that away for a monogamous relationship? The same person for the rest of your life!' She laughs as if someone has just said something ridiculous. 'That is not how men are made.'

Gabriel's face remains blank. 'A few months back, do you recall hearing about a girl who was murdered in one of the brothels in Camden? She was killed by one of her customers.'

She rolls her eyes, her face dejected, her voice lacking its previous energy. 'Of course, nothing happens in this world without me knowing about it.'

'Who owned that brothel?'

She sighs. 'I'm not a snitch.'

'Is that where all the politicians used to go?'

'We're just looking for Jed Smart, Mesrine.' I say, gentler this time. 'Anything you can give us… anything you know about him or a place that he might have been to.'

'Ludmilla Romkova.' She drawls reluctantly.

'And who is that?'

'She ran the boutique near Mornington Crescent. Before one of her girls died, she used to organise secret parties in hotels and sometimes in big mansions in the countryside. Lots of powerful people would attend.'

'People like Smart?' I ask with eager impatience.

'I would have to ask her.'

'How do we find her?'

She shakes her head.

'How do we find her Mes?' Gabriel insists.

'I don't know. She has not been around for a long time.'

'You need to reach out to her.' I insist, forcefully. 'I want her to tell us where we can find Jed Smart. We need to have a conversation with him in private.'

'And why the fuck would I do that?' She yells, outraged. 'Why should any of us help you?'

'Because if you don't…' Gabriel steps in. 'I won't rest until I've pulled every string at the NCA to have this fucking place gutted, turned into a halfway house and the both of you arrested.' He shouts, his temper finally landing in the room like a fourth presence.

CHAPTER FORTY-SIX

GABRIEL

Lex slams the car door, leaning her head on the dashboard before typing on her phone.

'What are you doing?'

'I need Keys to locate Ludmilla Romkova. We might have pushed Mesrine too far. Ludmilla could be going into hiding as we speak.'

'And if she comes through, how long do you think it will take Ludmilla to find Smart.'

'A day, maybe two.' She shrugs.

I tense, waiting for her to say something more.

She turns away, looking out the passenger window, watching groups of people fan past The Red Door. Her phone chimes and she looks down, reading the screen.

'Keys come back to you?'

She holds up her phone. 'That's what Ludmilla looks like.'

'Ok.'

'We'll sit tight until Keys has something on her whereabouts.' She reverts to watching passing pedestrians. 'Who knows? Mesrine might even bring her to the club.'

'Lex, can we talk abou…'

'I think we should wait in silence…' she states smoothly, '…enjoy some quiet time.'

'Alright then.'

She closes her eyes and rests her head back on the seat. I wait a few beats, certain that any second, there will be a tirade of abuse hurled in my direction: a full-on dressing down. I jerk my knee, trying to stave off my own impatience, forcing the part of my brain that so desperately wants to open up a conversation, to let go. *If she's willing to move past it, then we should leave it at that.*

Her eyes open, she glares at me. 'Honestly Gabriel, your sleeping with Mesrine Roche undermines everything my family has done in this city.'

'That's your takeaway?' I cross my arms. 'I can only fucking apologise for jeopardising your reputation in the criminal underworld, Alexandra.'

'You've given the Corsican Mafia leverage. That conversation could have been a lot easier.'

'You should have just let me handle it.'

Her eyes bulge. 'The fact you had to step in to get the information is not how this should work. It made me look weak.'

'Well naturally, that was the plan... ruin your status in the underworld.'

She shakes her head, unimpressed by the sarcasm.

'You think I slept with her to get back at you? Not everything I do is about you.'

'What were you thinking paying for sex!' She blurts out as if the words have tumbled from her mouth without her consent. 'The point of looking like you is that you shouldn't have to.'

I look away. 'I didn't.'

'Hmm?'

'I didn't pay her.'

'You didn't pay her?' She repeats, slower and louder.

'No...' I confess quietly.

'Just...' she throws her hands over her face. 'Don't speak anymore.'

'You don't think I didn't hear exactly what you said to Tino Caruso a week ago?'

'How is that relevant?'

'I'm just saying, I'm not the only one who had other interests.'

She grits her teeth, saying nothing.

'Aldyn and I would meet at Mesrine's Club. He would give me updates on how you were doing.' I admit hesitantly. 'A few times, I'd stay on for a drink.'

'A drink.' She scoffs.

'Fine, loads of fucking drinks.'

'At least you're being honest now.'

'Look, I was drunk, it was stupid, meaningless, honestly meant nothing. Less than nothing. If it's any consolation, I was hammered, and my performance likely wasn't good.' I continue rambling, aware I'm making it worse. 'Take comfort that you've only slept with me sober.'

'Oh that makes me feel so much better, thank you.'

'You know it meant nothing, Alexandra.'

'Then why did you keep going back? You've crossed boundaries! There's something between you now that can never be undone.'

'Because I had sex with her?' I ask, astonished. 'It doesn't make her special, Lex. There's been so many other...' I stop, swallowing the words, trying to adjust the smirk on my face.

'Finish that sentence.'

'You get the gist.'

'Gabriel...this isn't funny.'

'I'm not laughing.'

'You'll be burning that bed in Oxfordshire for one thing.'

'Nobody has ever spent the night with me in that room.'

'What about Meyer?'

'I couldn't... that will always be our house to me.'

She shakes her head, irritated I've swerved her off track. 'The point is it's created obstacles we don't need, an enemy I can't afford.'

'Right... we're back to pretending this is about your reputation.'

'What else is it about!' She shouts. 'She knows intimate details about you, Gabriel. That is not a woman you want to know *anything* about you! And not only has she seen your *unbelievable body*, she also claims to know your sexual preferences.'

'There was no exchange of any preferences, no toys, no special moves, no nothing.'

Her eyes screw shut. 'I'm asking you to spare me.'

'Listen, what's done is done. I can't change it. If there were terms and conditions to you leaving me, you should have sent them in writing; made it very clear who I was and wasn't allowed to sleep with.'

'Next time, I just might.'

'Next time... nice.'

We both brood in awkward silence. I listen to the tapping of her fingers on the window, the repetitive sound conveying the fury still simmering under the surface.

'You left Alexandra.'

'I'm aware.'

'I didn't think you were ever coming back.'

'Got it.'

'I was just trying to get over you.'

'By getting under a dominatrix?'

'She wasn't in character when we...'

'What was she then?'

I shrug. 'Just her.'

She chuckles an unsettling sound. 'You mean *Mes*?'

'Mature.'

'I hope you've got yourself checked since…' She murmurs pointedly. 'God knows what's crawling around in there.'

'Yeah, I did thanks.'

'Properly?'

'No, actually, I went to a back street doctor in Peckham.'

She scowls at me, unamused. 'You could have had your pick of women. Anyone! But you choose Mesrine Roche, the only other woman with proper influence in organised crime.'

'When can you admit that this is less about the threat to your position and more about the fact your feelings are hurt?'

'She's barred from my club.'

I catch the undercurrent of pain in the husk of her voice. 'Alexandra…' I turn to face her. 'The second I saw you in Monaco, whatever and whoever came before instantly became irrelevant. Nobody is you.'

For a moment, her face relinquishes some of its hardness, her shoulders wilting as if surrendering the rage until her expression switches again. 'Can you just admit that you did it to hurt me?'

'Has it?'

'Huh?'

'Jealousy doesn't make you less impressive to me. You can admit you're human.'

Her phone buzzes and she quickly reaches towards the dashboard. 'Keys says he's going to need a few hours.' She reads before pocketing her phone. 'I need to get out of this car.'

CHAPTER FORTY-SEVEN

GABRIEL

Aron Palmer, the AA chairperson, waits by the door. He's wishing the group a good week as we fan out of the hall into the evening sun. He stands a head shorter than me, his body a block of sinew and muscle. Palmer's dedication to his physique is a prime example of addiction not being cured but merely redirected. He used to head up cybercrime at the NCA until he had too much to drink and caused a pile-up on the M25, nearly killing two civilians. He was good at his job and didn't buy into the politics that came with being in charge, but he was never the same after that. Once he'd got out of rehab, Scotland Yard offered him a position, less senior but an opportunity all the same. He said he couldn't go back to law enforcement. He thinks he deserves a life sentence, a punishment for his actions. Despite all the work he's done, he is still racked with guilt.

'Nice to have you here, James.' He grips my hand, shaking it. 'You feeling alright?'

'It's not easy starting from scratch.' I admit.

'Listen, I've been there. Most of us have. You're standing here now mate, that counts more than falling off the wagon.'

'I'm trying.'

'You got a good support system?'

I look over at Lex, who waits for me, leaning on the bonnet of Aldyn's 4x4, her hair tousling in the breeze. 'I'm one of the lucky ones.'

'Where were you before?'

'Islington.'

'Good bunch.' He grins. 'Lively.'

'It was good, but I needed a new start.'

'You should check in with them.' He suggests in a way that seems more like an order. *Typical ex-copper.* 'They'd want to know you were ok.'

I dig my hands in my pockets. 'To be honest, the thought of telling them I fell off isn't easy.' I disclose. 'I was clean for five years.'

He shrugs. 'They will just be happy to hear from you. You got a good sponsor?'

'Yeah, someone I've known for a long time.'

He offers a sympathetic grin. 'You're on the right track.'

'I hope so.'

He pats me on the back. 'We're stronger than we think.'

'Listen,' I step closer. 'I was hoping you could help me with something.'

Scepticism flashes in his eyes. 'Work?'

'I need to reach out to someone.'

His expression falls flat. 'Someone unreachable, you mean?'

'Someone you're well acquainted with.'

Palmer looks over his shoulder before leaning in.

'Eden.'

His face breaks into a grin, chuckling for a few seconds before the realisation dawns on him. 'You're not serious?'

'I'm working an op. I need some information from him.'

'For what?'

'Can't say.'

'Eden isn't the sort of person you just bring a box of cookies to in prison, James.'

'Can you help?'

Engines hum as people fire up their cars. Palmer looks back to the car park, his legs practically twitching to leave. 'There's no way I can get you a face-to-face.'

'A call will do fine.'

'It will have to be recorded, as per prison regulations.'

'No can do. This has to be off-book.'

'I'm retired, James.'

'We both know you've got the contacts.'

'Fuck… you're still pushing the limits.'

'I'm not recruiting him if that's what you're thinking.'

'Eden will run rings around both of us. The fact he's in prison is a minor miracle, I won't do anything to jeopardise that.'

'I'm under no illusion but you know I wouldn't ask if I didn't need to speak to him, Aron.'

'You need to remember that despite not being near a computer for nearly three years, he is still one of the most dangerous men in the world.'

'Not something I will ever forget.'

'Give me a few days.' He nods. 'I'll see what I can do.'

'I owe you.'

He raises his eyebrows, backing away. 'Big time!'

I watch him leave, breathing out the tension in my body. *It's a risk but one I'm willing to take to get ahead.* The moment of relief is short-lived when a slender figure steps into my peripheral vision. I would recognise the overpowering scent of Chanel No. 5 anywhere. My mother stands ahead, her long raven locks falling over frail shoulders. Her chocolate brown eyes regard me with superior judgement as if she's already holding back something she's desperate to say. I catch the falseness in her smile and suddenly realise I've never seen her without lipstick on. She's a very attractive woman, Camina James. Made all the more striking by her expensive designer clothes and overpriced handbags. My father has always proudly labelled her the picture of perfection. Never a hair out of place. For someone who is supposed to be in the business of helping others, she sure spends a lot of time on herself.

'Hello Darling.'

'What are you doing here?' I ask curtly. *Edward must have sent her to pry.*

'It's lovely to see you too after so long.' She steps in for a hug, her skeletal body digging into me. 'You look better. Given up drinking again, I see.' She kisses me on the cheek, rolling her eyes when I wipe her lipstick away. 'Is that the flavour of the month?' Her eyes switch to Lex. 'Will she say hello?'

I exhale. 'Why are you here?'

'Have you spoken with your father?'

'Not recently.'

'He's worried. We both are.' She looks back at the hall with disapproval. 'AA groups can be triggering.'

'It works for most.'

'Not all.' She offers a pointed look.

'If you happen to find the cure to addiction, let me know.'

'Gabriel,' she sighs, disappointed, 'I've told you time and time again to come and see me, but you never take me up on it.'

'Because you haven't...'

She gives me a questioning look.

'You haven't found the cure.'

'How will you ever know?' Her phone rings. She looks down, beginning to rummage in her handbag. 'It's your sister. I'll call her in the car.' She eyes Lex again.

'Do you want me to introduce you?'

'Is it serious?'

'Yes.'

'Do you think you're in love with her?'

'Yes.'

'Another time.' She offers a smile that doesn't reach her eyes. 'I've got a client in an hour. A child whose parents are divorcing. She's awfully upset, keeps scratching hateful words into her skin. Trauma really is very sad in children...' She murmurs, searching for her phone again. 'Right better call Lily back. *You* could call us every now and again.'

'I'm relatively busy.'

'Hmm.' She narrows her eyes in Lex's direction. 'I thought you liked thin women.'

'Excuse me?'

'All your ex-girlfriends were tiny, darling. Model thin, like your sister. It's what you're used to.'

'I went to an all-boys boarding school.'

'What about that one at Cambridge... she was gorgeous.'

'You think I should get back with her?'

She offers a dismissive look. 'You're very handsome, you really could have anyone you wanted.'

'Ok... well, this has been nice.'

'Gabriel.' She crosses her arms, looking pensive. 'Are you happy?'

'I was until about ten minutes ago.'

She tuts disapprovingly. 'You may refuse to make an effort with me but you're still my son and I know when you're not... settled.'

And yet despite being one of the world's leading psychologists, you still do fuck all about it. Just like Janie. 'I'm good, Camina.'

'Mummy will suffice.' She sighs. 'Honestly, Gabriel, petulance is usually a cry for attention.' She pauses. 'Will that girl look after you?'

'We look after each other.'

She shrugs, giving up on the conversation. *Finally.*

'I've got to go.'

'It would be good to meet her properly.'

'I have a feeling you've all you need to know.'

'Goodbye, Gabriel.' She drops her gaze, tapping at her mobile.

Wandering over to Lex, I take a deep breath and look up to the sky, silently asking the Universe what the fuck it thinks it's doing to me.

'Everything ok?' She asks, her tone wary.

'Unbelievable.'

'You want to talk about it?'

I peer over my shoulder. My mother remains on the phone, pacing in front of her car, her forehead wrinkled with displeasure.

'Maybe later.'

'And the meeting?'

'Tough.'

She nods, aware that I'm not in a sharing mood. She steps forward, placing her hands on my face. 'You're a very impressive man, Gabriel James.'

'Not to her.' I utter, surprised by my own words.

'She doesn't see you, but she doesn't need to. Because I do.' She holds my gaze for a moment. 'You know you can talk to me about anything. I will never judge.'

'I know.' I offer her a small smile, grateful that she offered to wait here. 'Any news?'

She drops her hands and climbs into the driver's side. 'Keys has located Ludmilla Rumkova. She used her credit card at a café in Harrow. He managed to track her from there. She's staying in some seedy B&B.'

'He's good.' I mutter, impressed. 'No word from Mesrine, I take it?'

'Radio silence.' She twists her mouth, staring ahead. 'Gabriel, I was jealous.' She turns. 'Really jealous.'

I smile, taking her hand. 'I know.'

'And it's my own fault. I left to give you a life, to give you freedom, it was yours to do whatever you wanted. I had no hold over you.'

'You always have a hold over me. Since the moment I saw you crouched by that broken bike in Cambridge.'

She glances up at me, a softness returning to her golden eyes. 'She's still banned from The Athena.'

'I can't imagine she'll be going anytime soon.' I pull her into me. 'There's no place for her between us...' I'm cut off by the sudden buzzing of my pocket. I slide out my phone and put it on speaker. 'Yep?'

'Update! We managed to locate Smart.' Collins announces, her voice urgent. 'He's been abroad. His plane lands at Heathrow Terminal 5, 6pm.'

CHAPTER FORTY-EIGHT

ALEXANDRA

'*Smart lands in a private aircraft.*' Collins' voice calls through my earpiece. '*He'll be escorted from the plane to a private lounge, taken through passport patrol and into a waiting car. There's roughly a fifty-metre stretch where he will be accessible, just after the border, before he reaches the car. OVER.*'

'*I'd say you have just under thirty seconds to place the burner phone and tracker on his person.*' Gabriel adds; his voice conveying just how much he hates this plan. He's already made it through security and currently waiting in departures.

'*TECH, do you have eyes? OVER.*'

'*Surveillance feed from your body cam is good.*' Keys responds. '*Meyer is canvasing CCTV for any unwanted company.*'

'*All looks clear from down here so far.*' Gabriel observes.

'*I'd suggest you clear security on the south side.*' Meyer instructs. '*It'll be quicker.*'

'*Your TAC comms won't trigger anything, but you just have to avoid going through the body image scanner.*' Gabriel says. '*If you don't set off the first screener, you'll be fine.*'

'*After you're through,*' Meyer continues, '*head towards Gabriel at Gate 14. There's a fire exit opposite the Gate. Let us know when you're there and Michael will disable the alarm. Once you go through that door, you'll reach a corridor. Smart will cross that hall after passport control in roughly half an hour.*'

'*Thanks.*' I murmur, carefully weaving my way through the crowd of trolleys and suitcases. '*Sounds simple enough.*'

'*Unless Smart recognises you before you can even get close.*'
Gabriel mutters. '*In which case, you just have to get back to me at Gate 14. We have an exit plan.*'

'*Roger that.*'

Reaching security, I watch the faces of eager and excited holidaymakers; some rifling through their hand luggage, others using their boarding passes as a fan to beat the stifling heat, a few people frantically stuffing liquids into clear plastic bags.

'*How's it looking? OVER.*'

'*No outside interference. You're clear.*' Meyer replies.

I reach up to take my baseball cap off when two heavily armed airport officers appear on the other side of the screeners. They stand with dead straight backs, their fingers resting on the triggers of their huge guns, their eyes scouring the crowds, canvasing the area with determined precision. A short, bald man dressed in a black and purple *Heathrow Airport* uniform loudly instructs me to remove my hat and place it in the tray. Stalling for time, I begin patting my pockets, pretending I've mislaid something. True to form, the travellers behind me begin tutting and sighing at my lack of airport etiquette.

'Madam!' The bald man's voice becomes more shrill and impatient. 'Please remove the hat.'

I raise my head, offer a quick smile and throw the cap in the tray. Heathrow's *Employee of the Year* offers a satisfied nod before moving on to his next victim.

With subtlety, I return my attention to the armed officers as I collect my bag. The stockier, slightly paler of the two positions himself in my direction. I slowly look away, busying myself with my rucksack and searching for my boarding pass. Eventually, I swing the bag over my shoulder, replace the hat and walk straight past them with a relaxed pace. There's no reason for either of them to recognise me but my heart is still thrashing in my chest, my stomach burning with anxiety.

'*I'm through.*' I whisper, passing a group of students in matching Jesus hoodies. '*Going down to departures now.*'

'*We see you on the feeds.*' Keys replies. '*You've got twenty minutes until Smart lands. OVER.*'

'*Just enough time for a Wagamama's.*' I joke, feeling an overall sense of relief as I approach the escalator.

'*What's your order?*' Keys asks. '*I always start with the chilli squid.*'

I stop.

My body freezes.

'*Alex?*' Keys voice rings in my ear.

I meet the cold stare of the man standing ten metres away. I know that face. His dark and unnaturally detached eyes watch me, like he's been waiting for my arrival. A smirk dances on the corner of his lips. A look that says he knows things beyond anyone else's comprehension. I want to tear my eyes away, but I can't. I won't because that's what he wants. He wants me to wilt in his presence. He wants weakness. He wants fear. Finally, he nods, offering a salute before turning with casual ease and disappearing into the crowd.

'*Lex?*' Gabriel presses. '*What's going on?*'

'*VIPER.*' I murmur, taking a second to gather my thoughts. '*He's here.*'

'*What? The suspect from Port Latakia?*' Gabriel demands.

'*Yes. The unidentified suspect. The tall, creepy guy. OVER.*'

'*Alexandra…*' Collins stutters. '*Are you sure?*'

Adrenaline kicks in. My brain snaps to attention. '*It's definitely him.*'

'*Describe him to me.*' Gabriel orders.

'*White male. Pale. Roughly six foot, perhaps a little taller. Navy blue long-sleeve shirt, jeans. He's headed towards the shuttle.*'

'*Got it.*' Keys interjects. '*I'm following someone who matches his description on the feeds. Tracking him through departures. OVER.*'

'*Tell me where he's headed.*' Gabriel adds.

'*You both need to get out of there.*' Collins announces urgently. '*If VIPER has seen you, this op is compromised. It's not safe to approach Smart.*'

'*Forget Smart.*' Gabriel insists. '*This is the priority.*'

I march quickly towards the shuttle, shoving my way through a heavy stream of people. '*We need to find him, Alison. That man is a threat to everyone standing in this airport. He's connected to Almasi. We need to bring him in.*'

'*Jesus Christ.*' Meyer whispers. '*It's confirmed. The images on CCTV match our images at Port Latakia.*'

'*Keys, you need to figure out how he checked in, what passport, what flight.*' Gabriel commands.

'*You two have another problem.*' Keys informs.

'*What the hell is bigger than this?*' I say, searching through the mob of travellers.

'*There's a special ops team on site, headed in your direction.*'

'*Where?*' I turn over my shoulder. '*Who?*'

'*Just passed through security. Am cross-checking their faces with our database profiles. You and Gabriel need to lay low.*'

Fuck. I swerve into a shop, feigning interest in a stack of swimsuits.

'*Lex where are you?*' Gabriel asks.

'*I'm in Reiss. Trying to maintain cover. You?*'

'*Men's restroom.*' Gabriel whispers. '*I think I saw the suspect come in here. Keys, can you confirm?*'

'*On it.*' Keys replies.

'*Negative.*' Gabriel says suddenly. '*It's not him.*'

'*I think we've lost him.*' Meyer informs regretfully.

'*You both need to get out.*' Collins insists. '*If you're not back at this van in five minutes, I'll drag you out. The lead is dead. OVER.*'

Ignoring her, I exit and briskly walk along the next parade of shops. '*Gabriel, your position. OVER.*'

'*I'm headed towards Gate 14. VIPER might be here for Smart. It's a long shot.*'

'*Keys, Meyer, you need to find him again.*' I request. '*Forget the special ops team, make this a priority. OVER.*'

'*We're trying. OVER.*'

'*TAC team lead operative is Agent John Rikers.*' Meyer declares. '*He works in the Special Activities division for Defence Intelligence.*'

'*Rikers....*' I say, recalling the name.

'*You know him?*' Gabriel asks.

'*He was part of an op I worked in Afghanistan.*'

'*Alex, he's coming up on your six.*' Keys reveals. '*There's a Boots Pharmacy on your left, get in there. Rikers will pass you with his team. He won't see you. OVER.*'

'*Roger that.*' I dip into the aisle, keeping watch on the shop's entrance.

John Rikers. In 2016, Rikers' black ops squad were helping the CIA locate Taliban explosive sites. Rikers and his team stumbled upon an IED factory in the mountains. They were ambushed. Simon Haines, Wayne Gibbs and I were assigned to an extraction op. When we got there, Rikers was the only one left.

'*He's passing you in five, four, three, two....*' Keys pauses. '*He's stopped. Alex, they've all stopped.*'

'*What are they doing?*' Gabriel's voice increases in pitch.

'*Alex, you need to get out of there.*' Keys voice urges. '*They've stopped outside the shop.*'

'*I'm on my way!*' Gabriel says urgently.

'*No, stand down. Don't come here.*'

'*They're there for you, Alex.*' Keys informs quickly. '*GCHQ received a red flag alert just seconds ago. You were identified through CCTV at Heathrow. Special Activities is coming for you.*'

I watch the shop's entrance, waiting for Rikers and his heavies to pile around the corner. '*Gabriel stay where you are. Do not come in here. Keys, there's a black book under my bed. It has every useful contact in the criminal underworld. Everyone my father ever helped. You'll need that network.*'

'*Lex... stop,*' Gabriel implores. '*Nothing is happening to you.*'

It's the last thing I hear before pulling my earpiece out, crunching the device under my foot. An alarm sounds above my head. Shutters begin descending at the shop's entrance. Ten operatives surround me, quickly filing under the metal, their expressions unreadable, their faces covered by thick, black balaclavas that reveal nothing but their dead stares. Each of their guns is aimed at me, their fingers poised on the triggers. One of the TAC team lurches forward, yanking my arms behind my back, buckling my knees until I drop to the floor. My hands are cuffed, my head tugged backwards so my eyes land on the tall, statuesque man looming above me. He looks different in a suit; somehow more intimidating than when he was wearing full military combat gear and holding an AK47. He crosses his arms, regarding me without warmth or recognition. But the scar that marks his top lip confirms his identity. *Agent John Rikers.*

CHAPTER FORTY-NINE

ALEXANDRA

The door opens. The room illuminates. I lift my head from the table and straighten my shoulders as much as my cuffed hands will allow. John Rikers throws a thick file on the table before taking a seat. His sudden movements send a wave of cheap aftershave across the room. He opens the file without looking up. My eyes trace the scar across his top lip. It almost forms a perfect *S* shape. If the shooter had been six inches to the left, John Rikers would be dead. The bullet merely grazed him. It still caused enough damage for him to have the lower half of his face reconstructed but at least he has one. Finally, he looks up. He has the same almond-shaped brown eyes as Gabriel, just with more intensity and less warmth. He stares at me with contempt. I don't know what I expected. Nothing about Rikers has ever been friendly. He's all hardness and authority. Even when thanking me for saving his life, he offered a handshake. We'd been stuck in the mountains together for over ten days. You expect that experience warrants a hug, at the very least.

'I find it disappointing for us to be sat on opposite sides of this table, Christofi.'

'Well, I'm sorry to hear that John.'

He sighs, opening the file. 'Do you know why you're here?'

'Catch up? For old times sake…'

'This will go easier if you-'

'Why don't you tell me why I'm here, rather than us wasting time playing a guessing game.'

'You booked a flight to Turin under an alias.'

'Did I?'

'Carla Borino.'

316

'Never heard of her.'

'That flight ensured you were in Terminal 5 at the same time the Defence Secretary was travelling back from a state visit.'

'I don't have access to his iCal. So I wouldn't know.'

'What were you doing in the terminal?'

'Do you interrogate every ex-soldier leaving the country?'

He starts reading from a list. 'Bahrain, Jordan, Saudi, Syria, Qatar, Turkey, Cyprus. Quite the year you've been having.'

'I like the Middle East.'

'I would have thought you'd maxed out your time there.'

'It's always sunny.'

He scoffs. 'Up until a month ago, you were a ghost. No record of residence, no employment details, no travel history. Not a peep since you left the army.'

'You've been looking me up.'

'I like to keep tabs on people I've worked ops with.' He pulls several images from the file. 'Suddenly, you're on the system and wow....' He whistles through his teeth. 'Your record paints quite the picture.' He slides over a picture of Diren Paytak's body lying on a gurney in the morgue. 'An intelligence informant, shot dead by you.'

'Paytak was, in fact, a criminal who was trafficking children....'

He drops a second picture in front of me. I'm walking beside Kristine Kingley on Southgate High Street. 'Links to the disappearance and subsequent murder of Kristine and Samantha Kingley.' He retrieves a handful of CCTV snapshots. I'm standing next to Tino Caruso in Hotel De Paris. The other shows me talking to Raheem Kamani in reception. A final image presents me following Gabriel down the corridor to his hotel room. This has Edward James all over it. Not only has he made my records public, he's planted evidence so every intelligence agency in the world is on my back.

Rikers taps his index finger on Tino's face. 'Caruso is the facilitator of the Taliban's opium trade in Europe. Raheem Kamani is an ex-intelligence agent, wanted for defecting to Syria. And this….' He lifts the image of myself and Gabriel. A picture that thankfully only shows the back of his head. 'If I found out who this man is, I'm certain it would tell an interesting story.'

'I'll save you the time. He was a one-night stand.'

'Seems convenient.'

'I'll tell you what's convenient… how all of this intel just became available out of the blue. Don't you think that's a little odd?'

He stares at me for a beat, clearly considering the question. 'What is your interest in the Defence Secretary?'

'He's not my type, sorry.'

'There are no flights from this airport booked in your name.'

'You're kidding?' I roll my eyes. 'God, some airlines are just useless.'

'This isn't a joke, Christofi.' He sits up in his seat, pulling at the collar of his suit jacket. 'You're connected to the death of a minister in the Home Office, then you just so happen to be in the same place as the Defence Secretary, at the same time, twice in less than ten days.'

'What is the Defence Secretary so worried about?'

Rikers swallows slowly, his eyes betraying his discomfort for less than a second before he clears his throat and returns his gaze to the file. 'Would you like to know what I think?' He sits back in his chair and crosses his arms. 'I think you gave everything and more to your country. You fought battles that our own government didn't understand. You risked your life over and over. Paid other people's debts. Yet the army still got rid of you when they found out who your father was. All the good you'd achieved was erased because of your surname. They labelled you a gangster's daughter and that was it.

Erased. And now I think you use your skills in other ways. I think you're a mercenary to the highest bidder. There is no loyalty to your country. That has long passed. It's about money.'

'Who would the highest bidder be in this instance, John?'

He hesitates. Then it hits me. Granted, John Rikers is a square and socially inept but he's a stand-up citizen. He's never been corrupt, it's not in his makeup. He wouldn't protect Smart's misdeeds. He doesn't know the truth about the MOD and the Compliancy program. This is about something else. There has to have been a threat made against Jed Smart. Something that's got Riker's special activities team looking into everyone his boss has interacted with recently.

'I can't tell you the truth if you don't explain why I'm here.'

'Who are you working for now?'

'I would never work for anyone that intended to harm this country, let's put it that way.'

'That remains to be seen.'

'If you think you know so much about me, Rikers, why don't you take a look at my military file, the testing, the psyche evaluations? Do you think I would have been accepted to my unit had they believed I was capable of working against my country?'

'You passed all your psyche tests.' He concedes, flicking through the folder in front of him. 'You also achieved 99% on the military aptitude tests and 99% in all your physicals, even beating some of the men in your class.'

'What a modern perspective....'

'You were the smartest person to graduate in the history of the SAS. Your metrics were so high you had MI6, MI5, GCHQ knocking on your door. But you refused them. Why?'

'What has my career choice got to do with anything?'

'You had the potential to put your mind to good use.'

'I didn't want to be sat behind a desk.'

'You wanted to be on the ground?'

'Exactly.'

'Which provided you direct access to multiple high-value targets and enemies.'

'Right…' I exhale, understanding exactly where this is going. 'You think I choose B- Squad because I was planted from the beginning to infiltrate a SAS tactical unit, get access to contacts in the Middle East, China, Russia and trade intelligence secrets.'

'Your father had quite the criminal network.'

'Yeah well, I paid the price for that. The army eventually kicked me out.'

'I've read Sergeant Haines' reports on your performance during yearly training exercises.'

'I passed every single one, consistently.'

'He writes that you have trouble controlling your emotions.'

'Who do you think convinced Haines and Gibbs to carry you through the Afghani mountains when you could barely breathe through your fucking mouth? They wanted to leave you, John. That's what becomes of people who switch off their emotions.'

'You're very good at what you do. I'm just doing my due diligence to ensure you're on the right side of this.'

'The side of what!' I shout, slamming my fist against the desk before trying to slow my own breathing. 'Tell me why I am here.'

He takes a breath to reply but a swift knock on the door draws his attention away. He stands, allowing his chair to fly back against the wall. It's the only sign he's rattled. The door swings open before Rikers has time to reach it. A short man with broad shoulders and half-moon spectacles stands in the doorway. He, too, wears a suit. The jacket is double-breasted, which makes him look squarer than the average person. He has long grey hair, which has been carefully combed away from his face. The gel shines brightly under the harsh lights.

'Paul Brown, Director of Security Appointed Intelligence, Secret Intelligence Service.' He flashes his identity card. 'I do apologise for the intrusion. I believe your team have been notified.'

'We were told S.A.I.B.R would be sending a full team.'

'Just me and two of my agents behind the glass.' He offers a quick reassuring smile but his eyes spell haste. 'Whilst I appreciate you are simply carrying out your duty here Agent, my division received intel that a key suspect to our international investigation was in Heathrow today. We dispatched our Agent here, who's an MI6 registered asset.' He gestures towards me. 'Everything you need to sign the asset over to us is in your office.'

Flustered, Rikers looks between Brown and the mirrored interrogation glass as if waiting for someone to intervene. 'With all due respect, Director, I'm going to need some time to go through the paperwork, and to discuss this with-'

'I invite you to take your time, of course.' Brown gestures to the door. 'Obviously, a fair bit of it is redacted, we're not able to disclose all the details but my agents will provide you with a sworn statement from the Prime Minister that this asset is under our charge.' Brown motions to the thick file resting on the desk. 'With regards to whatever offences you are here to discuss. It would be worth noting that these are covered under Section 29B of the Regulation of Investigative Powers Act. Our asset has immunity whilst in our charge as an undercover officer. It's all in there.'

Rikers frowns. 'Right.'

'I'll need a few minutes alone with my agent if you wouldn't mind.'

Rikers swallows, his throat bobbing with concern. Finally, he nods, muttering something about contacting his superiors before leaving the room. Brown listens by the door, waiting for the sound of Rikers' footsteps to dull before taking a seat.

'We have roughly ten minutes, give or take.'

'Out of the frying pan and into the fire...' I mutter, feeling dejected. 'You work for S.A.I.B.R.'

'I know who you are.' He clasps his hands together, his eyes intent on mine. 'And we both know who put you here.'

'Edward.'

He nods. 'He's an opportunist.'

'Why stick your neck out for me?'

'There's an impending terrorist attack involving all major London airports.' He straightens. 'We've been watching carefully.'

'Ok....'

'Which is how I know you saw VIPER today.'

'Do you know where he is?'

He shakes his head.

'His identity?'

'We suspect his name is Andrew Magnusson.'

'Magnusson...'

'You've heard that name before.'

I nod. 'Ex- British Intelligence. Was supposed to have died in the 7/7 bombings. He used to own the lab facility just outside of Monaco before it was declared derelict. You don't think he's dead?'

'We do not.'

'Why are you telling me this?'

'Because...' he sighs. 'We can't seem to get a grasp on this thing. And we're running out of time.'

'You cannot let them win.'

'Yes, well... it appears no matter how many obstacles are put in your way, you invariably inch closer to the truth.'

'All the intel I have, you have. You have everything from the facility. You have Flint. You have all his correspondence with Smart.'

'A few weeks ago, Gabriel stood in my office and assured me you were the best at what you do. An ex-SAS soldier with no ties, no responsibilities.'

'I'm just one person.'

'And yet you do not give up.'

I scoff. 'You know how many men have sat opposite me like this, stroking my ego, telling me they need me or how much their division could use someone like me? I'm not cutting a deal.'

He chuckles. 'No deals, no rules. My division doesn't exist. And neither do you.'

'So what is it you want?'

He lifts himself from the seat briefly, pulling something from his back pocket. 'Is this the man you saw today?'

I stare at the image. It's a grainy headshot. It's bad quality but I can still make out the shape of the face, the eyes and the SIS polo top. He looks younger, less weathered. His gaze carries more energy. 'That's him.'

'This was taken during Magnusson's first week in the service. And it's the only image of him that exists. There are no digital copies.'

'He worked hard to wipe his existence from the world.'

'The Defence Minister, Jed Smart, was due to travel back to London Heathrow from a visit to Jordan this evening.'

'But something tells me he didn't make it back to London, did he?'

'What do you know?'

I shrug. 'It would explain why I'm being held by Defence Intelligence.'

'He's dead.' He waits, watching the information sink in. 'His plane was bound for Jordan. He arrived, carried out the first two days of his ministerial duties. Three days ago, he cancels everything else. He travels to Damascus by car. Checked into a hotel. Sometime after that, he died.'

'Cause of death?'

'Not determined. His body was flown home from Syria today.'

'That's how Edward got Rikers on my case.'

Brown holds up his index finger. 'We both know Jed Smart was purchasing special ops agents called Compliants on the black market from The Singularity. And we both know he was training them to work for the MOD. Smart was a key witness to help us bring down Higgs.'

'It's either The Singularity or Almasi who are responsible.'

'Precisely.' Brown stands from his chair, beginning to pace the room. 'And I have to choose whether my division intends to win the battle or the war.' His words create a chill in the air. He shakes his head as if the defeat has already occurred. 'With the help of Higgs and The Singularity….Almasi is going to destroy our home. That's my battle. It's the battle of every domestic intelligence division in this country.'

'You said it involved airports… Hadid Waqif mentioned something similar to David Fallows.'

'Using Compliants, Almasi is going to stage four attacks. These Compliants are going to rig bombs to trains arriving at London airports. The goal is to create the ultimate chaos. My team are working with SO15 to determine who Almasi will be using and how these attacks will take place. The PM has signed off on every resource we have at our fingertips to ensure we stop this. But ultimately, with our efforts on this, we're ignoring the head of the snake.'

'You need a team who will go after Magnusson.'

'Intel suggests that Andrew Magnusson has been in this country for the duration of Smart's trip.' Brown takes a deep inhale, considering his next words. 'And just so happened to be at Terminal 5 at the same time the Defence Secretary's plane landed.'

'That is no coincidence.'

'We don't know who Smart met in Syria. But whoever it was, it was likely on the instruction of Magnusson. And it got him killed.'

'Syria is where everything originated. The camps, the shipments, now Smart's death.'

'Syria is a lot to contend with, Alexandra. It's not just The Singularity. You've got MI6 ops all over the place. SO15 undercover agents. CIA black sites. It's a political minefield.'

'Which is why you won't send any of your own agents out there.'

'Like I said, my division doesn't exist and that's how it has to stay.'

'Which is why you want me to go, presumably.'

'I'm under no illusion that you've been operating alone. You will have to tell the others to stay behind.'

'You know as well as I do that won't happen.'

He looks at the floor, a semblance of sadness crossing his brow. 'I have nothing to offer you, Alexandra. No support, no immunity, no resources.'

'I understand.'

'If you get caught by ISIS, you're on your own. Run into Syrian rebels, you're on your own. Picked up by another agency, you're-'

'I get it.' I look up at Paul Brown, meeting his eyes. 'I know the probability of making a return journey.'

'At least try to convince James and Collins to stay put.'

'They lost out to The Singularity too. It's their fight just as much as mine.'

He takes a long breath before nodding slightly.

'No matter what happens. I'll go to Syria, I'll find Magnusson and I'll put an end to all of this. Just help us get out of the country, that's all I ask.'

CHAPTER FIFTY

GABRIEL

The captain switches on the seatbelt sign as Tino Caruso's private plane hits a pocket of turbulence. The small aircraft rattles from side to side, shaking vigorously through the clouds. Collins whimpers opposite me, gripping the armrests. Lex presses her forehead against the window, staring at the wing whilst clutching my hand with white knuckles.

'It will stop soon.' I reassure her.

She turns and flits her tense eyes to mine.

'And if we go down; the g-force will knock you out anyway.'

'For fuck's sake...' Her lips lift. 'You're so annoying.'

'It's not like you've spent years jumping out of planes.'

'Precisely, it's the sitting in them I don't like.'

'Your luggage could be the issue.' I smirk. 'Didn't they teach you to pack efficiently in the army?'

'Yeah and it was a pain in the arse.' She rolls her eyes. 'Anyway, you have OCD.'

'Thank God one of us does.'

'Are you done?' She throws her hand over my mouth.

'Not nearly.' I lean down to kiss her.

Collins loudly clears her throat, breaking the moment.

'Shouldn't the pills you took have knocked you out by now?'

'They're not ketamine, Gabriel.'

'Shame...' Keys whispers with his eyes closed.

'Got any spare?' Lex asks.

Collins rummages in her handbag, popping a white pill from the sleeve before handing it over. 'People in glass houses...' She raises her eyebrows at me, catching the disapproval on my face.

'Pills were never my thing.'

'These help me relax.'

'Did you have a bad flying experience?' Lex asks.

'Never liked it.' Collins explains. 'And I had a terrible landing in Nice. What about you?'

'I was in a helicopter crash in Afghanistan.'

'Show off.' Collins utters under her breath.

'Should we get this briefing underway?' Emily leans forward, politely trying to get everyone's attention. 'That will be a good distraction.'

'Yep, let's.' Keys punches in a code on a small iPad.

'What we know so far is that Jed Smart is dead.' Collins begins. 'Allegedly killed in Damascus. Imran Almasi is planning a large-scale attack on all major airports in London using Compliants. And lastly, we all suspect that Augustus Fox, the founder of A Better World, is actually Andrew Magnusson, the British Intelligence operative who supposedly died in the 7/7 attacks.'

'Who is Higgs?' Aldyn interjects over the aisle. 'You have discovered Fox, Magnusson, Flint, Smart. But how do they connect to Higgs?'

'One of them must be Higgs.' Emily suggests. 'Higgs has to be a code name for something.'

'Keys, can you update us on the intel Brown shared about Smart.' Collins requests.

He squints at his screen. 'Paul Brown claims Smart travelled from Jordan to Syria, more specifically Damascus, to meet a contact with supposed links to The Singularity and the Compliancy program. I've narrowed down a 17-hour window of when Smart checked into the Hotel Dame Rose and then when the Syrian Security Forces were called to the property due to reports of a death. Cause of death is listed as a heart attack.'

'That window will help us determine who else might have been around at that time.' Collins says enthusiastically. 'Good work, Michael.'

'I've run a check on all guests that would have been staying in the hotel at the time and nothing stands out. I'll need to spend this evening going through CCTV. Any help would obviously be appreciated.'

'Yeah, we can do it in shifts.' Lex suggests. 'I'm certain Smart was murdered. He was in good health according to the medical records Keys obtained.'

'Exactly.' Keys agrees. 'Someone in that hotel knows something.'

'Another reason why Syria is important...' Emily interjects, gesturing for Keys to hand her the iPad. 'S.A.I.B.R found evidence on Flint's laptop that he was tasked with prepping Almasi's Compliants for explosives training. Flint was running some sort of immersive program. Emails from Almasi mention a facility in the Syrian desert.'

'Could that have meant Za'atari camp?' I ask.

'I think this is different.' She clarifies.

'That could be where Andrew Magnusson creates Compliants.' Lex suggests. 'And that could also be where he is right now.'

Lex stands as soon as the seatbelt sign is switched off, mumbling something about needing the toilet. Watching her climb over me, Keys quickly unclips himself and follows; both of them disappearing to the back of the plane.

'Before you start...' Collins says, eyeing me. '*You* are more Michael's type than Alexandra is.'

'Did I say anything?'

Keys returns after a few minutes, settling back into his seat. 'Alex just had to run something past me.'

'Got stuck in the loo.' Lex says, appearing a moment later.

'Keys said you had to run something past him...Was it how to unlock the door?'

'Should have got your stories straight.' Collins mutters.

I stand from my seat, mere inches from Lex's face. 'Let's talk for a minute.'

Lex closes the door to the small bedroom cabin and leans against it, her face filled with unease. 'Look, it's not important. I'm just asking Keys for a fav....

'I don't care.' I grip her shirt and pull her towards me.

She grins, surprised. 'So *this* is what you wanted to talk about?'

'Yesterday, I thought I would never see you again.' I mutter, lightly grazing my mouth against her lips. 'Today, we're on a suicide mission and we've got about 15 minutes before we land in Cyprus for the layover. Time is of the essence.'

'We need to have a proper chat about Brown, Gabriel. I need you to know the stakes...'

'Later...' I carefully pick her up and perch her on the edge of the dressing table. Towering over her, I grip her hips and gently pull her into me, craving the feel of her body against mine. I tilt her chin to meet my gaze before taking her mouth, my tongue finding hers in an instant. She moans, wrapping a hand around the back of my head, her breathing becoming more urgent as she begins to fumble with the buttons of her shirt.

'Let me...' I whisper, grabbing the material and ripping it open, quickly discarding the top on the floor.

She enfolds her legs around me, laughing a hot, breathy exhalation as her long hair flows down her bare back. Dropping to my knees, I begin snaking my tongue down her chest, grazing the swell of her nipple with my teeth, urgently seeking to taste other parts of her.

She whispers my name, her fingertips digging into my skin, her nails tearing at my shoulders.

'Gabriel?'

I straighten, looking over my shoulder.

Lex bolts into a seated position.

'Gaaaabriel?' Collins' voice calls out again.

With my heart still racing, I follow the sound of her voice to the ceiling, locating a tannoy speaker tucked in the corner.

'James?'

Irritated, I slam my finger on the intercom. 'Yeah?' I try to calm my heavy breathing. 'What is it?'

'We're due to land at Episkopi base any moment.'

'We'll be out in a minute.'

'Clearly you'd both forgotten where you were...' Her disapproval oozes through the speaker.

'Gabriel...' Lex whispers, zipping up her jeans. 'I need another top.' She gestures to the buttons discarded all over the floor.

'Your suitcase is in the hold.'

'You always keep a spare T-shirt on you.'

'How do you know that?'

'I know you.'

'You want me to go back out there alone?'

'Oh my God...' She grins. 'You're scared of Collins!'

'Aren't you?!'

'Please go and get the shirt.'

'Fine.'

Predictably, Collins' judgemental glare greets me when I return to my seat. I peer down at the dishevelled neckline of my T-shirt and quickly realign it before running a hand through my hair with a wry smile.

'You needn't think you're amusing.' She grumbles.

After a few minutes, Lex marches out of the cabin, holding her broken top together before snatching my rucksack off the floor.

'I forgot.' I add apologetically.

'Everything alright?' Keys looks up, waving an index finger at Lex. 'Your shirt looks a little…'

'Shut up Michael.'

'No, it's just you seem to have lost some… Ow! Fuck.' He clutches his leg.

Lex smiles back innocently, tossing her ripped top on my lap before throwing one of my crisp white T-shirts over her head.

'When we land in Cyprus, then what?' Keys asks, still rubbing his knee.

'We'll have to disembark and get escorted to the base whilst we wait for the clearance from Brown to enter Syrian airspace.' I reply.

'Remember that The Singularity aren't the only threat in Syria.' Lex says, taking her seat again. 'Trust nobody, say nothing, not even to the soldiers you speak to at Episkopi base. Everyone will be given a back story. You need to memorise it like your life depends on it.' She glances over to me. 'Because it does.'

CHAPTER FIFTY-ONE

ALEXANDRA

A heavy wave of exhaustion hits me as I close the door to Gabriel's hotel room and amble down the musky red corridor in search of the elevators. I said I couldn't sleep, suggesting I should go for a walk to clear my head. Being extremely tired himself, Gabriel didn't offer much protest and I assured him I didn't need company. He was half asleep when I left but I'm certain he still detected something was off. *He always does.* Checking over my shoulder, I let out a long sigh and reach to push the button for the lift, fiddling with my key card in my other hand. As I wait, my mind begins to wander; thinking about the next few days and what it will take to find Andrew Magnusson.

Sensing a lingering presence a few paces behind, I flit my eyes to the window at the end of the hall, checking the reflection. A blurred, petite figure stands a few metres back. *Emily.*

'Alexandra, can we talk?' She takes a few steps back and lets herself into her room, holding the door open for me.

I approach hesitantly. 'Sure...'

She drops onto the bed, clearly nervous. It's as if she's rehearsed a speech but can't figure out how to start. 'Gabriel recruited me for S.A.I.B.R., did you know that?'

'I did.' I lean against the wall opposite her.

She smiles. 'I was in awe of the fact he'd flown up the ranks at the NCA. Enlisted by MI6 to start his own taskforce at such a young age.' She falters. 'I don't recognise him anymore, to tell you the truth. Forgive me for saying this, Alexandra, but is that what becomes of the people around you?'

I look away, knowing there's truth in her words. 'Honestly, Emily… it's a question I've agonised over countless times.'

'That's why you left him.'

I nod.

'And yet here you both are.'

'He means the world to me.'

'But you're allowing him to chase something that you know cannot be beaten.'

'I have tried to do this without him. It's not what Gabriel wants. I have learnt to respect his choices.'

'And the rest of us?' She laughs, shaking her head. 'It's not like we can be heroes, right? Brown won't acknowledge we're even here. Win or lose, we'll just disappear into operational no man's land. Nobody will talk about what we hoped to do, what we wanted to achieve.'

'War has its own rules, Emily.'

'And what kind of war is this?'

'Brown might stop Almasi's attack in a few days, but he's under no illusion that someone else will crop up. He is merely treating the symptoms of Magnusson's existence. But until we cut the source away, the fight isn't finished.'

'I'm scared…' She whispers. 'I don't want to become nothing to my country because they think I went rogue.'

'I'm scared all the time.'

'But you did this for a living, and you survived.' She grips her fingers to her forehead. 'Every time you survived.'

'Every time I started an operation, I realised that nobody, not even my father, would know the truth of what I was doing or who I was fighting and why.'

'Then why did you continue? It's thankless. It must have caused you so much trauma, so much pain.'

'Because I looked at the team I was doing it with, and all I saw was bravery and strength. I wanted to be like that; to operate in the shadows. I wanted our enemies to be afraid in the same way they made innocent, helpless people afraid. Nobody at home would ever understand the sacrifices we made to keep them safe, the dangerous people we fought, the near misses, the suffering we went through. But we knew.' I place my hand on my chest. 'We knew that we were protecting our country, we knew what we did mattered. And deep down, my father would always know who I was, despite what anyone told him. It's good to have fear. It's real. It means you're strong.'

She grimaces. 'How can that be true?'

'You're still here, aren't you? You didn't run.'

'I desperately want to do this; I want to help those children, but I'm scared of the decisions I've made. I'm scared of the person who made those decisions.'

'*And* you're scared.'

She looks up, confused.

'You want to do this. You want to help those children *and* you're scared. Being scared doesn't erase the others.'

'Wow.' She scoffs. 'You had a really good therapist.'

I smile. 'I had a really good Dad.'

'I just don't feel I'm up to this.'

I turn to face her. 'You're the best forensic analyst MI6 has ever had. You're used to being exceptional. And this situation makes us all feel vulnerable. But the reason you're on this taskforce is because you are exceptional, Emily. You want to make a difference. Everything you do matters to all of us. Be scared.... I'm terrified. And it is a strength because it means you want to live. Living is so much harder than giving up.'

'Initially, I thought it made you hard, all the death and the pain.' She says as if the observation has just drifted into view. 'But it hasn't.'

'You just… you can't let it win.' I make to stand, holding out my hand to pull her up. 'You've got this. We're a team. And I want us to get out of this more than anyone. Trust me, I'm not here to di…'

The sharp ring of my phone cuts me off.

'One second…'

'Fuck me, I almost had a heart attack. I've been texting you like!' Keys whispers urgently. 'I nearly rang Gabe, and you know how that would have gone down.'

'I'll be with you in a minute, can you hold on?'

'No it's a go right now, Alex. The thing we spoke about on the plane…It's on.'

I swallow, my mouth turning dry. 'He's here… In Damascus?'

'Yes. Hotel Europa.'

'Did he come alone?' I murmur, glancing at Emily.

'He did.'

'I'll be there in ten.'

CHAPTER FIFTY-TWO

GABRIEL

Lily has a ladder in her tights. She keeps pulling her thick black dress down to try to cover it. My mother presses her hand over my sister's fingers, urging her to keep still.

'It got caught on the pew…' Lily whispers.

The music begins and my mother struggles to pull herself to stand, almost as if her knees might give out at any moment. I take Lily by the shoulders and force her to switch with me in case they do. She doesn't protest, likely, she knows what I'm doing. The violins come in with a slow, melodic sound. On the Nature of Daylight. Why did my parents have to choose something so sad? Janie would have hated the heavy melancholy of this event. Her favourite song was Dreams. The number of times I had to listen to Stevie Knicks singing the same thing, over and over. Now all I want to do is put it on and picture my sister jumping around the living room with that joyful look on her face.

My mother's shaking hands clutch her order of service as the precession makes its way down the middle of the church. An enlarged image of Janie stares at me. I look away, unable to bear seeing that bright, beautiful smile. We know the truth now. My sister wasn't smiling on the inside. The back of my father's head moves into view, his right shoulder props up the corner of the wicker coffin that holds Janie's body. I shift my gaze, grit my teeth and face forward. From the corner of my eye, I can see Lily looking up at me. My jaw is clamped so hard I feel my face shaking. She takes my hand, forcing my fingers apart. I squeeze hers tight, wishing I could transfer the agonising ache in my body, just for a moment. I twitch to my left, expecting to see Janie shuffle in next to Lily. I still look for her everywhere. We grew up as a three. Two feels like an unfinished sentence. Our triangle is missing a side.

Jesus Janie, I wish you would come back and alleviate this fucking horrible sadness inside of us. I'm desperate for you to know that I'm sorry. I'm sorry that in your last moments, I was so physically close but emotionally unreachable. I'm sorry I dismissed you that evening. I'm sorry I didn't see the signs. If I had just got out of my own head and looked up from the TV... If I had really thought about why you were lingering downstairs for so long when usually you run straight up to your room. You were looking for a reason to stay. I was meant to be the one to give it to you. I'm your big brother. I was meant to protect you. I failed you, Janie. I failed.

I let go of Lily's hand and wipe the tears from my face with the back of my clenched fist. Desperate for a distraction, I look over my shoulder. A tall, lanky, dark haired boy shuffles along a pew before he comes to stand against the wall in the corner. His suit looks too small for him. His wrists shooting out way beyond the length of the arms. He seems startled as we lock eyes. He looks around my age. How did he know Janie? Was he a friend?

'Gabriel!'

I sit up in bed and turn on the light, confused by the frantic hammering at the door.

'Who is it?' I run my hands over my face repeatedly, noting the moist remnants of tears. *I haven't dreamt about Janie in years.* Shaking my head clear of the memory, I check the time. *Three AM. What time did Lex leave?* The knock comes again, more urgent this time. 'What is it?' I growl, throwing back the duvet.

'Gabriel! I need to speak with you.'

Emily. 'Fuck.'

I pause, giving myself time to think. *Do we have to do this now?* Lex has been telling me to speak with her for days. Our last conversation seemed pretty final but out of respect it's only fair we try to draw a line under it properly. I hope she knows how much we need her on this team. Admittedly, I got caught up with everything in Italy and smoothing things over with her was low on the list. I yawn, trying to gather the energy before swinging the door open. 'Hey look, it's late… how about we…'

'Gosh, are you alright?' She looks up at me, her tone thick with worry.

I clear my throat. 'Why?'

'You don't look good, Gabriel.' Her accent makes it sound so matter-of-fact, like a GP delivering bad news to a patient.

'Thanks?' I move aside as she enters the room, frantically fiddling with the ends of her hair.

'We need to talk.'

I turn to face her. 'Yeah, look I'm sorry we haven't spoken…'

'Did Alexandra tell you where she was going?'

'Huh?'

'Who is she meeting?'

I hesitate. 'What are you talking about?'

She frowns, conflicted. 'She's gone.'

'I'm not following.'

'Alexandra has gone to meet someone.' She drops down on the edge of the bed. 'We were in my room. She got a call. Then she left.'

'What the fuck are you talking about?' I stalk to my phone, rip it from the charging cable and dial her mobile.

'She's gone, Gabriel.'

I dial again, waiting until it reaches voicemail.

'Are you hearing what I'm saying…'

Furious, I slam the phone down before frantically picking it up again and dialling for Keys. 'Where the fuck could she have gone in Syria?'

'She said *he* was in Damascus. Do you know who that could be?'

I look around the room, wracking my brains. 'I have no idea.'

'Did she say anything earlier?'

'She was here about an hour ago, I think.' I squint, trying to work it out. 'She said she needed a walk. I told her to stay in the hotel.'

'Well, she was with me for a bit and then she got the call.'

'It doesn't make any sense.'

'She must be somewhere in the city.'

'And you didn't hear a location. No hints of who she was meeting or where?'

'Europa...' She nods her head at the floor. 'I think the person on the phone said Hotel Europa.'

I open the wardrobe, rifling through drawers, trying to find clothes.

'Let me come with you!' She calls out. 'You don't know what you're walking into.'

'Stay here.' I rebut, quickly throwing on jeans and a T-shirt.

'You shouldn't go alone.'

'Go find Collins.' I stalk towards the door. 'Tell her what's happened, tell her I'm going to check it out and to stay near her phone.'

'It's not safe. Fox could know we're here.' She cries out, breathless. 'Gabriel, at least take Aldyn!'

CHAPTER FIFTY-THREE

ALEXANDRA

Damascus is an unforgiving place. That is what Simon always used to say. He had a knack for looking at the world with such pessimism. I guess you would if you spent ten years leading a squadron of elite killers. But I don't see what he saw. Despite the hour, various hotel guests drip in and out, none of them paying me much attention as I observe them from behind the black silk wrapped across my face. Two children read under a table whilst their parents share coffee, struggling to stay awake. Another woman sits alone, listening to music, and scribbling determinedly into a notebook. A group of teenage boys play cards, yelling enthusiastically now and again. There's an infectious buzz in the air. This is one of the oldest cities in the world, it's seen tragedy, endured pain but it's still here. Humanity is good at that, getting back up in the face of destruction. I sit at a table in the corner, watching the bar's entrance, my fingers tearing apart the edge of a sugar packet. A waitress, who looks too young to be working, approaches and asks if I'd like anything to eat. I respond that just a drink would be fine. She nods, telling me she'll fetch the menu. She returns quickly, handing me a laminated booklet.

'Two araks please.'

I look up, startled. I hadn't expected him this early.

'Are you trying to kill me?'

'I mean, it would only be fair.'

Wayne Gibbs takes a seat.

The waitress returns with two glasses of the strong anise spirit; the only booze we had to hand on every tour in the Middle East.

'Hello, Angel.' He winks.

He still has that strong, cockney accent. The one that could be heard above everyone else across camp, accompanied by that warm, wheezing chuckle. Wayne Gibbs settles into his chair before turning over his shoulder. 'You've deliberately sat me with my back to the door.'

I raise my eyebrows, regarding him with a smile.

'Smart cookie.' He says, nodding.

'You look well for a dead man.'

'Yeah, it's not all bad…' He looks around the bar.

'Still running?'

'On and off.'

Gibbs takes his drink, holding it up between us. 'To Charlie McGuire and *leaving it at the door*.'

A wave of sadness hits me. I hear McGuire's voice. The words he'd say after every op. The phrase that helped us put the killing aside when we returned home. My throat runs dry, picturing McGuire sitting across this table now. *God, I wish he was here to see this. Wayne Gibbs alive.*

'You know what happened to him?'

'I heard he'd passed…' he sighs. 'And I got word how.'

'He was far too good for this world.'

'It must have changed Rhiannon, what happened to us. I guess I got lucky.'

'The Foreign Office brought her home.'

'Did you put her down?'

I nod.

'You did what you had to.'

'And you… what happened to you?'

'I escaped.'

'When?'

342

'They were keeping me at some gaff in Beirut. Some high up in the Lebanese army. His place was attacked by the FSA. They took me.'

'I thought you said you escaped?'

'You bring me here at 3am to interrogate me, Alex?'

I shake my head quickly to protest.

'Nah, I'm messing...' he laughs. 'It was an escape...of sorts. Not at first. They were brutal fuckers. They've got their ways. We've got ours. But when they realised I was in Lebanon working towards the same goal...' He leans in, lowering his voice. 'When they understood that I hated Assad just as much, and the reason I was captured was because we were spying on the Hez lovers.' He straightens, 'Well, they softened up a bit. Things got better... they started to accept me as one of theirs.'

'They let you go?'

'About three years back.'

'But you stayed...'

'What did I have to go back to? Never had any family. B-Squad was my tribe. And for all I knew these past few years...you were all gone too.'

'We left you.' I clench my teeth together, trying to stop my mouth from shaking. 'We just left.'

'Haines gave orders. You followed.'

I roll my eyes. 'Especially me.'

'He had a hold on everyone. Not just you, Al.'

'God, Wayne. We shouldn't have left you there. It was wrong. It was-'

'Hey...' he reaches across the table. 'Don't do that. Guilt is useless. Gets nobody nowhere. It all turned out for the best. I have a life now. I have people that I care for. What I'm doing feels like the most important mission I've ever had.'

343

'You're helping the Free Syrian Army?'

He nods. 'When the FSA took me to their camp in the North. I met some boys; westerners who gave up their posts and decided to do their bit.'

'How so?'

'They're good lads. Ex-military. But they've still got their head in the sand, no pun intended. Their minds won't let them leave even if they wanted to. So they stayed back. And now they're training the Northern Storm Brigade. There's six of us.'

'So you live with them, the rebels?'

He looks around. 'They deserve peace. They've been accused of siding with terrorists and all sorts. The FSA isn't the problem. You and I know that.' He shakes his head. 'Saddam was best left where he was. Assad...' He scoffs.

'You like it don't you?'

He offers a curious look.

'You like helping them.'

'It feels right. We're not being told who to assist, who to ignore, who to attack. Me and those other lads, we're finally directing our skills where we choose... because we know it's needed.'

I smile, noting the satisfaction in his eyes. *He's found his calling.*

'Well, you get it.' He frowns. 'So tell me...What are you doing out here?'

'You can't run from the past, no matter where you go.'

He grins. 'That's a fire I've not seen in a while.'

'There's been a lot of pain and a hell of a lot of loss.' I breathe in, trying to find the courage to say the words. 'And after all that, I needed to know where you were. Not because I thought you might come after us, not like Rhiannon. I just... I've lost so much in such a

short space of time. If there was a chance that you were out there…
that I could gain something…'

'You had someone find me…'

'I have a friend who's very good with computers.'

'My boys could do with someone like him.'

'They're good? Your boys?'

He nods with pride. 'They're fucking good, Alex.'

'I'd like to meet them.'

'One day.'

I hold his gaze.

'You want to meet them now.'

'I need your help.' I reach forward. 'Wayne, we really need
your help.'

He downs the rest of his drink. 'What is it? CIA? MI6?'

'Independent.'

'I'm listening…'

The door swings open.

I look above Wayne's head, catching a tall figure storming
through the bar with intent. 'Oh shit.'

Gabriel's furious eyes examine everyone, his perfect face set
in a thunderous glare.

Wayne follows my gaze. 'He yours?'

'Mmhmm.' I say as his eyes finally land on me.

'Can't keep under the radar with those looks. Attract way too
much attention.'

'Shh, he's coming over.'

CHAPTER FIFTY-FOUR

GABRIEL

It's a mixture of feelings when I do finally see Alexandra…

Relief that she's ok.

Rage that she left.

Confusion as to who the bloke is opposite her.

'What do you think you're doing?'

'Sit down.' Defiance hits her eyes. 'Don't make a scene.'

I look around the reception before pulling out a chair and reluctantly taking a seat next to her. 'Who are you?' I ask the broad, heavily bearded man opposite. 'Do you both know what time it is?'

His sharp brown eyes regard me with amusement before he breaks into a grin and looks to Lex. 'He's a charmer.'

I turn to her, waiting for an explanation. She gives me a look that tells me she wants me to be nice.

'Wayne…' He says, offering a thick hand covered in dirt-smeared scars. 'Officer Wayne Gibbs, Northern Storm Brigade.'

'You survived.'

'Ahhh.' He looks over to Lex. 'He knows about me.'

'Formerly B-Squad, Special Air Service,' I say. 'You're meant to be dead.'

'That's the one.' He signals to a waitress. 'You want a drink mate?'

'Just a water, thanks.'

'Nothing to put a bit of hair on your chest?'

'I'm an alcoholic.'

'Same here.' He quips, ordering another round.

I look at Lex. 'You didn't think the two flights we took out here would be a good time to tell me you were meeting someone in Damascus, in the middle of the night?'

'Look...' Gibbs frowns at the table, waving his grubby hands in the air as if searching for something in the depths of his mind.

'James.' I say, filling in the blank. 'Gabriel James.'

'Listen Gabriel... the who, the what, the why doesn't matter. Alex found out I'm alive. She wanted a meeting. Here I am.' He laughs. 'The point is, I'm not dead. I'm happy to see my old friend... and she tells me you need my help. So let's cut this alpha male shit, mate. We both know you're much taller, much smarter, much better looking than me. I'm just here to see my friend.' The waitress sets his drink down, he reaches out quickly, knocking back the whole thing. 'So now we've got all that out on the table... what can I do you for?'

'You still train?' I ask, eyeing him up.

'It's the only thing I know how to do... killing nasty people.'

'You do that on your own, do you?'

'There's a group of us. Ex SEALS, SBS, SAS. All the acronyms.'

'You ever come across any of the jihadist cells?'

'All the time but I train with the FSA. And my boys don't mix with terrorists. Assad will have you think we're all in one friendly commune. But you and I both know that's not the way it works.'

'What have you heard of Almasi recently?'

He shrugs. 'We've taken out some of those lads. Never come close to *him* though.'

'He's back, Wayne.' Lex and he exchange a knowing look. 'We have it on very good authority that he's going to attack again but this time, it'll be different. He's stepped up his game. Nothing like you or I have ever seen in the B-Squad days. But there's a bigger picture and we have to be careful where we share our intel. Almasi's got backing from an organisation with major government connections.'

'Bloody hell, Alex. How'd that all come about?'

'He's working with a group called The Singularity. It's run by a man named Andrew Magnusson, an ex-British intelligence agent who went rogue at some time during 2005. Magnusson has a program that essentially targets orphaned children from Za'atari migrant camp, brainwashes them and trains them as elite soldiers. These kids are programmed to blend in, to act without any emotion. They are the most obedient, primed, skilled assassins in the world and Imran Almasi has an army of them. Magnusson is selling these soldiers to people in positions of power. He doesn't care who, as long as his business continues.'

'Who else?'

'The Ministry of Defence.'

'Two opposing sides?'

Lex nods. 'There could be more, we just need to find him. We think he has a facility out here somewhere. MI6 have intel that Almasi is going to use his soldiers for a large scale attack four days from now. This kind of attack will cause anarchy. It could destroy London as we know it.'

'Kids?' Gibbs widens his eyes. 'They're doing this to kids.'

'They've been doing it for years.'

'Fuck me...'

'Do you have access to weapons?' I cut in.

He nods. 'Got Obama to thank for that. He sent the FSA a load of artillery in 2013. Still got a bit now. And I've got an elite team of six fuck off soldiers.' He says proudly. 'They're as good as any of us in the forces ever were...'

'Wayne...' Lex wrings her hands in her lap. 'I wouldn't expect you to ask the FSA to fight on our behalf. They shouldn't have to. But the others you mentioned, the six of you. If you could help us… that would be…' Lex looks to me, 'we just need to get to that facility, find Magnusson and put an end to this. All whilst keeping under the radar.'

'That is quite a story, Angel. And it's one hell of a fight.'

'We know the risks.' She says, with desperation in her voice. 'We know we won't survive without help.'

Wayne Gibbs exhales, knotting his hands together. He stares down at the table for what feels like hours before finally resting his eyes on Lex. 'It would be an honour to serve with you again.'

Lex's shoulders drop with relief.

Wayne looks at me, tipping his chin slightly. 'You alright with that, handsome?'

'If Alexandra trusts you, then so do I.'

He smirks, turning to Lex with raised eyebrows. 'Got yourself a modern man.'

'We'll give you the full picture, start to finish. But it can't leave this table.'

'Copy. Whatever you say, stays wi….'

He's cut off by the sudden buzzing of my phone. I pick it up, recognising Collins' number.

'James.' Her voice sounds rushed. 'You need to get here now.'

CHAPTER FIFTY-FIVE

GABRIEL

'What the fuck happened?' I look around the room, observing the various bullets burrowed into the wall. Aldyn stands by the door in his boxers, straining to hold back Raheem Kamani, the doctor who approached Lex in Monaco. A body is propped at the end of Collins' bed. The man's head is slouched over his shoulders, his chin resting on his chest as blood seeps from the fatal wound on his skull, down his uniform and onto the cream carpet. An ashtray is discarded on the floor, the glass smeared with blood and brain matter. Crouching down, I examine the gun in the dead man's hands.

'I was asleep.' Collins starts before clearing her throat. 'That man there...' She gestures to the floor. 'He came in, tried to attack me.'

'He's one of those.' Aldyn barks. 'He has a chip.'

Lex drops to her knees, carefully lifting the suspect's head. 'He's a Compliant.' She stands, wiping blood against her black jeans.

'A what?' Gibbs asks, bemused.

Lex marches over to Kamani, pulls out her gun and presses it against his forehead. 'Stop wriggling.'

With fearful eyes, he stills; his chest the only part of him moving as he breathes. The image jerks something free in my mind. The familiarity of his sunken, pleading eyes tugs on a memory.

'This guy...' Gibbs interjects, standing above the bludgeoned body. 'He attacked you?' He points at Collins. 'And you killed him?' He gestures to Aldyn. 'With your bare hands.'

Aldyn nods.

'So who is that?' Gibbs points at Kamani.

'Sorry...' Collins frowns. 'I think the question is, who are you?'

'He's Wayne Gibbs.' Lex throws out. 'We can trust him.'

I scan the space again. Something's not adding up. Collins, in a hotel dressing gown, standing at the foot of the bed. Aldyn, in his pants by the door, holding Raheem Kamani. The dead body. Blood on Aldyn's hands. I glance back at the bed. Aldyn's gold watch rests on the bedside table. I look at the watch, then at Collins, then back to Aldyn.

'Gabriel.... I...' Collins starts.

'Nope.' I hold up my hand. 'You don't need to go there.'

Lex's face drops as her thoughts fire through the same pattern.

Aldyn takes a breath to speak. 'We don't have to explain anyth...'

'No, no.' I shiver. 'You're all good.'

Collins rolls her eyes and places her hands on her hips. 'The attacker had a key, he let himself in. If we hadn't been awake...'

'Yeah, we get the picture.' I insist again.

'This isn't a joke, Gabriel.' She snaps, her face reddening.

'Kamani, explain what you are doing here, or you will soon be joining the man on the floor.' Alexandra insists.

'I helped...' He pleads, holding his hands up. 'Please, please! I was just here to help!'

'We need to move.' Gibbs looks back at the door.

'Hold on! We just met you.' Collins says before glaring at me. 'Explain!'

'I contacted Wayne.' Lex jumps in without shifting her eyes from Kamani. 'We need him. He can help us.'

Collins narrows her eyes. 'I thought you were dead.'

'Join the club.' Gibbs says, offering a cheerful grin before it drops. 'But can we have this catch up later? Because right now, we have to go.'

'Please, I promise I'm just here to help.' Kamani insists, his face glowering with sweat. 'Please don't kill me.'

'Explain what the fuck you were doing here!' I demand, standing behind Lex. 'How did you end up involved in this?'

'That man...' He gestures towards the body. 'He was sent to kill you... all of you.'

'How do you know that?' Lex asks.

'He has been following me too. I managed to lose him and run counter-surveillance. I tailed him here.'

'Who does he work for?'

Kamani shrugs. 'Whoever sent him does not want you here. They want you to stop!'

'And what exactly are you doing here Kamani?'

He hesitates, his eyes darting wildly around the room.

'We don't have time for this. Run an interrogation when we're all safe.' Gibbs implores, analysing the group. 'Is this all of you?'

'There's two more.' I reply, staring at Kamani, an overwhelming sense of dread filling my stomach.

'Get them up. We'll go to my camp. You'll be protected.'

'How long will that take?' Collins asks.

'Two hours...roughly.'

'He's right.' Lex says assertively. 'We can't stay here.'

'You can't just take me!' Kamani shouts. 'Where am I going?'

'Listen to me.' Lex raises her voice. 'If what you are saying is true, then it's only a matter of time before they send someone else. You'll need our protection.'

He blinks rapidly. 'Can I get my things? I have my laptop, there's very important things, it's very important.'

Lex drops her gun. 'Gibbs, are you ok to grab his stuff, we might need it.'

'Give me the address. I'll see what I can do. You lot need to pack and get out of here. Everything you can carry. But leave that suitcase.' He gives me a knowing look before he turns to the rest of the group. 'We need some way of getting rid of the body.'

CHAPTER FIFTY-SIX

ALEXANDRA

We slow at the approach to the North Storm Brigade checkpoint. Four men in weathered military uniforms step forward, their fingers hanging on their triggers. They squint through the sun, trying to get a read on our identity. Gibbs unwinds his window on the driver's side and juts his head out, shouting in Arabic before putting the hand brake on and getting out of the car. A haze of heat swells from the bonnet as we wait. The soldiers fervently question Gibbs, their eyes drifting over his shoulder every now and again, studying us suspiciously. Groaning, I lean forward and drop my head in my hands, resting my elbows on my knees.

'Are you car sick?' Collins calls from the back of the jeep.

'No.' I inhale a deep breath, trying to move past another nauseating wave of unease.

'What is it?'

'The last time I was in the desert, I was on my own, running ops for Edward.'

She says nothing but I sense a weight of expectation in the air.

'I feel responsible for you.'

'I'm flattered.'

'All of you.'

'You're spinning out. Take three deep breaths...'

'This desert isn't kind, Alison.'

'We'll be fine.' She responds curtly.

Straightening, I look out to the landscape, noticing the tops of tents poking up from the valley, white canvas tips sticking out above the long grass. Having satisfied security checks, Gibbs steps back into the vehicle and the FSA soldiers jump into action, opening the gate.

'We'll take Kamani to the compound.' He points at a building in the centre of the valley. 'The boys will guard him there. There are some tents at the edge of camp for the rest of you.'

'And the six?' I ask. 'Where are they?'

'They're doing a run in Homs. They'll be back later.' He swings the jeep up a verge, manoeuvring in between heaps of sand and dehydrated grass. He brakes suddenly, narrowly missing a group of shirtless men jogging with strained faces, steadily holding a timber log above their heads. With sweat-slicked heads and determination brimming in their eyes, they continue ahead, reciting military cadence calls.

'Drills.' Gibbs explains, noticing Collins' shocked expression in the rear-view mirror. 'You remember that Angel?'

'All too well.'

'We'll stop here.' He kills the engine, tips his glasses off his face, and jumps out, signalling to Gabriel in the truck behind.

Doing my best to ignore the blistering heat, I hand Keys and Emily their stuff. They head towards the compound whilst the rest of us unpack the cars.

'Are you going to explain why you have taken me to a Syrian rebel camp, Miss Christofi?' Kamani holds his bound hands in front of his face. 'Are these people going to treat me as their prisoner?'

'We're just taking precautions.'

'Please untie me.'

'We will.'

Gibbs jogs over. 'You come with us, Dr Kamani; we'll get you fed. Angel…' He points to the east of the camp. 'You, James, Collins, and Wolfe dump your stuff over there. There are facilities you can use in the compound.' He pauses, eyeing my face. 'You alright mate? You look green.'

'Dehydrated.' I reply, unwilling to divulge that our decision to come here has left me riddled with anxiety. 'I should come to the compound, help get Kamani settled.'

'Don't worry.' Gibbs grins. 'We got this... control freak.' He winks, grabbing Kamani before traipsing through the sand.

Collins and Aldyn follow, their bags in tow. I exhale, watching their blurred figures disappear in the smog.

'What's up?' Gabriel asks, leaning against the boot of the jeep, concern marring his dark eyes. 'You're wringing your fingers. You only do that when something's wrong.'

I look down at my hands. *He knows me too well.* I sit next to him in silence, not knowing how to answer his question. Being back in this environment with Gibbs is giving me a nostalgic sense of a past life mixed with a startling realisation. With the amount of training, preparation, planning, and skill that was required ahead of our operations in B-Squad; I'm beginning to wonder if we've rushed out here. We're out of our depth; relying on the very man I abandoned, someone I've not seen in years. What if captivity has changed him? He has every reason to betray me, to make me suffer. Never mind the fact we're seeking help from a foreign militia in the middle of barren, unforgiving terrain. A place that takes no prisoners.

'Lex...' Gabriel drops his bags and steps in, resting his hand against my forehead. 'You're losing all colour in your face.'

'This was a mistake.' I confess, staring at my sand-covered boots.

'Huh?' He runs his fingers down my cheek. 'What are you talking about?'

'I didn't think this through. He could be working with them.' I gulp past the dry panic in my throat, my brain throwing out the risks, racing down a list of *what-ifs*. 'I've brought you all here, risked your lives. We've made a mistake, Gabe.' I drop my chin to my chest. 'We need to get Kamani. We need to go.'

'Here sit down.' He guides me to the boot of the car. 'Have some water.'

I nod, taking the bottle from him, swallowing huge mouthfuls. *Something occurs to me suddenly*. 'Why…' I pause, glancing up at him. 'What are you doing?'

'Rehydrating you.'

'No, why are you so calm?'

He exhales, taking my shoulders, pivoting me to face the valley. 'Look.'

'Yes, it's a sandpit…' I say, exasperated.

'Look again.'

I sigh, squinting through the sun.

'See… there.' He points towards the Compound.

Gibbs peels off from the group, handing Kamani to a group of FSA soldiers before he calls out to someone. A woman turns, her face breaking into a wide grin. The basket in her hands falls to the floor, and she starts running. Two children joyfully dash after her, their happy voices chanting songs. Gibbs stretches out his arms, and she falls into them. He kisses her on the forehead whilst the little girls run in circles. He laughs and kisses her again, savouring a moment of holding her close. The children pull at his shirt and eventually, he lets her go to chase them, making pretend monster noises whilst they squeal with delight.

A smile creeps across Gabriel's face. 'I'm pretty sure Gibbs isn't working for The Singularity.'

I look across the sea of tents, using my hand to shield my eyes, spotting more families; women chatting animatedly in groups carrying piles of clothes, a group of girls skipping, mothers laughing; watching their children playing in the sand, men sit around their tents, playing cards, passing around a box of cigarettes. Amidst this bare, dusty wilderness is so much life; vibrant, happy pockets of life. More than I've seen anywhere, for a long time.

'It's going to be ok.' Gabriel says, pulling me into him.

My mouth trembles against his chest, unexpected tears escape, running quickly down my cheeks.

'You made the right call.'

CHAPTER FIFTY-SEVEN

ALEXANDRA

'Holy shit...' Keys says with disbelief.

'What is it?' I move closer to his screen.

Gabriel strides into the compound's incident room carrying a box of guns. 'Lex, are you...' He stops, immediately taking in the energy between us. 'What's going on?'

'We have access to Kamani's laptop.'

'You hacked it?'

'He gave me the password.' Keys says, embarrassed.

'Gabriel, Smart was meeting Kamani in Damascus. He was promising him asylum in the UK.' I say, reading Keys' screen. 'Smart left Jordan to meet with Kamani to get information on The Singularity's sales to Almasi.'

'Huh?' Gabriel frowns.

'Smart didn't know that Magnusson has been selling Compliants to Almasi. It seems Kamani blew the whistle and told Smart about it. Agent Rikers told me Raheem Kamani had defected. Which means he was a wanted man as far as British Intelligence was concerned. Kamani arranged to meet at the Hotel Dame Rose and was going to trade Smart the low down on Almasi's plan for safe passage back to England.' Keys explains. 'But Smart died a day before they were supposed to meet.'

'Magnusson found out and killed Smart.' Gabriel says, putting the box down. 'He must have figured out Smart was digging a little too deep. Or Raheem Kamani was bait.'

Keys nods. 'It appears Smart thought the British Government were the only people with access to Compliants. He wanted to take The Singularity down. It says it right here.'

Collins enters, her glassy eyes reading our faces. 'Why do you all look like you've seen a ghost?'

'Look at this.' Keys exclaims, almost jumping out of his seat. 'Look at the correspondence here.'

I look up to Collins. 'Smart was going to strike a deal with Raheem Kamani.'

'That means Magnusson knows Kamani flipped sides. He'll be out to get him.' Collins surmises.

'That's if he did flip sides.' Gabriel mutters. 'We need to speak to him.'

'Might he be more inclined to share information if it's just Alex?' Keys suggests.

'Why's that?' Gabriel asks, crossing his arms.

'I mean…' He cranes his neck. 'Look at you like.'

'It's fine,' I insist. 'I don't mind speaking to him alone.'

'What if he…'

'Can someone mic me up.' I interject, ignoring the look of protest on Gabriel's face. 'You can listen from in here or stand outside the door.'

'Just remember he's a large part of this. He's not a victim.'

'She doesn't have a history of being soft.' Keys murmurs.

'Received and noted.'

Collins rummages through a few rucksacks stacked in the corner of the room. 'Here…' She holds up a small device, attaching it to the top of my T-shirt. 'Keep the mic visible, so he knows we're listening.'

'And I'll be right outside.' Gabriel insists.

Collins catches my eye with a knowing look. 'You're good.'

Kamani stands at a window overlooking the sand dunes. His room is a little small, but an effort has been made to make it homely. There's a writing desk by the window, a narrow bed covered with colourful blankets and various different cushions are nestled against the far wall. There are steps to the left of the doorway that lead down to a bathroom. I even notice the corner of a stone bathtub. I take a large stride into the room, careful not to step on the prayer mat in the centre.

'Ms. Christofi…' Kamani says with his back to me.

'Are you hungry?' I eye the clay jug on the desk. 'Do you need more water?'

He turns and leans on the window's wooden ledge. 'You're going to pretend you're here as a host?'

'We need to talk.' I take a sit on the thin mattress.

'I tried to save your lives and you treat me like this.'

'There's some gaps I need you to explain. We're just taking precautions.'

'Ask your questions.'

'You say you were running counter surveillance on the man that was following you.'

He nods.

'Who sent that man?'

'I cannot be sure. Perhaps my employer. Could have been someone else looking to find out information.'

'Do you have access to vital information, Raheem?'

'Some might think so.'

'Is that why you approached me in Monaco?'

He shakes his head. 'I was foolish.'

'How did you know who I was?'

He looks at the door. 'Some things are better left buried.'

I sigh. 'Ok…but you clearly aren't working with The Singularity anymore?'

'I'm not.'

'Which is why you were due to meet Jed Smart at the hotel.'

His face drops. 'Where is he?'

'I'm sorry.' I shift my gaze. 'He's dead.'

He closes his eyes as if his last lifeline has been ripped away.

'Raheem, we can help but I need you to explain from the beginning.'

He closes his eyes. 'There's nothing you can do for me. You won't stop him, Alexandra. Without Jed Smart, my true part in this is lost.' He sighs as if the mere notion has drained all the energy from his body. 'We need his resources.'

'That's not true.' I lean forward. 'We have more than enough. I need you to tell me where the facility is. I need you to point us to Magnusson, Higgs, everyone involved. We can protect you if you help us.'

'Magnusson...' He frowns. 'What do you know?'

I stand. 'Andrew Magnusson, the man who allegedly died in 2005, didn't really die. He left the country and assumed a new identity as Augustus Fox. He started the Compliancy program.'

'Magnusson became Fox, yes.' He confirms, his voice hoarse.

'And who is Higgs?'

He watches me cautiously.

'What's the matter?'

'I don't understand your question.'

'Everything has led back to Higgs since the beginning. Higgs coordinated the trafficking of thousands of children out of the camps with Diren Paytak. He is the man everyone answered to.'

'That is not possible.'

Irritation spikes my heart rate. 'Higgs exists.'

'Yes, Higgs exists.'

'What... ok so who? Who is he?'

'Not who.'

'Raheem, you're not making sense.'

'Higgs is not a person. It's part of the program.'

'No.' I shift the weight on my feet. 'How is that possible?'

'Higgs Boson is a serum created for the program.'

I think back to Icarus. *You're nearly there... it's fascinating.*

'He's never been a person.' I mumble. 'Magnusson created this all by himself?'

He closes his eyes. 'Magnusson created it, and I oversaw it for years. I put them under, seeded out the ones with potential.'

'The children?'

His expression tumbles into self-revulsion. 'I listened to them beg for their parents, ignored their pleas to go home. I told them it was alright when their hair fell out from the stress and the trauma. I buried the ones who couldn't take it, wiped the personalities of the ones who could. It took years to perfect the serums, to get the chip to function properly.'

I think back to the deadness in Hope Clarke's eyes. The dull, muted shade of her skin as if she had spent an entire childhood indoors. I clench my teeth, biting back the urge to tell Raheem Kamani that he deserves a long, sufferable death.

'You think I'm evil...' He crosses his arms, lowering his head. 'I think it too.'

I stay silent for a time, listening to the waves of my own breathing. Kamani doesn't move, doesn't even try to offer excuses. We simply allow ourselves to sit uncomfortably in the pit of guilt and shame that fills the room; the look on his face reminding me so much of my own broken conscience.

'I came across a group of children once in Islamabad.'

Kamani raises his head, watching me carefully.

'They'd been tortured, beaten, brainwashed. They needed someone to speak up for them. Their whole lives, nobody had. They had no one and nothing. Nothing but misery and fear. They were going to harm people… a lot of people.' I twist my lips. 'They didn't know any better.'

'You killed them?'

'I know what it's like.' I look up, meeting his sad, desperate eyes. 'Hating yourself so much you want to break free from your own skin. Wishing for even ten seconds of relief, praying to be anyone but you.'

'Then you see me.'

'I know how it feels.'

'And now you think you can be the voice for the children of Za'atari?'

'Don't you think it's time someone was?'

'I don't deserve your help.'

'But they do. All I can think about right now is how I wish I'd come in here armed or how quickly I can get out of that door, grab a gun, and turn it on you before you have time to hide. In the short time we've sat here, I've run that scenario in my head over and over and over again. I want to kill you because you are one of few people I've met whom I can actually lay some blame.'

'Do it.' He hisses. 'I would rather you did.'

'I need you alive.'

'They told me I was changing the world.' He raises his voice, spit flying from his mouth. 'Imagine someone who looks like me, offered bursaries, scholarships, grant after grant. All so they could place me in one of the most pioneering psychiatric programs in the world. Working with a team of people who produce the real phenomenon. Exceptional subjects with remarkable talent. I wanted a piece of it.' He tears at his hair. 'I wanted to be recognised for that work!'

'Who is they?'

He focuses on the mic attached to my shirt and his eyes flit to the door. 'Magnusson and his team.'

'He groomed you.'

'Excuse me?'

'He used your vulnerabilities against you, financed your entire education, primed you to become what he wanted.'

'I was never extracted.'

'But Fox or Magnusson, whatever you want to call him, he gave you a way out of poverty, right?'

He sighs, sitting on the bed. 'Did you ever believe in something so badly; you'd do anything to make it work? Anything to reach that point. Just to prove you could, to show the world you were more.'

'Many, many times.'

'One day, I just... I woke up.' He shakes his head as if reliving the memory. 'There was a girl. Akilah. We brought her to the program when she turned eight. I knew she was different from the moment I met her.'

'How?'

'We don't allow the children to have personal possessions. They wear grey tunics. Nothing has any colour. We don't want them stimulated unless they're in session. Even their living quarters are neutral. And Akilah... she just had this spirit.' He smiles. 'Nothing I've ever seen before. She saw light in everything. She was constantly being isolated from other children for telling stories at night, calling out through the walls so they could hear. She'd comfort the ones that were homesick. She'd tear pieces of her tunic apart to make bows or pretend it was a teddy bear. She'd find ways to give the things she made to the other children. She'd lost her parents in Aleppo, come to Za'atari with nothing, made new friends, and then was taken by us to the facility. Despite that, nothing could dampen that spirit.'

'Until you…' I say, hastening a guess.

'She was strong, intelligent, quick thinking. She passed all aptitude and physical tests. She aimed to please. She enjoyed talking about politics. She respected authority. She was the strongest candidate we'd seen in years. And then the extractions started…' He swallows. 'We couldn't…' He breathes deeply. 'Numerous times, we'd get her into Compliant stages. And once a child is under, once they're successfully in Compliancy, Flint would usually start them on the physical simulations. But then, some days would pass, and she'd be back again, smiling, telling stories, singing to the other children. And after a few months, she started to understand. She realised she wasn't meant to become lucid after such a short time. She recognised that her accidental defiance didn't please us. So she began to hide it, pretending to be in Compliancy. We'd run tests to check if extraction was successful but even then, it became hard to know when she was in and when she was out. Sometimes, just before we put her under, she'd watch me in the lab, tracking me… like a caged animal waiting to get out.'

'At eight?' I say, disbelieving.

'We hadn't turned something off, Ms Christofi, we were switching it on. And the more I saw her, the more I felt she was goading me, daring us to continue. *Train me up. Make me a monster. Then watch me come back.* She had more fight in her than anyone I've ever met.'

'You're using the past tense.'

He looks up, his eyes tearful.

'That's why you wanted out?'

'We received word that one of our first ever Compliants had become unstuck in Russia. Her mind was unravelling.'

'Hope Clarke.'

'Magnusson knew it wasn't working with her. After that, he said he couldn't take the risk. The Higgs program wouldn't tolerate any further anomalies. And Akilah...'

'She was one.'

'Precisely.' He whispers. 'She would have been the best... if only they had known how to control her.'

'How many Compliants have The Singularity sold to Almasi?'

He shrugs. 'Ten, at least.'

'Are they ready? Are they trained?'

'Yes.' He admits shamefully. 'Dr Flint trained them. They are the best.'

'Where does Almasi take delivery?'

'He has a place in South Sudan.'

'You've been?'

He nods. 'Just once.'

I catch his reluctance. 'If you really want to help, then prove it by telling us where to find Almasi and Magnusson. We have to stop this. We have to stop the attack.'

'I could show you on a map.'

'Thousands of innocent people might depend on this information.'

'What do you know about the attacks?'

'We know the plan is to hit major London airports.'

He regards me coolly. 'That's not the plan, Ms Christofi. That's the distraction.'

CHAPTER FIFTY-EIGHT

GABRIEL

Wind blows across the dunes; tents flapping wildly with the gusting current. I cover my face, shielding my eyes from grains of sand cutting across my vision. Collins and Emily rush ahead, hauling barrels of water back to their camp. I allow myself a moment to take in the landscape, part of me wishing we could stay here forever; live a simple life, escape the rest of the world. Raheem Kamani's face floats into my mind, illustrating a faint memory. I try to grab it, hold onto it, make it a solid, tangible thought but it drifts into nothing again, like smoke disappearing into the sky. *What the fuck is happening to me?* I rub the base of my palm against my sternum. *There is something important waiting in the depths of my mind. Why can't I remember?* I arrive at the entrance of Keys' tent, trying to hide the strain on my face. He's crouched over his rucksack, muttering as he searches for something.

'I need you to do a few things for me.' I announce.

He looks up, startled. 'Is Alex all finished up with Kamani?'

'She will be soon.'

'And you don't want her to know about this, which is why you're here whilst she's busy.'

I offer him a blank stare.

He exhales. 'I'm not good at secrets, mate.'

'You kept Wayne Gibbs a pretty good secret.'

'For less than 24 hours like.'

'Keys, this is important.'

He dives his hand into his bag and pulls out one of his many laptops. 'Take it I'll be needing this?'

I pick up a scrap of paper from the wooden stool he's using as a desk. 'Got anything to write with?'

He digs through a pocket, handing me a pencil.

'I need you to log into this account.' I scribble down the information. 'Use these details.'

He leans over my shoulder. 'If it's hacking into GCHQ – I won't be able to do it alone. They've bolstered security big time.'

'You won't need to hack anything.'

Frowning, he reads my writing. 'MI5…. That looks like a classified account.'

'Don't ask and you won't be complicit.' I hand him the note.

'How have you managed to get these details?'

I hunch as the top of my head skims the ceiling pole. 'Best you don't know.'

'I wondered why you and Alex get to sleep in the compound.' Keys shrugs. 'Now I know.'

'Can you do it for me or not?'

He exhales a long, loud breath. 'If I log into that from here, they will trace my IP address, we will be toast.'

'Not with that.'

'I don't think you know how this works…'

I meet his frantic eyes. 'You need to trust me when I say these login details are untraceable.'

'That's not possible.'

'Keys,' I step in, losing patience. 'Do you think I would risk us getting caught with something as simple as this? Do you think I would ask you to do this knowing it would put all of us in danger, serving up the woman I love on a platter?'

He waivers, still thinking. 'I don't.'

'You will not be tracked if you use these details.'

He looks between his laptop and the note in his hand as if one or both might burst into flames. 'The only way you could have access like this... untraceable, undetectable access is if you'd created a ghost profile. A way of accessing the data without a peep...' he trails off, squinting into the distance. 'You're a very skilled man, Gabriel, but I know you can't do this.' His eyes widen. 'You used another hacker.'

'I need you to search an operational code name. Once you find the code name, you can access a classified, unredacted file.'

'Who?'

I take the note and scribble the full name.

Keys frowns. 'Again, I have to ask why?'

'I need to know if there's any way the person on that piece of paper might have ever had contact with Raheem Kamani or Andrew Magnusson.'

'Gabe...wha...' He splutters. 'You seriously think that's possible?'

'Magnusson worked with someone before he faked his own death and became Fox. I want to know if this person was involved.'

'How did you come to that conclusion?'

'Something Kamani said.'

'Right, well...' He looks down at the note. 'I'll see what I can find.'

'Thanks. I owe you.' I feel even hotter suddenly. Sweat trickles down my face, I wipe it away with my forearm.

'Why don't you just ask Kamani yourself?'

'Don't trust him.'

'And this is all a part of this strange thing you have against him.'

'It's a feeling.'

'There's only two people in the world who could have given you this ghost, Gabriel. If anyone in government finds out you used a hacker to create a profile with clearances higher than the fucking moon, you will go to prison for the rest of your life. You know that, don't you? Using the credentials of a...' He grips the ends of his hair, like pulling it out from his skull is a better option. 'How am I meant to explain that to Alex? If I'm the person who helped put you behind bars.'

'Keys...' I step in, 'get your shit together. Stop asking questions you know I'm not going to answer.'

'Who did you go to?' He asks, sounding hurt. 'To get the ghost profile, who did you pay?'

'You're acting like I cheated on you.'

'Alex isn't going to like this.'

I sigh. 'I want to make sure I'm right before I...'

'Agent James.' Kamani's voice cuts in, his face appearing between the white folds of the tent's entrance.

I tense, irritated. 'Not now.'

'I see you are busy.' He backs away. 'When you are done, Ms Christofi needs us all in the briefing room.' He makes a prayer sign. 'Please.'

I stare at his hands, focusing on his long, lanky limbs. The tangled thread finally resurfaces from the depths of my mind. 'Ok yeah. I'm coming.'

CHAPTER FIFTY-NINE

COLLINS

I peer around the corner of a doorway, finding Wayne Gibbs standing above a scattering of documents, examining each one laid out in front of him. Mismatched chairs surround a large wooden table. Two sofas are tucked at the end of the room, with stacks of books on either side. Gibbs walks over to one, picking up the steaming coffee mug perched on the pile closest to him. A small kitchen sits behind him with several battered pots and pans lying on the drying rack.

'It's not much but it's home.' Gibbs walks back to the table, placing his drink beside him. 'Fancy a cuppa?'

'No thanks.' 'I reply, taking in the collection of children's drawings that have been pinned to the wall. A collage of scribblings; pictures of the sun, campfires, friends and their favourite teachers. 'You do a lot for the children here…'

'We try.' He smiles, taking a seat.

Alexandra enters, her expression slightly strained.

'Where's Raheem Kamani?' I ask.

'I sent him to get Gabriel.'

I raise my eyebrows. 'Is that a good idea?'

'Where's the other two?' Gibbs asks. 'The pretty girl and the big fella. Your fella…' He nudges his head in my direction.

I stare at him, taking a second to absorb what he's saying. Alexandra begins sifting through the documents on the table, pretending she didn't hear.

'You know the petite girl and the Eastern Europ-'

'Aldyn is making some calls, checking on his business at home.' Alexandra interjects without looking up.

The fact she felt the need causes my body to heat. I can feel the skin on my neck reddening, the sensation creeping up to my face. I refuse to look in her direction and instead busy myself with a notepad and pen. It's not like Alexandra and Gabriel haven't constantly blurred the lines between professional and personal for years. Every poor soul in a five-mile radius has been involved in the trials and tribulations of their turbulent mess. The one time I slip up just so happens to be the time every person on the team rushes to my bloody bedroom. That is some luck. *One time. Slip up. Who am I really trying to convince?* I might be too ashamed to admit it out loud but deep down, I know I'd do it again. *Aldyn Wolfe, for God's sake. How did it come to that?*

'We can fill Wolfe and Meyer in later.' I say, offering my most stoic voice. 'Should I look for Gabriel? If he's in one of those moods, we might struggle speaking to Raheem Kamani ever again.'

'They need time alone.' Alexandra insists.

'What are you thinking, Alex?' Gibbs asks, intrigued.

'Kamani has more to say.'

'Gabriel has been nothing but hostile towards him since he showed up.' I respond. 'Why on earth would he tell him anything?'

'It's a feeling I have.'

'Well, I hope he manages to get it out before Gabriel kills him in the desert.'

'Kamani jumped at the chance to find Gabriel and bring him to the briefing room.' Alexandra sits up, crossing her arms. 'There's more to that.'

Gabriel marches through the door with a face like thunder. He's followed by Raheem Kamani, who trails in, his eyes glued to the floor. Raheem takes a seat, clamping his hands between his knees. Without a word, Gabriel drops into a chair beside Alexandra. He's become a complete misery since Kamani appeared, clearly there's something about the man that gets under his skin. Right now, he's wound up like a spring. Alexandra quickly glances in his direction, her expression troubled. Pushing Gabriel and Kamani together might not be working as well as she hoped.

'Dr Kamani,' She starts. 'I think it's important you share what you know about the Palmyra facility and Andrew Magnusson's plan, with my colleagues.'

Kamani takes a breath before explaining everything in slow, methodical steps; describing Magnusson's motivations in changing his identity and how he took extraction and Compliancy to the next level. As he moves on to outline the moment Imran Almasi became involved; Gabriel sits forward, analysing every word, examining every twitch on the man's face.

'Could I just get a few things straight?' I interject, looking up from my notes. 'Magnusson worked for another British Intelligence Agency, then the 7/7 bombings happened, and he used it as an opportunity to move the Compliancy program to The Ministry of Defence?'

'Yes. He became Fox and some years later; he approached Jed Smart with the concept of Compliancy.'

Gabriel's eyes narrow. 'And this intelligence agency, the one he was at before, who was it?'

'MI5.'

The colour drains from Gabriel's face, rage twitches in his eyes. 'And an agency like MI5 just accepted that their groundbreaking Compliancy program died with Magnusson.'

'You have to understand, Mr James, the Compliancy program was so secretive, nobody else knew about it. Magnusson's colleagues at MI5 might have eventually suspected what he'd done but they could never admit it existed. They couldn't simply ask the Ministry of Defence for it back.'

'And when did you join the program?' Gabriel asks, narrowing his eyes.

'Some time after Magnusson started working with the MOD.'

'You sure about that?'

'Dr Kamani,' I interject, moving the conversation forward. 'You told Alexandra that the airport attacks are a distraction...I need you to tell us more about this please.'

He hesitates.

'Well go on...' Gabriel demands.

Alexandra gives him a look, one that hopefully encourages him to exercise a modicum of patience. *Someone has to.*

'The attacks will happen on August 5th, as you know. The targets are Stansted, Luton, Heathrow and Gatwick airports. A Compliant will rig devices to the front, middle and back of the eight thirty-two train arriving at Stansted, the eight-twenty at Luton. Same with the eight twenty-nine arriving at Heathrow and the eight thirty-six arriving at Gatwick. The bombs will be enough to take most of the terminals down with them.'

'And you're telling me that despite the amount of people this will kill, it's not the main event?' Gabriel asks.

Kamani shakes his head. 'The attacks are a means to something else. Imran Almasi is a pawn. Magnusson is merely using him to create a catastrophe.'

'Jesus Christ.' Gibbs turns to face the wall behind him.

'What is the bigger plan?' I ask. *We have to get everything out on the table, no matter how hard it might be to hear.*

'When the attack happens on the city, all resources will be put into finding the perpetrators and preventing another one. Your country is very resourceful but even you do not have enough manpower to cover four attacks of that nature and keep the city safe. The whole country will have its focus trained in one very specific direction.'

'Which is a distraction from what?'

'When the attacks take place, the Prime Minister and various other government officials will be transported out of the country, on separate aircraft, to a safe place. The proposed plan is that those flights will never make it to their intended destination. He wants to create maximum chaos.'

'Magnusson is going to have the Prime Minister murdered and like he did Smart?' I suggest.

'I know it seems ludicrous.' Kamani shrugs. 'But this is Andrew Magnusson's lifelong mission. And I don't think he would have killed Jed Smart. He was priming him to take the Prime Minister's place. He needed someone he already had in his pocket.'

'With all those people in government gone, Magnusson will indirectly run the country.' Gibbs mutters, staring at the floor. 'Almasi attacks, Magnusson uses it as an opportunity to gain control of the country, Smart was to become the front man.'

'Exactly.' Kamani whispers. 'And he will succeed because The Singularity already have Compliants that infiltrated the government many years ago. He will succeed because he has the money and the resources.'

'Except now Smart is dead.' Gabriel rebuts. 'Did he know about Magnusson's plan?'

'That's not how Magnusson operates.' He insists. 'Once Smart was there, Magnusson would ultimately have the country in his control. More Compliants would be placed in important, influential positions in government. Andrew Magnusson would be one of the most powerful men in the world.'

'Rinse and repeat.' I say, looking between Alexandra and Gabriel. 'Which means, Dr Kamani, you could be right, Andrew Magnusson wouldn't kill Smart. Smart was part of his plan. Even if

Magnusson discovered Smart was working against him, he had more than enough leverage on him to ensure he played to his tune.'

'Magnusson needed Smart.' Kamani insists. 'He spent years cultivating that relationship.'

'What made you approach Smart and tell him about Almasi?' Wayne Gibbs asks. 'That was risky.'

'He was my only way out.' He looks at his hands. 'I didn't tell Smart the whole plan. I didn't want him to think he had a chance of becoming Prime Minister off the back of it. All he knew was that Magnusson was selling Compliants to Imran Almasi. He was willing to give up his involvement in the program to stop it.'

'How noble.' Alexandra murmurs. 'Will Magnusson still attempt this coup even with Smart dead?'

'He will find a way to make it work. He would have had a plan B. Someone to replace Smart. It won't be easy, but he won't give up.'

'Brown will need to know about the attempt on the PM's life.' I glance at Gabriel. 'S.A.I.B.R and SO15 need to know there's more to this.'

'I'll call Brown.' He suggests. 'I'll tell him what we know about Magnusson's actual plan. I'll ensure GCHQ and SO15 are aware.'

Wayne Gibbs scoffs. 'That lot are so uptight; the PM won't be able to sneeze without them knowing.'

'Which is what we need.' I say, crossing my arms.

'The thing is…' Kamani starts, thinking to himself. 'Even if you stop this attack in three days. Magnusson will find another way. He already has Compliants infiltrating your government. He's a patriot of extremes. He believes the country is damaged. He thinks he is the only person who can fix it. And to do that…' He holds his hands out. 'He thinks it needs to be destroyed.'

'So we need to find this Magnusson, Fox fella… and we need to put him down.' Wayne Gibbs insists. 'How many facilities are there?'

'Two.' Kamani answers quickly. 'One in Palmyra City, another near Monaco.'

'And the one you worked at is in Palmyra?' Alexandra confirms. 'Which is what? Five hours from Za'atari camp?'

Kamani nods. 'It's a facility built under the city.'

'Will Magnusson be there?' She asks.

'He is there until the attacks.'

'Is it easy to approach?' Gibbs asks.

'There are cameras on the road, outside the building, and everywhere inside the facility.' Kamani explains.

'Keys can help with these.' Alexandra announces. 'He'll be able to hack the feeds, then record a loop of footage. He'll overlay that onto the real CCTV. So we can approach the facility without being detected.'

Gabriel stands and begins to pace the room. 'And when we get into the facility, what then?'

'There's a changeover in security.' Kamani explains, picking up a pencil and drawing on the blank sheet of paper in front of him. 'At ten every night, the shift changes. Security Team A clocks off and goes to minus four, disarms and leaves. Security Team B arrives and disperses across minus three, minus two, and minus one. But A usually clocks off a little earlier. B take their time. There's about ninety seconds where the floors are empty.'

'My suggestion is that we send in two teams.' Alexandra reaches over the table, swivelling around Kamani's sketches of the facility. 'We have Team ALPHA, who arrives first and infiltrates the west entrance here during that ninety-second window. ALPHA head to minus four and deal with Team A, then move to minus three and minus two to get the children out. Team BRAVO will enter the facility from the east entrance... here.' She taps her hand on the paper. 'Whilst ALPHA is working on the children, BRAVO handle Security Team B.'

'ALPHA must not let Security Team A sound an alarm or they will have both teams on them. They will be outnumbered.' Kamani says, looking around the table.

'Fine.' Gabriel says. 'Makes sense.'

'ALPHA need to secure as much as the west wing as they can.' Kamani continues. 'Once you reach the labs, a member of staff will sound an alert. You have no choice. There are too many nightshift workers, you won't be able to stop them. When the alarm goes off, Magnusson will be moved to a secure room on the lower east side of the building. He has three Compliants that escort him everywhere. He will go with them. They are very advanced.'

'In terms of ALPHA and BRAVO...' Gabriel starts. 'How are we making that decision?'

'James, you could join ALPHA with Boots, Jake, and Sully.' Gibbs leans to pat Gabriel on the shoulder. 'Me, Fenwick, and Ronnie make up BRAVO. Collins, you, Aldyn and Meyer will be in trucks about half a mile from Palmyra. Dr Kamani, we need you to drive the fourth. Then we evacuate the children to those vehicles.'

'Sounds reasonable.' I agree before turning to Kamani. 'Will four trucks be enough for all the children?'

'If they are the ones I have seen outside, then yes.'

'Good.' Wayne Gibbs says with satisfaction but his expression remains hesitant, almost as if he has something else to add but stops himself.

'You think I didn't notice you weren't assigned to a team, Lex?' Gabriel grumbles without looking up.

I inhale a deep breath, summoning the energy to mediate this inevitable confrontation. The predictability of this conversation is almost excruciating. Nothing gets past him; she should know that by now. Gabriel raises his eyebrows, waiting for a response.

'Someone needs to get Magnusson.' Alexandra says quietly.

'How are you planning on doing that?'

'We could put a bird on the roof.' Gibbs adds. 'It drops you in, you kill Magnusson. It gets you out.'

Gabriel turns his attention back to Kamani. 'Is that possible?'

Kamani straightens his shoulders as if being questioned in court. 'That sounds straightforward.'

'Then why don't you do it?' He snaps back.

'He won't fit through the vent,' Alexandra offers, holding up a sheet of Kamani's rough drawings.

'I explained to Ms Christofi that there is a vent from the roof. It is laid out as an L shape around the east section. You just need to make sure you are there before Magnusson. You need to take the Compliants by surprise. You'll have to shoot them all dead.'

'You really trust what this guy's saying?' Gabriel cuts in, his face erupting with outrage. 'Someone who broke into our hotel in the middle of the fucking night?'

I frown, taken aback. *What has got into him?*

'What he's saying checks out, lad.' Gibbs advises carefully.

'You're not going up against Magnusson alone, Lex. You need to think up another way.' He stands abruptly. 'Let me know when you have a revised plan.'

'Gabriel!' I assert. 'We don't have time for this.'

'Even if by some miracle Alexandra makes it out of there....' He continues, ranting. 'We can't just execute Magnusson, Alison. We need him to tell us where all the Compliants are. Brown will want him alive.'

'You don't need him.' Kamani admits, quietly. 'I have enough.'

'Alexandra has executed a number of operations long before you were back in her life.' I raise my voice. 'This is what she does.'

'Find another way.' He warns, his voice laced with an unnerving sense of restraint.

'There isn't one, Gabriel.' Alexandra rises from her seat, crossing the room and placing her hands on his face. 'This is the only way.'

He refuses to meet her gaze, instead staring over her head, the weight of his controlled silence setting the whole room on edge. Like the clock has stopped ticking and we're all waiting for the bomb to detonate.

'It's the only way.' She repeats, clearly sensing the cracks of vulnerability beneath the outburst.

'Find another one.' He says finally, before turning away and throwing the door open so hard it slams into the wall.

'I'll try speaking to him.' I say, attempting to break the tension. 'I'll see if I can get through to him.'

'He's just afraid.' Alexandra mutters, staring at the empty doorway as if Gabriel might reappear.

CHAPTER SIXTY

ALEXANDRA

Memories of the past few weeks disturb my sleep: *Hope Clarke thrashing in her chair, her fingernails clawing for relief, spittle flying from her mouth as her body jerked out of control, the pride in Flint's eyes, the eagerness and excitement in his voice.* My eyes stutter open. I squint at the ceiling, swallowing the rise of bile in my throat. My hands grip the sheets. *I'm back in the lab, waiting for the hot current to stop searing through muscle and tissue. The terrorist from the Wharf bombings stands over me, blood dribbling from a gnarly bullet wound in his neck.* Screwing up into a ball, I reach for Gabriel, craving the feel of him, needing to know he's close but his side of the bed is empty. I sit up. My brain jolts into awareness. Standing, I grab his jumper from a chair in the corner and creep lightly down the hallway of the compound. It's quiet. Only the hum of the generator can be heard as I tread the uneven floor. Reaching the briefing room, I peer in, expecting to see him hunched over the table, formulating an alternative plan but that, too, is empty. Padding to the storage cupboard, I grab a small pistol, load it, and continue the search. *Where could he have gone at this hour?* A light breeze rushes sand through the front door, depositing grains of it over my bare feet. I look out across the camp; white tents stand illuminated by the moon. I strain my gaze to the horizon, hoping to spot Gabriel's tall figure walking between the long grass. *Maybe he just needed some time to clear his head.* Taking a deep breath, I turn and head for the stairs. *Or perhaps he's with Kamani?* The thought panics me until a muffled pounding catches my attention. Angling my head towards the sound, I wait, listening out. It comes again. Puzzled, I shift down a second smaller passageway to the back of the building. The noise increases as I approach the room at the end; a short, sharp tapping accompanied by heavy breathing. Tensing, I use the end of the gun to nudge the door open. A large, dimly lit room comes into view; an area containing two tatty gym benches with a scattering of dumbbells, an old rowing machine, and boxing equipment in the far right corner.

Gabriel has his back to me. A punchbag swings from the ceiling, its chain rattling under the force of his fists. He stops, wiping sweat from his forehead before looking down at his hands, adjusting his wraps. I allow myself a few indulgent moments to soak him in. My stomach clenches, noticing the furrow of his brow, the darkness in his eyes. He's dealing with something, something he's keeping to himself. *Should I let him figure it out? Would I just be interrupting his outlet of stress?* I shake my head in answer to my own question. *We need each other.* When it feels like we should struggle in isolation, that's when we need each other the most. I approach quietly, trying not to disturb his flow. He doesn't notice me at first, continuing to expel short, sharp breaths. I watch as he beats the bag with determined power, throwing a right hook, slipping to the left before dropping an uppercut, the bulk of defined muscle in his biceps rippling with intensity. Eventually, his eyes flit to me and he straightens, steadying the bag, his chest heaving.

'It's three in the morning.' I say, taking a seat on a bench.

'Couldn't sleep.' He grabs a bottle, squirting the water into his mouth, avoiding eye contact. *He's shutting the world out tonight.*

'You need to use gloves.' I nod at his bruised hands. 'Wraps aren't enough.'

'All these ones are too small.' He places the bottle down, focusing his attention back on the bag.

'You're not ok are you?'

He exhales, exasperated. 'Lex...'

'Don't Lex me. I know what it looks like when you're deep in something, when you're struggling.'

He shakes his head. 'Not everything has to be done to a death, Alexandra.'

I smirk. 'I was waiting for that.'

'What?' He snaps.

'The lashing out. First, it's the silence. Then you lash out to get me to back off.' I murmur, adding, 'most people do back off.'

He stares as if weighing up his options. 'But not you.'

'Not me.'

'Whisky helped me sleep.' He admits.

'Ok...'

'There's a lot of shit going on in my head at the moment. I'm....' He sighs, almost as if resigning the thought. 'Sobriety is just dredging up a lot. Everything alcohol kept at bay.'

'We've been through a lot, Gabriel.'

'Just pisses me off.' He slams another punch into the bag.

'You can talk to me.'

His eyes shift away as he thinks on something. 'You don't want to listen to that.'

'If it helps you, I do.' I hesitate, wondering whether to push it.

He stays silent, removing the wraps from his hands.

'I don't want to wake up with you gone in the middle of the night, so we need to work it out.'

'Fuck, I don't know.' He takes a seat on the bench opposite. 'I don't want you anywhere near Raheem Kamani. I don't trust him. I don't want you in this fight against Magnusson. I want you far away from that facility. I can't stop thinking about all the ways our plan can go wrong.'

'Can you think of another way we can take it all down?'

'No.' He confesses. 'I can't and it's killing me. After everything we've been through, everyone we've lost along the way, it doesn't seem right that we're resting everything on Kamani. He was a part of that program for years. I'm not losing you again.' He whispers, his face tense and filled with angst. 'I'm not putting your life in the hands of someone I don't fucking trust.'

'I promise I'm not going anywhere.'

'That's not certain.' Tension invades his eyes as if his mind is wandering to a place he's not sure he can come back from. 'This is a crossroads, the turning point between us.'

'How do you mean?'

'This is the moment where I put my foot down and it saves your life. I'm not taking chances anymore. Please don't go into that room Lex. You join BRAVO or you don't come. That is within my control and I'm saying no.'

'This is what I'm trained to do.'

'If you go into that room and I lose you...' He breathes as if he can't bear the thought.

'Don't you think I feel the same about you?'

He closes his eyes. 'When you were gone... I used to have this recurring dream. I'm in bed asleep and I wake to your voice whispering my name in the dark. *Gabriel, Gabriel.* Again and again. Then you climb up on the bed, you lie down next to me and you hold on as if you're never letting go. In the dream, I think to myself... she's come back. She's finally given in because she can't stand for us to be apart anymore. And then...' He trails off uncomfortably.

My mouth runs dry. 'Then...'

'I'm able to drift to sleep knowing I don't have to miss you anymore, it feels good.'

'Why's that so bad?' I ask softly.

He raises his head, his eyes filled with so much pain it makes me want to look away. 'Because it isn't real. It was never real. I would wake up and the reality would sink in. You weren't really there, and I was still alone. So I'd have a drink to blur the heartache, then drink some more to forget missing you.' He scoffs. 'Even though you're here now. You're right there. I still can't sleep because it's eating me alive; the fear that I'll wake up and you'll be gone again. This time, I don't have the drink to numb everything. I just have to take it. Feel it all the way we're meant to.'

I crouch down in front of him, taking his bruised hands in mine. 'I know it hurts, but it is the greatest privilege… to feel.'

'That's…' his eyes expand. 'That's what you say to me.' His jaw firms, his brain working to digest this. 'It happened?'

I nod slowly.

'It was real?'

'A few months after the funeral, Edward requested me back to the UK. It was so hard; being home, knowing I couldn't be close to you. I just wanted one night. One night to feel something again.'

'I thought I made it up.'

'You didn't. I was there.'

'I stayed in that house just in case you came back, so you had somewhere to return to.'

I lean forward, gripping his arms. 'The point is I will always find my way back to you.'

He pulls me into his lap, gently pressing his beautifully etched mouth to mine. We trade kisses back and forth and I relax into him, savouring the moment of all the pain dissipating. Gabriel takes my face in his hands, the look in his eyes intensifying. The air shifts suddenly as I set my legs on either side of him, tracing both hands up his vest, my fingertips caressing the well-defined grooves of his stomach. He groans with satisfaction, his tongue finding mine as he hauls me closer with demanding necessity. His hands tighten reflexively against my hips, and I rock against him, driving a growing ache between my thighs, running my fingers through his messy hair. He tilts his head, his lips travelling over my jaw and down my neck, frantically unzipping my hoodie before discarding it on the floor. Returning his attention to my body, his eyes blaze with a restless yearning; a look that sets my blood on fire. My core tightens in anticipation, craving the reverence of his touch. He pulls his vest over his head, and I stroke my thumb lightly across the marked wound on his shoulder. He watches me, his eyes fierce on my face, the beat of his heart raging against mine until suddenly, he takes my mouth with searing possession, his rough hands sinking into my tangled hair. His skin: hot and damp against my bare flesh, spurs my desire further. Gripping his powerful arms, I wrap my legs around his waist, caging him to me. Holding me tightly, he stands from the bench, lifting me off my feet and laying me gently on the floor. He removes his shorts, a ghost of a smile touching his lips before he glides his tongue over my throat, between my breasts and across my stomach. His chest heaves with expectation as he slips my underwear over my knees. Watching with deep fascination, I spread my legs, offering myself to him.

'I need you to tell me nothing will happen to you.' He breathes, his possessive gaze stirred with vulnerability.

'Gabriel, please…'

'Tell me.' He repeats, displaying perfect restraint.

I squirm beneath him. 'Nothing…' I shake my head, fixated on his perfect mouth, 'I'll be fine.'

'Say it.' He commands.

I swallow, composing myself enough to speak, knowing he needs to hear the words before lust seizes control. 'Nothing will happen to me.'

He barely lets me finish before he takes my mouth again, absorbing my harsh, panting breaths as he thrusts into me, both of us becoming lost to instinct.

CHAPTER SIXTY-ONE

GABRIEL

'Right ok, so let's go clockwise.' Gibbs stands at the head of the table in the common room, waiting as everyone settles in. 'Gabriel, Alex, this scary fucker is Boots.'

Hunched over his food, Boots raises one hand. He has a scar that travels from his left nostril, diagonally across his lips to the cleft of his chin. He uses his other hand to shovel food into his mouth, never once looking up from his plate.

'Next up is Sully.'

An older man with the broadest shoulders I've ever seen nods a quick hello. Boots jokes across the table, referring to Sully as a human triangle. Sully tells him to fuck off.

'This guy wearing the cap...' Gibbs continues. 'This is Ronnie.'

Ronnie tips his hat slightly, revealing small beady eyes between a red beard that covers most of his face.

'He always wears that because he's receding.' Another bloke quips in a midwestern accent, adjusting the red bandana that hides the burns on his right temple, covering most of his forehead on that side. 'Nice to meet you both.'

Gibbs gestures to him. 'This handsome chap is Jake.'

'Good to meet you.' Lex offers.

'And last but by no means least... Fenwick.'

'Like the shop in London.' A bald cockney man winks, his dark eyes lingering on Lex for a beat too long.

'Lads, this is Alexandra Christofi. As you all know, I served with her.'

'I've heard about you.' Jake slurs in his American accent. 'People used to say that if you woke up with the Angel stood above your bed, you had every reason to shit your pants.'

The group laughs. Boots makes a lude joke about counting his blessings. Gibbs stares him down until his eyes return to his food.

'Fellas... this fine figure of a man is Agent James, MI6.'

Their faces land on me, the mere mention of MI6 spurring all kinds of judgement behind their eyes.

'How much do you know?' Lex asks, pulling their attention away. 'How much do you know about why we're here?' She elaborates assertively. Alexandra is accustomed to being the only woman in the room, their uncooperative gawping doesn't faze her. If anything, it spurs her on.

'We know enough, Miss.' Ronnie offers, finally.

'Officer to you.' Gibbs interjects.

'With all due respect, Officer. We know why you're here.' Jake announces, playing with a cigarette between his fingers. 'We know people...FSA brothers. Good people who have lost children. Taken...' He stops, baring his teeth. 'Gibbo told us what you need.'

'So what's your POA?' Ronnie asks curiously.

Taking charge, Lex stands and paces the room, explaining the operational specifics, constantly anticipating questions and holes in her theories. She continues laying out each unit's strategy with a play-by-play account of what each person needs to do. The group remain silent, watching her intently, listening to their individual tasks and responsibilities.

Jake whistles. 'This ain't your first rodeo.'

'The question is...' Fenwick interjects. 'How much we getting paid for this job?'

'Fucking unbelievable.' Gibbs mutters.

'He's right, Gibbo.' Jake interrupts. 'We got our lives here. Our families.'

'You run shit all the time for me!' Gibbs exclaims.

'Yeah for you.' Fenwick responds. 'To protect the people of this camp.'

'We're doing it for free.' Sulley mumbles. Jake and Fenwick fall quiet. 'Those kids aren't so different from the ones here. The ones we've pulled from rubble, saved from bombs. They deserve our help.' Sulley locks eyes with Lex. 'You got an intel source on the ground that says this Magnusson guy is there?'

Lex examines him across the table, making all kinds of deductions. 'Not on the ground.'

'Then what?'

'We have a source here, with us. He says Magnusson is at the facility, along with the evidence we need to put him away and stop the program altogether.'

'That's it…' Jake starts. 'That's the intel?'

'So there's a chance we could go in there and find nothing?' Sully asks.

Lex straightens. 'The intel is good.'

'And we're supposed to trust your say so?' Jake replies.

'Magnusson is there.' I say, glaring at Jake. 'And so are a group of children he's kidnapped from Za'atari migrant camp.'

Jake exhales, balancing his cigarette behind his ear. 'You plan on taking the whole thing down?'

'All of it.' Lex replies, her face set in a hard line. 'I'm not stopping until all those children are safe and the program is gone. Not until Andrew Magnusson is dead. That sound good to you?'

He curls his lip, impressed. 'Yep.'

The rest follow his lead, mumbling their agreement sporadically, a few more enthusiastically than others. Lex looks to me, relief flooding her face.

'Then it's a good'n.' Gibbs stands. 'Let's get ourselves fed. Meet at sun-up. That's 06:00 hours. We'll rehash the POA. Make sure we're green to go for tomorrow evening. Sully, prep the birds. Fenwick, you need to meet our drivers. Alex can intro you.'

'James…' Jake murmurs, turning his attention to me. 'You need kitting out. I'll show you the toys.'

'James!' Gibbs calls out. 'After you're done, come join us for dinner. There's usually a bit of singing, good food. You lot can get to know more people from the camp.'

'I'm told the women are already quite fond of you.' Jake sniggers. 'Come with me, pretty boy.'

We stride out of the briefing room, taking various turns down narrow corridors until we reach a set of stairs leading to a basement. 'In here.' He takes a few steps down before looking up at me. 'I'm not planning on killing you, don't sweat.' He shoves a heavy door open with the whole weight of his body, disappearing underground.

Following him down, I look up at floor-to-ceiling shelves stacked with equipment.

Jake reaches up and yanks a few boxes down. 'Helmet… night vision.' He frowns before pulling out an old bottle of whisky. 'Someone's got a stash.' He grins, screwing the lid before taking a swig. 'Want some?'

'No thanks.'

'Come on… it's the good stuff.'

'I don't drink.'

The bottle drops from his mouth to his side. 'No shit. Seriously?'

'Seriously.'

'Why's that?'

'Just trying to be a calmer, more peaceful person.'

He laughs, looking up to the ceiling. 'I hear you.' He sets the bottle down and walks to the shelves at the back of the room. 'You got any of this already?'

'Not much.'

'You know how to use it?'

'Sure I can figure it out.'

He scoffs, pulling down another box. 'Assault pack. There's extra ammo, knives, scissors, GPS, all sorts of useful stuff. Have a look through. You got a pistol, right?'

'Yep.'

'You can have an MK46 or an M4A1. The A1 has a grenade launcher. But I doubt MI6 let you play with the big boys.' He looks me up and down.

'The A1 is good.'

'You sure?'

'Positive.'

He shrugs, taking the rifle carefully off the wall. 'And in here...' He beckons me to a battered wardrobe. 'We should have armour. If you're lucky...' He rummages through. 'Boots used to wear something your size before he got too fat.' He hands me a vest, sniffing it before grimacing. 'Try that on.'

I throw the body armour over my head. 'Seems alright.' I unstrap it and pull it off again. I catch the sudden look of surprise on Jake's face. 'What?'

He nods to where my T-shirt has ridden up, focusing on the fading bruises across my ribs. 'I heard you'd been through the ringer for Christofi. Bullet wounds, broken bones.' He whistles through his teeth. 'She must be one hell of a ride.'

'Careful, I only said I was trying to be more peaceful… not that I was.'

'I like you, James. You're a lot like me.'

CHAPTER SIXTY-TWO

ALEXANDRA

I sit on a trunk by the fire, finding joy in watching the group. Gibbs and Fenwick pass around plates of food. Sully shouts encouragement to a group of boys who sprint eagerly after an American football. Boots crouches next to a handful of FSA soldiers, accepting their offer of a beer before they *cheers* their cups. More people join us, and I shift my eyes across the camp. There are men, women, and soldiers chatting excitedly: their conversation a hubbub of curiosity and anticipation amidst the arrival of new dinner guests. A boy runs past us with a toy truck in his hands. An older woman shouts out, warning him to be careful. He glimpses at me as he passes, the innocence in his eyes throwing me back to Islamabad. *Simon's voice. The IEDs. The dryness of the ground. The way it absorbed their blood in an instant.*

'You need to eat.' Gibbs appears, swigging from a carafe.

'Is that arak?' I hold out my hand.

'Is that a good idea?'

I raise my eyebrows at him until he gives in, handing me the drink.

'Usually, I can't shut you up the night before an op. Remember Haines used to tell you to take a walk, get all that pent-up energy out of you.'

'I remember.' I take a swig, my whole body burning from the strong liquid.

He leans forward; his kind eyes regarding me. 'You're still as good as you were then, Angel. You came here to do a job. The context changed, but you didn't.'

I sigh, sifting my boots through the sand.

'I heard on the tape…what you said to Kamani about Islamabad…' He lowers his voice. 'Is that why you're doing all this Alex?'

I hand him back the carafe. 'You first.'

He smirks, taking another swig. 'Might have something to do with it. I'd tell you to forgive yourself but I'm still trying to figure that one out.'

'We knew better.'

'I know, mate.' He pats me on the knee. 'We're trying to set the world right now. Try to remember that when you're in the middle of beating yourself up.'

Collins and Aldyn approach with children running between them; laughing, and singing to each other, chanting playfully in Syriac. Aldyn leans into Collins and points towards the horizon. She shields her face from the evening sun, her gaze seeking something out before she breaks into a smile. I follow their eyeline, curious to see what caught their attention. Gabriel strides across the sand, his long legs surrounded by a group of children following him through the grass. Three boys and two girls gallop after him, asking him questions, studying him whilst he answers. The smallest girl hands him a stick and he stops, crouching down to her level; smiling and saying thank you. Taking her hand, he walks over to flat ground and draws a few lines in the sand, the girl follows with excitement. The other children watch on, their faces alight with joy. Gabriel beckons one of the other boys over and hands him the stick, explaining the rules. The boy turns to his friends, grinning before stepping up to the square. Gabriel drops to his height, pointing out where he can draw his mark. The boy smiles, nodding enthusiastically, enthralled by this new game. The rest of the group fidget with anticipation, itching for their go. Another smaller, younger girl runs over, gently tugging on the back of Gabriel's T-shirt before her mother intervenes, apologising for the intrusion. Gabriel laughs, assuring her it's fine as the toddler reaches out to be picked up. The mother shakes her head, laughing with embarrassment. Gabriel bends down and takes her daughter in his arms. The little girl beams, touching Gabriel's face, curiously twiddling his hair. Amused, Gabriel sets her back on the sand, talking to her for a while. She gleams with pride, motioning for him to wave to her friends. A swell of emotion overcomes me. *The pure joy, the simplicity.* Keys stumbles up the ridge, calling Gabriel's name. Gabriel gently pats the little girl on the back and waves goodbye before stepping closer to Keys. The atmosphere changes as the two of them begin to chat somewhat intensely. Gabriel listens carefully, his eyes sliding back and forth as he takes the information in. My heart drops as I acknowledge the sudden hard look on his face. It's the kind of expression he adopts when he's knee-deep in shit. *The peace never lasts.*

'I think the lads are impressed with James.' Gibbs knocks me into the present again. 'And this lot aren't usually a fan of MI6.'

'Yeah well... he has his moments.'

He snorts, amused. 'He's not out of place, is what I'm saying.'

Through the crackling cloud of smoke, I watch Gabriel jog over to Raheem Kamani, who sits opposite us by the fire. The two of them exchange a few quick words before Kamani gestures towards the compound.

'Something is up...' I murmur, watching the two of them disappear with Keys.

'Stop worrying so much. I've asked Jake to keep an eye on him anyway.'

'Thank you...' I take a long breath, trying to settle my mind. 'Who is that... over there?' I ask, needing a distraction.

He looks up at the slender woman guiding a group of toddlers to sit cross-legged in front of the fire.

He smiles. 'You saw her when we arrived?'

'I did.' I admit, smiling.

'Like I said, I made a life for myself here.' He stares at her, his eyes alight with something more than just the flames.

'She seems lovely.'

'That's Gamila…. She's been teaching the kids. Trying to give them as much of an education as she can. She just wants them to have something, you know. Something to hold onto.'

'How many children are in the camp?'

'About one-twenty in this one. Gam teaches around eighty in total, she thinks.'

'Wow…'

'In the caves.' He signals behind him. 'In case of airstrikes, that's the safest place. Most of the children sleep there, too.'

'These are your people now.' I say, watching two girls braiding each other's hair between their mother's legs.

'Most came from Douma. After the chemical attacks.'

'Gibbs,' I whisper, placing my hand on his. 'Why are you risking all of this… for us?'

'Bit late to back out now.' He winks. 'See that little sweetheart there…'

A tiny girl with long dark hair tears bread into pieces, reaching her hand out to feed a collection of hens. Her long, thick eyelashes flutter with joy as the chickens hop around her with excitement.

'That's Hafsa. Her father suffered fatal injuries after the first attack. We found her hidden in a cellar. She hasn't spoken a day since.' He shakes his head as if he can't comprehend the suffering. 'Then this week Gam and some of the others, they taught her to ride a bike…' He chuckles proudly. 'She laughed for the first time since we found her. And she's laughed every day since, mate. That's what I want. For all of them. I want them to be kids. Camps like Za'atari aren't a life, we know that. And we do what we can to support but at least it's better than what awaits with evil fuckers like Magnusson in the world. These children have been through lifetimes of hell. They were born into a warzone, and he uses that to his advantage.' He drops his head. 'I just want to see more of them laughing.'

'Me too.' I smile at Hafsa, twiddling her fingers in her curly dark hair, chatting to the chickens. 'Me too.'

Making my way back to the compound, I link arms with Keys. Both of us crane our necks to the clear night sky, trying to distract ourselves from the weight of tomorrow.

'I always feel better…' I confess, 'when I consider what's up there. It makes everything we stress about here feel so insignificant.'

'It freaks me out personally…' Keys admits. 'Apparently, that fucker is constantly expanding and I for one, would like to know where it's going.'

'Nobody knows.'

'And that is the freaky part.'

'Doesn't the possibility of the unknown give you hope that there's so much more to life than this?'

'It gives me anxiety is what it docs Alex.' He laughs. 'Jesus, you really are brave.'

'What were you chatting to Gabriel about earlier?' I ask suddenly.

He stops in his tracks, dragging me to a halt.

'I know there's something going on.'

'He asked me to look into Magnusson's records again. He thinks we might have missed something.'

I frown. 'Have you got them?'

'Not yet. I was going to run a search tonight. I think he's just trying to cover all bases. Make sure he has all the intel on Kamani before you lot storm the facility on his instruction.'

'He has a real issue with Kamani.'

'You should speak with him. Ask him what's going through his head.'

'I already did that.' I sigh. 'Last night…'

'He's really good at shutting people out.'

'Usually when he's struggling the most.' I murmur, pondering the thought. 'I do get some of what he's feeling. It's hard after everything we've been through; knowing it's all coming to a head, knowing it's the end and not being able to see a future beyond it. He doesn't want to trust Kamani because he's scared to consider an outcome where we succeed. It's much easier to go against something that seems too good to be true.'

'And you? What do you think?'

'I'm trying to stay pragmatic. I've seen a lot of men feign remorse for their actions to serve their own agenda. I don't see that with Raheem. I believe he wants to make amends. And I have to trust that he has done everything in his power to help us get into that facility. Nothing goes according to plan. Not in our world. But I'm prepared for every eventuality.'

'You and Gabriel, you're true survivors.'

'I want him to believe that too.'

He stops again, taking both my hands in his. 'I wanted to thank you…' He sighs. 'For coming to me, for bringing me here.'

'Are you being sarcastic?' I grin.

'You've made me feel good again, like I'm worth something to the world… helping people for once.' He clears his throat, his squinting eyes trying to recall something before raising his head. '*You must thank your own worth for what I grew to be, for the demon lurks under the angel in me.'*

'That's beautiful. What is it?'

'A poem my Grandmother used to read …' he takes a breath. *'We are bound soul to soul by life's holiest laws. And if I am an angel – why, you are the cause.'*

'Will you find it for me when we get home?'

'I will.'

'Thank you.' I put my arm around him as we trundle through the sand. 'You're still going to run the club for me, right? When we get back. You're not going to become a philanthropist and ditch me?'

'Mate.' He smirks. 'I'm not going anywh…'

His words fall away.

I follow his eye line.

Gabriel and Emily stand close together, the former's expression torn between anguish and irritation. Seeing us, Emily quickly leaps back, creating distance as she wipes tears from her face. My mouth drops open slightly. I look between them. Emily excuses herself, scurrying away towards the tents. Gabriel runs a hand through his hair, a battle raging behind his eyes.

'I'll urm… I'll see you in the morning.' Keys whispers sullenly, patting me on the shoulder before walking on.

'Night.' I utter.

Gabriel plasters a false smile on his face. 'I was looking for you.' He takes my hand, lacing his fingers with mine before kissing my wrist. 'Come to bed with me.'

I wrap my arms around his waist and step into him, nestling my head against his chest. His body relaxes, clearly taking my affection to mean I've moved past the strange encounter. But in truth, I'm listening to the intensity of his heart rate. And it's racing. Racing like never before.

CHAPTER SIXTY-THREE

GABRIEL

The moon hangs above the dunes, its glow blanketing the sand. I sit, casting my eyes over the camp. It looks so peaceful at night. The welcome breeze causing ripples on the canvas of the tents. I lean to my left and run my hands through the tall grass on the verge. Its ends rustling in the wind.

'I need my beauty sleep, you know.' Keys huffs, climbing the hill. 'Could we not have met closer to the Compound?' He stops, noticing the rucksack in the sand next to me.

'Thanks for doing this.'

He doesn't move his eyes from the bag.

'Keys?'

'Yeah…' He sits down next to me, pulling a folded piece of paper from his pocket. 'I don't feel good about this, you know. Alex knows there's something wrong. She senses you're holding back and you've made me lie to her face.'

'I needed to know for sure myself.'

He nods. 'I get it man, I do.'

'This is the only copy?'

'Yep.'

I take it from him, unfolding the edges. Keys sits in silence, waiting for me to read the information. His breathing is heavy. I'm certain he's noticed a change in mine. That or he can hear the pounding of my heart in my chest. I scan the words, the unredacted details of Andrew Magnusson's intelligence record, right from when he was first recruited. *MI5. Doctor of Cognitive Psychology*. I grip the paper, continuing to read until I reach the bottom. It's everything I expected but seeing the evidence laid out in front of you is another feeling entirely. I drop the note and look to the compound where Alexandra currently sleeps, completely oblivious to the truth. I pull a lighter from the side pocket of my bag and set the paper alight before throwing it into the sand.

'I'm sorry, Gabriel.'

'I need you to keep this to yourself for now.'

'They need to know.'

'The plan doesn't change.'

'How long can you expect to lie to them all?!'

I look over at him and nod. 'When they're up, you can tell them.'

'And what about you?' His eyes drift back to the rucksack.

'Where will you be?'

'I've sent you a list of instructions.' I pass him a pad of paper. 'Everything the team needs to know is in there.'

Keys turns it over in his hands for a few moments before looking back at me. 'You know some people are surrounded by family. Picture perfect setups. They've got siblings, cousins, aunts and uncles coming out of their ears. And yet, they still feel alone. The truth is it doesn't matter how many you have to go home to. All you really need is just one person. One person to have your back no matter what. One person to pull you up to the surface and tell you to breathe.'

'Who is that person for you?' I ask.

'It used to be Mario.' He smiles. 'He always came through, even when my own mammy couldn't bear the sight of me.'

'He didn't give up easily.'

'Stubborn through and through.' He scoffs. 'That's where *she* gets it from. That pain in the arse determination.'

'You know, I saw anger in his eyes right before he went. He didn't want to leave her behind.'

'He loved her very much.'

'I was meant to be that person for Janie. I'm supposed to be that person for Lex. But all this time, I've been failing. I'm failing because I keep bringing the danger back into her life.'

'You are the only person who has ever known how to save her, Gabriel.'

'This could have ended a long time ago if I had just opened my eyes. I can't let her walk into that room with Magnusson. She shouldn't be within one hundred feet of him. It's not what her father would want.'

'Regardless of what's on those intelligence records, you are her person. She needs you.'

'I'll never replace Mario.'

'No....' Keys admits. 'But you push her to own the darkest parts of herself. You make her feel alive. You make her feel human. You know every inch of her. And if you leave, it will break her.'

'How can I let her confront Magnusson knowing what I know?'

'Let her make her own decisions. You can't deal with this alone. She'd want to protect you.'

'She can't continue to pay for other people's mistakes.'

'It's not your fault. None of this is your doing, Gabriel.'

I close my eyes, dropping my head. 'This whole fucking time, it was right there.'

'Please tell me what you're going to do?' Keys whispers.

'It's all in there.' I turn to him, deliberately ignoring the question. 'ALPHA and BRAVO need to storm the facility as originally planned. They need to take down the security teams and get the children out. Leave Magnusson to me.'

Keys begins frantically shaking his head.

'Listen, I've already set things in motion. You need to make sure Alexandra sticks to the plan.' I stand, throwing the backpack over my shoulder. 'Relay the message. If they follow the instructions I've laid out, it will be simple.'

'No, no. She is going to kill me for this. For letting you go.'

I pull out a gun, cock it and point it at his chest. 'I left you no choice.' I start to back away. 'I told you that if you didn't let me go quietly, I'd shoot you.'

'Please don't do this.'

'Take care of her, Keys.'

I leave him standing on the dunes before walking towards a line of parked trucks. It will take me a few hours to reach Palmyra but by the time Lex wakes up, I'll already be in the facility.

CHAPTER SIXTY-FOUR

COLLINS

I pull back the entrance of the tent and take a deep breath, inhaling the cool, crisp air. Sleep has decided to evade me tonight. For hours, I've been dreaming about waking up in blood soaked sand. Bolting upright, I kept feeling the ground around me to make sure it wasn't real. What is impossible to escape is the fact we're all going to that facility today and there's a chance some of us aren't coming back. That very thought has been circling my head all night. I cast my eyes over the trucks. All of them have been efficiently packed with medi-kits and other necessary provisions. *Ready and waiting.*

Yesterday, Team ALPHA and BRAVO ran a kit check. According to Alexandra, every operation requires a sort of *dress rehearsal*. It's a timed exercise where operatives practise putting on their battle gear, checking everything is in order. Alexandra did it twice. The first time was for Gabriel's benefit. He's a fast learner but she wanted to make sure he knew the order of things. *Ballistic Vest. Integrated breathing device. Weapons. Grenade. Radio. Googles. Helmet.* The strain that's existed on Gabriel's face since he entered this camp deepened even further. Alexandra's precision: the detached and methodical way she rigged that equipment unsettled him. It made him realise there was no arguing with her place in this. She's the best person for the job. The only person to take Magnusson down. He hates it with every fibre of his being that he knows that she has to be in that room.

'Can't sleep either?'

I turn, startled.

Keys lingers in the doorway of the compound, clutching a steaming mug.

'Jesus Michael, you scared me.' I place my hand over my heart. 'What are you doing up?'

He averts my gaze. 'Something has happened, Alison.' He looks at his feet, sifting sand beneath his boots. 'I made a mistake.'

'What...' I clear my throat, my voice hoarse. 'What is it?'

Keys nudges his head over his shoulder. 'Come sit down.'

'You're worrying me.' I whisper.

He guides me into the briefing room. 'Coffee?'

'No just tell me what's going on.' I take a seat, gesturing for him to do the same.

He reaches into his pocket, pulls out a USB and places it on the table between us. 'This....'

I pick it up, turning it over in my fingers. 'What is this?'

'I need you to look at it.' He slides his laptop over.

I shake my head. 'Whatever it is, I need to hear it from you.'

'I'm not meant to say anything.'

'Tell me you're not working for them, Michael.'

His mouth drops open, a gasp struggles up his throat. 'I would.... I would never ever betray this team. Not ever.'

I breathe a sigh of relief, briefly closing my eyes. 'I just had to check. I'm sorry.' I hold up my hands. 'I'm sorry. I had to make sure.'

'Jesus...' He runs his hands over his head. 'I don't know how to put this into words. But I fucked up, Alison. I really fucked up.'

'Just say it.'

He exhales. 'Gabriel is gone.'

My stomach drops. 'Where has he gone?'

'He wanted me to look into something for him. I did what he wanted. I looked into it. I gave him the information. Everything is on this USB. He saw it all. He....' Keys exhales. 'He left.'

'Left to go where?'

He throws his hands over his face, beginning to pace. 'That's the thing. There's nothing we can do. Not now, Alison. It's too late.'

'Where has he gone, Michael?'

'To the facility. He said we had to stick to this plan.' He gestures to a pile of handwritten notes on the table. 'He wrote it all out. He wants us to go to the facility as planned. We have to get all the children out by midnight. We have to be clear of the facility by a mile's radius at least…' He trails off, shaking his head. 'I don't know, once you see what's on that USB, you'll get it. I couldn't believe it but-'

'Keys! Take a breath. What's happening at midnight?'

'Air strikes,' he whispers, his voice strained. 'Gabriel has spoken to Agent Rikers. The guy from Defence Intelligence.'

I feel the blood drain from my face. 'Agent John Rikers?'

'Yeah.' He watches me closely. 'Rikers is going to deploy air strikes at midnight. He is going to hit the facility.'

'Air strikes.' I utter the words again.

'That's why we have to get the children out by then. That's why we have to be clear of the location.'

'And Gabriel? What about Gabriel? You should have come to me the second he left!'

'I was going to wake Alex up but he told me this was the only way. He said if I wanted to keep her safe, I needed to leave it be. He said she can't continue to pay for his mistakes. Once you see what's on that drive, you might understand.'

I stand from my chair, my hands gripping the table in front of me. 'How long?'

'Sorry?'

'How long has he been gone?'

'A few hours at the most-'

'So he'll be there by now!' I raise my voice. 'He's bloody gone to keep Magnusson in that facility. He'll be in there with Magnusson when the missiles hit! He'll die in there Michael!'

'Once he saw what was on the USB, he just closed off. Wouldn't see sense.'

'What is on the USB?'

He drops into the chair opposite me, his expression rigid.

'What's on the USB, Keys?'

The sound of Alexandra's voice travels through the room, injected into the air like an electrical shock. Both of us look up. Keys' mouth opens and closes. He hesitates, his face collapsing with shame.

'Forget it….' She enters the room, standing at the head of the table, her face set in a hard, determined line. 'You can explain on the way. Just tell me exactly where he is. Tell me where and I'll tell you how we're going to get him back.'

CHAPTER SIXTY-FIVE

GABRIEL

The sharp stench of chemicals knocks me awake. Wincing at the intense pain at the base of my skull, I try to sit up, resting my back against a wall. I'm in a holding cell, a bare clinical space with nothing but a single bed and a small table, neither of which were made for an adult. A child cries in the distance, their desperate pleas fading as their body is seemingly dragged further away. An older, more authoritative voice commands them to be quiet before a beeping starts. A door clicks, plunging the facility back into an uncomfortable stillness. This place is truly soulless, the air is filled with a heavy sense of despair. Ignoring the throbbing of my head, I approach the cell door, trying to see through the small glass window.

'What did you do wrong?'

I jerk back, looking behind me.

'I saw them bring you in.' A small voice calls out.

'Hi…' A sharp stinging sensation causes me to bring my hand to my mouth, feeling the wound on my lower lip.

'Did they hurt you with the zapper?'

'No…' I lean in against the wall. 'What about you?'

'Sometimes…'

'I'm really sorry about that, pal.'

'They said when I'm bigger, it will stop, and I'll just feel brave and strong. Do you feel like that?'

'Sometimes.' *This kid can't be more than six or seven.* 'What's your name?'

'Abeer.'

I think back to Lex and Pakistan. 'Nice to meet you…' I swallow hard. 'How old are you Abeer?'

'Five and two months.'

'Cool.'

'I'll be big soon.'

'And how long have you been here?'

He doesn't reply.

'Days or years, do you think?'

'I can't remember.'

'They can hear everything I'm saying, can't they?'

'Yes.'

Boots echo from down the hall and I look up to the cameras on the ceiling. I plant my feet, braced for whoever's coming.

'Will they use the zapper on you?' Abeer asks. 'Can you help me?'

'Yeah, pal.' An armed guard appears in front of the glass window, and I clench my fists. 'I'll help as much as I can.'

'Against the wall.' The guard demands, tapping the door with his weapon. 'Against the wall.'

'Or what?'

He raises his eyebrows. 'Or we'll punish someone else for your defiance.'

Immediately, I drop my hands and do as he says.

The guard punches his finger on the keypad. 'You and I will get along just fine if you behave.' He sizes me up with just a hint of apprehension in his cold glare. 'If you try anything funny, that's a whole other story.' He motions ahead. 'Out.'

'See you soon, Abeer.'

'Walk.' The guard commands, pressing his rifle into my spine, marching me down the corridor.

I peer into the other cells, each of them presenting a different scene; some are empty, others contain sleeping teenagers, a few have doctors crouching over beds with drips and various medical equipment, some children lay peacefully, barely moving, others stare at the blank walls ahead.

'Where are we going?'

He remains tight-lipped, guiding me to a stairwell that leads to a narrow, dimly lit hallway. The eerie stillness reminds me of being the only one left at school. Whenever my mother was late, which was often, I'd kill time and roam the empty halls. Knowing everyone had gone home for the weekend, there was a certain freedom to wandering around after hours. *No teachers. No rules.* I became accustomed to the calmness of a place once the masses had left, felt more attune with the surroundings. For those short hours, it was mine. But for obvious reasons, this is quite different. Magnusson's facility hosts a wicked hollowness. Despite the fact we pass multiple labs, several operating theatres and various other rooms of people working on test subjects, it's a deep, merciless trench.

'Stop here.' The guard orders, sliding his card over a digital console. It flashes green and the wall next to us drifts to the left. He gestures ahead.

I slip through, stepping into an even darker space. He shoves me forward. I throw my hands out ahead of me, my palms slamming into metal.

'What the fuck....' I grunt angrily.

He grips the back of my neck, swiftly slamming my head against the door. 'Open it.'

Pain splinters across the bridge of my nose, my entire face feeling like it's been shattered into pieces. 'Fuck you.' I spit, fighting every instinct not to retaliate.

He leans around me, pushing down on the handle. 'In.'

I glimpse the scar on the back of his neck, the incision that tells me I'm standing with one of Magnusson's adult Compliants.

'Couldn't have just done that the first time.' I pinch the bone between my eyes as I'm shoved into a brightly lit room.

'Agent Gabriel James, Secret Intelligent Service.' A rasping, sickly voice announces.

I blink past the welling of my eyes, struggling through double vision. A figure faces a glass window that looks out to nothing but a few square metres of rough, rocky earth, as if the room has been buried beneath a canyon. Battling to focus, I watch as he turns, presenting a long, gaunt face, balancing on a lank, willowy body.

'So who's it to be... Augustus Fox or Andrew Magnusson?'

'Bravo.' He applauds, sitting down, his neck stooping over his chest, like a branch sagging after a stretch of heavy rain; his figure twisted and distorted by a lack of sun and fresh air. He wears a white lab coat, which covers a cream shirt, and brown suit trousers. It's an outfit that could easily pass for 1950s communist Russia. Despite the lack of light, his presence casts an even heavier shadow in the room; a lurking toxicity that makes you feel sick to your stomach. His eyes, his skin, even his fingernails carry a discolouration; like he emanates poison.

'This is a wonderful surprise....' He holds his hands out, seemingly delighted, like a grandparent receiving an impromptu visit from their favourite grandchild.

His attention shifts over my shoulder, and I turn, following his contented gaze. The first Compliant exits and a brunette enters in his place. Her movements are determined, a fresh bandage covers her left hand, tightly wrapped over the space where her fourth and little finger should be.

'There she is...' Magnusson smiles with pride. 'Agent James, meet Sigma.'

Sigma offers no reaction to Magnusson's greeting or his introduction before setting her mechanical glare on me. Her cold eyes meticulously scan every inch of my body as if assessing the risk of leaving me standing in the middle of the room. The door's hinges groan again as a second person enters.

'This one Delta?' I mutter sarcastically.

'Zeta.' Magnusson smirks, enjoying the ceremony.

Zeta presses his back to the door, his hand hovering over his weapon before he prowls the perimeter of the room, eventually coming to stand protectively next to Magnusson, like a well trained Apex predator. A thick, reddened scar runs down the middle of his face, it appears, at one time, an opponent might have tried to peel him in two.

Magnusson moves, perching on the edge of his desk, his nails tapping the carved wood. 'You and The Angel. A most extraordinary pair. Please...' He gestures to the chair in front of him. 'Have a seat.'

'I'll stand.'

'See...' He raises a bony index finger. 'That! Strength of character like no other. Tell me...' His yellowing eyes fire up with excitement. 'Tell me why it is you came.'

'I'm here as a courtesy.'

'Oh yes?'

'We've taken out all your key players. This program is done.'

His eyes narrow.

'This facility will be destroyed.'

'You've come to negotiate.'

'It's more than you deserve.'

'It's a wonder you're stood here really...' He muses. 'I'm told you're an addict.'

'I'm giving you the chance to live.' I add, ignoring him. 'You can walk out of here alive. We'll take you in, keep you away from everyone who wants you dead. And in return, you'll tell us everyone who's involved in this sick fucking thing.'

'Or...'

'Or you stay here with me, and you die.'

'Oh you too?'

'I'm here to make sure that happens.'

'You're willing to go down with me.'

'If that's what it takes to wipe you, your program and this awful fucking place off the face of the earth, then yeah.'

'What if I run?'

'You won't.'

'You're sure?'

'I know your type.'

He nudges his head quickly. The Compliants shift; their movements rapid. Zeta lurches forward, his weapon pressing into the front of my skull. Sigma's gun jams into my left temple. Our bodies positioned in a near-perfect right angle.

'Look at me, James.' Magnusson commands, his face inches from mine. 'Look at me...' He clicks his tongue until my eyes rest on his nasty face. 'There you are. You're so similar. This dogged air of authority everywhere you go. Everyone is beneath you. Nobody quite as sharp. I think you're here because you finally know the truth.'

'I told you why.'

'Say it.'

'It's over.'

'No, no, no.' He waves a fragile hand. 'Why did you come alone? Tell me the real reason.'

I exhale, enraged that he takes so much pleasure from this.

'I just want to hear you say it...' He beams, his expression filled with delight. 'Why did the handsome hero come alone? What makes you think you can walk into my home without being killed on the spot, Gabriel *James*?'

'You know-'

'Ah ta ta… tell me with your own words.'

My stomach turns, his snide words taunting me.

'Come on, Gabriel. How did you come to learn that you were invincible?' Magnusson lures as if coaxing an injured animal to walk again. 'Come on…' He grins. 'Because…'

'You created the Compliancy program with my father. It was founded by MI5. By you and Edward James.'

'There it is.' He sighs, looking relieved. 'The truth will set you free. How did you come by that information exactly?'

'Raheem Kamani.'

'Such a talent. It was your father who found him, nurtured him. You remember him, do you? The first of Edward's little pet projects. Did Raheem tell you the full story? Did he tell you why he ultimately chose to join me?' He doesn't wait for an answer. 'Your father practically brought him up, treated him like one of his own, paid for him to live in a nice flat, funded his education. Raheem joined our operations unit at MI5 when he was just twenty-three years old. And he wouldn't have been there without Edward James. Then, out of the blue, you get offered a place at Cambridge, you tell your father that you want to go into intelligence. Suddenly, Edward had a new interest. Poor Raheem was instantly put on the back burner. You see, the thing is with Edward, he uses people, he plays a dangerous game of favourites. And when he's finished well…' He makes a cutting motion across his throat.

'I'm under no illusion that he's a good man.'

'Things weren't working out at MI5, so naturally, we left to expand the program's true potential. Your father didn't think big enough. He wanted to own my creation for himself.'

'Well it's over for both of you now.'

'The hunt for The Singularity all but destroyed your life.' He continues, ignoring me. 'And yet Edward was right there all along. Right in front of you. He'll always be there. Every time you look in the mirror.' He rests his palm on my right shoulder, gently caressing the area of the bullet wound, his voice drifting between his lips as if trying to catch a passing thought. 'Tell me, when you lie with The Angel and her hands trace these scars, do you think of me?'

'You don't think I know how to get into someone's head.'

'Oh, I have no doubt you're the best.'

'I assume you're not taking me up on the offer of surviving?'

'A captain never abandons his ship.' He waves a hand.

The Compliants drop their weapons.

I grit my teeth, unable to temper the wave of defeat. This was inevitable. Magnusson was never going to surrender but hearing him confirm that, allowing him the autonomy to decide my fate with a few simple words, fills me with anger. I admit there was a small wish he would surprise me, that I'd leave here with him and step out of the facility only to find Lex standing with Collins, Gibbs, and the boys. I picture her marching towards me with furious eyes, irritated for taking matters into my own hands. She might give me the silent treatment, tear me down a few pegs for leaving, but we'd both be alive. And that is all that would matter. My mind stalls on an image of her face. The wild hair, the golden eyes, that infectious, loud laugh. I'd trade anything to hear it again. But I left knowing the probable outcome of this decision. I grappled with it, agonised over it. There is no other way. Alexandra will no longer risk her life for the actions of my family. This is my responsibility. I'm prepared to die to put it right.

'You're no coward, I grant you that.' Magnusson chuckles as if reading my mind. 'What a match you are for her…'

An alarm sounds. A warning that wails three times before stopping abruptly.

Zeta grips my arm.

Sigma pivots towards the door.

Magnusson hurries to his computer screen, examining it. His face lifts with amusement. 'Our Angel! The Angel has come for Gabriel James.' Magnusson watches me with intrigue, enthralled by the devastation on my face. 'Into the lion's den…' He murmurs with delight. 'Just like I thought she would.'

CHAPTER SIXTY-SIX

GABRIEL

Magnusson hums to himself, a tuneless, irritating sound, as he picks up a small black remote and points it at the wall to my left. Shelves stacked with various books, framed doctorates, and old photos of him standing with politicians, slowly shift to the side.

Alexandra is thrust into the room.

She's hunched over, clutching her ribs as a third Compliant pushes her ahead. This one is almost as wide as he is tall, with bleach-blonde hair and narrow, determined eyes. He grips her hair, dragging her across the room. Despite his strength and the ease with which he handles her, he's slightly out of breath, his knuckles reddened and bruised. She gave him a good run, at least.

'Thank you, Tobias.' Magnusson nods at the third assassin.

Lex continues to emanate a slow wheezing, clearly struggling to breathe. She winces, attempting to straighten up. Her eyes dart to mine and her face tenses, analysing my bloody nose and split lip.

'Welcome my Angel.' Magnusson marvels in her increasing anger.

'Are you ok?' She rasps, still looking at me.

'It's a fucking wonder you were in the army.' I growl. 'You haven't followed a single instruction since I met you.' I keep my eyes trained on the floor. *She was supposed to be safe, supposed to live. She shouldn't be here.*

'I really do find the two of you so fascinating.' Magnusson offers a sadistic smile. 'It's a classic, isn't it? Who loves who the most? Who will trade their life first? You can't *both* win.'

'Shut up, Magnusson.'

'Have you told her?' He continues, jeering. 'Does she know what Daddy did? Has it changed your perception of her? The woman you love agreed to work for the founder of the program you vowed to defeat. Chasing me on your father's behalf, not really knowing who or what she was hunting.'

'Keys told me…' Lex glances at me, her eyes filled with worry. 'You could have come to me; I would have helped…'

'Silence!' Magnusson's sharp eyes pierce her face. 'He's here now. That's all that matters.' I feel a hand on my shoulder before I'm pushed to my knees. 'I've decided that we're going to play a game.' Magnusson declares. 'Lift your T-shirt, please Gabriel.'

Sigma sets a portable machine next to me, efficiently threading out the wires, waiting for me to obey.

'Come on now, play along.'

She attaches two lap-pads to my chest, another to my temples.

'No!' Lex protests, panic striking her face. 'No! Do it to me!'

Tobias thrashes her backwards, pinning her to the wall.

'Do it to me instead!' She pleads, straining against his grip. 'Put me back in it. I'll do it. Not him!'

My heart sinks.

She was broken after her experience in the lab with Flint and yet here she is, desperate to take my place.

Ignoring her pleas, Zeta pulls me to my feet, leading me into the seat opposite Magnusson.

'It's alright…. Master James is far too complicated for extraction, Angel.' Magnusson laughs, a long, condescending sound whilst pointing his remote to the glass behind him. It darkens, fading into blackness. A ring of orange light appears. 'You both insist on feeling everything so very deeply, I think you could benefit from seeing how it governs you.'

Tobias grips Lex's arms and tugs her writhing body across the room before dropping her into the chair next to me. Having finished connecting me to the EEG machine, Sigma places it on the desk and takes an obedient step back into the shadows.

'Alexandra, I'm going to ask you a series of questions and you're going to answer them truthfully.' Magnusson holds out his hands. 'Don't lie. Trust me I'll know.'

'If you harm him…'

'Yes, yes.' Magnusson dismisses.

I glance the time on his monitor. *Ten twenty-six.* We need a new plan. Lex cannot stay here to die. She won't pay for my father's decisions, not anymore.

'We'll start easy…' He looks up to the ceiling like a child in a game of eye-spy. 'Alexandra, do you love Gabriel James?'

'Yes.' She spits begrudgingly.

The EEG machine whirs, the screen ahead illuminating as words appear in a list.

Magnusson looks up, reading. 'Sharp increase in dopamine and oxytocin but he's fighting it. There's a spike in cortisol. Alexandra, my darling, your love stresses him more than it pleases him. Now that is interesting.'

I glare at him, my eyes scorched into his face.

'Now Angel, tell me… what do you know about Higgs?'

'It's a serum you created to brainwash children.'

'Ahhh…' He hisses as if reeling from a hot surface. 'You make it sound so base.' Magnusson tilts his chin. 'Higgs is a serum, yes. But it's based on Higgs Boson, which has been a theory of psychologists for decades. It was introduced in the early seventies to erase trauma from patients with acute psychosis. We used visual cues to understand emotional triggers that told us where to sever the link.'

421

I check the time again. *Ten thirty.* I have to stall long enough to ensure he's here when the missiles hit. *I have to stall. Lex has to leave.* 'Why did you start this?'

'Really, Gabriel... that is a question for Daddy.'

'There must be a reason you chose to continue his work.'

'My work.' He points a finger into his chest. 'It's mine.'

'So tell me, why go to such great lengths... why build the second facility? Why sell Compliants to Smart? Why use Almasi as a scapegoat to take over the British gov....'

'Because!' Magnusson shouts, his face reddening. He takes a breath. 'Because *my* program, *my* Compliants, *my* influence is going to fix everything that has been broken in our country for a very long time. We're laughed at by our Western allies; bullied by Russia, China, America. And, of course, they're mocking us. Their people are more highly skilled, they have better weapons, superior intelligence. Over the last twenty years, we have become a joke! As a nation, we have started to reward weakness. We open our borders to anyone, welcoming useless, worthless people who don't give anything back. They suckle on the teat that is this country's welfare system. We have a shortage of doctors, scientists, engineers. Nobody wants to do the hard jobs anymore. British people are lazy, slovenly; consumed by social media platforms that the Chinese created just to keep us quiet, like offering a toddler a lollypop. And we take it. Our government willingly allows us to dumb ourselves down because it makes us easier to control. I will get this country back on track. I will reclaim our power. People I worked with in MI5, good, honourable people... they gave their lives for this country to prosper; to protect our core values.' He exhales as if he can't even believe what he's saying. 'They would be horrified.'

'And you think you're saving the country by stealing children from refugee camps and training them to infiltrate governments. You think you're protecting it by encouraging terrorists to blow up airports?'

'When do you think Britain has been at its strongest?' He raises his thin, sparse eyebrows. 'War! We were the most powerful during times of hardship.'

'You're essentially reducing our society to nothing so you can rebuild it in your image.' Lex says, incredulous. 'Exactly as you do with your Compliants.'

'A black hole Singularity...' Magnusson holds his hands out with pride. 'From nothing comes everything. He who can destroy a thing has the real control of it.'

I return my eyes to the clock. *Ten forty.*

'What stage of Compliancy are the three musketeers?' I interject, tilting my head to his Compliants.

'They are fully trained.'

'And the children you've sent to Jed Smart?'

'They've had some good, intricate training already. They're obedient, they learn fast.'

'You shipped them over, then what?'

'The UK government has a training facility off the coast. We give them the entire training program.'

'Almasi got them already made though, did he?'

'He has his own requirements.'

'He doesn't even realise he's being used by you, does he?'

'Needs must.'

'How many of your Compliants have you deployed into positions in the UK Government?'

He laughs.

'How many are waiting for the go-ahead to murder the British Prime Minister?'

'Oh, you have taken a deep dive into my world, haven't you Gabriel…' He offers a tense snarl, narrowing his eyes. 'You are more like Edward than you'll ever know.'

'What happened with Hope Clarke?' Lex asks suddenly. 'She was the first Compliant, wasn't she?'

Magnusson's expression freezes for a split second before he recovers. 'Every masterpiece has its flaws.'

'She became lucid, and you didn't know how to get her back under?'

'One rotten apple needn't ruin the whole orchard.' He sits up, straightening his jacket.

'So you started this program in Chateau Noir with Edward?' I continue, pressing him.

'That's where it began, yes.'

'Then, in 2005, you faked your death so you could separate yourself from Edward and MI5. You moved into new territory, started a contract with the MOD.'

'Gold star.'

'When did you start training them to infiltrate the UK government?' Lex asks, clearly hoping this time he might actually offer an answer. 'How many are operational at this moment?'

'Let's get back on track.' Magnusson insists.

'No.' I respond defiantly, reaching under my shirt, ready to rip the wires away. 'You've made your point.'

'Would you prefer we hooked her up instead?' He warns, waving a finger.

I drop my hand, feeling the spike in my heart rate before the machine reacts and the screen bears the truth; I grit my teeth, watching the words appear, every raw emotion exposed to the room. *Adrenaline, Cortisol, Norepinephrine. Ten forty-six.*

'Good.' Magnusson says, satisfied. 'Tell me Alexandra…why did you agree to work for Edward James?'

'I…' She stops, her voice cracking. 'I believed it would save Gabriel's life.'

'I don't need you to be hooked up to the machine to know you're lying to me, Angel.'

Lex frowns. 'Edward offered to wipe Gabriel's record, to keep everything we had done under wraps if I joined the hunt for Higgs. He would have gone to prison otherwise.'

'No doubt it was a factor in your decision, saving Gabriel. But what's the main reason? Come on… let's get it all out on the table.'

'I have no idea what you're talking about.'

'Oh but I think you do, Alexandra.' He grins. 'Come on, tell us…' He waits. 'No? How about I venture a guess? I think Gabriel deserves to know why you broke his heart, don't you?'

'He knows everything.'

'You couldn't give yourself to him anymore because you were consumed by revenge. After watching your sister murder your father, you wanted people to suffer. And you knew you had to put everything behind you to achieve that goal. Nothing was more important than the need to avenge Mario. Nothing more important than becoming a monster.'

Lex fails to hide the misery in her eyes.

'You knew Gabriel would hold you back. You loved him deeply. Much as you do now but there was no place for his love in your life anymore. In order to become brilliant, you had to switch it off. You had to push him away.'

'We get the point you're making Magnusson…'

'Am I near the mark?'

'Yes.' She admits quietly.

'Decrease in serotonin and adrenaline.' Magnusson cranes his neck, reading my results. 'Wow, you're quite literally causing him pain.'

The EEG machine continues humming. I shift in my seat, refusing to look at the screen again. *I don't need it to tell me what I'm feeling.*

Lex stands from the chair, her fingers gripping the portable machine. 'So we're guided by our emotions; we saw children suffering and we wanted to punish the people responsible. I lost my father, and I sought revenge. I love Gabriel James and I'm frequently irrational because of it. We feel... everything. We're flawed. We're human.'

'But what if you weren't? What if you allowed logic, statistics, and rationality to guide you? This is the price you pay for love... Pain.' He waves his hands in the air. 'Then you let Edward get the better of you – his greed has ruined you both.'

'It's not about greed.' I say pointedly. 'You took his work and sold it to his enemies. He wants to punish you.'

'I am beyond his reach.'

'Are you?' Lex snaps.

He trains his attention on me. 'This is what you like about her, isn't it, James? She's a warrior. Scrapped her whole life for significance.'

Anger boils under the surface, rippling through my blood, but I keep quiet, not wanting to give him the satisfaction.

'The truth is Angel...' Magnusson continues, 'you're an insult to the order of things. Your place was in the criminal underworld. But the army put you on the front line to tick a box. This country has gone mad. Talent, skill, ability mean nothing anymore. But if you're a minority, well then, you hold the golden ticket. Straight to the top you go, all so they can show you off and tell others how modern they are.

426

But does any of this performative nonsense save lives, defend cities, prevent disease? I'm taking all the vulnerable, the weak and I will make something real, something tangible.'

'You're the fucking monster.' Lex yells.

'Angel, behind every milestone of human history stands a monster.' He laughs around the room as if performing to an audience. 'Your whole life, Alexandra, people told you that you were special because that's what our society does. We take the downtrodden and we give them value. Tell me... has that helped you thrive? Look at you, you have no discipline, no obedience, no respect. And since you started this crusade, you've done nothing but prove me right. Then there's Gabriel James; blinded by love, wishing for things that can never be, he'd tear out his own guts if you asked him to. But all he's got to look forward to is more death, more disappointment. It's not like you can give him a future. You can't even keep a child long enough to give him a family.'

'Enough!' I bellow, slamming both fists into the desk, the glass cracking under the force. All three Compliants draw their weapons. I rip off the lap pads, throwing them down. 'One more word in her direction and I will strangle you in that fucking seat.'

'Aggression is anger in action.' Magnusson muses, signalling for his protectors to stand down. 'A burst of adrenaline signifying your desire to take immediate protective charge. You're not attached anymore but I can tell you what's happening inside. Your heart rate accelerates, your blood pressure rises, your rate of breathing increases. You've got increased blood flow to your limbs and extremities. Your body is priming you. See... see how she controls you.'

He stands, buttoning his jacket, twitching his head in command. Zeta marches towards Lex, knotting his hand in her hair before he yanks her head back. She cries out in pain, the silver of a blade settling against her skin.

'Now Gabriel…' Magnusson starts. 'I'm going to need your full attention for this next part.' He leans down, placing a large bottle on his desk, followed by a single empty glass. 'But I can't imagine that will be very difficult.' He mutters, knowing my focus is entirely occupied with the knife. 'She'll be fine if you play one last game.'

He unscrews the cap, pouring the liquid into a tumbler before sliding it across. I turn, instinctively catching the drink in my hand. I stare down at the golden fluid, my mouth salivating. My mind sputters like the picture of an old television, every sense homed in, mesmerised by the drink's proximity.

'No!' Lex shouts.

'Come on… have a sip.'

'Stop it.' Lex demands. 'Please don't…' She bends backwards, trying to keep the tip of the blade from drawing blood.

'Drink it.' Magnusson smiles, his lips spreading across protruding lips.

'Gabriel, please…' Lex begs. 'Don't give him the satisfaction.'

'You gave her your life, your career; you take beatings and bullets in her name. Everything you do is for her. But not this. This is yours. It's for you. Just for you. You deserve this, Gabriel. It's the only thing left in your control.'

Lex continues struggling, trying to break free. Zeta lets her go before swinging his hand in the air, backhanding her hard. Her head whips back, her body hurled towards the wall. She recovers quickly. With determination set in her eyes, she lunges for him. Zeta draws his weapon, clicks the safety, and fires a shot at her feet.

'I'll do it!' I yell, pulling Zeta's attention to me. 'I will do this, and you let her walk out of here.'

Magnusson pauses, thinking about it.

'You can keep me. That can be your parting gift to Edward. But Alexandra goes.'

'I won't leave!' Lex screams.

Magnusson nods. 'If you take the drink, Alexandra can leave before our government gives us the firework show.'

'No.' Lex wails, dropping to her knees. 'Please.'

Zeta looms over her, resting his gun against the crown of her head.

'I do this, and I have your word?'

Magnusson nods. 'Be done with it, or we will kill her... simple as that.'

I look down, examining the whisky; temptation grappling with flashes of restraint.

'Please,' Lex sobs. 'Please don't.'

Ignoring her, I take a breath. Grip the glass.

'Bottoms up.' Magnusson jeers. 'This is what he will do for love...' He flits his gaze to Lex. 'Destroy his sobriety. Demolish his oath. All to save your life. Do you think you're deserving of his sacrifice?'

Keen to shut him up, I throw the drink back, my body burning with a concoction of ruin and relief.

Pleased with the outcome, Magnusson pours again. 'Might as well do the bottle.'

I swallow another.

And another.

Then another.

'Why...' Lex cries. 'Why are you doing this?'

'This is the danger of attachment, my love.' Magnusson lectures. 'Look! Look at Gabriel! Drinking from the poisoned chalice, consuming the one thing that he knows will destroy him. Because of you. Because nothing good comes of loving you, Alexandra. Nothing of value. Nothing of use. You must have realised by now that you are and will always be his downfall. You would both be better off if Dr Flint had completed his work at Chateau Noir.'

My eyelids drift heavy, the world becoming more and more unfocused. My mouth slackens, my movements less determined.

'One more my friend. Then we'll let Alexandra go, release her into the world to do more damage. It's not the desired outcome but...' he shrugs, 'that was the deal.' Magnusson tips the last dregs of the bottle into the glass.

I straighten, turning to Lex; weary and defeated. 'To leaving it at the door.'

Her eyes lock to mine, her expression quietly transforming. She shifts slightly, planting herself steadily. I inhale a sharp breath downing the final morsel of liquid, screwing my eyes shut and dropping my chin to my chest.

Magnusson walks towards me, raising his head to peer into my face. 'That's it, Gabriel. Get it all dow....'

I shoot up, spurting a full mouthful of whisky into his eyes. He recoils, his torso folding over his knees. I swing to my left, shattering the crystal into Sigma's face. She dives her fingers to her weapon, but I kick it out of her hand and smash her backwards into the wall. The crown of her head hits the edge of a shelf, leaving a smear of blood across the wood. I grip her shoulders and slam her a second time, knocking her unconscious. I turn to find Lex. She leaps up, thrusting her foot into Zeta's chest before shooting her elbow into his face. Having assessed which one of us he thinks poses a larger threat, Tobias pulls out his gun and charges towards me. I drag Sigma's comatose body in front of me as he fires bullets. Pulling the pistol out of the holster around Sigma's waist, I fire two quick shots at Tobias. He quickly dives over Magnusson's desk, hiding from view.

'You good?' I call out to Lex.

She nods, wrestling the knife from Zeta's hand, slicing it through the air with meticulous precision. The blade draws a narrow slit across the base of his throat. Zeta drops to his knees, his face frozen with shock, his hands twitching towards the wound before the light behind his eyes dulls.

The scene distracts me for a second too long. Tobias reappears, jumping up to launch another tirade of gunfire. He fires off two more shots. I barge Lex to the side, moving her out of harm's way but she cries out in pain, dropping to her knees. Dragging her behind one of Magnusson's lounge chairs, I note the blood seeping from her left shoulder. Taking the knife from her right hand, I rise and hurl it at Tobias. With an effortless shift of his weight, he ducks out of the way; the blade lodging itself in the wall above his head.

I fly towards him, narrowly avoiding a second flurry of bullets. Hooking my arm around his throat, I punch the gun from his hand. He links his left leg around my knee and twists me onto the floor, coming to quickly straddle my chest. I strain against him, my fingers gripping his wrists, struggling to keep his hands from reaching my throat. He hurls his head forward, headbutting me. The world becomes blurred. I blink rapidly, knowing I've released control. His weight bears into me, all ninety-plus kilograms crushing my windpipe with an overpowering hold. My mouth claws for air, my brain feeling as if it might protrude out of my eyes. I tear at his fingers, wheezing for oxygen, my legs scrambling, kicking against the tiles, my body bucking violently, refusing to surrender under his vice-like grasp. The veins in his face explode with effort, his eyes bulging from their sockets as he drives the full weight of his body against my trachea.

Suddenly his head is whipped back, his body disappearing. A sound fills the room. A quick and recurrent beating, accompanied by a bellow of rage. Disorientated, I try to sit up, my lungs battling to draw breath again.

'You ok?' Lex appears above me, blood splattered across her face, soaking her blonde hair.

'Where's Magnusson?' I rasp, warily.

Her eyes widen with panic. He emerges, hooking his arm around her neck, dragging her backwards, the tip of the knife toying with Lex's throat.

'Stop!' I reach for Tobias's discarded weapon, aiming at his head. 'You think you can end her life before I end yours?' I shout.

'Don't come any closer, James...' He warns.

The alarm system starts up again, its siren blaring into the room. I look at the clock. *Eleven twenty-four.*

'Let her go.'

'After everything she's done to you...breaking you over and over and over!'

'Let her go!'

Lex nudges her head slightly, catching my eye. She's telling me to shoot. She's confident I'll hit him first time.

'Final warning Andrew.' I shift my grip, ready to end his miserable life, when a shrieking voice cuts through the air. Lex drops to the floor, covering her face. Two bullets pierce Magnusson's chest. Reaching forward, I pull Lex behind me. Magnusson drops to his knees, blood spreading rapidly from the holes in his torso, seeping into his shirt. He sways slightly before collapsing to the floor. I adjust my aim, speedily training my gun at the figure behind, shouting for Sigma to drop her weapon.

'It has to end...' She hurries out, turning the gun on herself, propping it under her chin. 'I just want it to end!'

'Stop!'

Fear flashes in her eyes. She places her finger on the trigger. The cold shadow of obedience having completely disappeared.

'Put it dow-'

The final discharge of the bullet cracks into the air.

CHAPTER SIXTY-SEVEN

ALEXANDRA

'You two planning on hanging around for long?'

Gabriel swings his weapon to the door, taken off guard.

Wayne Gibbs appears, his hands and face smeared with blood. 'Don't worry, it's not mine.' He says, adjusting the strap of his rifle before checking his watch. 'But we do really need to go before Defence Intelligence lights us all up.'

'Wait.' I grimace, leaning over Magnusson's desk, collecting his laptop, and chucking it to Gibbs with my right hand.

Gabriel turns, noticing me wince with pain. 'You need medical attention...'

'It's just a flesh wound.'

He strides towards me, holding my face in his hands. 'You weren't meant to come here. Why didn't you just do what you were supposed to? I wanted to keep you out of this.'

'You broke our promise... We're in this together.'

'You sacrificed so much for this cause already. Magnusson was my responsibility.'

'You should know I will never give up on you. We come for each otter. That's what we do. It's what we always do.'

He drops his head wearily. 'This isn't your battle anymore.'

'If it's yours, it's mine.'

'Edward...' He screws his eyes shut.

'When did you suspect?'

'Ever since I saw Kamani in Monaco, it's like an alarm has been going off in the back of my head. It just kept getting louder. He was at Jane's funeral. It didn't make sense before but Magnusson said my father took Kamani under his wing in the early days.'

'Jesus, Gabriel.'

'Do you understand why I needed to make this right? This is so intertwined in my past.'

'Not alone.' I run my hand over the defined line of his jaw. 'You never needed to do this alone.' I pause, thinking about Edward. 'He knows you know?'

'Yes.'

'Is that why he's backing Brown and Defence Intelligence to take out the facility and Almasi?'

'Because he's afraid.'

'You did what you had to. You made the right choice.'

He looks at my arm. 'Are you going to be ok?'

'Are you?' I ask, nodding to the empty bottle.

'Gibbs! Have you got a medi-kit?' He calls out, ignoring me.

'Gabriel, we don't have time.'

Gibbs steps forward, pulling various medical equipment from a rucksack. 'She's right.' He looks at Gabriel. 'We'll put it in a sling, clean you up. But you need to get to the trucks. ALPHA and BRAVO are in full bloody swing mate. We've taken one floor already. Got half the kids out. There's another load we need to get to.'

'We'll strap you up…' Gabriel says, without moving his eyes from the bullet wound, 'then you get to the trucks.'

'I'm not leaving you behind. Not like this. You had a whole bottle of whisky Gabriel.'

'I'm good.' He shrugs, offering a lazy smile. 'Perks of being a drunk…'

'You shouldn't have done that for me.'

'As long as you're here at the end of all of this, I'll be fine. Anyway, you're no good with one arm.' He insists, dousing a cloth in alcohol, cleaning my wound before Gibbs applies the bandage.

Gunfire resounds down the hall. Gibbs loads his weapon and treads carefully to the door. 'Ronnie and Fenwick have our six, but we need to hurry.'

'Sully?' I ask, looking across the room.

His shoulders slump, shaking his head.

No.

Gabriel looks up, his eyes searching mine. 'You're going to be ok...' He says, noting the exhaustion in my face. 'Lex.' He tilts my chin, trying to get me to focus. 'Don't be a hero. Get to Collins and the trucks.'

'No...' I reach forward, touching his cheek. 'Not without you.'

'Listen to me...' He smooths the edges of the bandage before gently moving my arm into the sling. 'We have a house, a dog, a few kids and loads of other mundane shit normal people do waiting for us after this.' He takes my head in his hands. 'I need you to be ok.' He says, checking my sling. 'Remember your promise to me?'

Tears pool in my eyes. I nod quickly.

'Say it.'

'Noth...Nothing will happen to me.'

'Good...' He kisses me quickly before he stands, pulling me to my feet. 'I love you Alexandra and I need you to keep that promise, so don't fucking break it, you hear?'

'Please... please don't leave.'

'Come on you two.' Gibbs storms back into the room. 'James, we need to go. Alex, if you want to be stubborn, then get to minus three, there's another group of kids we didn't account for.'

Gabriel breaks contact, backing away.

'You best come back, James.'

He nods, grabbing his weapon. 'I always come back.'

The Dark Angel

I sprint down a dark corridor; trying not to let my mind wander to ALPHA and BRAVO. Focusing on the moment, instead, where we're all reunited; the time where we can reminisce on how all of this was worth it; trading war stories. I'm out of breath by the time I reach the door to the stairwell, my fingers tingling in my left hand. I try to ignore the surge of blood running down my arm. The bandage has bought me some time, but I reckon I've roughly got ten minutes before I pass out. I lied. The bullet is very much inside my body and with every inch of movement, it tears just that bit deeper, destroying the surrounding nerves and tissue. I shove through the door, and dash up the stairs to minus three, checking over my shoulder for any stragglers from the facility's security team. Eventually, I step onto the lab floor; limping past a few men and women in white coats rushing around, collecting vials, others tremble under their desks, covering their ears, clearly terrified by the intermittent tirade of gunshots from down the hall. Feeling woozy, I glance down at my pale arm; this is going to happen quicker than I thought. *What if you don't have time to get the children out?* A shuffling at my feet pulls me from the thought. I look down to see a petite woman in a white lab coat, cowering under the counter.

'Are you a doctor?'

She nods, whimpering.

'What's your name?'

'Ad...' Her voice trembles. 'Aditi.'

'Do you have a scalpel and a pair of tweezers?'

'Urm.... I think so.' She looks around nervously. 'Yes, somewhere.'

'Stand up.' I lean down, struggling to pull her to her feet. 'I can't lift you; you're going to have to do it yourself.'

She hesitates.

I angle the gun with one hand, pointing it at her head. 'Stand up.'

Slowly, she rises from the floor, holding her hands in the air.

I grimace, pulling my arm out of the sling. 'I need you to get this bullet out of me, ok?'

Abruptly, she turns to the desk behind, collecting equipment.

'If you pick up anything I didn't ask for, I will shoot you Aditi. And I would really prefer if I didn't have to.'

She halts, turning over her shoulder before nodding.

I roll up my T-shirt. 'If I pass out, do not stop. Keep going until it's done. Find something to stop the bleeding and then you wake me up.'

'Yes ok…yes.' A sharp focus arrives in her eyes.

'If my pulse drops out, you take me in there.' I point to a room with three-sixty glass, and what looks like a dentist's chair in the middle. 'You use that defibrillator, and you bring me back.'

She frowns.

'I know what you do in here. I know you have the means to bring me back. Ok?'

'Yes.' She repeats, this time much more certain. 'It's ok, you don't have to worry. I will get it out.' She grips the scalpel in her hand, her expression determined.

'I'm trusting you with this job.' I drop to the floor, leaning against a cupboard door. 'If you help me, I will get you out of here, ok? There's an FSA camp a few hours away. You'll be safe. Nobody here will get to you.'

'Ok. I can use this?' She reaches up, presenting a surgical stapler. 'To stop the bleeding?'

I raise my eyebrows. 'Fuck it, why not.'

CHAPTER SIXTY-EIGHT

ALEXANDRA

I jolt upwards, shooting my hand out, tightening my grip around the neck of the tall, blurred figure standing over me. He grabs my wrist, gulping for air, straining to pull me back. I climb up to my knees, pushing all my weight behind the action.

'Alexandra... Alex...andra please.'

My brain refocuses. I quickly let go. Raheem Kamani coughs, massaging his neck.

'Kamani...'

He splutters. 'You were out of it.'

'I'm sorry....' I say, a little dazed.

'That's ok... it's ok.'

I peer down at the bullet wound in my arm; freshly cauterised and bandaged up. Aditi bursts through the door suddenly, her arms stacked with vials and more bandages. Kamani raises his gun.

She freezes, her panicked eyes looking between us. 'Something to wake you up.' She raises a shot of adrenaline.

'It's fine.' I drop my hand over Kamani's weapon. 'She's good.'

'You will take me with you?' Aditi asks, flinching as the sound of gunfire increases. *It's getting closer now.*

'Yes, you can stick with us.' I shuffle the sling back over my head. Kamani helps me, glancing over my shoulder with worried eyes.

'I have to get in that room...' He mutters. 'There's more children on the other side.'

I follow his eye line to a heavy set of doors before looking at Aditi. 'Can you get us in?'

She nods, digging in her pockets and pulling out a card.

'This is the last group.' Kamani takes her card, rushing across the room. 'Collins and Meyer from your team, they helped get the others out.'

'You're sure?' I call out to him. 'Just this group to go?'

'Yes.' He smiles, hopeful. 'About six, I think.'

The doors fly open. I stand, following Kamani into a bleak corridor of white cells. Each one has heavy silver doors and a digital keypad.

'How the hell do we get these open?' Reaching the first cell door, I peer through a tiny window. A small, blonde girl is huddled under her bed; she clutches a grey blanket which is screwed into a ball. Her eyes are squeezed shut, her face plainly terrified. 'How do we get them out?' I repeat, examining the entry sensors.

Kamani grabs Aditi by the shoulders. 'Please… you must know how to get them out.'

She responds in frantic Syriac, shaking her head as tears roll down her face.

'What is she saying?' I sense it's not good news. 'Aditi, you're not leaving here unless all those children are out.' I grab her wrist and check the time on her digital watch. *Eleven thirty-seven.* 'In twenty-three minutes, we're all going to be blown to dust.'

'I have access to four cells. My pass can open just a few.'

'You can only get four children out?'

'For security purposes.' Kamani explains. 'Nobody is given all access.'

Whimpering resounds from the second cell to my right. I approach the glass, noticing another little girl covering her face. She's peering at me through a small crack in her fingers.

'Hey…' I say softly. 'Sorry, we didn't mean to scare you.'

She parts her hands, glimpsing one eye through the gap.

'My name's Alexandra.'

440

Curiosity crosses her dainty little features, and she shuffles to the end of the bed, offering me a little wave.

'Alexandra, we need to get moving.' Kamani demands.

'Unlock the four you can get access to.' I murmur without dropping the false look of reassurance on my face. 'Get them out. Let me deal with the rest.'

Kamani shouts instructions behind me, relaying the message. Aditi races down the hall, frantically swiping her pass.

'Anya.' The little girl calls out softly. 'My name is Anya.'

'That is a beautiful name.' I smile.

'Do you know my mummy?' She climbs to her feet, wandering to the door. It breaks me how little effort it takes for children to trust you. *Magnusson counted on that purity.* 'Is it time to go home?'

'Yes, it's time to go home.' I force a smile and look to Aditi, who shakes her head. Anya's cell is not one she can open, which means this little girl is destined to be left behind.

CHAPTER SIXTY-NINE

GABRIEL

Jake goes down, taking a hit on his left side. I clamber across the floor, trying to reach him. Bullets tear through the lab; machines spark, wires ignite, test tubes and various medicine cabinets explode around us. Glass lies everywhere, thick shards of it surrounding several lifeless bodies with blood pooling around them.

'Pineapple!' Jake shouts, throwing his arms over his head. Unable to move, he turns towards a cabinet for cover. *Military code for Grenade.* I hear the ominous jingling of metal on the tiles before my body is lifted from the ground. Objects soar off the surfaces, flying overhead as if a giant has thumped its fist in the centre of the room. A roaring boom burns through my ears, blasting into my brain. My back hits the floor, my right arm cushioning my head. I lay still, blinking up at the crumbling ceiling.

'James?' Jake's hoarse voice calls out. Dragging myself to sit, I glance through the thick cloud of smoke and rubble, trying to locate my weapon. A man rounds the corner. I jump to stand. He raises his gun, his finger braced on the trigger until his head explodes from the power of a bullet to his skull. I shift out of the way, watching a second shot strike him. A pink mist bursts from his body, descending into the air before he falls to the floor.

'You there, James?' Jake calls.

'Hold on.' I yell, making my way towards his voice.

I find him propped against a glass door, his face cut to pieces, his assault vest torn to shreds. The material of his T-shirt has burnt into the skin on his shoulder.

'Had better days…' He grins.

Hearing more voices from the west corridor, I take the top of Jake's vest and haul him up to stand. 'We need to go.'

'I'm just going to slow you down.' He croaks.

'We have one floor to go, mate.' I support his weight. 'You'll manage.'

'No, give up!'

'We're getting out together!'

'Leave me damn it! You won't make it if you take me.'

'No fucking way.' I pull him close to my face. 'It's two flights and I'm not leaving without you.'

'Can you get me some gum… It's in my top pocket.'

'Unbelievable.' I rummage, pulling a piece out, gently pushing it into his mouth.

'Always gotta stay fresh brother.' He smiles.

'Exactly.' I dip to hold his weight across my right shoulder, flinching suddenly when the door marked fire-exit flies open.

'Let me go.' Jake struggles, scrambling for his weapon.

Gibbs backs through the exit, clearly returning gunfire.

'You on your way out?' He calls, eyeing Jake's paling face.

'First class ticket.' Jake jokes.

'We need to get to the ground floor.' I inform. 'The convoy is waiting.'

'Time check.'

'Eleven forty.'

'Plenty.' Gibbs winks at Jake, discreetly taking stock of his injuries. 'Come on then, solider. Let's go!' He slings the strap of his weapon across his chest before reloading the ammunition. 'I'll watch your six.'

We move slowly and I brace to heave Jake up the first flight of stairs. 'How's your angle?'

'Clear so far.' Gibbs murmurs, treading carefully.

We round the corner, approaching the second flight. I tighten my free hand around my weapon.

'Might take a vacation after this.' Jake coughs with false optimism.

'Yeah....' I lug him up another step, trying to keep my tone light. 'Where you thinking of going?'

'Figure I should change it up a bit... the jungle maybe.' He breathes, attempting to laugh before he starts spluttering, blood dribbles from his mouth. His body sinks heavier.

I pull him up, leaning him against the wall, wiping the bloody saliva from his chin. 'Jake...' I search his eyes. 'Stay with me buddy. You have to stay awake, ok? Stay with me.'

Gibbs follows closely behind. 'That our way out?' He signals to the door just three steps up from where we're standing.

'The golden ticket.' Jake utters, his eyes weary.

Gibbs jumps up to the top of the staircase and raises his weapon, firing three bullets at the door. Checking the damage, he hurls his boot against it to release the lock. It doesn't budge. He tries a second time. Then, a third.

'Here.' I signal to switch places.

Forcing my weight at the door, I strike my foot hard against the panel, only stopping when gunfire resounds from below.

Swearing, Gibbs peers over the rail. 'Come on big lad.' He urges. 'Get us the fuck out of here.'

The surge of bullets echoes louder, mixed with the sound of heavy boots. Trying not to focus on their proximity, I slam my weight against the door, bellowing with frustration, battering the lock again and again until finally, it relents and the latch releases. I jump down, rushing to support Jake. We both drag him into the open air.

'Stop… stop. I can't.' Jake wheezes, his weight pulling us both back. 'I can't fucking… go any further.' He holds his side, the skin on his hands completely obscured by the thick ooze of blood.

'Yes, you can! We're nearly there.'

Gibbs turns over his shoulder; distracted by the sound of enemy commands being directed roughly fifty paces behind. 'Carry him!' He yells, gripping his rifle. 'I'll cover you…. just get him to that convoy James!'

'Make sure you get there too!' I shout before pivoting down to lift Jake over my shoulder. His body becomes limp, his arms drooping over me. I start jogging towards the meeting point, navigating the dry, uneven ground. *There better still be at least one truck.* I try not to think of Lex, instead concentrating on racing between the rubble and debris of the ancient city. Jake's pulse has slowed. He's lost a lot of blood but if we can get him flat in the next one to two minutes, there's a chance we can save his life. I pause for a few seconds, trying to catch my breath and check my watch. *Eleven forty-seven.* Eight minutes to get far enough away from the blast radius to not suffer any damage. Eight minutes to get Jake to safety. Eight fucking minutes to ensure we've evacuated every child from that facility. *Eight minutes to do a hell of a lot.*

'James!' Gibbs calls from behind, swiftly catching up. 'There they are…The trucks!'

I squint into the distance, making out the blur of headlights at the foot of the hill.

'Come on, give me some of the weight.'

We shift Jake between us, practically dragging him the last one hundred metres. My lungs burn for air, sweat covers my body, my clothes feeling heavy and wet despite the dark sky. Eventually, I spot Collins loading children onto the first vehicle.

'James…' Kamani jumps down from the boot.

'Can you help him?'

He steps forward, examining Jake. 'Lay him flat.'

'Can we put him in the truck? Can you work on him there?'

'Yes, but I will need someone else to drive in my place.'

'That's fine... I can do it.'

With Gibbs' help, I lift Jake onto the metal floor of the truck. Small, frightened faces of young children look on, their innocent eyes fixed on the state of his battered body. I pull his vest off, exposing two bullet wounds near his kidney.

'Put pressure on it.' Kamani hands me a cloth.

'Everyone get out ok?' I ask.

He places his hand on top of Jake's chest. 'I need another medi-kit. There's one at the front, on the passenger seat.'

'I'll get it.' Gibbs jumps out.

'Raheem... did everyone get out ok?'

'Blood in the airway.' He murmurs with his ear to the base of Jake's throat. 'I'm going to have to clear it.'

I kneel beside him. 'What can I do?'

'Start CPR.'

I lean over Jake, pressing lightly into his chest, only stopping to allow Kamani to make an incision in his throat.

'Who is that?' Collins' panicked voice calls out.

'Jake.' Gibbs replies, climbing back in.

'Two-minute warning.' Collins informs solemnly.

'Where's Lex?' I ask, still pumping air into Jake's lungs.

Kamani halts for a split second before continuing to free Jake's airway.

'Kamani...'

He looks up, his eyes loaded with regret.

'She still in there?'

I already know the answer.

He nods before returning to the wound. 'Minus three.'

'Gibbs… take over.' I command, shifting away.

'You what mate?'

'Take over!' I yell, waiting until he moves next to me, his hands shadowing mine. 'You got him?'

'Yeah.' He says, continuing CPR. 'What are you doing?!'

'She's still in there.' I tell him over my shoulder, leaping out of the truck, sprinting back towards the facility.

CHAPTER SEVENTY

ALEXANDRA

'Keys! Keys! Can you hear me?'

'Alex! What the fuck...'

'Listen...' I rush out. 'I'm on minus three in the facility. There are two children stuck down here.'

'Alexandra, you have just minutes to get out of there.'

'Please, I can't leave them. I can't get into their cells. I've tried everything. I'm out of bullets. The doors won't budge.' I choke back the sobs which are so desperate to spill out of me. 'I need you to tell me how to hack the system. There's a digital keypad on the doors.'

'Alex...'

'Yeah?'

'I have to be there. I can't do it from here.'

'Wha... what do you mean?'

'There's no central system for me to get into. I have to manually look at each one. And there isn't time for me to teach you to do it yourself.'

'Fuck.' I whisper, dropping the phone.

Keys' voice continues explaining through the receiver.

'FUCK!' I shout, storming into an empty cell, trying to think up a new plan. *There is always a way. I'm not leaving two children to die in here. No way. That is not an option.* There is another way. I just need to think.

'Alexandra, you have to get out.'

'I will never be able to live with myself if I leave, K.'

'You have people that will be ruined if you don't make it out of there. Please get out!'

I hang up the phone and hurl it on the floor, throwing my hands over my head. 'Ok...' I take a breath, noticing the time on the cracked phone screen. *Eleven forty-seven.*

Distant crying resounds from the six-year-old boy in the other cell. Anya calls out to him, reassuring him that everything is going to be just fine. I slide down the wall and close my eyes. They can't die like this. Not scared. I have to comfort them somehow; fill their last minutes with something more than just terror.

'Who wants to hear a story?' I announce, with as much excitement as I can muster, banging my head against the wall.

'Will we go to heaven, Alexandra?' Anya asks.

I close my eyes, my body aching from the fear in her voice. 'Shall I tell you a story about a very brave Prince and Princess?'

'Is it a fairy tale?' She asks.

Her voice is much louder than before.

My eyes fly open.

'Are they very brave, the Prince and Princess?'

I knock my knuckles against the surface.

'Hello?' She calls out in response.

'Yeah.' I turn to kneel, dropping my ear to the wall. I knock again, then again, then again.

'Alexandra?' Anya calls out from the other side.

I knock again.

'They're thin.' I mutter. *The internal walls are paper-thin.*

'Are you starting the story now?'

'One second!' I jump to my feet, racing back to the lab. Searching the room, I pick up a fire extinguisher, testing its weight before sprinting back to the empty cell.

'Anya, stand back and cover your face!' I shout, thrusting the heavy metal against the wall, beating at the plywood again and again.

The material begins to crumble, breaking and collapsing piece by piece.

'I'm scared!' She shouts.

'It's ok!' A small gap forms, becoming increasingly bigger. Anya's eyes light up as she sees my face.

'Come here.' I hold out my hand, helping her climb through. 'Stay right here. I'm going to get your friend, ok?'

She nods. 'He's shy.'

'What's his name?'

'Oti...'

'Ok.' I say, creating a gap big enough for me to slip through. Racing across Anya's cell, I reach the far side and heave the extinguisher against the wall. My body shrieks at me to stop, my injured arm pulsing with exhaustion, the stitches ripping open. Dust sprays from the crumbling wall and into my eyes. I stop, checking the time again. *Eleven forty-nine.* Having weakened the fortifications, I start kicking my boot through the rest of the boards. Finally, I pummel my foot through a large crack. Gasping for breath, I squint through the dust, finally seeing Oti's terrified expression.

'Hey little man! Come here!' I hold out a shaking hand. 'Come on, I'm getting you out of here.'

He tucks his chin to his chest before tentatively stepping towards me, climbing through the narrow space.

'Anya, can you run next to me? I'll carry Oti. He's smaller and not as fast.'

'You're bleeding...' She observes quietly.

'That's ok, it's just a scratch. You have to keep up, ok?'

Her lip shakes, her bright green eyes heavy with fear.

'Anya.' I crouch down. 'I bet you can sprint super-fast.'

She nods proudly.

'Can you show me? Show me how fast you can go... when I say. Ok?'

'Ok!' She replies, re-energised.

'We've got this.' I pick up Oti, who grips my shoulders. 'You ready?'

'Ready.'

'Come on, let's get you home.' I sprint through the lab with Anya scurrying alongside. 'You can do it.' I encourage whilst looking out for signs that will take us above ground. Locating the fire-exit, we race for the staircase. I continue cheering Anya on, offering more praise as we climb upwards. 'We're going to make it out of here!'

'Yeah...' She agrees, out of breath and using the handrail to hoist herself up. 'We will!'

Reaching the top, I deposit Oti safely before rushing to Anya.

'You did so well!' I heave her off the floor. 'Come on, I'll help you with the last leg.'

'I nearly did it all...'

'Just this last bit, alright?' I pull her up, resting her on my hip. 'Remember to follow me through the city to the big trucks.'

'Then I'll go home?'

'You'll be safe.' I say, not knowing what home looks like for her anymore.

We burst through the door into the cool air of the desert. Oti clutches me tight, his face hidden in the crook of my neck. I beckon Anya to follow me across the ruins, imploring her to be careful as we dash towards the convoy. Tears of relief and exhaustion are whipped away by the wind as we race towards the last remaining truck. Squinting, I think I make out the shape of Alison Collins standing with her hands on her hips. The closer we get, the more I see of her; a knowing smile is etched across her face, her eyes alight with a relief that matches mine.

'Jesus, you're cutting it fine.' She says, bending to pick Anya up. 'Go right to the back, sweetheart.'

'Thank you for waiting.' Still trying to catch my breath, I set Oti down in the truck, settling him between two other children. Another little boy, roughly his age, takes his hand immediately.

'We're safe now.' Anya calls out to him, affording a small smile in return.

'Keys called me. He insisted you'd find a way out.' Collins pats me on the back, leading me to the front of the truck. 'Come on, you can breathe later. We need to get a real move on.'

I jump into the passenger side, reaching for water. 'I didn't see who was back there with the kids…'

'Fenwick and Boots.'

'Gabriel?' I ask. 'Where is he?'

She starts the engine before accelerating away. 'He came out with Gibbs and Jake. Jake was hit pretty bad. Gabriel was giving him CPR. Kamani is with him in the other truck. They're still trying to fix him up.'

I reach for Collins' radio, tuning the frequency. *'Gibbs. Come in. OVER.'*

White noise fills the van before a build in static. *'Hello Angel.'*

'You made it out.' I smile.

'Nine lives…Me.'

'And Jake?'

Silence.

I take a deep breath and tap my fingers on the dashboard.

'He's got a few nicks. But I think he'll survive.'

'Good.' I exhale. *'Can I speak to Gabriel?'* I wait, looking out of the window, still unable to believe we made it out alive; the last ten minutes feeling like an utter blur. *'Gibbs?*

'Yeah?'

'Gabriel? Is he good? Can I speak to him?'

Collins frowns, staring ahead at the road. She's picked up on my concern.

'Gibbs. Can you hear-'

'He's not with you?'

My stomach flips. My breath faltering.

'No. I've got Boots and Fenwick.'

Collins nods her head vigorously. 'He was tending to Jake.'

'Gibbs, Collins says Gabriel was tending to Jake in the back of the truck with you.'

'You said you saw him?' I turn to Collins. 'Did you see him?'

She hesitates, her mouth opening and closing.

'Did you see him or not?'

'Yes!' She nods her head quickly. 'Yes! He was in the truck with Kamani. He was there with Gibbs!'

I pick up the radio. *'Gibbs, he was with you. He was with you and Kamani. OVER.'*

'He went in back for you.'

The sentence echoes in my brain like a tormenting tune. *He went back in. He went back in for you.*

'Turn the car around.' I demand in a voice that doesn't sound like me. 'Alison! Turn the car around.'

'Alexandra we can't...'

'Turn the fucking car around!' I slam my hand against the dashboard. 'Turn it around!'

A low, vibrating rumble fills the sky. Almost as if the world is being shaken like an eight-ball. The car trembles, throbbing under the shuddering roar of an RAF Typhoon.

'Stop!' I scream, peering up at the hazy sky.

'Alexandra please!'

I load my gun and point it at her head. 'If you do not stop this car. I will shoot you. And I will get out anyway.'

She exhales a shaking breath, pressing the brakes. The vehicle comes to an abrupt halt. I open the door and fly out, sprinting towards the facility as the deafening thunder increases. I shrug out of my sling, forcing my left arm in sequence with my right, charging towards Palmyra City. I look down at my hand, sodden, blood haemorrhaging from the freshly open wound. All pain and awareness of my body are stamped out by the sheer need to close the distance between myself and the entrance to that facility. I jump over debris, kicking up sand, my boots pounding dirt, my heart feeling as if it's being tugged forward, pulled back to him, hoping by some miracle that Gibbs made a mistake. The earth shakes beneath me. But I won't stop, I won't falter. He's in there. He's in there somewhere. *We come for each other. We always do.*

The rolling boom of the jet's engines shoots through me, my breath becomes lodged in my throat, the mere notion of living today, tomorrow, the rest of my life without him is hampering my rationality. I look up to see the white plumes of the missiles hurtling towards their target. My throat makes a strangled noise. My heart burns with pain. My lungs become two heavy slabs of thick concrete.

It detonates.

CHAPTER SEVENTY-ONE

He watches me tear the damp paper coaster into pieces, discarding flurries of it onto the table before taking another sip of his beer. His dark eyes regard me over the rim of the glass. He licks his lips, his gaze still fixed on mine until he places the pint back down.

'Have you always been mildly destructive?' *He smirks, nudging his head towards the pile.*

'I have a lot of anxious energy.'

'Do I make you anxious?'

'Only when towering over me in a dark alley.'

'I'll be sure to avoid it in future.'

'I think that's wise.'

'What year are you in?'

'Second. You?'

'Same.'

'College?'

'Fitzwilliam.'

'I see...' *I nod knowingly.*

'What's that look for?'

'Nothing.' *I shrug.*

'You think you've got the measure of me now?'

'Fitzwilliam boys aren't that hard to read.'

'You want to put it to the test?'

I raise my eyebrows, intrigued.

'What am I thinking?' *He stares at me blankly, like I'm the most disinteresting thing in the world.*

'You're trying to think of something clever and profound to tell me about Fitzwilliam boys to prove me wrong.'

He smiles. 'Incorrect.'

I laugh. 'Ok, what were you thinking....'

The smile fades. He meets my curious stare. 'One of your eyes is bigger than the other. Only slightly. And you have the least symmetrical face I've ever seen.' He shrugs as if he's just listed off directions to a stranger. 'But it's also the most beautiful.'

'Alexandra.'

Slow, silent tears creep down my cheeks before a whimper escapes my mouth.

He's gone.

I rock back and forth, trying to picture somewhere else, another time, another day. 'Please...' I tip my gaze to the sky, pleading. 'Don't do this to me again. Not again.'

'Alexandra...' Collins appears at my side, crouching next to me. 'Come on, darling.'

'Are you sure he went back?' I look up. 'Did you speak to Aldyn? And Emily?'

Her head twitches, her face disintegrating into hopelessness. Her glassy blue eyes screw tightly shut. 'He isn't with them.'

'No.' I whisper. 'God no...'

'Come on.' She tries to pull me up.

'It's not possible. He isn't...' I shake my head, unable to comprehend. 'He didn't die, Alison.'

That word and Gabriel should never be in the same sentence.

Never.

'He wasn't supposed to die. Just tell me he didn't. Tell me he didn't die. Can you? He isn't gone.' I beg. 'Can you tell me that?'

Tears race down her face. 'I can't...' she sobs. 'I can't.'

I turn away, suddenly needing to vomit as if my body is physically trying to eject grief. It's like I've swallowed a vial of despair that my insides are just not able to digest.

'Come on…we have to go.' She says, rubbing my back. 'The children, Alex. We have to get the children to safety.'

I flinch, hearing the radio in the truck.

'That's the others. They're well on their way to camp by now.'

'I need to find him.' I whimper. 'Please Alison, we need to find his body.' I take her hands, gripping her wrists. 'Please don't make me leave here. I can't leave him. He doesn't belong with those people. He belongs with us…'

'Alexandra…' her voice cracks and she takes a deep breath. 'We will come back. We will come back for his body.'

'Tell Gibbs to come back. I'll wait here. They can come back. I'll just wait here.'

She swallows, looking down at the ground. 'Let me contact the others.'

I sit, shivering on the end of a rock, reminding myself to breathe in and out as my brain serves up images of him.

'How many girls have you said that to?'

With a smug arrogance, he holds up his hand, making a zero with his thumb and index finger. It's the sexiest thing I've ever seen.

'Do you date much?'

'That's a very intrusive question for a casual Thursday night drink.'

'I'll take that as a yes.'

'I've been on some dates, sure.'

'What was the worst date you've ever been on?'

He smiles, narrowing his eyes. 'You don't do small talk, do you?'

I screw my hands shut, digging my nails into the skin. This is the very moment my memories of him will be the clearest, the most crisp. After a while, you don't remember the person you lost. You just recall the ghost of them.

'You're in shock.' Collins returns, handing me a sweet. 'You need the sugar.' I take it from her before she fiddles with the buttons on the radio, pulling it up to her mouth. *'ALL STATIONS from NAVY SQUIRE. Come in. OVER.'* It buzzes back with more interference. She presses her finger down. *ALL STATIONS from-'*

'-a kilometre...east. OVER.'

Collins pauses, frowning at the radio.

'ALL STATIONS from NAVY SQUIRE. Come in. OVER.' She repeats as more static fills the air.

'-down the tunnel.... Out by the...'

I stand from the rock.

We both stare at the radio.

It falls silent.

'This bloody thing. Aldyn can never use his properly,' Collins whines frustratingly, slamming her hand against it. The radio sputters again, louder this time. We both jump.

'- caves... out of a tunnel.'

'Wait!' I yell. 'Don't touch the frequency.'

'...the same caves.'

Collins' eyes widen.

'Who is that? Is that Aldyn?' Nerves leap from my chest and into my stomach. 'Alison, who is that?' Both of us gawk at the radio like it might spontaneously combust.

'Where is-'

I shift from one foot to the next as more static comes. I feel sick. My head spins, the ground swimming beneath me.

The radio hums again. *'...did she get out?'*

It's not Aldyn.

I grab the radio from Collins, holding it tight between my palms. *'Gabriel!'* I shout, my voice hysterical. *'Gabriel is that you?'*

Collins' face is frozen with anticipation.

My heart rockets against my rib cage.

A few more minutes pass and nothing comes.

Just silence. *More silence.*

Feeling dejected, I sit down again, my stomach returning to knots, hope dissolving once more. Collins places the radio between us before she drops down next to me with a long, deep exhale.

'Lex?'

My head snaps up. *That can be nobody else.*

I exhale a laughing breath. 'It's him…' I look to Collins, clutching the device. 'It's him… right?'

'It's him.' She looks up at the sky, laughing with disbelief. 'Ah thank Jesus Christ.'

'Gabriel? Please tell me where you are!' I scan our surroundings, stepping up onto a mound of rubble to get a better vantage point, knowing I won't fully believe it until I see him with my own eyes. *'Where are you?'* I ask again, squinting through the ash cloud. *'Gabe… can you hear me?'*

'Here….'

Confused, I look down at the device.

'I'm here.' His voice cuts through the smoke.

I break into a wide grin. He limps towards us through a thick fog, his handsome face bloodied and bruised, his clothes torn and covered in dirt. Without a second thought, I race over the rubble, never before so impatient to touch him, to feel him with my own hands. The person, just moments ago, I thought I'd lost forever. Jumping up, I leap into his arms, wrapping my legs around his body, clutching his shoulders tightly. I lean back and examine him closely;

needing to ensure this is real. After so much loss and pain, fate has finally afforded us something. *He's here. He's right here.*

'You're bleeding a lot...' He comments with typical Gabriel fashion. He sets me on my feet, holding me steady, pulling up the sodden sleeve of my T-shirt. 'After all this effort to find you, please don't bleed out on the way home.'

'I won't, I promise.'

'Come on,' he pulls me close. 'Let's get you to the truck.'

'I thought you were gone. I was...' I stop, craning my neck to kiss him. 'How?' I whisper against his lips. 'How did you get out?'

He strokes my face. 'I knew there was a tunnel on minus four. When I couldn't find you, that's where I thought you'd gone. I went down there after you. It brought me out by the caves.'

I close my eyes and wrap my arms around his neck, inhaling the scent of him, relishing the feel of his skin against mine, silently thanking the universe for allowing me this. *For bringing him back.*

CHAPTER SEVENTY-TWO

GABRIEL

'You know it would be so much easier if you would just let me do this outside, where there's proper light. It's too dark in here.' Emily says, trying to stitch the deep cut above my brow.

'I don't mind if it leaves a scar.' I reply, sitting between Lex and Jake, both of them hooked up to IV drips and various medical wires.

'*You* might not…' She murmurs, narrowing her eyes, threading another stitch. 'Nothing's going to happen if you step out for five minutes, Gabriel. She's fine, she just needs rest.'

'I don't want either of them to wake up alone.' I wince as she sews another hole.

'Ok, well.' She dabs the wound before picking up the metal bowl from the side and throwing the needle in. 'Sorry if it's not straight.'

'Is she awake yet?' Keys asks, appearing in the doorway.

'No.' I glance at Lex's bruised face, her pale lips slightly parted. 'Any updates on Almasi?'

'Airstrikes in Turkey, Sudan, Syria.' Keys mumbles without taking his eyes off Lex. 'It's all over the news.'

'There'll be an inquest.'

'I'm sure our government can come up with something creative.'

'No doubt.'

'Good news is that Collins has spoken to your boss at MI6.'

'What does Brown have to say for himself?'

'Well, as today is August 5th, all airports have been evacuated. All non-essential flights have been grounded for the next forty-eight

461

hours whilst both S.A.I.B.R. and SO15 ensure they've apprehended everyone connected to the attacks. The PM is in a secure, undisclosed location for the next two weeks at least.'

'They think they stopped it?'

'Collins says they're confident the attack has been foiled.'

I let out a long sigh of relief, running my hands over my face.

'Collins has sent Kamani's testimony to Brown. It details everyone he knows to be linked to Magnusson in the UK government. She says everything they've got on Magnusson's laptop will be enough to shut down the MOD's Compliancy training facility.'

'Good.' I look at Lex. *She should be hearing this, too.*

'In light of the circumstances, Edward has dropped Alexandra from his shit list. Collins says to tell you that Brown wants you back ASAP but not to worry because neither of you is going to prison.' He takes a long breath. 'Jesus, I can't believe I remembered all that. And before 10am too. I need a drink.'

'What we having...' Lex's voice drifts through the room. Her eyes flicker open, a ghost of a smile playing on her lips.

'Welcome to the waking world.' Keys chuckles.

I breathe a small sigh of relief. 'Hello stranger.'

'How long have I been out?'

'Two days nearly....' I stand and help her sit up properly, taking both her hands in mine, trying to warm them up. 'You're cold.'

'Just bad circulation.' She dismisses.

'Shall I shut that window?'

'Has he been like this the whole time?' She asks Keys, her eyes widening.

'Neurotic?' Keys raises his eyebrows. 'If you think Gabriel is bad, you should have seen Aldyn.'

I laugh, shaking my head. 'Yeah he's been driving me mad, googling all these conditions.'

'He's a hypochondriac.' Lex shrugs. 'Who knew...'

'I'm glad you're back with us, mate...' Keys says softly, 'Camp was too peaceful. Nobody does chaos like you.'

She looks around the room. 'Are we in the compound?'

'Yes.'

'Why didn't you take Jake to a hospital?' She looks over her shoulder, immediately questioning me. 'Is he ok?'

'He just needs rest. The boys did a supply run. He's got what he needs. Kamani has a friend from Aleppo, another doctor. He's visited to make sure he's healing ok. He's coming back tomorrow.'

She notices my lingering amusement. 'What?'

'Control freak is back.' Keys scoffs. 'How long did that take, Gabe?'

I look at my cracked watch. 'I'd say under a minute.'

She rolls her eyes. 'I'm catching up!'

'I know...' I bring her fragile wrist to my mouth.

'I'll leave you two to catch up,' Keys adds. 'We'll chat later Alex.' He blows her a kiss before backing out of the door.

Lex raises her hand before looking off to the side, her mind elsewhere.

'You have more questions, don't you?'

She smirks.

'Go on...' I laugh.

'How are the children?'

'The children are fine; Gibbs has been working with his contacts to have some of them reunited with their families. We're organising support for the ones who were subjected to... you know.'

'How are you feeling...' She asks nervously.

'I haven't had another drop since the lab.'

'That's not what I meant.' She whispers softly. 'I want to know how you're doing.'

'I know… I've reached out to my sponsor. Collins is keeping an eye on me in the meantime.'

'Gabriel…'

I look down, feeling discomfort in my chest. 'If you put me back there, I'd do it again.'

'It wasn't a moment of weakness. It was courage. Remember that.'

I nod at the floor, shoving all intrusive thoughts away, the shame feeling lighter now that she's here. *It wasn't weakness.* That is something to hold onto.

'Have you been getting any sleep?'

I hesitate, wondering if I should lie but she always sees right through me anyway. It's why she asked. 'I've not really left this room, to be honest.'

'Gabriel…' Her expression switches to concern, a fire returning to her eyes, 'you need to look after yourself.'

'And now you're here… with me… I will.' I lean over her, kissing her on the forehead, tucking a blonde wave behind her ear.

She rests her head back on the pillow, glimpsing up at the ceiling, a single tear running down her cheek. 'I really, *really* thought you were gone.'

'I know…' I reach out and catch it with my thumb.

'You made me promise nothing would happen to me, but you didn't do the same. I just…' She swallows, closing her eyes. 'It hurt so much. It broke me. I still feel it, even now.' She rubs her chest. 'I thought I would die right there with you.'

'Listen…' I gently take her face between my palms. 'Look at me. I'm right here. It didn't happen, it wasn't real. I promise you I'm not going anywhere. I can't even leave this room.'

She laughs, flashing a bright, beautiful grin. 'We can go live our boring life now, can't we?'

'That we can.' I smile. 'Where do you want to start?'

'Maybe a dog…'

I grin. 'That's the priority, is it? Not marriage or a house.'

'A Westie would be my prefere…' She pauses, a sudden gleam in her eyes. 'You mean that?'

'I thought you wanted a boring life.'

'So I'd be your wife…' She suppresses an excited grin as if trying the word out for size.

'That's how it usually works.'

'Can you get in here with me?' She pats the sheets.

I carefully move onto the bed. She settles her head in the crook of my arm, her fingers tightly gripping my chest.

'Do you think we can really have all of that?' She says, relaxing into me. 'Everything you just said.'

'After everything we've been through, a mortgage and a wedding will be a breeze.'

'Ask me…' She looks up. 'Ask me again.'

'Alexandra Christofi, will you be my wife?'

'Forever.' She whispers, taking my hand.

CHAPTER SEVENTY-THREE

ALEXANDRA

We stand on the hill between the long grass, our feet sinking into the sand, watching our lanterns take flight, drifting gracefully into the night's sky, sailing amongst the stars. Gabriel takes my hand, both of us fix our eyes on one lantern in particular. One that sways in the wind with a list of six names. *Charles McGuire, Theresa Stanley, Amber Brookes, Mario Christofi, Hope Clarke and Thomas Sullivan.* I smile up at the sky, thinking of my father and how much he would have loved this; something so beautiful in his honour. I wish I could tell him we did it. We took them on, and we won. We ripped Magnusson's evil out of the world. Not one of us gave up until it was done. Mario wasn't a perfect man, but he had principles and if he believed in something, he'd fight. That's what he taught me. *If you're still standing, then you have fight left. Use it. Use it to protect people who can't do it for themselves.* Gibbs, Jake, Fenwick, Boots, and Ronnie move to the front of the crowd, their rifles carefully balanced between their shoulders. With the help of Boots, Jake takes a knee, his shaking hands smoothing out a neatly folded Union Jack on the sand before he rises again. Gibbs calls out the drill command and all five men stand to attention. I've seen this countless times before but a chill still travels up my spine. This time, I'm not going back into battle. This time, it truly feels like the end. A bugle rings out as we watch the final lantern drift from view and I think about all the near-death encounters, the pain, the loss, the sacrifices made by everyone standing in this crowd. I'm one of the lucky ones. Battle was the life I chose. Others had war thrust upon them, with no influence over their fate. That is why we do what we do. They are who we stand for.

'I wish things could have been different for Sully.' I say to Gibbs as he drifts back towards us.

'He was waiting, Alex. He couldn't live a normal life, not after his wife died. He wanted to get back to her. He always said that.'

'From the short time I spent with him, I could tell he was a good person.'

'One of the best.' Gibbs says wistfully before stepping in, regarding Gabriel and me with mischief in his eyes. 'You two want to think about staying here permanently? The kids love you. Though, you might have to fight some of the local women for James. There's quite a queue.'

Gabriel laughs, slapping Gibbs on the back.

'Come on you lot.' Collins weaves her way through the dispersing gathering towards us. 'There's arak waiting by the fire. Gabriel, you can have a mint tea.'

'The smell of arak is enough to keep me sober for life.'

'You go ahead.' I tell Gabriel. 'I'll just be a minute.'

'You good?' He asks, still feeling the need to check every five minutes.

I nod reassuringly and he kisses me on the head before jogging after Collins. Gibbs and I stand on the hill, watching the community flow back towards the camp. Children laugh with delight and amusement as Gabriel jogs up behind Keys and playfully nudges him out of the way before continuing on. Keys breaks into a sprint, yelling after Gabriel, doing his best to catch up. Collins shouts at them both to grow up before she and Aldyn burst into laughter.

'It's really something… when they're all happy.'

'If Haines could see us now, eh?' Gibbs smiles.

'He wouldn't believe it.'

'Where you off to next?'

'To tell you the truth, I'm not sure.'

'You don't want to go back to London?'

'It just doesn't feel like home anymore.'

'I assumed you'd take over from your old man....'

'I'm handing that over to Aldyn...'

'I'm sure you'll dip in from time to time.' He winks.

'Never say never,' I smirk.

'It's ok, you know...'

I frown, watching him find the words.

'It's ok to feel lost when you reach the end of
something...even something awful.'

I hesitate, following his eye line. 'You really think it's the
end?'

'You don't?'

'With everything that's happened, all the shit we've been
through, I never actually considered we'd get to this place. I don't
know if either of us knows how to do normal.'

'You need to find yourselves a place to call home.
Somewhere you can make a fresh start.'

I nod, thinking about his words.

'You got a place like that?'

'I think so...' I smile. 'Yeah, I think we might.'

'It's going to be alright, mate.' He pulls me into the crook of
his arm. 'You're allowed some peace.'

'I'm worried we've become too used to chaos.'

'You'll always have each other for that.' He winks. 'Find your
home, find your peace and enjoy your fucking life.'

We reach the campfire, climbing over logs to take a seat. I
nestle in between Gabriel and Aldyn, enjoying the relaxed way the
group chats over the fire. This is the first time we've ever been fully
present, with no prospect of death or suffering around the corner. No
wondering if that will be the last meal, the last laugh, the final smile.

Tomorrow is never promised but there's a little hope now. A glint. A spark in everyone's eyes that wasn't there before.

Gabriel dips his head, his lips brushing my ear. 'Everything alright?'

I take his hand, absorbing every inch of his face. I lean up to kiss him, whispering against his lips. 'Everything's perfect.'

CHAPTER SEVENTY-FOUR

ALEXANDRA

ONE MONTH LATER

Looking out over St James' Park, I watch the rain slink down the glass. The muffled patter of water soothes me somehow. It's a quiet night. None of the usual noises you'd expect from Central London. Barely any traffic, no sign of people. The temperature has dropped since I arrived thirty minutes ago.

My head turns only slightly when he eventually powers through the door. Cursing under his breath, he shakes his umbrella dry before turning on the light. Seeing me across the room, he gasps. He stumbles back and his hand instinctively shoots out to a side draw.

'No point.' I collect a handful of bullets from my pocket and pour them on the floor; watching them bounce away. 'You thought I wouldn't sweep the place.' I pull my own weapon from my waistband. 'This one's loaded, though.'

Panicked, Edward James glances at the camera in the top left corner.

'Yeah, that's off.'

'What are you doing here?' He asks, his voice hoarse.

'Sit down.'

'Can I at least take my coat off?'

'Sit... down.' I repeat.

He moves slowly across the room, lowering himself into the leather chair behind his desk.

'Keep your hands visible.' I lean over him, moving the paperweight out of arm's reach. 'I'll take that, shall I?'

'Why are you here?'

'Just thought I'd pop in...'

He scoffs, looking up to the ceiling. 'Gabriel doesn't know.'

'He doesn't.'

'Do you think that's wise?'

'Glass houses and all that...' I murmur.

'So come on.' He hisses, impatiently. 'What is it?'

'I'm here to tell you a collection of short stories...'

'I don't have time for games.'

'Oh, this isn't a game... far, far from it.'

'Just say what you need to say.'

'You might want to pour yourself a drink.' I gesture to the cabinet by the window.

He narrows his eyes and strides across the room, still exhuming the usual show of arrogance. He twists the cap from a bottle of whisky, and pours himself a glass.

I wait for him to settle back into his chair. 'A little girl goes missing in a small town in Hungary. The police there are understaffed and grossly underpaid. The people who took this little girl bribe one of the junior officers on the police force, imploring him to hide evidence concerning her whereabouts. He takes the money, does what he's told, and regrets it for the rest of his life. That's part one.'

Edward exhales as if he's already bored.

'Part two. There once was a very clever man working for MI5.' I gesture to him. 'He and another very clever doctor put their clever heads together to outsmart all the other government agencies across the world...'

Edward takes a few gulps of whisky.

'The man and the genius doctor developed a program... a program that erases memories, removes attachments, and extracts emotions from a person's mind. Essentially making them a blank canvas. With an elite training program and the right psychological conditioning, they created what we would one day call a *Compliant*.'

'What is the point in this?' He laughs, stiffly.

'They started carefully. Taking orphans that nobody would miss, trialling the program where they could. Luckily for the doctor and the clever man, the program was successful. That's when they started getting braver... taking more children. Using youth as the ultimate cover. The Russians did it with child soldiers, so why couldn't they? Nobody would suspect a sixteen-year-old girl as a spy. But the doctor... he saw how much MI5 relied on him and his ideas. He knew he'd created something special. Like nothing ever before. So then came a turning point. When the 7/7 bombings happened, the doctor used it as a chance to take his invention beyond the realms of the Security Service. He faked his own death and disappeared.'

'I have already discussed this with my son. So is it money you want?' He splutters. 'Money for your silence?'

'I want to hear you say it....'

'You've not let me get a word in edgeways.'

'Gabriel doesn't even know the half of it. Admit it was you blackmailing Jake Roe. Admit you murdered Jed Smart.'

'What on earth makes you think that?'

'Raheem Kamani came to me in Monaco. He told me to stay away from James. Your son was standing behind me at the time, so naturally, I thought he meant him. But he didn't, did he? Kamani was telling me to stay away from you.'

He stares at me blankly. For once, with nothing to say.

'You founded the program with Magnusson and there began your hunt for vulnerable children. Hope Clarke being the first of them. Poor Roe was just in the wrong place at the wrong time when you needed someone to cover up evidence in her disappearance. He thought he would do this one thing for you and that would be the end of it. But Jacob Roe was sorely mistaken because you never let anyone off the hook, Edward. When you got wind of Higgs and the fact your son was investigating the suspect involved, you started to panic. You knew what Higgs meant and you started digging a little deeper. That's when you discovered that Magnusson was still alive and using A Better World under an alias, to continue the program you created together. So, you set a plan in motion to protect yourself. You put Jake Roe on a taskforce with Alison Collins and had him fabricate a story about finding evidence of weapons sales on the dark web. Roe was instructed to slow down the NCA's operation whilst becoming your canary, searching for Higgs where you couldn't. You deliberately made everyone think Higgs was a person. Someone tangible that the NCA would have to search for but it would keep them off your scent. Tell me, how many times did Jake Roe nearly kill your own son trying to protect your secret?'

'What an extraordinary imagination.'

'After Olivia attacked us, you attempted to disband the taskforce, but you were limited in what you could do, you wouldn't turn Gabriel in. So you got me in a room, and it all came together. You could emotionally blackmail me into finding Magnusson for you, ensuring Gabriel was nowhere near the investigation. You split us up but kept me close, trying to control where I put my efforts. The plan was to use me like you did Roe. Then, once I'd got close enough, you'd kill me and get on with what you needed to do.'

He looks away, a slight twitch in his right eye.

'You underestimated me, Edward. I was closer to finding Magnusson than you had ever been. Your plates were spinning out of control, so you went back to using Jake. He told you about the meeting with Hadid Waqif and Fallows. That's when you hired a sniper to execute them in Battersea.'

'Do you have any evidence to support these wild accusations?'

'Then, when you found out we were all in Monaco, that was too high risk for you. You couldn't have your son getting wind of the Compliancy program. Roe promised Lucas Caruso the one thing he couldn't resist. Calabria and money. Caruso took the bait and gave me up. When that didn't work, when Gabriel stopped Icarus Flint from frying my brain, you urged Roe to do it again, to use the Italian Mafia to get rid of me.'

'This is all conjecture.'

'Roe gave it away, Edward. When he was pointing a gun in my face, he said… *I had to find a way to separate you from him.* Not *them.* But *him.* Then, later, when Caruso insisted on keeping Gabriel back, Roe lost it. He couldn't agree to that. You had instructed Roe to find a way to make me disappear. But not Gabriel. That wasn't part of the plan. Roe couldn't allow your son to disappear as well. Caruso wasn't supposed to touch Gabriel. Since Olivia attacked us eighteen months ago, nobody has been allowed to go near him. The sniper's bullets miraculously stopped when Gabriel appeared in Battersea.'

Placing his drink down, Edward rises from the chair, wandering to the mantlepiece on the far side of the room. Stepping in, he examines a picture of Camina with her three children before gently rubbing his thumb over Gabriel's joyful, gapped tooth grin. 'He was about twelve in this. Always smiling.' He stares down at the image for a time. 'That all changed when Janie died.'

The mention of Janie James sends a sharp pang up the middle of my stomach and through my chest.

'His entire adult life, he's fought so hard to avoid being like me.' He chuckles to himself as if enjoying an irony.

I move to stand opposite him. 'I read Magnusson's decrypted file.'

'You mean the one you accessed through Leo Eden?'

I frown, feigning ignorance. 'Leo Eden is in a maximum-security prison.'

He exhales, repositioning the frame on the mantelpiece.

'A member of the team had the foresight to remove this particular nugget of information before Gabriel had the chance to read it. But I've seen it. The un-doctored file cites three people who worked on your program and the Higgs Boson serum. I have to admit, I did think it was an odd pairing. Why would a Doctor of Cognitive Psychology have anything to do with an Intelligence Officer in MI5, even if, by that point, you were the Deputy Director of Intelligence. Would there be any reason for you two to cross paths? Unlikely. So, I knew there had to be a link, something or someone that brought you together.'

He glares across the room, his eyes spurring me on. I tighten my grip around the gun in my hand.

'The lies, the double-crossing, the attempted murders, the successful ones, the blackmail. You have gone to great lengths to protect that third person, Edward. It's been staring me in the face. I don't know how I didn't see it before. Maybe I just didn't want to admit that there's an ounce of similarity between you and Gabriel.'

'And what is that?'

'We both know Gabriel has committed a long list of crimes to protect me. I'm the one person he would do anything for.'

He tilts his chin, gazing down at me with false superiority.

'And that triggers you because it's what you have been doing for decades. Devoting your life to protecting his mother. A world-renowned psychiatrist, cognitive therapist, and psychoanalyst. She is the reason you met Andrew Magnusson. She is the true source of the Higgs Boson serum, the Compliancy program. She built the infrastructure. I think her work was born out of losing your daughter.

She couldn't understand how she'd failed her. With so many things in your control, it must have torn you apart, knowing you couldn't save Janie from herself.'

'We wanted to help people!' He shouts, losing all sense of restraint. 'You think it's smart, standing here and telling me everything you know about my wife. Do you think I can let you live?'

'I think we've just discussed the reason you won't do anything to me, Edward. I don't think that's a battle even you're ready for.'

'We didn't...' He rubs his shaking hands through his hair. 'We couldn't understand how... how could Lily and Gabriel be fine. But Janie... it was a sickness, a darkness infecting her mind.' He looks at the floor, spittle crawling down his chin. 'Andrew and Camina created Higgs Boson to try and help agents with PTSD. Then we just...' He sits back in his seat. 'It just developed. We saw a way to create something phenomenal. The Russians, the Chinese, the Saudis... they had nothing like it. Nothing at all.'

'Gabriel thinks you were chasing Magnusson because you wanted to punish him for stealing your work, but it's only been about protecting his mother.'

'Please Alexandra. Please leave her out of this!'

'Your secret is safe...' I confess cautiously.

He hesitates, puzzled. 'What... Why?'

'Gabriel struggles enough with the fact one of you did this. It will break him to know it was both of you.' I turn for the door.

He follows me, his expression manic. 'Please Alexandra... wait.'

Stepping forward, I press the gun into his sternum, looking him dead in the eye. 'If you even think about harming my family, I will kill both of you. You've underestimated me once before. Don't make that same mistake again.'

He nods, his eyes desperate. 'What are…What are you going to do? What are you planning on doing to Camina?'

'Nothing.' I exhale. 'You're both already living in hell.'

EPILOGUE

TWO YEARS LATER

RAE

I yawn, trying to keep my eyes trained on the winding road ahead; this isn't the sort of place you'd want to drift to sleep. The roads are narrow and there's a seemingly endless drop on the left-hand side. I check the rearview, ensuring nobody has picked up my trail. Clear for now. The front tyre slips down a pothole just as my phone starts buzzing. The sudden jolt of the car causes it to fall down the side of the passenger seat.

'Fuck.' I pull over, reaching down. A name flashes up in bold letters. *Not now.* I cancel the call, switch off the device, pull off the back and remove the SIM card. I'll get a new one at the airport.

Stepping out of the car, I stand on the edge of the mountain, gripping the phone and the sim in both hands. *This is the way it has to be.* Taking a deep breath, I throw them into the trees below before pivoting on my heel. A row of small cafés catches my eye across the street. I peer through the sun, practically salivating at the smell of fresh coffee. Two men sit outside: each one sipping espressos, basking in the summer rays, and conversing passionately in Greek, clearly enjoying the simple pleasures of life. What I would give to be able to sit undisturbed and watch the world go by. I exhale and turn back to the car, catching my reflection in the window. A slightly distorted, saddeningly accurate version of me glares back. Hair matted. Dark circles. I look ill. I lean into the car and retrieve two wet wipes from the glove compartment, quickly running them over my face, around my neck and under my armpits. That will have to do. It's not a bloody beauty pageant.

I pull out onto the road, take a sharp left and indicate again before swinging the vehicle right, then another sharp right as the car rolls towards a set of wooden gates. With my heart tremoring, I cut the ignition and get out. No visible security detail. Then again, I'm told these two have the whole district on their payroll. They probably knew I was coming the minute I turned onto the mountain road. Peering over the gate, I see the red-tiled roof of a large Mediterranean villa, set amongst a forest of pine trees that climb the hill behind.

'Nice...' I whisper, ducking under the twisting jasmine weaved around the gate.

Arguably, the two most significant people in British Intelligence and no protection detail surrounding their property. That's when you know you're being watched from the shadows. A song by INXS softly plays through the house; Michael Hutchence's husky voice escapes from the open windows downstairs. The front door is already open when I step onto the wide porch. I glance around at the scattered lounge chairs, noticing a few colouring books and several Barbies tucked between cushions. I pull my hair off my face and clear my throat. *No mistakes can be made.* I see a large brass knocker attached to a heavy door and tap it a few times.

'Can I help you?'

I raise my head. Gabriel James has a reputation for being handsome. But experiencing the scrutiny of that face is an entirely different experience. His eyes possess a boyish softness mixed with disconcerting darkness. My body appears to rise in temperature. He leans in the doorway, looking me up and down.

'I'm sorry to just barge in here like this... I urm...'

'You didn't.'

'Hmm?'

'We were expecting you.' He nudges his head to the three armed guards behind me. *Where the fuck did they come from?*

'How did you know?'

'Aldyn Wolfe.' He crosses his tanned arms, amused.

'Yeah, he's been helping me.' I linger my eyes on them for a beat too long before whipping my attention back to his face. *Rae, stop looking at his mouth.*

'We trust Aldyn. What is it you need?' He raises his eyebrows, waiting for an answer until a child calls out for him. He turns, placing his body in front of her protectively before crouching down and picking her up.

A gorgeous little girl stares back at me with curiosity. She has his dark eyes, both striking and warm at the same time, with a beautiful mane of wild blonde hair. Her mouth puckers into a pout. 'I used Mummy's lip gloss.'

'I told Mummy you're too young for that.'

'Who is this Daddy?'

'I think it's the woman Grandpa Aldyn told me about.' He says in a voice that's clearly reserved for her. 'But I'm just waiting for her to tell me why she's here.' He turns back to me, his eyes narrowing slightly. His other hand has disappeared behind his back, the sinew of muscles in his forearm flexing. Likely because he's holding the gun tucked into the waistband of his jeans.

'I'm Rae.' I rush out. 'Rae Murphy.'

'I know who you are, Rae.'

'Gabri-' I hear her voice before she appears next to him. *Wow.* Alexandra Christofi. An impressive face to match an impressive reputation. The woman who gave up everything to protect her country, safeguarding our way of life. Now I see where the little girl's hair comes from. That and the strawberry shaped lips. Alexandra's large golden eyes regard me suspiciously before she leans to her right, her hand also vanishing.

'Rae.' I repeat. 'Rae Murphy. Aldyn Wolfe... he told me where to find you. He said you could help.' Forgetting everything Aldyn told me to do, I quickly dive into my pocket for identification. Alexandra flinches, stepping far enough forward so her daughter can't see the pistol gripped between her palms.

'Go slow.' She instructs me.

'Lex...' Gabriel groans.

'Phoebe, sweetheart...' Alexandra utters whilst studying my ID. 'Why don't you go find Grandma Ali?' She tucks the pistol into her denim shorts.

The little girl rests her head on Gabriel's shoulder and clings to his neck. 'I want to stay.'

Gabriel holds her in front of him, kisses her on the cheek and sets her back on her feet. 'Why don't you ask Grandma if you can feed the chickens?'

Phoebe's head snaps up excitedly. 'Yes...' she shouts, quickly dashing across the porch, only stopping to quickly retrieve one of the Barbies. 'And then I'll show you and Mummy later.'

'Sure but go slowly...' Gabriel warns.

Phoebe makes only a little effort to slow down before calling out for her Grandmother eagerly.

'How old is she?' I ask, hearing an older woman responding beyond the path.

'She's two.' They both say in unison.

'She's adorable.'

'She's a whirlwind.' Gabriel murmurs, winking at his wife.

'You said Aldyn sent you?' Alexandra gestures to a table and chairs, taking a seat.

Following her lead, I lower myself into the cushions, fighting the urge to lie down and close my eyes. Both of them look at me sceptically, waiting for me to elaborate.

'Murphy…' Her eyes convey a hint of mistrust. *She's sounding me out.* 'Any relation to Sam?'

'Sam was my brother.' I admit. 'You knew Sam?'

She nods. 'I liked him… a lot. I'm sorry for your loss. He was a good man, really good at his job.'

'I know this is out of the blue. I'm just…' I sigh. 'I really need to talk.'

'Aldyn is like family…' Gabriel starts, his eyes watching me closely. 'He's Phoebe's Godfather. If he's sent you to us. He must trust you.'

'He's been a real help to me.' I admit cautiously. 'He used to help Sam out a lot before he got in trouble.'

Alexandra nods. 'I remember he connected Sam with some contacts. Off the books.'

I smile. 'Sam never played by the rules.'

'Is this connected to him?' Alexandra asks. 'Is that why Aldyn sent you out here?'

'Sort of… I'm here because I'm looking for someone.'

'Who?'

I take a long breath. *Get it out Rae. Just get it out.* 'Eden.'

Their bodies still, their expressions intensify.

Exactly the reaction I was expecting.

'A few years ago, I worked on an operation to detain Leo Eden. It was thought he possessed highly classified information that was a threat globally. I was on a team tasked with tracking that intel, getting it back and locking him away.'

Alexandra leans forward, waiting for me to continue.

I hesitate. *Stick to the basics. Just the basics Rae.* 'We took Eden in, but the intel was lost. Nobody knows where, exactly.'

Gabriel shifts in his seat, knowing what's coming.

'Recently he helped you...' I meet his eyes. 'Leo helped you uncover who was behind The Singularity.'

'You want to know where he is?' Gabriel utters, irritated. 'We made a deal. We can't give you his location.' He snaps, his tone abrupt, all evidence of the doting father completely disappearing. In his place sits the intense figure of a man Aldyn Wolfe warned me about.

'You'll have to excuse my husband, Rae... he doesn't like surprises.'

And now the charm offensive. Wolfe used the term *smiling assassin* to describe the woman he calls his daughter, citing her as more dangerous than Gabriel because you hardly see it coming. Most people can't imagine this beautiful woman capable of even a fraction of the extended list of things she's done for British Intelligence.

Gabriel continues to glare at me, his jaw shifting slightly.

'But you know where he is?'

'Rae, you have to understand,' Alexandra starts, 'Eden went from being the golden boy of UK Intelligence to the world's most wanted man in a matter of months. We pulled a lot of strings to get him released. And to tell you the truth, the only reason we were successful is because half of the people we had to deal with were being investigated for working with The Singularity. They agreed to release Eden for a lesser sentence. I guess what I'm saying is, we worked hard to get Eden out and to keep him safe. To go back on that now would be madness.'

'If you investigated Eden,' Gabriel starts, 'then you know exactly what he's capable of, to even be sat here having this conversation is putting all of us at risk.'

'Why do you need to find him?' Alexandra asks.

'Lex...' Gabriel warns.

'I just want to know why.' Alexandra murmurs.

'We're not going down this road.'

'Gabriel, it's just a conversation.'

'Sorry, you wasted your time, Rae.' He stands from his chair. 'We can't help you.'

'Sit down.' Alexandra demands.

'Are you looking to make me a widower?'

'Sit down...please.' She repeats more softly.

He rolls his eyes before reluctantly taking his seat.

Alexandra leans over to him and places her hands on his face. 'Nobody is going anywhere. This is just a conversation, ok?'

Gabriel hesitates, his eyes tempering. In that moment, I realise he isn't all bravado and arrogance. He's full of fear; terrified of losing the woman sitting in front of him, the person he loves the most in the world. It makes me like him more, seeing this vulnerability. He inhales, taking her hand and kissing it before placing it in his. I look away, feeling like I'm intruding.

'Aldyn did say that he knows Gabriel well enough that I might leave here empty-handed.'

'But you still came?' Alexandra asks, intrigued.

'I don't expect either of you to tell me where he is.'

'So what is it you want?' Gabriel asks, his hand tightening around Alexandra's.

'I only came to pass on a message.'

'What is it you want us to say?' Alexandra asks, her interest piqued.

I clear my throat, meeting her gaze. 'Someone is coming for him. Someone from our past. And they think the best way to get there is through me.' I clear my throat. 'And our son.'

Music that inspired The Dark Angel

Eye for an Eye
UNKLE

Never Tear Us Apart
INXS

NFWMB
Hozier

Berlin
RY X

Let You Go
RY X

Bird Set Free
Sia

Breathe Me
Sia

Unstoppable
Sia

This Is What I Mean
Stormzy

Movement
Hozier

Another Love
Tom Odell

Inside
UNKLE

Drop Dead
Holly Humberstone

I Get It Now
Fjord

Back to You
Benjamin Gordan

Bitch
Ruby Amanfu

Somewhere A Clock is Ticking
Snow Patrol

Nina Cried Power
Hozier

Salt
RY X

The Yawning Grave
Lord Huron

Thistle and Weeds
Mumford & Sons

As It Was
Hozier

White Blank Page
Mumford & Sons

Cosmic Love
Florence + The Machine

Uprising
Damned Anthem

Francesca
Hozier

Acknowlededgments

Thank you to everyone who continues to ask about my writing and has kept the fire alive with book two; I am forever grateful. Thank you for reading, for encouraging me and for making this all worth it.

Thank you to Henry who has read and edited this book more times than he would have liked. You are the best!

And lastly, thank you to the people whose stories and experiences have shaped The Burnt Child and The Dark Angel.

Printed in Great Britain
by Amazon